THE STRATEGIC INTELLIGENCE FRONT

UNEARTH

BOOK ONE OF THREE

NICHOLAS P CLARK

On an otherwise uneventful evening, there is a breach in the White House; an encrypted message is found on the President's computer. The White House is subjected to a lockdown, and an emergency meeting of the inner caucus and select high ranking military generals. As the meeting progresses, there is a heated debate about the origin of the encrypted message, some in attendance even believe it was a threat from another country, with the best guesses being Russia. The software engineers within the white house security are called to trace the origin of the message.

A tech report shows that an encrypted IP Address embedded into the server used to send the message come from a Russian based hackers group computer, The Russian government house. The general's beckon for an aggressive militaristic response to Russia's aggression, but other officials, and the president, decide to undergo a stealth operation instead, to find out the plans of the Russian government.

Elsewhere, both the Chinese and Russian government receive similar messages and after decrypting locations the messages were sent from, the Chinese discover that it was sent by the Russians and the Russians discover theirs was sent by the American government, thereby turning nations against themselves. Back at the White House, a government official in top security meeting is excused by an aspiring politician and they leave together. Outside they discuss the proceedings of the meeting.

(Here we discover the mole in the president's cabinet, he however does. not know the task force)

This official then hands over a tape recording of the proceedings of the meeting to the politician and the politician leaves.While the official is away, the rest of the meeting agrees to launch an undercover mission so as to infiltrate the Russian government. The president gives a go-ahead for a special CIA task force to be launched and for records of its existence to be scrubbed as soon as the team is in place and sent on their mission.

At the Russian and Chinese meetings, a similar approach is taken, with all nations involved deciding to lay low about their received messages and plans.

Contents

CHAPTER ONE 1

CHAPTER TWO 6

CHAPTER THREE 12

CHAPTER FOUR 18

CHAPTER FIVE 25

CHAPTER SIX 29

CHAPTER SEVEN..32

CHAPTER EIGHT 39

CHAPTER NINE 44

CHAPTER TEN 48

CHAPTER ELEVEN 53

CHAPTER TWELVE..59

CHAPTER THIRTEEN...62

CHAPTER FOURTEEN 67

CHAPTER FIFTEEN..72

CHAPTER SIXTEEN 80

CHAPTER SEVENTEEN 85

CHAPTER EIGHTEEN...91

CHAPTER NINETEEN 99

CHAPTER TWENTY	105
CHAPTER TWENTY-ONE	110
CHAPTER TWENTY-TWO	115
CHAPTER TWENTY-THREE	121
CHAPTER TWENTY-FOUR	125
CHAPTER TWENTY-FIVE	130
CHAPTER TWENTY-SIX	137
CHAPTER TWENTY-SEVEN	144
CHAPTER TWENTY-EIGHT	221

CHAPTER ONE

"Russia exploring options for potential cyberattacks on U.S. energy sector, FBI warns. 6 hours ago,"

"FBI 'concerned' about foreign cyberattacks on critical US infrastructure. 3 hours ago,"

"Americans must prepare for cyber warfare - Experts say. 12 minutes ago,"

The headlines all said the same things, in spite of the artful play on words in every article he had seen, and that was forwarded to him, The President was sure all he had read was alike; A blatant disrespect of his orders to keep what had transpired the previous day a national secret!

With his tablet in one hand, he clutched the cocktail he had ordered an hour ago; bourbon, Angostura bitters, sugar and garnished with a cherry. He needed to let off steam, he had to be calm, he had to think, for his sake, and for that of every American.

Storming out into the Truman Balcony, on the second floor of The White House, a security detail following close by, he resignedly slumped into the chair he had ordered to be placed there.

There he sat, staring at the water fountain as it toiled endlessly, and gracefully, living its life for the sheer purpose of aesthetics, not having to answer to a scared, angry populace that would turn on you if they saw it fit to do so.

Thoughts of press conferences and public hearing, with flashy cameras and annoyingly inquisitive media personnel made him want to throw his glass as far as he could, but he didn't.

"Wallace Jefferson James, now is not the time to lose your cool" he reassured himself. He had to be strong, to be a figure of hope; he had a job to do, and he would be damned if he didn't do it properly.

Behind him, he could hear his security detail mutter something. Then he spoke out loud.

"Mr President Sir?" The security detail called to him; it seems that his attention was needed in the main house.

"What is it, Cooley?" He replied, his eyes rolling into the back of his head. He tried to hide it, but his annoyance at being disturbed caused his eyebrows to furrow so much that Agent Cooley apologized for the disturbance.

"I'm sorry to disturb you sir, but it's the First Lady on office line two, sir." Agent Cooley replied.

"Could you put her through to my tablet here? I'm really not in the mood for a conversation on the office phone" He requested.

"Alright sir, I'll get to it right away" Cooley replied, muttering back into his jacket, and the microphone that was planted there.

"Sir?" Came Cooley's voice again.

"What is it now Cooley?"

"She wants to video chat now sir" Agent Cooley requested, keeping his tone as respectful as he could.

"Tell her to call my tablet" The President sighed.

"Alright Sir" Cooley replied, relaying the president's message over to whomever he was on the phone with.

As The President sat in his chair, he began to think of his wife, his first lady.

They had met when He was young and running for senator in his home state of Missouri. Back then, she was a journalist who came to him with evidence that showed indecency towards women, sexual assault, and several incidents of unlawful conduct and financial crimes by his opponent, an aging stateman who had hung unto power for a long time.

Although they lost the elections, the women involved in the lawsuits that followed were ensured justice, financial compensation, and an America with one less predator, and corrupt politician.

"We might have lost the battle, but we've won the war" She had said.

In appreciation, he offered her drinks, a place on his team, and his heart as well. A few years later, they had tied the knot.

Wallace had always wondered what it was that fascinated him about her; it could be her eyes, they glistened in every light, or her hair; thick, black, yet shiny.

Maybe it was the way she talked, or it was…

"Hello? Wallace!" He had snapped back to reality.

"Hey, Marie, I'm sorry, I just got lost" his eyes welling with tears as he let out a yawn.

"I know, you've been staring at me since you picked up. Are you okay Wallace? She asked.

"Yeah, not exactly, you've seen the news right?" He was gesticulating wildly.

"I have, it's terrible. How did that happen?" She asked.

"Well, that is the thing, it hasn't even happened yet. At least not to everyone." He replied, waving his free hand wildly.

"What do you mean?" She asked.

"You know how you have a farm, then you have the test animals, you know? The ones in the back that make all the milk, and all the noise?"

"I don't think I follow, but go on?" She requested.

"I'm sorry, I'm just rambling" He replied, cupping his hand over his mouth.

"It's nothing, you hear? Just be good, okay?" She replied, letting out one of her infectious smiles.

"I hear you Marie, I do. I'll try" He shrugged.

I make no promises. He thought.

"You better be good and get some rest too. I know it's probably 12 there already." She replied, looking at her watch.

"11:43, but yeah, I need sleep" he said, looking up from the screen. He smiled sheepishly.

"You definitely need to. Listen, I have a speech to give in an hour or so" She replied, turning to her assistant, "Joyce, how much time do I have?"

"About an hour and a half, ma'am." Came a voice in the background

"Alright then, Wallace?" She called, turning to face him again.

"Yeah, babe?" I have about an hour and a half before I can go give my speech"

"I'll want to hear it then, don't I?"

"How about you do that in the morning? Get some rest"

"Alright, alright."

"And tell me what you think when you hear it!"

"Haven't I heard it already? Isn't it the 'Flower, space' one?" He asked.

"No, it isn't. It's the one with all the metaphors, I didn't read it to you"

"Oh, alright then. I'll call tomorrow to give you my feedback"

"Alright then, one more thing, tell Junior that I said to..."

"Tell him what? You know the boy doesn't listen to no one but you"

There was no response, all that was on the screen was a frozen image of his The First Lady.

"Honey? Honey!" The President called. Turning to his aide, he beckoned on him to come forward.

"Cooley, tell the tech guys that the Wi-Fi is down for some reason" He requested, but Cooley wasn't there. President Wallace became worried. After yesterday's scare, it would not be advisable for him to be alone.

"Cooley? Cooley!" He called, but there was no answer. As he walked away from the balcony, and headed west, towards the Oval Office, all the while scrolling through news articles.

Inside the Oval Office, he whistled as he grabbed a couple of documents that the Secretary of Interior had forwarded through her assistant to his desk. It had something to do with a wildlife fund he championed.

Wallace had not expected the presidency to be as tedious as it was. Sure, it was not a park ride, or a cotton ball, but he had expected at least a titanium pellet thrown at once in a while, not an entire barrage of alloys of titanium, chromium, and platinum.

"Metaphors" He chuckled, peering at the title, and recalling the name of the fund.

"Wildlife Security Fund" he read, then he sighed. He had been so overwhelmed that he had forgotten such a pivotal part of his overall campaign, so much so that he had to be reminded by a bunch of appointees, and they by those they had appointed.

As he turned to leave, making an agreement with himself to not go to sleep till he had scrutinized the papers and given an approval, Agent Cooley stormed the Oval Office, accompanied by several other agents.

"My President, are you alright?" Agent Cooley asked, his eyes darting as he searched for possible assailants.

"Yeah, take these. I'm heading up to bed" he said, handing him the files, and turning to acknowledge the swarm of agents in the room. "Is something wrong? Are you guys having a party here?"

"No Sir, but can I see your tablet for a sec, Sir?" Agent Cooley requested, grabbing it before he could get a response.

With swift movements, he dropped the tablet on the floor and cracked open the screen with his heavy shoes, stamping away with ferocity.

"What the hell, Cooley?" The President barked.

"I'm sorry sir, but the IT guys alerted us of a spy bug in your computer, Sir"

"And you thought that the best way to possibly get rid of it was to crack it open?"

"I'm sorry, Sir. We had to disable communication with the outside world"

Wallace was now pacing the Oval Office. He felt angry, ferocious, and especially helpless. Someone was playing a sick game on the most powerful nation on earth, and he was the face that was being poked at.

"Get me the IT guys!" he requested, ordering everyone out of his office.

"I don't want to see your sorry faces in here anymore, do you understand!"

In a single file, they all exited.

"Ants" He muttered, eyeing the glass of scotch that sat atop the desk by his left.

"Damn it!" He cursed, reaching for it, clutching it by the neck and wringing its top open. He proceeded to pour himself a fairly large drink. He then swallowed everything in one gulp, writhing as it burned the back of his throat.

Then he sat, like a man that has just become mad, or under a hallucinogen; in his pajamas, awaiting the arrival of the some of the best tech minds in the country he ruled over, and tipsy. He was on his third glass.

CHAPTER TWO

There was just something about the night shift; maybe it was the silence, or maybe it was the cold air, from the night and the air conditioning that hummed above their heads, chilling their bones as they tapped away at their keyboards, their eyes fixated at their screen, looking away only for the occasional glance at coworkers and to check the bag of chips. At least that was Kevin's story.

It was Carol who had alerted White House security of what she suspected to be a trojan horse in the president's device. She thought to be a listening device, to gain access to his conversations, thereby knowing his every move.

Although she thought it hypocritical, because that was basically their job; her job, to be exact. She was the only one that did it well.

While Kevin sat at this desk, using office Wi-Fi to download an upgrade to a game he played, she actually put in the work.

"IT guys, you're up! The president wants to see you" Cooley called, poking his head through the small office.

"Up? Where?" Kevin replied, peering up from his screen. He had been gaming and fought to keep a straight face, nervously clicking at the mouse to minimize the game he was playing.

"The president wants you guys in his office, right now" Agent Cooley replied, snapping his fingers, and pointing away from himself.

"Wait, excuse me. What does you 'guys' mean?" Carol asked. She looked bothered and furrowed her eyebrows as she asked.

"Carol, come on, you know what I mean. Please don't make this a big deal" Agent Cooley replied.

"No, I don't know. Not all of us are 'guys', Agent Cooley" She replied, grabbing her personal computer, and storming out.

"She doesn't like you very much" Kevin said, dropping a finished bag of chips in the trashcan as he walked out, his head cocking as he sauntered towards the Oval Office.

"And what you were doing wasn't exactly JavaScript, now was it?" Cooley called after him, his question making Kevin to walk more briskly.

As Kevin trotted to meet up with Carol, he looked back to find Agent Cooley, who had gone to the kitchen to grab himself some water and a slice of toast. The president had sent he and other agents away in anger, he hurried because he had to do his job regardless.

Before Carol and Kevin could knock on the door of the Oval Office, Agent Cooley was already down by two slices and was running up the stairs towards the Oval office when the president granted them entrance.

"You're the IT guys? Where's Cooley?" The President asked.

"We don't know Sir" Carol replied, muttering under her breath.

"Wait, so it's just you two? That's kind of impressive" He praised, leaning back into his seat, his eyes in a dance with the lights that hung above.

"So, which of you discovered this 'thing' on my tablet, it's a virus right? Thank God we don't have one of those in real life" He continued, taking another glass to his throat. He knew he had to drink less, but he craved the burnt flavor the scotch had.

"That would be Carol, sir." Kevin answered.

"Carol? Her?"

"Yes Sir"

"That's impressive! Thank you! You know, I am this close to having you explain everything to me, but I'm certain I would not understand a thing you'll say, so thank you" He rambled, even he knew that he was drunk.

"Thank you Sir" Carol was smiling.

"Oh, it's no problem, at least we know that we're safe with you, unlike some other people" He replied, eyeing Kevin, who was poking a bust of former president John Adams, who had been president from 1797 through to 1801.

"What is he doing?" The President asked.

"Hey, Kevin! Can you stop that?" Carol instructed, rolling her eyes.

"Oh, I'm so sorry, Sir" Kevin muttered, almost knocking down the statuette as he turned"

Heaving a sigh, The President continued; "You know, John Adams- the guy you were just admiring, Kevin- had a saying. He said that 'There are two ways to conquer and enslave a country: One is by the sword; the other is by debt'. We all know that whoever did this didn't come for his money, they came for blood! So, I call you here to ask a question"

"What is it, Sir?"

"Is it possible to send a message back to whomever is doing this? Do we have a direct, sort of link to them? Can we find them out, call them out, maybe? I don't know much about this computer stuff, which is why I need you here"

"I don't think that is quite possible sir, the signal seemed to disappear and appear periodically, making it untraceable and difficult to track, but we will conduct diagnostics and table a report by morning" Carol replied.

"I'll like that, thank you Carol, and Kevin; I've got my eye on you"

"Thank you Sir" Kevin replied sheepishly.

Together they filed out of the Oval Office, with Carol preparing to berate Kevin as they left.

"Hey, can one of you guys send an e-mail to the military generals, my cabinet too? I think we need to discuss this in the morning". Came the President's voice, calling after them as they went.

There was no response, although Carol had heard him. She was hell-bent on giving Kevin a piece of her mind.

As they walked down the flight of stairs that led to their office, she burst out at him.

"What is your problem, man?" She yelled. "Do you know whom that was?"

"I do, what about it?" He replied.

Carol was taken aback, his nonchalant reply rocking her. "Wait, so you do realize that we were just in a meeting with the President? Why did you act like that if you did?"

"Act like what?" He asked again.

"Like a complete wuss, man! We're supposed to be competent; we do work for the man!" She explained.

"Well, technically, he works for me. I'm a citizen of the United States and he is a civil servant"

"Not when you work within the walls of White House, silly!"

"Oh, right. I could have played that better, huh?"

"Oh, you could have! You could've gotten a different game plan!"

"Damn it! How do I fix this, wait up!" He asked, but Carol had already started walking away, she was pissed, and he knew it.

"You can start by tracing what's left of the digital footprint of that signal, we do have to get something across to the President's table by morning" Carol replied, running her hands through her locks.

"Damn it. The one time I take the night shift so that I can get away from my mom and her yelling, I get stuck with deciphering a threat to national security" Kevin grumbled.

"Believe me, I'd much rather prefer to have Ebenezer back on the night shift with me, but he's out of town seeing his Nana. Think of this as a great pickup story for the hotties you'll get when you go to bars" She replied.

"You think I'll get hotties?" He asked excitedly.

"Get to work Kevin" She replied, walking away from him, rolling her eyes as she did.

"Alright damn, but I'll need some dinner first" She could gear him running towards her, then he ran past her, towards the kitchen.

*

The headache was sure worth it, because he had slept like a baby, a comatose patient, someone that just got knocked out…

"Damn, my head is spinning so much that my thought are flying everywhere" he muttered.

When he had taken five shot glasses of the scotch was when he knew he had to go to bed. All he could remember was the trip to his bedroom and how fuzzy his vision was. What amazed him was that he was tucked into bed as he woke up, even his alarm was set to wake him up an hour after his normal time.

Almost at that same time, he heard a knock on his door, and in came Agent Cooley.

"Good morning Sir, I trust you had good night's rest?" He greeted.

"I did, I sure did" He replied, rubbing his eyes. Slowly, he began a rather painful journey towards the bathroom, but he stopped at the door and turned to his aide who stood at the door of the bedroom.

"Thank you Cooley, it's quite a lot to take in to be honest"

"It's my job sir, nothing more" Agent Cooley replied.

"Neh, I'm welcome. I sure am" He laughed, closing the bathroom door behind him.

As he turned on the lights, he immediately closed his eyes, adjusting to the brightness was a task he wasn't ready for.

"Cooley!" He called.

"Sir?" He could head a quick shuffle of feet; Agent Cooley was already by the door before he could call for him again.

"You are good at your job, aren't you?"

"I try to do my best, Sir"

"Yeah, I'm going to be in here for a while, but I'll need you to go tell those IT guys to remind the cabinet about our meeting, and that I'll like to see them in the afternoon, probably around 3"

"Is that all, Sir?"

"Yeah, and I'll like some omelets, wheat bread and a protein shake, with a little coffee too."

"Alright Sir, coming right up".

"Also, turn on the television, I want to be able to hear it from here".

"On it Sir."

As he heard the door close, accompanied by chatter on the television, he turned to the shower and turned it on. Looking in the mirror, with his mouth full of toothpaste, he toiled at his teeth, hoping to preserve the smile that had gotten his numbers up a while back in a popularity poll. He knew he would be addressing the press soon, he had to be ready.

When the tub was at a certain level, he turned off the shower head and slid into the water; his perfect, lukewarm semi-pool.

As He soaked, he strained to listen to the conversation on the television, trying his best to pick up as much of it as he could.

"...that is just what it is; an undermininement of our national security"

"Thank you Josh, we hope the Presidency can come forward with an official statement as to what happened, and if the rumors are true. Up next we have Political analyst, Matthew Sorensson, happy to have your Sir"

"Ah, not this guy again" He grumbled, lathering himself with soap and sinking into the tub.

"...and that is where I have an issue with his policies on foreign interactions, you can't keep letting people in, you'll sabotage yourself, and in doing so, us all"

"But you do realize that there have been reports on the Chinese media about similar cyber-attacks, what have you to say about that?

"Well, I have no business with the Chinese, and I would concentrate on my own country, my own problems, thank you very much"

"Finally, Mr Sorensson, what words do you have for the President, what would you tell him to do?"

"I'd tell him to man up, buckle up, and come clarify these rumors so that every child can sleep at night peacefully, and every adult can wake up knowing they won't be attacked by the enemy. God Bless America!"

"Ladies and Gentlemen, that was Mr. Matthew Sorensson, this is Speak Politics, brought to you from the studios of the American Television Authority, ATA.

Until next time, I remain Hannibal Reece, thank you for watching and have a great rest of your day..."

As the news ended, the president heard a knock on his door, and then an opening. Quietly, he slid into his bathrobe and made his way to the main bedroom, turning off the lights as he left the bathroom.

Inside the main room, he could see a plate of omelets, a large sized cup of his protein shake, and a cup of coffee, all set to rest on the table beside his bed. Whomever had brought the food was already out before he got in, and he settled in to enjoy his makeshift breakfast, promising himself a full meal when he was done with his duties for the day, and the meeting he was to have.

CHAPTER THREE

Army General Larry Eisenhower had just gotten out of bed when he got a call from his counterpart in the Navy, Admiral Grant "Buster" McStephens.

Both men had known each other for a long time, right from their days where they had been in the same military class. Both men had developed a relationship that transcended the workplace, and they were even brothers-in-law, by virtue of the fact that McStephens had married Larry's sister, Grace, an author who had retired early from her accounting job at a Fortune 500 company to pursue her new-found career.

"Hey Larry!" Came his brother in-law's voice over the phone.

"Hey Buster, what's up?"

"Yeah, I'm heading out, I'm almost at the White House too."

"The White House?"

"Yes, Larry. The white house", came the response, "Didn't you get check your emails? The president wants to see us at 1500."

"Emails?" Larry asked, reaching for his laptop.

"Yeah, yeah. Mine came in this morning, quite early too"

"Really?" He asked, peering at his screen. "Give me a sec" He added, reaching for his glasses.

"Do you see it?" McStephens asked.

"Yeah, I do, what do you think it's about?" Larry replied.

"Huh? Haven't you seen the news?" He retorted.

"I'm off duty today, so I decided to sleep in. What's going on?" Larry asked again, this time he was yawning.

"The cyber-attacks? Tell me you've heard about them?" McStephens requested.

"Yeah, I have, but those are rumors, right?" Larry opined, scrolling through the e-mail.

"Apparently not anymore, if they were, we'd be enjoying our day off, won't we?

"You have a day off too?"

"Yeah, But I'm not lazy. I check my e-mail."

"At least I'm not a copycat, like you"

"What? When have I ever copied you?"

"Remember that shooting range out in Texas, I think it was '92"

"Oh, come on, we picked the same gun, get over it!"

"The exact same pistol!" Larry replied, both men were laughing.

"Get your lazy ass over to this damn White House Eisenhower! I'm out, the bar here is calling my name. See ya!" With that, the call was ended, and Larry set to prepare.

Eyeing the clock that stood right above the television in his room, he could see that it was a few minutes pass 12 PM, he knew he had to be out and about before 1300 if he wanted to beat the rush hour traffic and get to The White House in time.

Slowly, he walked towards his wardrobe, hoping to find a spare uniform in there somewhere. He was sure he had sent them all to the drycleaner's as he was going to be free for the next week.

Upon opening the wardrobe, he searched for a uniform, but all he could find were his suits. Sighing, he brought out a few possible options to choose from, before deciding to go with the plain grey suit he had gotten from his last son, Russell, as a birthday gift a few years ago.

He then went into the bathroom, but not before his stretching exercises.

"Ah, that'll get my blood going" He groaned, walking into the bathroom.

As he soaked in his tub, he chuckled. Buster had stolen his stretching exercises as well!

*

Admiral Grant "Buster" McStephens had just pulled into the White House when he was accosted by a valet who greeted him warmly and offered to park his car for him.

The boy, a freckled-faced young man, with curly hair and a goatee promised to handle his 1969 Mustang Mach 1 with care, complimenting him on his choice of car.

"I especially like the V-8, water-cooled engine on this one sir, you have great taste" He commented.

"And you are great at flattery. Here, for your troubles" Buster replied, squeezing a 100-dollar bill into the valet's hand.

The valet was so overcome with joy that he thanked him repeatedly, before getting into the car, revving the engine, and driving off excitedly. It was clear he did not hear The General's plea to "take it easy".

"Kids these days" he said, heading towards the main entrance.

"Once inside, he was escorted by an assistant who had been waiting for his arrival. This assistant directed him towards a waiting room, one where a bucket filled with ice that preserved the white wine it held was waiting for him.

Once inside, he poured himself a glass, and sat to enjoy the program airing on the television.

The assistant came back to him, this time with word from a case file containing reports of both cyber-attacks, the rumors, and the underlying truths, as well as word from the president himself, written on a piece of paper.

"Hey Buster!

Look, I'm sorry but we have to wait for everyone to arrive before we get started. I'm also sorry for making you wait in a small room, but it'll be best for me that I do not entertain guests at the moment, even highly placed individuals such as yourself.

I hope you understand.

Also, enjoy the champagne.

Signed

Wallace."

"Would you like anything else sir?" The assistant, a young woman, probably in her early thirties, asked.

"He sure is a busy man, isn't he?" He asked, ignoring her question.

"I guess he is" She shrugged.

"Yeah, He definitely is."

"Would that be all, Sir?" She asked again.

"Yeah, I want two things; your name so that I know who to call for, and a TV remote, thank you very much"

"Alright sir, if you need anything, just use the telephone beside you, and my name is Ethel" She replied, pointing to the telephone on the stool, right beside the cream-colored sofa he sat on. "As for the television, the remote control is over at the table there" she said, reaching for it.

"Thank you, Ethel" He replied, taking the remote from her"

As she left, he flipped through the channels, quickly switching it if they discussed the current political matters.

"I'm going to be hearing that in a minute, I might as well watch something else", he muttered, choosing to watch a rerun of a football game he had seen a few weeks prior.

"Yeah, at least we'll win this one" he said to himself as he set the remote controller down and took in the game. The Commanders were down by three points and needed to convert a chance to score a touchdown if they were to stand any chance of winning. It was all up to Wide Receiver, Rondell Mackey to get as creative as was humanly possible

"It's quite possible that the opposition has mastered their plays" said, the first commentator.

"I don't know, 20 years in this business, and I've known better than to underestimate anyone, especially when someone is backed up in a corner. especially at home, especially like thus!"

"Well, we'll see about that; the fans are leaving, the crowd has no cheer, except the opposition team, that is, and if they lose here, we could see them drop points"

"Watch out, here they go"

"Here's the Commander's quarterback, Quavon Scotson, you can see Rondell Mackey running down the sidelines here..."

"Oh, what a throw from Quavon, that had some serious steam!"

"...Rondell gets it! What an evasive move by Rondell, and another! Another! What a jump from the Chicago-born athlete!"

"Here we go! Here we go!"

"TOUCHDOWN!"

"I Don't believe it! The Commanders have done it! The crowd goes wild!"

The Admiral could not contain his joy, as he rose up and punched the air with his fist, muffling his own shouts of joy with his free hand.

As he sank back into the rather uncomfortable sofa he was sitting on, he glanced at his watch to see the time; it was almost past noon.

"Why Did I have to get here so early" he grumbled, grabbing the magazines that sat on the stool beside him.

As he scanned through them, one particular magazine seemed to catch his eyes, so much so that even he found it weird.

"The People's Music? Alright, let's have it. Probably some rapper flaunting a chain on page one, I bet" he said turning the pages, till he got to the center page.

"Selena set to release new music. After 26 years?" He questioned, wondering if her label had found an old computer with recordings she had done recently. After a few pages in, he was certain that he was bored out of his mind, he had a full dinner to get back to, and he was sure that it would be cold by the time he came up the front lawn.

He thought of inviting his brother in-law over, a hearty dinner was sure to take his mind off of his ex-wife, plus he would be around family again.

Almost immediately, the door opened and in came Larry.

"Speak of the devil! I was just thinking about you" he said excitedly.

"Really? What about?" Larry asked.

"Would you like to come have dinner at my place this evening, I'm sure Grace would love to have you"

"Sigh, okay then. I didn't have plans anyways"

"I knew that, but are going to wear that?"

"Wear what?" Larry asked, looking at his suit.

"You look like you're gonna be interviewed and then married, on the same day"

"I like this suit, it's stylish"

"And costs more than a used car too!"

"You're just jealous!"

"Of the quality of this suit? Yes. But am I jealous of your fashion sense, and the size of your brain, no I'm not!" Both men laughed, sighing as the laughter died down.

"Look at us! When my dad drove me to the recruitment center, I was sure I'd chicken out by the end of that week" Buster said.

"But now look at you, barely an adult and running the show at the biggest military in the world" Larry joked, reaching for the other glass of champagne that stood on the table.

"How about a toast?"

"Seems about right, plus there's no need to go into these meeting fully sober"

"I think you've got it all mixed up" Grant joked, as they clinked glasses and took sips.

Suddenly, there was a knock on the door, and Ethel came in, announcing that the president required the presence of both men.

"Show's about to start" Larry stood up and tapped his counterpart on the shoulder.

"Are you ready General" Grant asked, a look of concern in his face.

"Get out of here with that puppy dog face!" Larry replied, pushing him out of the way and exiting the room.

CHAPTER FOUR

As Ethel, the assistant, guided them towards the Oval Office, both men took in the sights, only stopping when they came up on a window that showed the Washington tower.

"Hey, you think Charles is going to be in there?" Buster asked, tapping his counterpart on the shoulder.

"I hope so"

"Why's that?" Buster turned to look at him, his response was damn near shocking.

"You know why, don't give me that look" Larry replied, walking away from the window.

"I don't, that's why I'm asking here!" Buster requested, almost in whispers.

"Wouldn't it be fun to get a rise out of him, you know, rile him up a bit?"

"I see where you're going with this, and I'm a hundred percent behind it" both men laughed quietly, like school children when they know the teacher is watching. Ethel was sure to be listening, but they didn't know she found it funny. Nobody liked Charles Boyd and making him secretary of defense only made him worse.

"Gentlemen, have a good rest of your evening" Ethel greeted, holding the door open for them, and brandishing a smile.

"Thank you Ethel!" both men chorused.

As she closed the door, Larry turned to Buster and said, "She sure is nice", to which he shrugged and walked away, saying.

"She's just doing her job Eisenhower, her job".

Both men took seats beside each other, sitting and trading whispers, which seemed to get even more frequent as Charles Boyd walked in.

For a man in his sixties, Charles Boyd looked rather agile, and aside his hairline, which was almost invisible at this point, and a limp in his left foot, he moved around quite easily.

"Gentlemen" He greeted, proceeding to take a seat directly in front of Eisenhower and McStephens.

"Boyd. Great to see you" McStephens greeted in response.

"Likewise," He responded, almost impatiently, sporting a fake smile and baring his teeth.

The whispers continued, with Charles stealing glances at both men, a glimpse of hatred in his eyes, but this only made them giggle more.

"Knock it off, gentlemen. We're about to discuss the fate of a country" Came a voice and a quick shuffle of several footsteps. It was the president.

"Good evening, Mr President"

"Good evening, Buster!" he replied.

"Good evening President Wallace"

"Good evening General Larry. Gentlemen, you remember our Director of the CIA, Mrs Rachel Colby?"

There were nods all around the room. Nicknamed "Iron Hornet", Rachel Colby was top of her class at military school, a ruthless firearms specialist who held the record for most accurate shots till a younger agent beat it a few years back.

Here she sat, quiet, trading smiles with all that sat in the room, a sharp contrast to her records in combat.

"Also, our Director of the FBI, Mr. Joaquin Taylor will be joining us via video chat today, his flight got delayed at the last minute, something about a faulty engine" President Wallace continued.

As he spoke, an agent placed a laptop atop the Resolute Desk.

"Good evening, ladies and Gentlemen, shall we begin?" Came Mr Joaquin's voice, alongside a hearty smile.

"So, now that we're all friends, can we get down to deterring our enemies?" President Wallace asked. "Who has a report to give? Hey Cooley? Where are the IT Guys?"

"They don't come in for their shift till 9 sirs, but they sent in a report stating what they had found. Its behind you sir" Cooley said, stepping forward.

"Oh, is it?" He asked, stepping away from the desk and picking out the report.

"Oh, here it is." He said, waving it about "Apparently, there are copies for everyone, bow thoughtful, Cooley could you pass this around, please?"

Cooley came forward, got a hold of the documents, and then proceeded to pass them around. All the while, the president was perusing the facts, his eyes darting at every corner.

After a long silence, he spoke.

"Item One!", He called, "Here it states that the IP address used to infiltrate the firewall of the white house emanated from somewhere between Europe, and Asia, and that further diagnostic search traced it to a region of Russia"

"Mr President, if I may, what the IT staff at the White House, alongside my best team at the FBI could decipher was just a fades digital footprint of the hackers IP, they- whomever they were- were smart enough to disappear and appear on our radar, half the time, bypass our firewall and listening in our conversations, well, the conversations with the white house" Mr Taylor summarized.

"On a scale of a hundred, how true do you say these facts are, Mr Taylor?"

"On a scale of a hundred? I'd say 80 percent Sir"

"I'd say a hundred" Secretary of Defense, Charles Boyd broke his silence.

"What?" The president was shocked, everyone was too. Charles Boyd was known to make rash decisions, but this seemed to defy even his streak.

"How sure are you Boyd?" The President asked.

"A hundred percent as well"

"I'm sure that you'll recognize the fact that these people are trained professionals who have done us the honor of painstakingly examining an otherwise faint signal and coming up with a working theory, I'd advise you tread with caution, Mr Boyd."

"Mr President, these computers will tell us what we want to hear, not what we need to, Sir"

"And what exactly do we need to hear, Mr Boyd?"

"That these Russians have it out for us? That it's the World versus The United States? That we need to bulky before we can be bullied? Pick a suitable one, I suggest we all do"

"Do you realize the implications of a full-on attack, even if it was verbal? Do you know the repercussions of that? Have you ever been in war, Mr Boyd? Rachel Colby asked, she was visibly annoyed by his outburst.

"I am capable of thinking outside the box, Ms. Colby. Thank you very much"

"Outside the box? Get this; you're not thinking outside the box, you're an astronaut in space, outside this globe that shields us, with no damn oxygen"

"See, there are fine lines here, and sometimes we have to cross them"

"Not when you risk burning both the line and the man that drew them! And its Mrs Colby to you!"

Both Eisenhower and McStephens sat in silence, both men had not spoken to each other since the meeting had begun and were contemplating what sides to be on.

McStephens was leaning towards a war; If they're brutish, why don't we do the same. Two wrongs not making a right doesn't mean you get knocked out of your own head and hospitalized.

He finally spoke, cutting through the rancor between Boyd and other members of this meeting.

"Sir, how about we give them a taste of their own medicine?" He said, all eyes turned on him immediately.

"What do you suggest, Buster?" The President asked, folding his arms.

"Why don't we do what they did? Attack The Kremlin, cause mass hysteria" he said, shrugging.

"Mr President, If I may. That will not be exactly possible", came Mr Taylor's voice again.

"And why is that" Boyd asked, visibly irritated.

"You cannot attack The Kremlin sir, its unethical, its borderline suicide, plus, this could just be an attack by an isolated group and not the Russian government in general"

"I'd be dammed if it ain't the Russians!" Boyd barked, springing up from his seat, and waving his and at the computer.

"But what if? What if it's the Russian government paying off a group of independent hackers to destabilize our systems? What if this was just a first wave in a series of otherwise covert attacks. The report, here in topic 6 states that it is almost certain that information was stolen. What if it was the launch codes? What if tomorrow, our nuclear arsenal detonates on our head?" He reasoned.

"Exactly! You cannot leave anything to chance"

"But there were reports in the Russian dailies ah5 a cyber-attack, not just on their government house, but on their entire capital city, half of the city now has information stolen from them" Director Taylor said.

"Yeah, an assistant brought this to my knowledge sometime yesterday, they say like ours, it's just a rumor"

"Don't you see the hoax? What power is strong enough to attack the Russians at the same time as they attack us?"

"Could be the Chinese?" The president replied, he and resurfaced from being deep in thoughts. "I mean, it can't be the British, Doherty and I are friends, plus they still haven't recovered from that entire business a few hundred years back"

"Well, I say we show the Russians and the Chinese who they're messing with!" Boyd was relentless.

"It could be the Chinese, but it would take more than a mobile VPN to mask an attack of that magnitude, more or less, there's no motive as to why either governments would attack us all of a sudden."

"No motive? These people don't like us!" Boyd was yelling again.

"So, help me God! Have a seat Sir!" Eisenhower finally burst out, silencing Boyd. As he surveyed the room, he was sure he could see Mrs Colby smile at him, almost.

"As you can see that this is how ancient civilizations got ruined? They looked too much like babies and didn't do anything when they were threatened!" He continued.

"You do realize that the first record of a vast civilization, the Egyptians got ruined because they wouldn't let a bunch of slaves go?"

"This is America, in the 21St century! Not some backward nation from before our founding fathers!"

"Oh, Shut up Boyd! We all know you won't be able to go to war, you're scared to pick up a gun!" Rachel retorted.

"I'm leaving" Boyd said, after a short silence.

Just then, there was a knock in the door, Ethel came in, requesting the presence of the Secretary of Defense, that an entourage from his home state of Milwaukee was here to see him.

"I was about to ask you to leave anyways" The president said.

Raging with anger, He darted out, oblivious of his limp and almost knocking Ethel, the assistant, over.

There was another round of awkward silence. All parties studied the report in silence.

Buster looked at his watch.

"6:45", He muttered, luckily he would not have to microwave dinner, but he had to leave in two hours.

"Sir" Rachel Colby finally spoke, breaking the silence, "I would advise we infiltrate the Russian government, possibly the Chinese too."

"How so" The president asked.

"Well, before this meeting, I was in touch with a couple of acquaintances from various parts of the globe and they made it known to me that the Russian security system in the walls of the Kremlin are a mixture of the old USSR encryption system, and a new more advanced system, and that hacking them would only be half-possible from outside those walls, ergo, we need agents within those walls"

"That's quite a stretch, don't you think"

"It's the only option we have currently Sir"

"I concur to this, honestly. This is the best we can do, as stealthily as humanly possible. Of we are found out, it could mean sanctions for you, the government, and the US in general.

"Put something across to my table by tomorrow morning, we'll see how it goes then. I want you two to liaise, and Rachel, I want a complete report on my desk by morning"

"Alright then Sir"

"Sheesh, that's it! Meeting adjourned!" He said, clapping his hands and grabbing his coat.

As they filed out the door, he called to them, asking for volunteers to speak with him at the press conference that had been organised concerning the rumors.

"That is what we will keep it as, just rumors. You understand?"

"Yes Sir" was the general answer, as they all filed out, leaving Cooley to bid farewell to the Director and shut down the computer.

As they approached the press room, they were welcomed by the unrelenting glare of flash photography.

"You see why I wear a suit?" Eisenhower said, turning to McStephens.

"Yeah, yeah" He replied.

"Alright, Ladies and Gentlemen of the press, we'll be taking 5 questions today, can we have them?"

The chatter began, every reporter was shouting at the top of their voice, beckoning to be called.

"Yes, you in the back" The president said, pointing to a man in a blue suit.

"Who do they say are responsible for the attacks?"

"Well, these rumors, I am sure you have heard them, have been spread by unscrupulous agents that want to sabotage the peace and tranquility of our state, another question? You with the brown notepad!"

"What strategies are the executive taking to solve this case of, as you put it 'mass hysteria'?"

"I would advise every citizen to be calm, we are on top of the situation, this too shall pass! Next please?"

"Should the average American be afraid?"

"Absolutely not, there is nothing to worry about as we are on top of finding out the not so merry pranksters behind these faux attacks"

"I see that you are accompanied by the Army General, Larry Eisenhower, and the Navy Admiral Grant McStephens, alongside the head of the CIA, Mrs Rachel Coldy, what roles do the military, and the intelligence agencies play in all this?

"Well, as you can see, my administration has got the finest of minds in any field of expertise and these fine gentlemen, and lady, were with me in my office, the oval office and we were discussing matters of national security, as we always do. This just happened to be a special meeting, seeing that you all have decided to grace is with your presence, next please?"

"Mr President Sir, I have but one question, are the rumors true?"

"No. I can say that as a fact. A fact I can stand upon. Nothing of the sort has happened, we are safe. God Bless America, have a good night ladies and gentlemen"

With this, they all walked out, each man towards his car, Rachel Dolby sought to call her driver and the president thought it wise to down a few shots of scotch.

"This better not become a habit" he muttered to himself. Deep down, he wanted to call his wife, and talk to her about stuff, but he was sure that whoever had staged this entire fiasco was watching and he would not want to give them any undue advantage.

"The Speech!" He remembered, rushing to his bedroom, and turning on the TV to search for it, his plans to have a hearty dinner completely forgotten, he sought to feed his soul instead.

CHAPTER FIVE

Exactly a week after the happenings at the White House, a phone rings in a small house in Rigby, Idaho. A man, who seems to be recovering from a hangover, stumbles in his way to the phone, but manages to pick up and mutter a greeting.

"A good day to you Sorry sack, your country needs you"

"Rachel? How did you get this number?"

"'Intelligence', son. Read between the lines"

"Nah, but you can never find me"

"Number 5, Aspen Drive! Kinda rhymes doesn't it?"

"What do you want?"

"From you, right now? Nothing actually. Just that there are two vans outside your door right now, and once I drop this call they're breaking in. I just wanted you to know that I don't want any more dead agents, have a good day"

As soon as he was off the phone, the man could hear his front door being broken into.

Resignedly, he chugged what was left of the energy drink he found beside his bed and knelt down, with his hands behind his head.

"So much for laying low" he muttered, right before they broke into his room, yelling loudly and flashing lights all over the place. Then came a sharp pain in his neck, and a whistling in his ESR, as the man fell to the floor, his eyelids dropping to eyes as they had become heavy. He was unconscious, and they dragged him out of the house, towards one of the vans, and way from a neighborhood that had not yet woken up.

*

The news reports would later read that James Edwards Rudolf, the construction worker who lived on Aspen drive, was abducted from his house at around 5 AM in the morning.

It would be few hours later before he would regain consciousness, and although he could that he wasn't in Idaho anymore, he was grateful that he hadn't been captured by anyone other than the man.

"What is this?" He asked, turning to see other recovering abductees beside him.

"Ah, Jabez. Mouthy as ever"

"Rachel? Is that you? Oh my god, I thought the Russians got me"

"Oh, they will" Rachel's voice came over the speakers again.

"What? What do you mean?"

"Nothing, nothing"

"What is this though, some secret facility? Have you guys finally figured out how to give is superpowers?"

"No, it's not that, we have them already"

"We have super humans. Hurray America! I mean, those other countries better not mess with us, right?"

"Exactly. You will be freed in a few minutes and given a meal to eat, have some rest. I'm referring to all of us, more importantly, those that can hear me. Good night, your country thanks you for your service" With that, she cut off communications.

Outside, she put a call through to the president, who was eager to pick up.

"How is it going over there?"

"Pretty great Sir, my team is here, and I didn't ask politely."

"Thank you Rachel, make sure no one knows about this as well"

"As always Mr President, you can count on me"

With that, she cut the call, reception up in the Unimak Islands we not really that great.

*

As the night fell, other abductees regained consciousness and Jabez saw it as a responsibility to calm them down, this he did by telling them that they had been kidnapped by their own government and were being held in a secure location. Although his intentions were to scare them, they all seemed to be at ease after he had told them, introducing themselves to one another and proceeding to eat their meals.

Apart from being a seemingly uneventful night, Jabez soon found out that they had been selected for sim sort of mission and each of them had experiences in espionage and intelligence gathering.

Skunk, or Jeffries Romelo had lived in South Korea for a while, and was fluent in several European, Asian, and African languages. An otherwise harmless looking fellow, he was cut like a typical businessman, choosing to sport the full head of dark, brown hair, and a pair of medicated glasses, which he didn't need.

Harry, or Ana Fritz was an underground artiste who had lived in Ukraine prior to her being abducted, a former soldier with two tours of Afghanistan under her belt, she looked the part of a simple girl, but bore the 'curse' that is a powerful woman.

Gemini, an African American who was a graduate of the Nigerian Defense Academy, skilled fighter who had fought in the war against the Boko Haram insurgents. His real name was Kehinde Shammah, or Treyvon Williams, his supposed twin brother.

Aria, or Azizat Ruski, a Slovakian beauty queen who had converted to Islam a few years prior so as to, in her own words, "Learn self-discipline like I've never learnt before".

She had formerly been a Buddhist and was skilled in several martial art styles, and the art of taking a perfect selfie.

"How is that even possible? And mind you, I mean the perfect selfie, and not the symmetrical masterpiece that is your face" Jabez asked.

"There are things that cannot be explained little man" Aria replied.

"I'm 6'1 here, what does "little" mean in Slovakia?"

"And I'm trying to sleep here!" Gemini growled.

"Did you not just wake up? How is it possible? You know, going to bed again? Especially when Aria's here, I mean, look at her!" He gushed.

"How about we look at her in the morning, Skunk-guy has gone to bed, so should you all"

"All right, Gemini well talk in lower voices, well use our inside voices"

"Excuse me, who is 'we'? I'm off to bed too, little man"

"Sigh, alright then. I guess it's wait till the morning time, isn't it?"

Everyone settled into their beds and someone in the control room turned off the lights.

"Do you know what would be fun?" Jabez asked, in the darkness.

"No!" They all chorused.

"Alright then. Sheesh, you guys are buzz killers"

It was a rather quiet night, and by the break of dawn, Rachel Colby was awake, and drawing a an to beat her rag-tag team into shape for what would be top-level espionage.

In the words of the president, "If the first attacks had leaked, I'm sure somebody somewhere would want about half a million Americans and the entire world to know that we are planning an attack on the biggest nation on earth, this would have consequences. Tread carefully."

CHAPTER SIX

"Good morning Sunshines! Rise and get to it" She called, banging at the door of the enclosure where they kept them.

"Good morning roomies" Jabez greeted, jumping out of bed, and heading for the doors.

Once outside, each person was given a change of clothes, a sponge, some soap, and a toothbrush.

"Fancy" Jabez commented, before he was forced into the bathroom.

After they had all had their baths and a serving of toast, eggs, waffles, and custard, they were directed towards a debriefing room where they met Rachel Dolby seated, awaiting their arrival.

"Have a seat" she said.

As soon as they had been seated, she stood up and began.

"Now, I'm sure all of you are wondering as to what you did to get here, whom you did it to, where it happened and all that is in between, well I am here to inform you that you didn't offend anyone, and that you were both too good at your jobs and also too much of a shitty person that we have to bundle you here" She paused, taking a deep breath.

"All of you are like plastic bottles, full of promise, potential, but you're cut, possible around the neck, or the ass, I don't necessarily give a dam! But you were 'cut' by the metaphorical blade that is bad luck, so much so that you we're thrown out of your respective fields, and they called back in this manner" She paused again.

"Now I would really love to go straight to the point, after that we would have to give you several papers to fill, these papers will state that you were not, after your last date as servicemen and women, accosted by the United States of America to do any form of job, or high-level, top-secret activity." Again, she paused, this time to catch her breath.

"So here is the deal, I'm sure you are all aware of this news story that trended last week, and that is somehow still alive in the news today? Well, it is true. The White House was attacked by people we suspect to be Russian hackers. Now the problem is that we would have launched a retaliatory attack, but we have to get access to the Russian systems without own hands, and that is where you come in; for the next few months, you are requested to go undercover in the Russian government House, otherwise known as the Kremlin and steal as much data as you can. any questions?"

"How do you plan on doing this?" Gemini asked.

"That is an important question, and for the next couple weeks, you will all be given new identities, as well as new training, with firearms, explosive, computer tech, all the bits"

"Another question, how many people know about this operation?" It was Aria who asked.

"At this moment, those who know about this are all in this room, plus the president who will be addressing you all as soon as the firewall at the White House is immune to compromise."

Question here, when will we have seconds? I feel kind of hungry at the moment"

"Jabez, you just ate, grow up. You're 35!" Rachel seemed to have lost it. She was not going to ruin an operation this delicate because the only person who could handle the team she was setting up in the field was also a man child with no regards for personal boundaries and a knack for sarcastic comments.

"It was a genuine request, in all frankness" He explained.

"Whenever you are hungry, get yourself to the dinning space" She replied, as calmly as she could.

"Thank you"

"Alright then, go through the paperwork. you have all day. Tomorrow we will begin training and remember to hydrate!" With that She left the hall and was back to her drawing board in no time.

"Hey, Skunk. What do you think her type is?"

"Who? Mrs Dolby? Isn't she married?"

"When has that ever stopped anyone from having fun?"

"I think morality does the stopping"

"Well, thank heavens I don't have that, but I might need to have a drink, you know? Loosen myself up, I'm not very chatty when I'm sober" he explained.

"I wonder how you can say that with a straight face, to be honest" Gemini spoke, but he didn't look up from his paper.

"You guys better not fight, odds are we'll be roommates for a few months, how about we try to be friends, alright?"

"Well said gorgeous, I'm off." Jabez said, signing on the paper and walking out of the meeting room.

"You didn't even read it! What if you just signed your body over to the government to be used as an experiment?" Skunk asked.

"I don't care, I'm American!" He shouted, darting off.

"Well, so are we!" Skunk yelled. "That guy is going to die first, my money is on him" he told the others, shaking his head.

"Or last, he looks like someone with a lot of luck"

"It's quite impossible that he has survived this long without at least a tincture of luck, it could even be that his mother prays for him"

"My mom is an atheist, she disowned me when I became Muslim" Aria shared.

"Well, isn't that a turntable? Is that even possible?"

Harry asked.

"It's my life now" She replied, shrugging.

There was silence as everyone. focused on their paperwork, cross checking every line and double checking every phrase as they read. They had heard stories of agents on foreign missions being bent over a barrel and they were sure to not want that for themselves.

As the others toiled, perusing the paperwork, and ensuring their safety, Jabez made sure that he had downed a bottle of Vodka before he retired for the night, long after the other had gone to bed. As he got to the sleeping area, he tripped over a stone at the entrance and lay there sleeping, it took the morning crew to wake him up.

CHAPTER SEVEN

"Mendez, tell them to get the chopper ready, I'll be at the helipad in 20" General Eisenhower said.

"Duly Noted, sir."

"Thank you" He replied, setting his phone aside and hurrying to finish his tea.

As he stood in his kitchen sipping his brew, his eyes wandering about his house, he turned to the table by the side of the dining area, where his picture with his ex-wife used to be.

He could see the frame for smaller pictures that rested on the table, and how he had removed them a while ago. Although he was grateful that she had not been given the house as part of the divorce settlements, her lawyers made sure that she got 40% of his investments, and another large chunk of his real estate.

"That's what you get when you marry a trophy wife" he muttered, wishing he had the same type of marriage his sister had.

It took the buzzing of his phone to jolt him from his daydream. Hurriedly, he reached for it, hoping to find a message from First Lieutenant Mendez, a soldier he had taken a liking to and made a personal assistant. It was the President.

"Mr President, good morning sir" General Eisenhower greeted.

"Good morning general, I hope I'm not interrupting anything at the moment" He spoke in hushed tones, breathing heavily into the speaker.

"Oh, no Sir. I'm just getting myself ready to leave for Fort Bragg, Sir." As Eisenhower replied, his voice showed as much concern as he could.

"The Fort Bragg joint?" The President asked, his voice had suddenly become louder, but still, it reeked of nervousness.

"That is correct Sir, do you need anything Sir?" Eisenhower requested, he had to be at a meeting later that day, his presence was needed on delicate issues.

"Yeah, I'll need you and Buster in my office. I got something to share with you guys, and I can't do it over the phone.

Damn, I can't even do it when phones are within listening distance of our conversations" H

"Is it that serious, Sir?" He responded, walking towards the stairs that led to the bedrooms, all the while staring at his front door, in hopes that the lieutenant at the other side didn't hear anything. Typical military man.

"I'm afraid it is, General. Have Buster meet us in the Oval Office in an hour"

"Alright Sir. I guess my trip will have to wait"

"It has to, because you'll get information to take to Fort Bragg"

With that, President Wallace had hung up the phone, leaving General Eisenhower with two calls to make; to put together the meeting in the oval office, and to cancel his Fort Bragg appointments.

"Mendez, the president wants me in the Oval today, tell the council they would have to go on without me, and keep a detailed sheet of what transpired"

"You got it Sir." Mendez replied.

"Thank you, and I want you waiting in the hall when I get out"

Heaving a sigh, he dialed Buster's home cell, bit he got no response.

"Grace is always at home, isn't she?" He thought to himself as he dialed the Admiral's personal line

"Switched off?" He muttered. "Where is this man anyways?" He had finished his cup and placed it in the sink. He thought to wash it, but he did not want water on his uniform so he promiser himself to wash it as soon as he got back, as well as not bother himself about one item in his house that was out of place.

With that he left his house, but not before double checking the lock on the back door, as well as a check on windows, and finally his front door.

"Are we ready to leave for the Helipad, sir?"

"Not exactly, Lieutenant. Apparently, the President has other plans for us today. The White House, please."

"...and on God's green earth it has been that was for a long, long time."

"So, what you're saying in essence, is that letting in more immigrants has contributed to the rumors of a hack on the American government"

"You're damn right, I'm saying it!"

"Well thank you for calling in Mr Isaiah. That's it on Politics Where It Hits! Until next time, I remain Shanelle Waters, have a good day, and God Bless America"

"Hey, can you turn that up?" He instructed the driver, a red-faced young man with spots of acne on the side of his face. He looked young, but rather neat looking, and quite tall as well. Eisenhower especially admired how he handles his uniform, he thought it reminded him of himself.

"Yes Sir, right away" the driver responded, Eisenhower thought his tone to be rather enthusiastic.

As he increased the volume, he realised that whomever the DJ at the station favored the oldies; Brenton Wood's funk classics, some Bee Gee Bees too, and when a song by Elvis came on, Eisenhower could see himself humming along to the tune, his eyes taking in the sights of Washington.

As his ride approached the gates of the White House, he thought to inform the President of his inability to reach Buster's cell, but he thought against it. He would have to tell him in person.

"Welcome Sir, the President is waiting for you" came a familiar voice as he stepped out of the SUV he had been in.

"Oh, thank you. Estelle, is it?"

"Ethel, Sir. But its fine" She had replied, waving his mistake away with a smile.

"Oh, sorry. Ethel. I hope that bubbly is waiting for me today too"

"Unfortunately, not sir, the President instructed to have you sent here right away"

"Is that right? No problem, it is too early to be drinking anyways"

"The President also instructed me to, as he put it 'confiscate' all mobile devices, Sir. If that is fine by you"

"What do you mean 'confiscate'?" Eisenhower asked, his eyebrows furrowing.

"Oh, it's just that there is a widespread panic in the White House and the president think that the phones have been tapped and there are listening devices in all of them" She explained, they were already up the stairs and walking through the hallway that led to the Oval Office.

"I see. I'll have to decline and keep mine on me, I have a crucial meeting at Fort Bragg that I needed to be at, but I'm here in the White House! I need to get information from my subordinates as to how it went" He explained.

"I'm sorry Sir, but he won't approve of it, He had been really..." She tried to explain

"It'll just be just fine. I'm sure he won't mind. Is he in here?" They were at the door that led into the Oval Office.

"Yes sir. Have a great meeting. If you need anything, just call. I'll be outside here with Agent Cooley" She offered, pointing to Agent Cooley who was assumed a stance of salute.

"At ease soldier" he said, brushing past the open door and into the white house.

"Did you get his cellphone?" Agent Cooley asked.

"No, he wouldn't give it up" Ethel explained.

"Well, stick around then, you'll get a call from the big man himself any moment now" Agent Cooley replied, grinning.

"I bet I am, probably with some big talk too" She sighed.

Inside, Eisenhower had taken his seat as the President talked on the telephone with someone else

"Well, we will have to brief you later, won't we? Goodbye" he said, walking over to drop the phone on his desk.

"A Good to you Mr President"

"And to you too General, have a seat" he said, pointing to the chair behind the General. "That was McStephens, and he says he won't be joining us, apparently he had to leave town early this morning, and that he was on a flight to somewhere else, I think he said Alaska, or was it Milwaukee?" The President said.

"We can continue in his absence, can we sir?" Eisenhower requested; he had begun to grow restless.

"Yeah, yeah, yeah. But first off, have you given your phone away to Ethel?" President Wallace asked.

"No Sir, I have a meeting in a few minutes, and I have to be updates on every development"

"And I'm having a goddamn crisis General!" President Wallace blurted out, he had grown red and was furious."

"I understand your concerns my president, but this is a secure line of communication here, and It will be quite helpful to the military of our nation that I be a part of this meeting."

"General, take the phone out please, do it for me" The President pleaded.

"Okay Sir" he replied, sighing.

"Ethel! Come in here!" The president called, and Eisenhower thou he heard the doors swing open.

"Sir?" She responded.

"Could you be so kind as to help the General store his phone in a secure location for as long as this meeting holds, please?" He asked her.

"Sure." She replied, coming forward. With an awkward smile, and a nervous reach of her hands, she collected the phone and tiptoed out of the room.

"Thank you Ethel" She could hear the President call after her.

"Thank you Sir" she muttered in response.

Turning his attention to a visibly furious general, the President said, "Now General, I called you here for one particular reason."

"And what is that Sir?" He inquired.

"I need you to push some weapons to a secure location, off the books" Was the reply he got, he was sure to have registered a look of concern on his face.

"Weapons? Secure Location? What is happening sir?" He asked.

"After our discussion last week, I decided to put together a small task for, and I saddled them with the responsibility of undertaking just a tad bit of espionage" The President explained?

"Sir, you did what?"

"When I realised that there could be spies in the government, and that we could be on the brink of a cyber war, or even a real war, I panicked, alright?"

"You panicked Sir?"

"Exactly! So, I had Director Colby put together a team of agents, off the record, you know?"

"Off the record Sir? Forgive me but I don't think I approve of this your plan, Sir."

"I appreciate your reservations General, but this is a step in the right direction here!" The President replied enthusiastically.

"I hope so Sir, but what about out agents already on the field?" Eisenhower asked.

"Following suspicions that some of them might have been compromised, we put together this team that'll go way under their own radar, thus, each team is not aware of the presence of the other" He explained.

"It's still not adding up Sir, what if these new crops of agents get attacked by forces?"

"As sad as it would be that that would happen, Director Dolby worked out a plan; She said they would be treated as tourists that had mishaps" The President replied, his enthusiasm seemingly gone.

"Let us hope that doesn't happen sir." Eisenhower saw it best to encourage him. President Wallace saw it fit to comfort him, he looked like he hadn't slept in days.

"What do you suggest we do Mr President?" General Eisenhower asked.

"We will need guns, and drill training equipment"

"Done. Anything else?" He inquired.

"Russian weapons too, exclusively if possible" He added.

"That is brilliant sir" Eisenhower commended.

"We will also need a way to get weapons into a safehouse, somewhere near Moscow, that'll be when the agents are on the field" President Wallace added.

"We will have to liaise with the CIA for that to happen, they might have safehouses, maybe inside Moscow that we can use"

"Excellent, how soon can you get the weapons?" President Wallace asked, he was starting to look impatient.

"I was on my way to Fort Bragg when you called, I could procure a few boxes. How would I deliver them, to where even?"

"Wait, I have the coordinates here, let me get them" President Wallace replied, searching through the papers on his table, muttering as he did.

After a short search, he found a yellow piece of paper, which he handed over to the General.

"Here, this is where I'll need you to drop them"

"54.7266° N, 164.2170° W, isn't that over in Alaska, the Unimak Islands?" General Eisenhower was curious.

"Yes it is, any problems?" He asked.

"Oh, no Sir, it just feels so remote, and random too" he offered, explaining his questions.

"Exactly what we were going for General, exactly!"

"But sir, that is about 5 thousand clicks from Fort Bragg"

"Well, it is 6598.31 kilometers to me exact, but you're getting the picture."

"But Sir, that is almost 2 days by chopper"

"Not if you use a plane, it isn't. What is the fastest and most discrete we got?" He asked.

"Eh, I have to make a few calls sir, I don't..."

"How about the Beechcraft C-12 Huron? Do you have one of those at Fort Bragg"

"As a matter of fact, we do, how do you know that? General Eisenhower was puzzled.

"Dolby. She wrote everything down. What a woman" he said, brandishing a sheet of paper that carried a list of requirements.

"Alright Sir. I'll check in with my subordinates and we'll get a pilot and a crew to check the airworthiness of the aircraft as soon as I get my phone back"

"You go do that, have a good one Eisenhower" he said, ushering him out of his office.

"You too Sir" Eisenhower saluted and turned to leave.

"Here you go Sir, sorry for the embarrassment" Ethel had jumped to her feet as he opened the door.

"Oh, it's no problem. Tell my driver to come around to the front gate with my car, please. I have to make a call to my assistant" he said, dialing Mendez's number.

CHAPTER EIGHT

As he picked up, Mendez informed him of his closeness to the White House, and that he was awaiting further instructions.

"No, Mendez. Go get the chopper ready, we are going to Fort Bragg anyways"

"Alright sir, right away" came the response on the phone, and General Eisenhower thought he heard screeching of tires.

"Easy there boy, don't overdo it" he muttered as he cut the call. Although Lt Mendez was a level-headed soldier, he was often too excited, especially when he was given an order, a soldier true and true, but there were times that General Marry Eisenhower wished that Lieutenant Mendez Alfonso would take a chill pill. He wanted this so bad that if he disobeyed a direct order on any occasion, he would hesitate to have him court-martialed.

"Easy there boy, don't overdo it" he muttered as he cut the call. Although Lt Mendez was a level-headed soldier, he was often too excited, especially when he was given an order, a soldier true and true. But there were times that General Marry Eisenhower wished that Lieutenant Mendez Alfonso would take a chill pill. He wanted this so bad that if he disobeyed a direct order on any occasion, he would hesitate to have him court-martialed.

He was already out of the front door, and as he stood in the sun, he could see his driver pull up around the corner. He seemed to increase his acceleration as he got to see him under the Sun.

"It's the trivial things" General Eisenhower thought.

"Are we headed somewhere else; General Sir" came the driver's voice as he turned on the Air conditioner.

"The helipad, please. The president wants me in Fort Bragg"

"Yes Sir" the driver said, turning the car towards the main entrance, where a small group of protesters had gathered calling for decisive action towards internet security.

As they drove past them, General Eisenhower could see their placards, and he was able to read quite a few.

"WE DON'T WANT TO GO BACK TO THE STONE AGE!"

"INTERNET SECURITY NOW!"

"PROTECT MY WIFI!"

"Easy, you sissies" he cursed. No matter how hard the government worked, the populace always seemed ungrateful, and although it was usually a faction, they were sure to put the Presidency under unnecessary pressure.

"Look at them, entitled teenagers who have done nothing for the government, but they expect everything done for them. It is sad isn't it" He had been bothered with how he was to smuggle the arms the president required out of Fort Bragg, and he needed to be distracted for a bit.

"Damn right Sir. I miss when it was cool to fight and might I say, die for one's country. Now they tweet about how they hate America, and get sad, and angry when the climes don't favour them"

"How old are you soldier?" He asked.

"I am 24, sir." The driver replied.

"And where are you from, solider?" He asked another question, he seemed like an interesting young man.

"Ohio sir, I was born in Heath."

"Heath? Where is that?"

"Right in the center, Sir"

"Do you like sports?"

"Yes Sir, I do. I'm a huge fan of the Buckeyes myself" The driver replied excitedly, shifting in his seat.

"That is quite sad, really" Eisenhower said.

"What is, If I may ask, Sir?" The driver seemed concerned.

"That you're not a Rams fan" The general was laughing. Somehow his mind seemed to stray back to the issue at hand.

"It's all about loyalty Sir" Eisenhower heard the driver speak in response.

"Say, soldier. How would you successfully evade a Cornerback that you know is coming for your legs"

"I played high school football Sir, and I don't mean to brag, but all I have to do is jump over them"

"Oh, we're referring to the big leagues here, Soldier. What would you do?"

"I'd create a distraction, then I'd feign several movements, you know, confuse the cornerback, then I'd jump up, above and past him. He'll be getting the grass from under his teeth do a week sir" The driver replied, rather enthusiastically too.

"So, you'd create a distraction first, is that right?"

"Yes sir!"

"How big of a distraction are we talking about?"

"I could hold out my free arm, and he'd think I'm signaling a teammate, or I could just charge for him as well, with quick feet, at the last seconds I could change my directions a few times and evade him"

"This is quite impressive Soldier"

"Thank you sir! Also, we're here!" He exclaimed, pointing to the helicopter, a UH-60 Black Hawk, freshly painted, with the US flag slapped across its side in a rather fashionable style.

"Ah there she is, Lucy" he gasped.

"Welcome Sir, I've been waiting" Mendez was running up to the car. A thirty year old son of Cuban immigrants born in the first year of his parent's arrival, Lt Mendez had grown up following orders, and learning the importance of hard work, his grandfather, a manager at a rather large cigar company, had sent his father to the United States in attempts to get him a degree, but his father had chosen to instead smuggle his girlfriend in with him, and not long after they had arrived, she was pregnant and he had to quit the University to make extra cash. He begun working at local restaurants, bars, and hotels as either a hand in the kitchen, a supplies manager or as a cook.

Although his grandfather had cut his father off, he took a liking to Mendez, pleading with gifts that his grandson be named after him. There were speculations that he wanted the young Alfonso to take after him, and eventually manage his Cigar factory, but from an early age, the boy was hellbent on wearing the uniform of the United States Army.

"Come to Cuba" his grandfather had said, but before his parent could stop him, he was already on his first tour to Afghanistan.

"The chopper is ready for you Sir" he smiled excitedly as he opened the door for General Eisenhower, the gap where he had lost a tooth and the scar on his lip standing out.

"Thank you Mendez, and you're coming with me to Fort Bragg!" General Eisenhower said, approaching the helicopter. As he walked, he reached into his pocket, searching for the paper holding the coordinates from the president.

"Alright Sir"

"We have a mission! Do you know how to fly a helicopter?" The general asked.

"Yes Sir, I do"

"Good, because you're flying this one. Tell the pilot to clock out for the day"

"Alright Sir" Mendez was already at the pilot's side of the helicopter, informing him of the General's decision.

Not long after that, they were in the air, and headed for Fort Bragg. As soon as they were away from the ground, the General spoke.

"Lt Mendez, can I trust you?"

"Of course, Sir!"

"Because we will need to do something off the books here. President's orders!"

"What exactly does he have in mind sir!"

"A smuggle! Russian weapons, to the Unimak islands."

"May I ask why Sir!"

"I don't know either Lieutenant, I am following orders, I suggest you do same!"

"Sir, yes Sir!"

"How was the council meeting?"

"It was rather uneventful without your presence Sir! Except for the discussion of the cyber-attacks on the White House, and an interception of foreign signals, probably for an attack on the Capitol and its systems"

"The capitol?"

"Affirmative Sir!"

"What did the head of the taskforce on internet security have to say about that?"

"Well, Major Groove says he has launched a full-scale investigation and that the identity of the criminals will be uncovered."

"Is that so?"

"Well, I mean, not exactly Sir. The team in charge was only able to uncover their location. Locations to be more accurate"

"Locations? Where are these locations?"

"Yakutsk in Russia, and somewhere on the outskirts of Weinan in China, at least that is what GPS coordinates say"

"Any chance these could have been decoy signals?"

"Still under investigation, but highly probable, according to the Tech team that filed the report."

"Thank you Mendez. Were there any comments on my absence?"

"Yes sir, but I told them that you had to see the president for important state business in a meeting behind closed doors"

"Good, good. Now we will have to devise a strategy for this smuggle to be successful."

CHAPTER NINE

"What exactly did they bring us here to do?"

A loud groan could be heard from other occupants of the room.

"Oh, shut up" came a strong voice.

"If you would just listen to me! Alright?"

"Look, say what you have to say and then shut up!" Aria barked. She had been frustrated enough and the last thing she needed was a man-child projecting his energies unto her.

"Hey easy there, I just have a theory, alright?"

"We're patient Zero for a new kind of disease!" He blurted, sparking another set of groans.

"Of course, you would think that!" Gemini's tone was harsh, just how he had hoped to sound.

"Look at the facts alright?" Jabez was sure to defend his beliefs, this irked the others to no end.

"Lay them out wise one, we're all curious here" Skunk responded, a sarcastic undertone could be detected by everyone but Jabez, who saw this as an opportunity to explain his theories.

"So, you see, they brought us from wherever they brought us from, and they kept us in a remote island, under the guise that they would send us to faraway lands on a mission that could be deemed suicide"

"Oh, shut up, keep it down" Gemini would not hear another word.

"Would you just listen? They brought us here, and now we're here, right? Has anyone seen a weapon? I mean one firearm that would aid us in weapons training. No? Because we are the weapon!" He exclaimed.

"Only dumb people take you seriously Mr Jabez, and I am not dumb." Gemini was adamant in his resistance. He knew Jabez's type; they would sow fear in the hearts of soldiers and then lead them on a charger, with afraid, pounding hearts, right to their demise. At least that is how his grandfather had died during the Civil War in his home country, where a captain had sold out his infantry in exchange for a seat of authority when the war was over.

"You should be scared, trust me. If you wake up by tomorrow morning and there are no guns, military training devices and all that, know that you are the weapon" He shrugged, turning to his pillow, but not before biding his counterparts a good night.

"Screw you man-child" someone cursed, but Jabez was already fast asleep, not even the plane that seemed to fly over them and the rather huge thud a few blocks away seemed to wake neither Jabez, nor his dysfunctional room of team members.

The morning was sun was not as bright as they would have hoped, but the air was cold, not to the extent that it would bite off a finger, but cold enough to make the teeth of whomever was out in just pajamas clench together in agony, but not when you're Jabez Glee and you're welding a bottle of well-aged scotch and a carefree attitude, accompanied by sleepy eyes and an early morning high.

Slowly, he wondered up the hill and towards the dining area, cursing himself for being awake that early and saying that a real man doesn't wake up until 4.

It was 5:39, but that was just according to the clock on the Director's wall. Rachel Dolby had just gotten off a prayer call with her husband when she looked through her window and saw her pick do team captain, with what seemed to be a bottle of alcohol, waddling towards the dining area.

Deep in regret, she shook her head.

"Damn Rachel, your first miss in a few years. Sigh" she muttered. Although she knew she was stuck with him, getting rid of him was quite easy; a few well-articulated calls and she would have him done away with and at the bottom of nearby water bodies. But she didn't do that, even when she had a direct order to protect her country at all costs.

It wasn't even pity, if it was she would have left him drunk and probably having unprotected sex with paid, but usually uninterested women, who in turn only gave a pitiful moan, practiced, and perfected by years of practice, and to the unfortunately unlucky, a baby, or even worse, a reason to take drugs that regulate sexually transmitted diseases.

"Hey Jabez!" She called, cracking open and window and taking in the frigid air.

He turned, searching for the voice. In the distance, he looked like a man lost in a sea of his own making, like if Poseidon forgot how to swim. A highly rated agent, he had succumbed to substance abuse once, when he had to find an arms dealer, but he just had to stop by his dealer's. Turns out the arms dealer and he had the same drug dealer, so in a rage induced by the substance he said he wanted to "sample" before he bought, he pounced on the arms dealer, killing him in the process.

In no time, all of Berlin was on him, and after 3 days of no sleep, with office agents trying their best to help him escape Berlin, CCTV footage of him falling after being shot in the back was uncovered and he was presumed dead. There was a quiet burial slated for the following week, but he resurfaced on the morning of the preparations, nursing an almost broken neck, and cut wounds that showed signs of torture.

"Who died" He had asked, even after seeing his picture surrounded by flowers at the memorial service held on office grounds.

Following a debriefing, by then Director of the CIA, they had all agreed to put the events of Berlin'07 behind them all, including Dolby, who at the time was assigned to taking notes.

But he had made a full come back and by the summer of 2013, he was in the field again, but this time he didn't relapse, he went and impregnated the daughter of the Mexican crime boss he was supposed to give Intel about. In the final hours of what was otherwise a stellar job, he had helped the daughter of the crime boss escape, who was a vital part of her father's operations and basically ran everything. She had played him, and it was said that she was not actually pregnant.

After being court martialed and placed under suspension with half his usual pay, he was reinstated, and he sought permission to track his estranged baby mama, Rosa, down.

He eventually caught up to her in Australia, and with one less bullet in gun and a wanted warrant because security cameras had captured the execution, he still managed to escape being arrested, this time unscathed, and eventually cleared his name.

Since then, he had been upstanding, and even won the employee of the month twice, possibly in 2017 or 2018. The he plummeted into a depression and has since been off duty or fired.

Now he was back, in her life, as she had given him another opportunity to prove himself, to earn his place in the circle of things. She was not sure about the other, neither did she doubt their credibility, but she was sure that Jabez was right for the job, even if he didn't want it.

It took a knock on the door to jolt her back to reality. Rachel Dolby took her time and make sure she had gotten herself together before she opened the door to whomever was at the other side.

"Jabez! Where did you get that from?" She screamed. He was holding an assault rifle and was almost as surprised as she was.

"Crate by the beach" he muttered, collapsing on the floor in front of her.

"There goes today's training" she thought to herself, as she dragged him inside the apartment and towards the fireplace, where she put a blanket over him and proceeded to phone the medical team she had chosen.

"...Olivier, come with a stretcher please" she pleaded, putting down the phone and rushing to get a kettle boiling so that she could massage his body with hot water.

As she struggled to save the life of the one person that almost half a million people's lives depended on, she be ga rethinking her life's choices, especially this one.

"Was he a good fit?" She asked herself.

Of course, he was! Unlike the other agents who possessed stellar accomplishments and had been sober since the day they were born, they made up for their non-consumption of alcohol in the number of bribes they took and the terrible judgments they had. Also, they seemed too "American", with accents that could be picked out in a European crowd, and habits that screamed "USA!". She didn't want that for this mission.

It was also best that the agents on this mission have no prior relationships with the other spies that were positioned in various parts of Russia, and recently, China too. Those agents may have been sabotaged and introducing familiar faces where they were could cause the mission to cascade on itself.

Although Jabez was a popular face in the earlier parts of the decade, this new crop of agents would not recognize him, as there were no honorary portraits placed anywhere. Even his name was not Jabez too! He had gone by the codename "Ichabod" during his agency days and was almost always away on a mission.

Also, he had changed, and as he lay helpless and cold, right in front of her fireplace, Director Rachel Dolby could we that he was a far cry from the young agent with dashing looks and a killer smile; he had grown and bore the looks of a man with a struggle, like a flower touched by thorns, greying too.

CHAPTER TEN

By the time the rest of the crew was awake, they were summoned to the meeting area where a surprise awaited them.

"Oh, yeah. This is it!" Skunk yelled excitedly as he trotted into the room, where he clutched onto rifle that was placed on the table in front of him.

"Is this AK-74M?" he asked, caressing the gun. In his excitement, he did a little tango, the gun as his dance partner.

"It sure is" Gemini replied, his eyes glistening.

"Look, I got the AK-12" Harry yelled, giggling.

"Is that the one with the 700 rounds per minute fire rate?" Skunk asked, rushing over to admire her gun.

"880–900 miles per second muzzle velocity? Sign me up!" Aria said, clutching her weapon.

"I am glad you love your weapons, but word reaching me is that we would not be having firearms training today. Your colleague, Mr Jabez Glee has become sick and needs a day or two to heal"

"Oh, come on! We cannot have anything good with him lurking around!" Gemini cursed.

"The Director has instructed that today be a day for team building exercises, where you get to know each other properly." The assistant said again.

"Can't we just shoot guns instead?" Harry asked, she looked like she was about to have tantrum.

"I'm afraid not, Ms. Harry. Have a lovely day. Breakfast will be ready soon, and you will be informed of that shortly." With that she ushered in more assistants who cleared out all the guns. An assistant had to nearly rip Skunk's weapon away, as he would not give it up. Gemini on the other hand, threw his to the floor, hissing in utter disdain, muttering curses.

"So, what do we do now?" Harry asked, looking at the other occupants of the room.

"I don't even know" Gemini said, running his hands his low-cut hair, cupping them on the back of his head and resigning to seat in the chair behind him.

"Who wants to share first?" Aria asked.

"Share?" came Skunk's response.

"Yeah, that's what we were told to do, isn't it?" She asked.

"Alright, I'll go first" Gemini said, standing up from his seat and taking a small stroll, turn in dramatically as he told his story. He seemed to be in a sudden good mood, and the other were sure he was masking his anger against Jabez.

According to him, He was the second child of twins born in a remote village in western Nigeria. Born to Yoruba parents at a time when his father was highly advised to take a second wife, seeing that his first was not going to give birth any time soon.

However, a few months prior to this arranged wedding, his mother had become pregnant and after a while, she gave birth to twins, whom she named after the proverbial twins, Taiwo and Kehinde. The boys were practically inseparable and indistinguishable as they grew.

As soon as they turned sixteen, their grandfather, a retired army general who saw it upon himself to make sure the boys turned out better than their father, an editor for a local newspaper, whom he had deemed a failure, he sent them to England, where he enrolled them in a military school. There they grew up, and by the time they were back in the country, they had become men; tall, physically attractive, and by no means less distinguishable.

It was here that the story would take a negative then, as Taiwo, the other of the siblings who had secured a job working in the police administration, was killed when disgruntled youth razed the police administrative offices. The offices were burnt to ashes, and according to reports, so did Taiwo. Kehinde was heartbroken and fled the country in a bid to start over without his brother.

He was quickly scouted by the MI6, the British intelligence agency and was set up with agency contract and assigned to Scotland Yard. It was there that rumors of a mysterious killer for hire surfaced, after several killings of quite important people in the London underworld died, then the entirety of the United Kingdom, then Europe at large.

He was charged with finding this killer and unmasking him, thereby bringing him to justice. He then begun a yearlong hunt, but for some reason, this unnamed assassin kept evading him, almost as if he knew what he was doing.

In a bid to alter his mind and find a new way to tackle the menace, he took a rather unconventional method of ingesting psychedelic drugs in a bid to come up with an out of the ordinary strategy, his time was running out and going back to the agency that had funded his yearlong expedition with no proof of success was not in the picture.

"It was on April 3rd, a few weeks before my birthday…" He was interrupted.

"Wait, so you took drugs to alter your thinking?" Harry asked.

"Yes, I did."

"Impressive" she replied to a look of approval on her face.

"Where was I?" He spoke.

"A few weeks to my birthday and I get this sense that I'm being followed. So, I get into an alleyway, and I wait for whomever is shadowing me to walk past so that I can make then unconscious, yeah? But turns out they're actually smart and I get drugged and dragged to who I assume is their boss. But that is where it gets interesting, because he sounds exactly like me!"

With the blindfold still on his face, He could hear the crime boss speak to the henchmen that brought his disturbances to his notice and promise to reward them well.

As the boss turns to address him, Kehinde calls out his brother's name, which surprises him and his cronies because he had not expected to be planning to execute his own brother, just yet.

Despite being the older sibling, Taiwo had always felt left out of certain things, like getting chics, friendship, and most times even his parent's love. Kehinde was always loved, respected, and in Military school, subordinates downright feared him.

He had joined the police to get the approval of his grandfather, while Kehinde had chosen to become a newsman, like their father, but for some reason he didn't feel at peace, maybe it was because his grandfather had lost his memory and could almost not remember anything anymore, or maybe because his father had always held a disapproving gaze when he was around.

According to him, when the youths had their riot, he saw it a perfect opportunity to escape, start afresh, and make a career out of taking his dissatisfaction with the way he was treated out on deserving people for money.

Kehinde on the other hand, was devastated and blamed himself for his brother's death, and was hellbent on avenging him. He had rebelled and taken his savings to go build a reputation in England and come back in the best future to police his community.

During their altercation, Kehinde said he was sure he heard his brother say that he wanted to come for him when he was done with mercenary jobs, and that he was the final peace in his puzzle of fulfilment.

Although the story did not end the way Kehinde thought it would, he knew he had to end his brother's life, although unwillingly.

It was after he had done this that he discovered that his brother had a child with a woman who knew him as Shammah, their family name, and that they had a child together. He swore to take care of the infant in ways that he could, agreeing with its mother to not disclose that fact that its father is dead.

"Would you want him to hate you when he grows up?" Aria asked.

"I don't" Gemini was in tears.

"Then tell him soon enough" she advised, comforting him.

"Dude, you liked your brother?" Harry could not get enough of his story.

"Is that all you took from that?" Skunk asked.

"Yeah. That and it can be made into a bad ass movie"

"That is true, I would see that." Skunk concurred.

"So why do they call you Skunk?" Harry asked.

"It's Ironic"

"No, it's not" She replied.

"It is!"

"It's not!"

"I say it is!"

"And I don't agree, there had to be a story there" "There is, but it doesn't leave this room, got it?"

Skunk has served in the military, on the walkway as a model, and even in strip clubs. His looks had attracted many advances, and from all genders too.

But lurking beneath the mask was a blood curdling urge to engage in combat. One morning, on a whim, he signed up to be drafted to Afghanistan, ditching his career as a model for companies that would lay him good money.

After 3 months of rigorous training, he was shipped to Afghanistan, and in less than two weeks since his arrival, all the friends he had made on the way over were either dead or injured. Still, he fought on, dating commanders, and engaging in combat of his own accord.

His brainless tactics soon got him in trouble as he was captured by a terrorist boss who thought to make a lesson out of him. Armed with pure skunk essence, the terrorist cell made sure he was well coated in the absolutely foul-smelling liquid before they let him go, earning him the name. As a result, he was told to remain in camp and in isolation till he could stop giving away their positions to the enemies and upsetting his fellow soldiers.

CHAPTER ELEVEN

After about a half a month or so, even when it had not completely worn off, he took it upon himself to attack the camp of the terrorist cell that had humiliated him.

Armed with knives, he slaughtered every last one of them, and according to stories in the army, you would hear a foul smell and while you are adjusting your nose to it, he would slit your throat.

Although he was reprimanded and sent back to the states for mental evaluation, his time as the skunk was surely impactful, and several stories were spun about his ferocious attack. They said forty-two men died that night, half of whom were sleeping.

Back in the states, he surprisingly passed his mental evaluation exams and according to doctors, he showed no signs of any mental illness, despite admitting to close friends that he had flashbacks of that night, as well as regrets.

With these stellar results at the evaluations, a desire to kill for one's country and a rather attractive face, he was recruited by a department in the CIA where he worked on cases that were deemed impossible, cracking them with little difficulty. He rose through the ranks and was just inline for a promotion in rank as well as widespread recognition when he snapped, resigned from his job, and disappeared. He was not seen for a long while, but he was In Europe and Africa taking mercenary jobs, in the shadows.

"Do you regret killing him" Aria asked a teary Gemini, she was comforting him, although he had said not to. According to her, he needed it, but he didn't know.

"So, who is next," Gemini asked, "I want to hear everyone's story today" he added, sniffling.

"Not me!" Harry was already out of the room. She said she was hungry and needed to grab a bite. Unwillingly, the rest followed, and the conversation was transferred to the dining area.

While inside, they all got rations, or rightly put, a misery serving of eggs, veggies, and watered-down coffee.

"Feels like prison again" Skunk said, to which everyone let out a hearty laugh.

"What do you think happened to Jabez?" Gemini asked when the laughter had died down.

"I don't know, but my guess is that he either tried to drown after getting too drunk too early, or he was smacked right in the face with his own bottle" they laughed again, this time even the dining area staff joined.

"But what do you think is happening in America?" Gemini asked, a look of concern had registered on his face. The laugher had died down, and so did the smiles that usually followed.

"A cousin of mine knows someone that lost all her cryptocurrency during one of the attacks" Harry said.

"Wait, they actually happened?" Aria was shocked.

"Yeah, they did. The government called them 'alleged' because they weren't wide scale like that" Gemini said, disgust was registered on his face. The yolk on his serving of boiled eggs was raw.

"Oh, I see. I thought it happened only in Russia to be very honest with you guys" Aria said, returning to her meal of oats and almond milk.

"Wait, Russia?" Harry was stunned.

"Russia? Are they victims as well?" Skunk asked. Gemini had gone to question the cook about the state of his eggs.

"I guess so. It affected people that had connected to Wi-Fi networks the most. They called it the biggest heist without a gun, everything from information to dead altcoins sitting at the bottom of crypto wallets were stolen." Aria said.

"Propaganda. That's what It is." Skunk wasn't impressed.

"I don't think so. I know people who lost things" Aria defended her claims.

"In person, or do these people know people that you know?"

There was silence, only disturbed by Gemini's shuffling of feet. He had gotten bacon instead, which he didn't like. He preferred his pork with a lot of peppers, not dry and salty.

"Exactly! All these might just be propaganda!" Skunk seemed excited, like a detective that had uncovered vital information.

"Or maybe not. What else could it be?" Harry asked.

"A deliberately outrageous plot by governments to spy on each other. To steal information from each other too!"

"So that's what we are here for? We're all thieves in our own rights!" Harry said.

"Exactly!" Skunk said.

"Not me. I've never stolen a day in my life. Well, except guns from dead perps when my own ammo is low, you know?"

"Yeah, unlike in the movies. Like I know that gun can hold only six bullets, why are you shooting with it for almost the entirety of the movie!" Harry concurred.

"Or like how the bad guys never land a single shot!" Aria interjected; her face lit up.

"Exactly! I have a few bullet wounds to prove that bad guys have extremely good aim' they all laughed.

"Guys! We're getting off topic here." Skunk said, interrupting the new lines of conversation.

"Come on man! Chill out for a bit!" Harry was not impressed anymore.

"That is how pawn die in a chess game, and pawn is even a dignified term for what we are" Skunk said.

"Slaves?" Gemini asked, looking him dead in the eyes.

"Yeah, yeah" he responded in nonchalance, before catching Gemini's cold, piercing, black eyes and he swiftly changed his opinion.

"So, if we're lower than pawn, and not exactly slaves, what are we?" Aria asked.

We're soldiers." Gemini replied. "We are not pawn, those are inanimate, and we are not slaves, because we chose this life and all our choices, individually and collectively, have brought us to this point, right here" He was standing up to go get seconds. A man that tall did not sustain himself on one serving.

"He is right, you know" Aria said, as the others watched him go.

"Yeah. But I still call propaganda!" Skunk was adamant.

"What are we going to do today, anyways?" Harry asked.

"I heard Chinese is involved in this, somehow." Skunk said, ignoring her question.

"China?" they both turned to look at him.

"You all don't follow the news?"

"I think their beef is with Russia though. Isn't it?" Harry said.

"How about we go to the beach?" Aria asked.

"That would be great, but now listen…" Before Skunk could continue, they had left the table, giggling as the left him with nobody to talk to.

"I just realized that you didn't share your story, Aria"

"Did you share?" Harry was laughing.

"Soon enough. But no pressure, am I right?"

"Yeah." With that they had left the dining area, and were chased by Skunk, who had not finished his food.

In the distance, they could see Gemini walking towards the sleeping area. A rather tall man with broad shoulders and a muscular build that seemed to be more of genetics than gyms, he kept his hair at a buzz cut level, and was clean shaven, but they thought he would look good in a beard.

Behind them, Skunk had caught up and was panting heavily, while asking if they had plans for the day, and that he had no ideas about what to do.

"How about we go to the beach?" Aria asked again.

"Oh, damn it. I'm in" he muttered.

"I'll run along and ask Gemini" Harry said, speeding off and disappearing into their sleeping area.

"I noticed that you didn't share, why Is that?" Skunk asked Aria as soon as Harry was out of sight.

Although she had been dreading the questions, she had braced herself for it and was sure her past would not trigger her anymore.

"Well, I did not get any opportunities, now did I?

"Looks like you had plenty to be honest" Skunk argued.

"It did not seem that way to he, at all"

"It sure did. Why do I feel like you ladies are hiding something?" He questioned.

"Ladies? I don't know about Harry, but I have nothing to hide, and as such when the time is right, I'll share. Is that right?"

As the approved their sleeping area, they could overhear a conversation between Gemini and Harry.

"...Swim? We won't be swimming, right?" He asked, to which she burst into laughter.

"What kind of spy doesn't know how to swim?" She was holding her stomach and crouched in pain

"It is funny, isn't it?" He, however, was not laughing.

"Yes it is" She gasped for air, but the reaction on his face only seemed to make it funnier.

"Let's go please" he urged, after he had taken off his shirt and worn something a bit lighter.

At the door, he found Skunk and Aria standing there, with Skunk nursing what seemed to be a scar of a knife cut on his elbow.

As soon as Harry joined them, they had headed to the beach, passing by what used to be the houses of the native occupants of the island before the government relocated then to the other side of the island.

Then they came up to a crate with just the word "Kalashnikov" on the sides and what seemed like an empty shell of a 5.45×39mm cartridge.

"This might have been what brought the weapons, and not the plane that brought us" Gemini chuckled.

"Jabez was wrong. Shocker" Aria added, to which everyone laughed.

"So, this is what caused that loud thud?" Harry had finally caught up to the rest of the crew.

"You heard it too?" Gemini asked.

"Yeah, if I had any weapons I would have investigated it"

"Yeah me too, I could sleep till 4 because of it" Gemini responded again.

Harry was surprised, she hadn't slept as well, "Me too!" She screamed.

"You guys didn't sleep?" Skunk asked, causing everyone to laugh.

As they descended down the rocks that had formed due to the many volcanic eruptions that had plagued the island, they saw a figure sitting in the distance.

"Who's that, didn't they clear out the inhabitants?" Harry asked.

"It says so in the handbook we were given" Gemini said.

Cautiously they descended from the rocks and towards the figure, who turned out to be Director Colby.

"Ma'am you scared us" Harry yelled.

"I did? How exactly did I do that?"

"We thought you were a spy of some sort!" Gemini responded.

"Aren't we all" she replied, to which they all shrugged. "Have a seat, I want to speak to you all about this mission. I was going to do so over at the meeting area, but it is quite lucky that you all found your way to me" she said, pointing to the sand all around her.

As soon as they had sat, Director Dolby heaved a sigh and began to speak.

"You all have questions, and that is a fact, but so do we; the US government that is. We have been attacked severally, at the White House, the Capitol, even a military base in Utah. All these are threats to national security, and in our day and age, that cannot be overlooked. You might have heard the rumors, maybe read a few things too". She said but was interrupted by Harry.

"Yeah, before you took away our phones" He commented.

"Safety protocol Harry. As I was saying, there have been rumors of attacks in other places too; Russia, China etc., but according to our intelligence reports, these might just be decoy attacks by both governments to shield the fact that they are the attackers and not some other sovereign state, or terrorist cell.

With that being said, despite the fact that you will be given weapons training, and coordinates for the location of a safehouse with an ample stash of guns and other supplies, you are not to engage physically unless otherwise engaged. You are also advised to keep a pistol native to the country of your assignment on you at all times, especially those who would be assigned to infiltrate the intelligence agencies of these countries."

"So, when do we leave?" Gemini asked, he head staring into the icy water, the waves crashing on one another seemed to make his skin crawl, but he braved it regardless.

"In a week or two, depending on the outcome of your training which starts tomorrow"

"Sweet!" Harry was excited, she would finally get to play with her new guns.

"If you will excuse me, I have a meeting with the president and several service chiefs, have a good day, agents" With that said, Director Dolby left them there, and walked back up the rocky sides and disappeared into the distance.

"First, I would check on the man child" she thought to herself, stop by at the infirmary before proceeding to her room for the meeting.

CHAPTER TWELVE

Although he was unsure whether the progress reports of the special team he had set up to investigate the matter at hand was capable of completing the task, he was particularly worried about the agent that was tipped to lead his team to success.

As he and several key members of his team waited for the Director of the CIA to come in for her daily report, he got news that General Eisenhower was enroute Washington via a motorcade and would be joining via video chat.

The President was skeptical about this approach to information delivery at the moment, but the engineers had allayed his fear, staring that they had coated his communications with layers upon layers of encryption.

Deep in thou, he didn't seem to hear the knock on the door, but as he turned to sit on his desk, in came Admiral McStephens, who greeted him with a salute. He was holding a tablet that showed General Eisenhower in video chat, and he too was full of good news.

"Good morning Buster, how was your trip?"

"Splendid Mr President"

"Good morning Eisenhower, and thank you for your service"

"All in a day's work, Mr President."

Alright then, have a seat, gentlemen. The Director of the FBI, and that of the CIA will be joining us soon. The Secretary of Defense, however, will not be joining us, he is speaking at a Peace summit somewhere in Africa, likewise the Vice President.

In walked, Director Joaquin Taylor, a tall man, balding and with rather thick looking facial hair, he muttered greetings, before unveiling a tablet and putting a call through to a waiting Director Colby.

After the usual exchange of pleasantries, the President began to speak, stressing the need for cyber security and for a stance to be made as soon as possible.

"Our agents have a picture of what they are to do Sir, we will have gathered necessary information in no-time"

Director Colby offered.

"Good. About the agent you said had fallen sick, what is the update on his condition?"

"Agent Jabez is recovering at a fast rate, he was not infected with anything contagious and should be ready to resume training in the coming days."

"Good, thank you. And you, Buster, any news on how we would get our agents into enemy territory?

"Our plans to incorporate their user details into several older servers and inventory reports are going smoothly, our agents are sure to have even parking tickets in their names dating back seven to eight years."

"Impressive, being believable is key here" he replied, turning to the tablet that the Admiral carried, "General, thank you for the delivery if the weapons, Director Colby has given news that she has received them"

"Like I said, Mr President, it's my duty to serve"

"Thank you. Director Taylor, what news do you have to give?"

"As The Admiral has said, we have inputted records for all agents dating back 30 years into the Russian systems, our work is impeccable, and our methods are thorough"

"Absolutely impressive, but about the locations of the signals though, what are we saying about those?"

"The points of interception still remain the same, and it would be advisable to visit these points in a bid to uncover these mishaps"

"And cyber security in the White House? What are we doing about that?"

"Well, Sir. My team is hands on all day to ensure that all devices within the premises are encrypted with high end encryption and immune to hackers and Internet pillagers. This is a fact I can be assured of..."

As she spoke, there was a sudden burst through the door, and in came the First Lady, accompanied by a running Agent Cooley.

"It's happening again!" She yelled, pointing her phone in the face of all that sat in the Oval Office.

"What is it, hon?"

"I can tell that I'm being monitored"

Instantly, there was a panic as the President grabbed the phone and dunked it in the jar of water that sat on his table, he ordered that all calls be ended, leaving Director Colby and General Eisenhower shut out of all communications. In a panic, he left the oval, escorted by Agent Cooley and the First Lady, but not before turning to Director Taylor and screaming,

"You have a week to get me answers! A week!"

As left, there was quiet, an uneasy feeling of both incompetence and discouragement, a union borne out of perceived mediocrity.

So, they sat in the Oval, the soldier with stellar accomplishments and a reputation for excellence, and the socially awkward, private analyst who had equally stellar accomplishments, but lacking in the charisma to brag about his. In silence they sat, each begging the other to leave first, but both not having the courage to lead the exit, sitting with heads bleed in thoughts.

"Good day Admiral" Came the Director's voice suddenly, but before Buster McStephens could respond, he was already out the door and into the corridor.

Outside, he used a burner to reach the Director of the CIA, who he informed of the president's deadline.

"Damn it! What happened?" Director Colby asked.

"Cyber-attack, on the First Lady's cell too"

"Damn it. A week huh?" She asked again.

"Yes."

"Thank you Director Taylor.

"You're welcome Director Colby, and whatever you're doing, do it quicker, times running out, the stock market could be next, and we don't want that"

"We don't" she replied, ending the call, and heaving a heavy sigh. Pressure was mounting, and she needed to be proactive. They all did.

CHAPTER THIRTEEN

Mornings that were cold as this one had not come around in a while. They seemed to defy the sun, striking just the same as its ever-burning glare. A barrage of both the cold, and the lukewarm, a mix that spoke volumes of the creativity of nature, or climate change.

The day was bright, but still it stung, so much so that if you kept your jacket on while indoors, no one would offer to take it away, or cast side glances at you, they'd even offer a beverage.

This, right here, was the day that President Wallace decided to expand his little project. A project that seemed to cost quite a lot in terms of funding, seeing that the agents that were recruited had to be compensated, especially during their mission overseas, and in lies as well. He had just shredded a military mandated piece of paperwork that sought to launch an inquiry into misplaced foreign artillery.

"Nosey bastards" he cursed, nursing the drink that Agent Cooley had poured him. Suddenly, realizing a fact that had stared him in the face, he reached out to Director Colby through a secure line he had set up for him.

"Director, I trust everything is going according to plan?"

"Quite so, Mr President. Our ailing agent is having a full recovery and would be getting back to preparations in no time"

"Good. He better. There's over four hundred million people depending on that man, and he chooses to freeze himself half to death? And be drunk? Where did you pick him up from Director?"

"I apologize for his behavior, Mr President, but he is a rather fine agent, with commendable performances in the field, and experience that will count when needed. Granted, he has his slips, and considering the fact that you did not give me enough time, or the liberty of employing my team to brainstorm on picking better agents, I'm quite sorry my picks don't meet your approval." She replied, her tone was angry, or tired, he couldn't tell.

"Don't get smart with me Director, you know why we could not involve your team!"

"I get that you are of the opinion that there are moles in the CIA, and also of the fact that you have denied my analyses and several proofs that showed a lack of such in my ranks." She replied, sighing.

"Director, I will not be having that conversation again. I will also advice that you pay less attention to logic and a little bit more of that attention to your gut" President Wallace admonished.

"Again Sir. I am sorry. What do you reckon we do?"

"I have handpicked several personnel for our project, chief among them is the one of the persons that first found out about the breach in White House security" he announced.

"Oh, is that so? What is his name?"

"Her. The question should be ' What is her name?' Director, don't be sexist"

"Oh, okay. Anyways."

"It's Carol. I don't know her last name, but we're about to find out" He seemed to be talking to someone in the room, so Director Colby listened closely.

Carol had just been escorted into the room by Agent Cooley. She looked nervous, tugging at the collar of the beach shirt she had worn. She was nervous, clearly so. I mean, she had thought it was cute, trendy, a shift from her usual monochromatic fit.

"Of all days to try something new! I look foolish!" She cursed, smiling abashedly as Agent Cooley opened the door into the Oval Office for her.

"Ma'am" She could hear him greet as she walked by. She wished she had his collectedness, his calm. She was a mess, all she could do was develop stuff on her computer, monitor the cyberspace of the White House, and make bad fashion choices! She wasn't cut out for meetings in the Oval Office!

"Ah Carol! Welcome" He greeted, all smiles. "Thank you Agent Cooley" President Wallace called, but the agent was already out in the corridor, the door shit tight behind him, scanning the hallway that led to the Oval Office for threats; a habit he had learnt from working where he did.

"Have a seat Carol. What is your last name? I didn't quite catch it" The President asked, jolting his guest back to reality, as she had not been paying attention.

"It's Duncan, Sir. Carol Duncan." She announced, tugging a loose curl behind her left ear.

"Well, Carol Duncan, I have something that I need to tell you. I hope to God that you keep it a secret, you hear me?"

"I hear you Mr President." She replied, her lips were dry, and so was her throat.

"Good, good. I'm recruiting for a team that's top secret, and not just secret like the public has heard rumors about its existence, I mean secret that the Vice President doesn't know. Hell! Even my wife doesn't know about it! And since you saved myself and our White House from external attacks once, I am giving you the opportunity to do the same, but on quite a larger scale here, are you following"

All she could do was nod and listen to her heartbeat loud in her chest.

I mean! He was the President!

Wasn't he? Was she dreaming? It had to be real.

Almost as real as the curses her brother had hurled at her when she picked up his shirt and said she wanted to style it for her outfit.

Although he had called her out as having no style, she went ahead with it anyways.

Outfits did not matter to her, so with her orange knee length skirt, and her hair packed in a bun with curls hanging along the sides of her face which he had grown to hate as it distracted her from her work, she set out to work, taking about 3 buses and a short between the first and the second to get to her Office, a small room she usually shared with one person, the present being Danielle, good old, quirky Danielle.

"She should have been called to do this, not me!" Carol was sure she felt a genuine urge to scream, but she was unsuccessful, the same way she was unsuccessful at listening to what the man that led her Nation was saying.

"Do you follow, Carol?" Was what she heard. But she wasn't following.

"Yes Sir, I am." She lied. "Normally these would be followed by a dump of paperwork that would be pretty self-explanatory" She muttered, shrugging off all doubts in her mind.

"And you're fine with going to the Unimak Islands?" The President asked, for what seemed to be the second time.

"Where?"

The President turned at his table, he seemed to be reaching for a piece of paper but stopped halfway in his quest to get it. As he turned, the look on his face was that of a confused man.

"What do you mean 'where'?" He asked. "We just had a conversation, weren't you listening?"

"I was Sir, but then I zoned out, I'm sorry Sir." She apologized, but he seemed to play off his initial seriousness.

"Don't be! You should have seen me when I met my first President in a private meeting" he said, laughing.

"Sir?" She was confused.

"Yeah, I think it was Clinton, was it? Oh, I was young, and he was kind of a fun guy, but the fact that he was the President of The United States kinda made me want to shit myself" President Wallace was laughing heartily, but all Carol could do was smile.

The room was quiet, awkward even. She had clearly not been listening, so it only seemed fit that he stopped talking. Impatiently, he stared at the door, as if he was waiting for someone to arrive with something. Then Agent Cooley came in, clutching a flash drive in his right hand.

Making his way to the center of the room, he walked over to the president, who was now seated at his desk. After he had whispered in his ear, he turned to Ms. Carol, who he beckoned to join them at the table.

With much more boldness than she thought to muster, Carol walked over to the table, where a blue flash drive awaited her. As soon as she got it, Agent Cooley walked towards the door, and back into his position.

"Here, Carol. The information on this flash drive was gotten from The Director of the CIA about a few minutes ago"

"Sir, I just want to assert my readiness to undertake any assignment that you want to give me." She said, grasping the flash drive.

"I'm sure of that. Be sure to get a good look at the information on the flash drive, and please, don't make any copies. It will automatically self-destruct after you're done." The President admonished.

"Thank you Mr President" she said, walking out.

"Hey, Carol!" He called after her. "How good are you with long flights?" He asked when she had stopped.

"Sir?" She was not sure he had heard him right.

"I asked how good you were with extremely long flights!" He repeated.

"I barely make it through them Sir" She responded.

"Well, brace yourself then, and nice shirt!" President Wallace shrugged, as he got back to the paperwork on his desk.

With that, Carol walked out of the office, unaware of what she had gotten into, or why she had gotten into it. If only she had listened!

As she walked into the hallway, past Agent Cooley and his colleagues who were tasked with protecting the President, she thought back to what he had said, about flying.

What did he mean? Where was she expected to go to? What questions would the flash drive answer?

The President, on the other hand, had received a call from Director Joaquin Taylor of the FBI.

"I am pleased to inform you sir, that we have made headways in the quest to find out how and where we were attacked, Sir" he said over the phone.

"Is that so? Well, I'm all ears, Director" President Wallace responded.

"Well, Sir. Our intelligence in Moscow is of the opinion that although the Russian government may be responsible for the attacks, there have been claims that they were also attacked."

"By whom?"

"We have no idea Sir"

"Wait a sec, have we had this discussion before, Director?"

"I don't think so, Mr President"

"Well, this information does not sound fresh to me. I need new intel, tell your sources to intensify investigations, and ask them about how the weather is in Moscow" He continued.

"Alright Mr President, I'll do just that"

"Director Taylor, be quick about it too, we don't have all the time in the world".

CHAPTER FOURTEEN

"..I'm out of ammo!".

"Me too!"

Where's Harry! Harry?"

"When was the last time you saw her?"

"I don't know, when was the last time we had a clear line of sight!"

"Everyone, calm down! We can work something out!"

"Or we can make a run for it!"

"Gemini wait!"

"I got a grenade!"

" That's good! We'll need to draw them in for that!"

"Which of you has the best throw?"

"I played softball for a while, maybe I can do it."

"Jabez? Where have you been?"

"I don't Know! I just got here!"

"We see that!"

"They're coming!"

"SKUNK WATCH MY SIX!"

"RELOAD!"

"Who has got eyes on the shooter!"

"I do! I'm taking him out!"

"I mean they're excellent shots, but do they have to be this lousy?" Director Colby thought to herself.

She had offered to supervise weapons training as Lt Mendez had errands to run, and although she was impressed, she was also a little bit disappointed.

So much so that when she got a radio call about Jabez's situation, she leapt at the opportunity to leave them all behind and race up the hill.

"Director, the patient is showing signs of life, but we will need your help to stabilize him." Came a radio message.

"Stabilize?" Director Colby was puzzled, but she made her way to the infirmary.

"I wonder what has happened to the man child now" Gemini said as she left. They had been in weapons training since the break of dawn.

It was 2 days since The President had moved the deadline for their readiness for combat, and although they enjoyed having firearms and combat training, the trainer that was sent to them was insufferable.

"How do you take something fun and make it less fun?" Harry had asked the previous day.

"You bring in Lieutenant Mendez" Aria had replied, to which they all laughed.

None of them knew how he had reached the island. They were clearly in the middle of nowhere and it was not hard to recognize everyone that had been there with them since the day they all got there

But then came Lt Mendez, probably out of the sky, with an attitude that reeked of hell, fire, and brimstone.

"With hi cliché phrases and that attitude? Uhm, I can't handle that!" Harry said as soon as the Director was out of earshot. They knew she would not condone their insubordination,.

"Ten bucks he says, 'Up and at em!' When we see him next" Skunk offered.

"We don't have any money; do you guys have money?" Aria asked, dropping her weapon.

"I mean, we don't, but you don't have yo pay right now. You can pay when the job is over"

"When we're all dead?" Gemini asked, backing all of them.

"Why do you have to be so negative man?" Skunk was distraught. "We're just trying to have fun here, now you've gone and ruined it"

"I'm just stating facts bruv, we're going to Russia, am I correct?"

"Yeah, so? What about Russia?" Harry asked.

"You guys don't know about Russia?" He was puzzled. "Well, I hope we don't find out what I mean, now don't I?" He added.

"What exactly do you mean?" Harry seemed quite inquisitive.

"Oh, nothing. Just try to not get caught, pray to whomever you serve that your cover is as strong as steel, and that the government doesn't abandon you when you need them most" He was back to loading his weapon.

"Sheesh man, way to spoil the mood" Skunk said, to which the others nodded.

"If you think he's doing a decent job, we've got his master coming in the distance" Aria said, as the turned to face the rest of the camp. They were at the at the rocky expanse that overlooked the beach, and the sea.

"Master? Nice choice of words. Real classy" Gemini commented, firing his weapon at the targets that had been set.

"Shit, It's Lieutenant Lame-dez" Harry cursed, turning to her weapon.

"Bets are closing everyone, who wants to play?"

"I bet 50 he says it" Harry said.

"I bet a hundred he says, 'why are you standing around like high school girls!'" Aria replied.

"I bet 200, on the high school girls' thingy" Gemini said, greeting everyone else with a smile. He had been hard on them, and that type of attitude was not good for boosting morale, especially when you were on a mission into the unknown.

As they stood, ready for whatever the Lieutenant was to throw at them, He seemed to be in a rather good mood, and instead of hurling insults and threats, he informed them that they had one more drill before they were to call it a day.

"I mean, you all have been training since 6 Am, and it's past five, so I think you all deserve a little rest. We go again tomorrow" He instructed, before turning to jog back up the hill and into the camp.

"Well, that was strange" Harry was the first to speak, the other only nodded in response. He had surprised them, dumbfounded them, even.

"So, I guess none of us won then?" Gemini asked after they had done their last round of shooting and had recovered their targets. He smiled, had hit the bull's eye severally, even at that distance.

"Well, you all lost, so technically you have to pay the booker" Skunk replied.

"And who is that? Aria asked.

"Me!" He replied, rather excitedly.

"I owe you a beer, nothing more" Harry said coldly, walking past him and towards the camp.

"Same" Aria said, laughing as he passed him.

"Do you believe those guys?" Skunk turned to Gemini, he had not said a word, yet.

"Yeah, they could've offered you a 6-pack each, which is what you're getting from me"

"A 6-pack? What the hell man? You owe the booker two hundred!"

"And I'm paying with a 6-pack. Be grateful, booker" Gemini said, walking past him.

"This ain't fair!" Skunk was now rushing to catch up with the rest of the crew.

"I agree" they all chorused.

"Then why are you guys treating me like this? Don't I deserve more?" Skunk was distraught

"Fine, you get three 6-packs, happy?" Harry replied, with Aria giggling beside her.

"Oh, I got a better idea" Gemini said.

"By all means, share with the class" Skunk said.

"How about you get... Wait for it..."

"What? Wait for what?" Skunk was confused.

"Nothing!" Gemini replied, running up the hill that led to the camp site, Harry and Aria following closely behind.

"Oh, come on!" Skunk called after them, as he struggled to catch up.

At the top of the hill, he finally got to them, but they had stopped to catch a break from running.

"What do you think happened to the man child?" Harry asked when he had gotten to them.

"I don't know, but I hope he's alright" Aria replied.

"I think he has been asleep for the past day or so." Gemini opined.

"Damn, must be hard. He hasn't gotten on anyone's nerves in almost two days, I wonder how he's coping in there." Harry remarked, to which the rest laughed.

"That part is true but imagine what it would be like if he woke up…" Gemini responded.

"We'd have to take two days' worth of insults and sarcastic comments in a few hours?" Aria had interrupted.

"Exactly." Gemini replied, walking up the island.

CHAPTER FIFTEEN

"That has got to be the weirdest dream ever, where am I?" He had finally woken up.

"Welcome back Jabez, Sir" came an unfamiliar voice.

"Son of a bitch!" he cursed. "I've been kidnapped by a beautiful woman!" He teased, rubbing his eyes.

"Easy Sir! You are at the infirmary" He had tried to jump off the bed, and the nurse assigned to him had reached out to grab him.

"Oh, I'm good, I'm good. I just wanted to how soft your hands were" he said, laughing.

"Don't get too familiar Nurse Amy, this one is a straight dog"

"Ah, if it isn't the biggest cock-blocker on the planet!" He had finally recognized a voice, and it was the Directors. He could also see her, but the room seemed too bright, and his eyes hadn't adjusted yet.

"Easy there, I could get you locked up for insubordination" She warned.

"Please, what could be worse than an Island in the middle of nowhere?" He asked.

"Thank you Nurse Amy, I'll take it from here" she said to the nurse.

"What exactly happened anyways?" He asked. "Cute shirt by the way, it really brings out the fun in your eyes"

"You were unconscious for a few hours, well over a day"

"I was what?"

"Unconscious, Jabez, I'm sure you were having fun when you slumped in his living quarters from being in the snow for too long, and being drunk"

"Damn, sorry about that" he had sat up in his bed by now, his eyes slowly granting him permission to see his environment. As soon as he could see properly, he stood up and attempted to walk out of the infirmary. "I need to get a bite, and a drink or too. I'm not sober enough to process this"

"Thanks to you, all alcohol privileges have been revoked. I had the crew I supervised dispose of every last drop of alcohol on this island into the sea"

"Damn it! What I wouldn't give to be fish right now" he thought. "But what about on cold nights? How do I handle that?"

"There are thermostats in every sleeping area that will regulate temperature, as well as warm blankets, and a fireplace"

"We didn't get a fireplace, did we? But you got one? Seems real fair, doesn't it."

"If I did not have one, you would not be alive right now, so be grateful"

There was silence, but Jabez kept searching for his shirt. Director Colby could see that she was sitting on it, so she took it as threw it towards him.

"Look, all you have to do is endure whatever alcohol addictions you have for the next month or so. Hell, two months, tops! Do this job and get paid! Handsomely too, then you can waste your pay on women and morbidly expensive alcohol that some European dude told you was worth twenty thousand because it was a hundred years old, you hear?" She was livid. All her plans, all her tactics, ruined by the same person that was supposed to be at the forefront of her plans.

"I hear you" Jabez responded, he was rather quiet, or maybe he was just sober.

"Do this and you'll never hear from me again. Plus, you might even be a couple million dollars richer.

"Did you say million?" Jabez was surprised.

"Yeah, I said it" She responded, her tone seemed rather nonchalant.

"Shit, I'm in" He seemed excited. "Let's do it for the ladies I'll be employing shall we?"

But the Director was already at the door. "I suggest you stay off the ground till you are due for training tomorrow, Nurse Amy will return with a plate for you"

"Alright ma'am!" He responded, laying back down on the infirmary bed.

*

"So, you really did wear it?" Layton asked, giving his big sister a stare that showed his disapproval.

"What do you mean? I pulled it off! You're just hating!" She replied, as she made dinner.

"You know, sometimes I wonder if we're actually related" He commented, laughing.

"Boy, you do realize that we have the exact same face?" She yelled, stuffing the leftovers in the microwave.

"But you still can't pull it off!" He was still laughing. "You do realize that you have no sense of style, right?"

"It doesn't pay the bills for your online video games now, does it?" She had gotten her comeback.

"Fair point, but the goal is to look like you live. I mean, you can afford this house, but can't afford a Gucci bag?" He mocked, this time he was seated by the kitchen counter.

"Well, If I do, guess who isn't going to college?" She was on fire!

"You really came prepared today, didn't You?"

"Yes, I did" She replied, doing a little victory dance.

"How was Work?" He asked.

"Pretty much the same." She replied, shrugging as she turned to the microwave, then as if she remembered something, she jumped back around and said, "The president and I had a private meeting in his office", smiles written all over her face.

"He wants to adopt me?" Her brother replied, laughing.

"Why are you never serious?" She asked, her hands by her waist.

"I'm sorry" he replied, still laughing. "What was it about?" He asked.

"Well, he likes my work on data security and think that I'll be a good fit for a new top-secret project he was running" She replied.

"That's great news sis" Layton replied, stretching out his hands and giving his sister a high five.

"And he asked me about how good I was with long distance flights, I don't even know why" Carol added, her brows furrowed as she was quite puzzled.

"I just hope you did not tell him about our trip to L.A in 2018, did you?"

"I just panicked for a small period of time, Layton"

"Sureee, the entire flight! Plus, what does he want you for anyways?"

"I don't know, but he did say that it was top secret, and he gave me this flash drive" She replied, reaching into her pockets to reveal the flash drive.

"Let me see" Layton said, reaching for it.

"No! This might contain US secrets"

"Yeah, I know. Which is exactly why I need to know what is on it" He was reaching.

"Layton stop! I only have a certain period of time to get the information on it before self-destructs" She warned, pointing to the chair where he had stood up from.

"You're lucky I'm not feeling like being pushing this night" He bragged.

"You're lucky I pay for that attitude" She retorted, turning to the kitchen again.

"What does that even mean?"

"It means sit down, shut up and digest some leftovers! You just growing up, no brains!" She teased, carrying her plate up the stairs.

"Yeah, at least I'm almost eighteen, and 6'3. What are you? 4'11?" He yelled after her.

"5'2, sucker!" She retorted again. He didn't win this time. Yay her.

As she shut her door and was about to get to work, she felt a surge of sadness. It felt like her room was haunted by a heaviness that was not alive but seemed to have a heartbeat.

Slowly, she set her plate on her desk, before reaching into her to reveal the picture of their parents.

"I'm stronger, Mom. He's a whole lot, but I'm stronger" she muttered, tears welling in her eyes

Their mother, Lana Duncan, a local journalist out in L.A, had given had just given birth to her brother when she asked for her daughter to be brought to her. The little girl had been woken up in the middle of the night by screams from her mom, and her dad losing his usual cool, sweating like a man who had just run a marathon, with his breath just as heavy. This girl would spend her night outside a labor room at the local hospital she had escorted her mother to on numerous occasions for checkups.

Innocent, and naive, she sat in the hall, right outside the labor, where she was greeted by nurses who told her that her "mommy was doing well", to which she would nod and smile as they left.

The sun showed signs of rising when her Daddy called her into the room, waking her up from a tiny nap.

She got into the labor room, where a few doctors left on her arrival. After she was in the room, and in the tight grasp of her Mommy, she was her Daddy leave, and her Mommy begged her to listen to her, and that she didn't have much time.

She could see her chapped lips, her pale skin, and her eyes that seemed to wander as she spoke, devoid of the life they held when she would call her to come hear her baby brother kick.

"I know you're only a kid, I know you might not understand anything that is going on, but I'm leaving you in charge" To Carol, her mother spoke words that she could not make sense of.

"You're right here Mom, and you're not going anywhere, are you?"

"I'm not, my baby girl. I just need you to promise me that you'll take care of our babies. The small, tiny one" she said, point to the crib beside her bed, "And the big one, that drives the car" She was now pointing to the window, where her husband stood facing the wall, his hands above his eyes.

Almost like a signal, he walked into the room, grabbing his daughter, and hugging her, before proceeding to hug his wife.

"There, there, Carol's in charge now" she said, smiling her last, as he ran her tired hands through her soulmate's hair.

"Hey Sis!" Carol felt herself get pushed back into reality, only this time it was her brother.

"What do you want Layton?" She yelled at him.

"You left your phone in the living room, and you have a call!" He yelled back.

"Bring it already!" She responded, to which the door swung open, and he walked in.

"Thank you, do you know who it is?"

"It says 'Private Line'"

"Close the door on your way out"

"Don't I get to hear this call?"

"You don't, now close the damn door, on your way out!" She commanded.

As she picked up the phone, she could hear an attendant say, "please hold on while you're being transferred", followed by the national anthem.

"Hey, Carol! Did you get a chance to look at our little flash drive?"

IT WAS THE PRESIDENT!

As if she had sat on springs, Carol stood up with so much force that she felt her breathing being cut short, and as she struggled to breath, she slowly came to the realization that the President of The United States was calling her, at home, to discuss matters of national security.

"Mr President? Sir?"

"Hello Carol, I'm quite sorry to call upon you at this type of hour, I hope you are not offended" Came his voice.

"Oh, no, no. No Mr President, it's no issue"

"Is that right? Well, I was just calling you about the matter of the flash drive. To be honest, I could not get a good night of sleep without knowing if you had gone through the files on the flash drive." He responded.

"As a matter of fact, sir, I was about to"

"Oh, good, good. I must have called early then, haven't I?" She could hear him laugh. A dry, forced laugh of a tired man.

"How about this, okay? If you are comfortable with being involved in this type of situation, which would benefit your country at large, how about you call this number tomorrow morning, and an SUV will show up and pick you up. Does that sound good?"

"Yes Sir, Mr President."

"Have a good night's rest, Carol. Don't forget to pack a suitcase!" He called after her, ending the call.

As soon as the call was over, in came her brother, his facial expression held so many questions, and almost all the innocence it had a few years prior, but now he was almost a man, and she knew he was not just friends with the Darlene character he kept texting.

"Who was that?" He quizzed her.

"Nobody" She replied, avoiding eye contact. He could tell when she was lying. Hell! Everyone could.

"Was that the president?" He screamed.

"Shut up Layton! And no, it wasn't the President." She replied.

"Then who was it? Huh? Who was it" She knew he was not buying it.

"It was a colleague"

"That you call 'Mr President'? Come on Carol, I might be the muscle, but I'm not stupid" He smirked.

"Boy, that was not anybody that you think it is! And even if it was, it is no concern of yours!"

"So, it was him?"

"Layton O'Neal Duncan, get your large behind out of my room this instant! Calling yourself that muscle, how about you muscle the trash!" She barked, pushing her brother out and shutting the door.

As soon as he had left, and she was sure that he was not in the hallway listening in on her activities, she opened her laptop and inserted the flash drive. Almost immediately a folder popped up on her screen, with the words "The Star-Spangled Cloak" as its title.

"Seems overly creative" She commented, shrugging as she clicked on the file.

Inside what she had deemed a rather poorly named file was information that made her feel like she was aiding a federal crime. From the detailed reports on several Russian spies whose identities were to be "cloned", to in depth analyses of her own reports using government satellites and even a thirty second footage from inside the Presidential Executive office.

Alongside that was a list of five rather strange names that she thought was a code for something.

"I mean, why else would 'Harry' be female"? I mean, there's a female 'Hilary', but 'Harry'? It has to be code for something"

She kept scrolling, until she found a list of people who knew about the secret project.

"President Wallace, Director Colby, Director Taylor, General Eisenhower? ME?" She screamed in shock, cupping her hand over her mouth at the same time.

There she was, beside the President, high ranking officials that literally held the country in their grasps, and her! Her! She was just an Ivy league graduate who was still paying off the last of her student loans! She just found out about this! She wasn't even sure what it was!

"I don't even know what it's all about!" She gasped. Her time with the flash drive was almost already over, so she powered through the rest of the stuff she had to read.

There were coordinates, a time sheet showing differences in time zones and when the "Agents" were to clock in.

"The agents?" She thought, scrolling down. There was sure to be something about these agents.

Aside the names she had seen earlier, which she had thought were codes, there was no other information on these agents.

Then she thought to herself; was she as expendable as these "agents"? Was that why she was called upon? I mean, she looked the part; naive, innocent, a mind that could be considered above average by some, thus labeling her as a criminal mastermind. Was she to take the fall?

"Your time is off, please remove the flash drive from your computer and wait for it to self-destruct" came a rather friendly voice. Carol heeded to its voice and unplugged the flash drive. Soon after, it smelt of burned wires.

Just to be safe, she took it to the kitchen and dunked it in water, before turning to the living room and noticing her brother asleep on the couch.

"Poor baby" She whispered, pouring herself a glass of orange juice to take up to her already cold plate of leftovers.

As she covered her brother with the blankets he had thrown to the floor, she glanced at the time.

"2:49?" She sighed. She knew The President was going to be calling her any minute, and that he had said something about her packing a suitcase.

Although she was not sure if he had meant it as a request, or as a command, she sought to pack one anyways.

As she walked up the stairs and towards her room, she thought about Layton. If she left, he would be home alone. She scheduled to make him a small budget once she had gotten to where she was expected to go, as well as food deliveries for as long as she was expected to be away.

"It'll probably be for a few days, right?" She asked herself, opening her door with her elbow, with a glass of water in one hand, and an extra helping of leftovers in the other.

CHAPTER SIXTEEN

"As expected!" She told herself, getting up immediately she heard it.

Her phone had rung at exactly five minutes past six. A little late, but she had expected it around that time anyways.

After packing her bags, she had lost the urge to go to sleep, instead ruminating on the files she had seen.

"Maybe the suitcase is so that I could go spend time with these 'agents', or just be in their general location, possibly?"

"What if this turns out to be another Presidential scandal? What if I become the face of controversy?"

"Where exactly do the coordinates point to?"

Thoughts like this clogged her mind, like small pieces of debris, clogging her mind and denying her sleep.

She spent all night googling the coordinates, trying her best to remember them, which she failed, cursing every time the search result did not yield positive results.

Now she was awake and awaiting the President's voice as she had been put on hold, again.

"Ah, Carol! Good morning!" Came his voice, surprisingly full of life.

"Good morning Mr President Sir" She replied. How exactly was did he sound so lively all the time?

"I trust you have had the time to look over my little gift to you?"

"I have Mr President." She replied.

"And what say you?" President Wallace replied, he had begun to sound impatient.

"Truth be told Mr President, Sir, I am still overwhelmed by the things I saw in those files, Sir" Carol confessed.

"It does get like that sometimes; it even makes you lose sleep" He responded.

"I could not possibly disagree Sir"

"Yeah, it's kind of crazy, you know? One day you're saluting a flag, barely learning the words to the anthem, and then the next day, you're the holder of nuclear key codes that can wipe out major cities"

"I can only imagine what that is like Sir"

"Don't. Because, Carol, you're living it." He announced. "What you just read is a top-level secret task force tasked with gathering intelligence from what we believe to be foreign aggressors. Only certain people know about its existence, and most of them don't even have the level of clearance necessary to get the full details divulged to them, but you do. No pressure, that is."

"Absolutely none Mr President" Carol replied, timing her breathing. Sweat beads had begun gather on her forehead.

"Good, good." He replied. "Well, now that that you know about it, you have two choices; accept my invitation to be a part of the change that the American cyberspace deserves, or decline, but you will be made to sign certain non-disclosure papers"

"I would love to serve my country, Sir."

"Good choice Carol! Damn excellent choice you've made!" He announced, heaving a sigh of relief.

"Thank you Mr President, Sir".

"Now, did you pack that suitcase I told you to? Because you will need it. Look outside your window, a black SUV would be pulling up right about now. That is your ride to the airport. When you are there, you will be escorted to the military hangar by the driver and from then on your flight would take off"

"I have one question, Mr President?'

"What is it Carol?"

"Where am I heading to?"

"I'm sorry, but that is on a need-to-know basis. We just can't risk it at the moment. There could be listeners right now, listening in on this conversation as we speak. But I give you my word that you will not be harmed during the time that you are to conduct this mission" He assured her.

"I understand that Sir."

"Thank you Carol, your country thanks you for your service as well." President Wallace said, ending the call.

As Carol sat on the edge of her bed pondering, her door swung open and her brother was standing there, grinning from ear to ear.

"That was him, wasn't it?" He asked.

"Layton, get out!" she commanded.

"It was him! I was right!" He yelled, disappearing into the hall as he performed a victory dance.

"Try that again and you're grounded!" She barked.

"Ohhh, not!' He was still dancing.

"Layton, come in here" She called, realizing what she had to do.

"Not again" She could hear him mutter in the hall as he strolled into the room.

"Look, you are right. That was the me president" she said, pausing to catch her animated reaction. There was none, only a smirk.

"I was on a night shift today, but according to the President, I have to go to somewhere to help do stuff that I have no clue about, hence, I'll be gone for a while." She spoke.

"How long?" Layton asked.

"I don't know, but by the looks of that flash drive, I'm guess it would be more than 1 week, are you okay with that?" She asked.

"I think so, hey text me when you land, okay?" He said, leaving the room suddenly.

"Layton, come back here" she called, but there was no response. She knew he had left to go find somewhere to cry. Her big softie was at it again. All talk, no action.

With that she stood up, looking through her window on her way to the bathroom, and there it was; a Black SUV with government plate numbers.

"Classic government" she muttered, rushing off, and into her bathroom.

As she stood under the pouring water, questions began to brew in her mind.

"How long has that car been there?"

"Did she have a tail on her, prior to this?

"Where was she being taken?"

"How do they know her... Oh wait! She works for them!"

"My fear of heights!" she gasped, her heartbeat had increased, and her hands seemed to become shaky, and cold.

"How am I going to do that? Not one! But potentially two flights?" She asked herself. "How will I handle that?"

Carol had just stepped out of the shower when she caught herself praying it was one of those things where they blindfold or even sedate a person till they get to their location.

"Damn it, Carol!" She reprimanded herself. "No wonder Layton thinks he's the stronger one" she said, her thought wandering back towards her brother.

Despite the fact that he was quite a popular athlete at his school, he seemed to prefer keeping a rather small social circle. He was friendly, and smiles at everyone, but he kept his distance, usually spending his lunch breaks in seclusion.

Carol always felt sad for him; he didn't know what it was like to have their mom around, and then losing their dad when he was about twelve in the plane crash. The exact same plane Carol would have been on If she did not leave for Washington a week before her father's flight. She was still in college then and had left early with her brother to allow her father sell off all the remainder of his really estate in Los Angeles. He was in meetings after meetings and would always check in with his kids, the last time being before he boarded the flight.

"Love you Lay Lay! Love You Mamas!" He had sent in what would be his final message to his children.

Carol had the television on and was working on a mini school project when she saw news of a plane crash on television.

"...in the early hours of today being the 14th of April, the passenger aircraft, Mave 236, had crashed just a few miles from the Ronald Reagan National Airport, also known as the DCA. Preliminary investigations are pointing to engine failure upon trying to land the plane, resulting in the crash, where at least 103 people were killed, and a further thirty-five were left with varying degrees of injury."

Carol could remember staring at the screen, the lights becoming fuzzy, and tears welling in her eyes. She wanted to believe that her father was alive, that he was okay, but she felt her panic levels rising. She felt helpless, and alone.

The trip to the Hospital in the morning was burdensome, traffic was backed up for what looked like several miles, but the wait at the hospital was far worse than she imagined, because everyone was busy, everyone was occupied, everyone was yelling. She had seen several families learn in tears, several others in far worse situations. One woman had to be admitted as she had passed out after hearing the news of her husband's passing.

When she had finally gotten hold of a young nurse, he seemed to be uncomfortable with what he was going to say, He looked like the type that was yet unfamiliar with divulging unwelcome news, and he fumbled with his words.

CHAPTER SEVENTEEN

"Hey, look. It's the man child!" Gemini said, pointing at Jabez's face as he walked up to join the rest. He looked like he had a limp in one leg, and struggled with his bad, nursing at his left rib cages as he cursed out anyone he came by.

"At least I know how yo have fun" Jabez retorted, defending himself.

"Fun? You almost got yourself killed mate! What if the Director had not opened the door? What if she wasn't awake?"

"Then I would have gone out a total Chad" He bragged.

"You are unrepentant, aren't you?" Aria asked.

"Like an atheist at Mass" He replied. "Is this the 74M?"

"Beautiful, isn't she?" Skunk asked. He had spoken for the first time since Jabez returned.

"Just like me" Jabez replied.

"Cocky bastard" Harry cursed.

"Well, at least I've got cock" Jabez retorted, immediately realizing that he was not thinking he continued, say in, "Moving on"

"Wait, what? What did you just say?" Harry asked.

"Moving on?"

"Before that, you said something else"

"Just like me?"

"No, no. Right after that"

"Moving on. I said, 'Moving on'" Jabez said, sporting a straight face.

"Sure, you do" Harry replied, to which the other burst into laughter.

"So, how was almost dying?"

"Uh, it was the best thing ever! Top of the lone experience" Jabez replied, sporting a hearty grin.

"Is that so?" Gemini asked, a look of doubt on his face.

"Is that sarcasm?" Aria asked.

"Absolutely not! It was pleasurable, arousing even. You should try it sometime"

"How about you try it again?" Hard remarked.

"How about I make you try it. I'd put two of these in the back of skull and sing you a lullaby" Jabez warned, brandishing his weapon.

"We have the exact same weapon big boy. Only that mine is loaded, and Aria is playing toss with your bullets."

"Hey, give me that!" He said, turning and snatching them away from her. "You win this time, Oliver Twisted"

"Oliver Twisted? What does that even mean?"

"Well, you look like a little boy, and you're begging for an ass whooping!'

"At least I don't bleach my facial hair"

Jabez turned, and stared at Harry for quite a while, watching as she loaded her weapon and fired it at a few targets.

"Are you gonna do something about it?" She asked, after she had shot a few targets.

"I am" He said, reaching to grab her, but instead of an attack, he went for a hug, saying, "I have missed you guys, bring it in. Even you Gemini"

As they stood in what was clearly an awkward embrace, Harry spoke out.

"That's enough! You ate suffocating me!"

"Just a little more, just a little"

"Nah, I'm out" Skunk said, breaking free, even though Jabez held onto his shirt.

Slowly they all broke free, leaving Jabez standing by himself.

"What have you guys been up to?" He asked, positioning himself and loading his firearm.

"You're looking at it" Gemini answered.

"Oh, I see. How did this get here exactly? Wasn't this place just a beach?"

"And it still is, clearly so"

"Yeah, but now there's bullets everywhere, and loud noises"

"Look, this is what we all love doing, right? Why don't we just do it, no questions asked, okay?" Skunk was not particularly chatty.

"Sounds fair to me." Gemini said, returning to his training.

"Soldiers! Drop your weapons and give me a jog to the end of the beach, plus a race when you are within hundred meters of your weapons! The last soldier gets the honor of giving me a hundred pushups!" Screamed Lt Mendez into a megaphone from atop the hill.

Hurriedly, and with curses on their tongues, they all let down their weapons and started jogging, leaving Jabez behind.

"Wait who is that?" He asked, but they were no longer within earshot, either that or they chose to ignore him.

"Hey, Soldier guy! I'm injured here! I don't think I should be doing this!'

"Then give me a hundred, Soldier!"

"Goddammit!" Jabez said, as he fell to the floor, collapsing on his side after his third pushup, muttering curses as he lay there. The sun was in my eyes, but his attitude had caught the Lieutenant's eye.

"You're going to be my new favorite now" he said. Jabez could see his somewhat maniacal grin.

"A few more days and I'm out of here" he muttered and resumed his punishment.

*

"Hey Sis! There's someone at the door for you!" Came Layton's voice.

"Coming!" Carol replied. His voice had saved her from any more hyperventilating.

Standing in front of the mirror, she tapped herself on the face to awaken her now sleepy eyes.

"Sis, there's a man in a suit at the door, he says he's looking for you" came Layton's voice thought the door.

"I said I'm coming!" She said, swinging the door open.

Carol was fully dressed, wearing a grey shirt she had sourced from a flea market a while back, she had on pants, blue to be exact, and a pair of sneakers she had bought to match with her brother's pair as part of an outfit for his 16th birthday. Although he had outgrown his pair, and has totally ruined them, hers still fit perfectly and were almost as good as new, seeing that she had only worn them a few times prior.

As she left her room with her suitcase, she met with her brother who was holding a Tupperware container.

"I made you a snack, call it breakfast, If you will"

"Thank you Layton" she said, hugging him. "What is it?

"Peanut butter and jelly. Yeah, I also took out the crust, but then I remembered that you like them, so I packed them separately."

"Oh, that is nice. I guess"

"You don't like it?"

"I do. I do. Thank you"

"Run along now, little soldier", He said, taking her bag from her and walking toward the door. As he was about to step out, the suitcase was taken from his hands by the rather sturdy hands of the agent that stood by the door. Silently, Layton walked back into the house, hugging his sister as she left.

"See you soon Lay Lay" she said to him, with tears welling in both their eyes.

"Eww, you're crying" he retorted, amidst tears.

"No, I'm not" She denied.

"Yeah, you are"

"So are you"

"I know. Word of this should never go out Sis, I have street cred to protect?"

"Street Cred? Boy you live in the suburbs!" She replied, pushing him out of the way.

As she walked up to the car, she could hear him say what was most definitely a clap back, but the intimidating presence of the agent made it difficult for her to turn back. She only did have a second look at her brother when it was time to make a turn around the bend and take off into the town.

"Ramen in the cupboards. Pizza money on kitchen counter. I'll book a restaurant for dinner once I get to wherever I'm going" She texted him.

"Lmao. Thank you MOM" He replied, to which she only smirked and slid her phone into her purse.

"House party?" He had texted again.

Carol could not believe her eyes. The Audacity!

"NO!" She replied, sighing.

"Everything okay back there, Ma'am?" The agent finally spoke.

"No. I'm fine. I just have a brother who wants to get his ass kicked." She spoke. "Could you organize that, by any chance?" She asked jokingly.

"Unfortunately, Ma'am, I do not do that anymore" The Agent replied.

HE WAS SERIOUS? Carol was sure that her heart bad skipped a beat.

"Is there any way I can be of assistance, Ma'am"

"No, thank you" she said, before rethinking her decision. "You don't happen to have a bottle of water here, do you?"

"I do ma'am" he said, popping open the glove compartment to display what looked like a mini fridge. "Sparkling or normal, Ma'am?"

"Normal, thank you." She answered, as she was handed the water.

After a long silence, she spoke again. "You do not have to call me Ma'am, you know?"

"I am aware your name Ma'am, but pride myself on professional conduct, so I refrain from first name basis in interactions"

"I see. So, what do I call you?"

"At the moment, Ma'am, I am your driver. My name does not matter, especially when you have a several pictures of my car, and probably a video of you entering my car with my plate number showing clearly. Your brother will send it to you any moment now too."

Almost immediately, Carol got a notification on her phone, where her brother had sent her a video with the caption, "No volume please".

"Tell him that you're in safe hands, Ma'am, and that the United States of America would appreciate if did not share any parts of my visit to your home with the general public.

"I'll do just that, sorry Sir."

"I appreciate that Ma'am." He replied. "We are about 10 miles from the airport, we will get there in no time"

The rest of the journey was mostly silent, except for the humming of the engine, and the rather noisy road users who wasted to time in flipping off anyone that didn't let them have the right of way. Usually, they would give the finger and then take their face away when they see the plate numbers, and the rather stern looming driver of what seemed to be a vehicle registered for use in the White House.

CHAPTER EIGHTEEN

"What do you mean by too many people on the island would complicate things?" President Wallace was furious.

"What I mean is that it would be quite pointless to bring more to the island, and that it would be best if they all worked remotely." Director Cby advised.

"You do realize that our cyber space is not safe?" He was waving his hands everywhere, his suit was on the floor, but he didn't care.

"I do realize that Sir. But a bunch of highly skilled personnel going missing with no tangible explanation by the government could spark some rumors, don't you think? I mean, yesterday I got an email on my private account from a news journalist that wanted to know about certain 'off the records, offshore' projects that we were working on" She further explained.

"What do you mean by 'We'?" He was puzzled, he sure needed clarity.

"The CIA sir. The only files linking you to our little project is in destroyed flash drive, probably in the trash can of your newest recruit."

"How sure are you that it is destroyed?"

"We have a chip placed in all our flash drives that shows when they are offline, and C47G is offline."

"So, what are you saying concerning our recruits?"

"Mr President with all due respect, it would be advisable that they all work remotely, and that they are not familiar with each other. My team on Identifications is working up fake I identification cards for all agents as we speak, on the fields, and in the safe houses."

"I see, but how about Russia? How do we get them to Russia?"

"They are to carry these fake Identities as their real ones. We are currently liaising with the FBI to give them back stories and reasons to going to, or returning to Russia, depending on what the back story is"

"Brilliant. Just brilliant" President Wallace commended.

"By the end of today, I would be issuing pass keys to a private internet that I would have set up with the computers of these selected agents.

"One last question, Director. How long would you estimate this mission to last?'

"With all honestly, Mr President, the infiltration of the Kremlin would have to be organic, as we can't just place agents in critical positions without arousing suspicions. We cannot also contact our own agents in the field. They are all A.W.O.L as we speak. Furthermore, the moral code of the Russian officials is one of strongest. We are yet to find a mole, sir." She explained.

"Give me an estimate, Director"

"Mr President, the variables are worth considering, Sir. It could take several months; it could take about a year too. A few weeks if we're lucky"

"So, we're in a rabbit chase with the prize being to gnaw off our own tails?" He gasped.

"Not exactly Sir. We each need to have a positive outlook."

"Get Director Taylor to find moles. I swear to God, me and that man don't speak the same language" He was rubbing his eyes. "I have a call to make right now" he said, cutting her off.

Immediately, he dialed Carol's cell, hoping she would pick up before she boarded the plane.

"Carol! Give the Phone to Agent Fowler" He commanded as soon as she had picked up.

"Mr President, Sir?"

"Agent Fowler, I want you to tell the captain that the flight has been cancelled and I would much appreciate that you drive Ms. Carol to her work shift. She will not be taking any flights today.

"Duly noted. Mr President, Sir!" He replied dutifully, prompting the President to hang up.

Agent Fowler was capable, more so than any agent that had been assigned to him, ever. But he was also rigid, and that was why he had preferred Agent Cooley to him.

As he sat, clutching a glass of gin, he called to the White House kitchen. It was almost afternoon, and the last time he had eaten was about the same time, but the previous day.

"What would you like Mr President" came a man's voice.

"I'd like a salad please, no dressing, unless its honey. Thank you." He replied.

"Coming right up, Sir" The voice replied, to which he ended the call.

"Cooley!" He called, as the door swung in almost immediately.

"Mr President, Sir" Agent Cooley answered.

"Could you get me Ethel, and another Suit? I think I have a charity thing this afternoon"

"Right away, Sir." Agent Cooley said, exiting the Oval Office.

Shortly after, Ethel appeared from behind the door.

"You call for me? Mr President?" She asked, clutching a time sheet and other paperwork.

"Yes, Do I have a charity thing today?"

"No, Sir. But you do have one tomorrow, by twelve, Sir"

"I see. I see. Another thing, are there any empty, secluded, but still comfortable offices available?"

"I'll check with the building's manager Sir; I have no information on that at the moment."

"If there is, have one furnished with all the tech gizmos a person would need"

"Gizmos? Sir?"

"Yeah, yeah. The uh... RV googles, is It?"

"Virtual Reality sir, VR googles." She corrected, biting her tongue as she did.

"Yeah, that one. It's a gizmo type contraption, isn't it?"

"I think so?"

"Look, furnish one of these offices in the best way suited for lady, but at the same time, one that is tech inclined. I'm working on a project, and I need someone to be in the best of conditions to deliver"

"Right away Sir."

"That will be all" he said, dismissing her.

As soon as she left, Agent Cooley came in with a rather dashing blue suit.

"Good choice agents, you do know your suits! But unfortunately, the thing I need for is tomorrow, take it back.

"On second thought, drop it here" he said, pointing to the couch.

"That will be all, thank you" he said, as the Agent resumed his position outside the door.

*

"Excuse me for a second, ma'am. I'll be right back" Agent Fowler said, going up into the cockpit to tell the pilot that the flight had been cancelled on the President's orders.

As she waited, Carol felt a hand on her bag, a baggage carrier had thought she was boarding the flight and offered to help, to which she declined.

After giving what seemed to be an unwarranted tip, the man left, and at almost the same time, Agent Fowler resurfaced from the cockpit, but stopped suddenly, as though exam in in Carol.

"Why is your suitcase open?" He asked, continuing his descent from the stairs.

"No, it's not, I locked it with my own…" She said, turning to the suitcase.

"I guess your laptop is gone too, isn't it?" He asked.

"Yeah. It is" she said, searching.

"Hold on to this for a sec, please." He said, handing her his tie, as he ran into the neighboring hangar.

"Did you get him?" She asked.

"If I did, I would not be breathless right now, would I? Also, I'd have another human, isn't that right?" His tone was angry.

"You don't have to be rude about it, I…" Carol wanted to defend herself, but Agent Fowler was having none of it.

"Shh. All nearby agents, requesting back up. Over" he had hushed her, to her shock. He had brought out his radio and was contacting other agents.

"You do realize that you are rude, and I can speak to the President concerning…" He had hushed her again!

"…suspect is male, hold on" he said, turning to Carol.

"Tell them what he looks like", He commanded, his tone was the perfect mix of calm and firm, but his ruffled shirt that betrayed his usually collected look said otherwise.

"Sorry, but that is not the way to speak to a lady"

"Does the lady want her computer back or not?" His tone seemed angry; Carol knew she had to comply. Angrily she snatched the radio from him.

"The suspect was tall, I could see his eyes, but he had black hair, and from the way he wore the hat he sure had long hair, and he had on the dark green overalls that workers at the airport wear" she said, all the while staring angrily at Agent Fowler.

"Copy that, moving out" came a voice through the radio, startling her and weakening her gaze. When she looked at Agent Fowler again, she was sure it was out of embarrassment.

"Give me that" he said, snatching it from her hands. "What kind of half ass description is that?" He questioned, a look of scorn on his face.

"That was the best I could do. I didn't take a good look at him" Carol said.

"And why is that? Why didn't you?" He was visibly annoyed.

"Because I was waiting for you to come out of the cockpit!" Carol has shifted the blame, but that only made Agent Fowler a bit angrier.

"You know what? Get in the car and give me your bag." He commanded, after he had taken a deep breath.

"Why? What do you want with it?" She was confused.

"The perp touched it, right? There should be fingerprints on it" Agent Fowler was already at the door of the car.

"The thing is…" Before she could speak, he had caught her off again. He seemed impatient.

"What?" He had interrupted her again, but she was too embarrassed to be offended.

"He wore gloves" she said, bowing her head.

"All available agents, I'll need a double sweep of the airport, watch out for any suspicious looking people with suspicious body movements" He ignored her, instead speaking into his radio.

"Get in!" He ordered, startling her.

"Where are we headed?" Carol asked, but he did not respond.

"I asked you a question, where are you taking me?" She asked again. This time they were outside the airport gates.

"Police Station, but not before you call the President and tell him of your misplaced computer?" He said, swerving past the tight corners.

"Is that necessary?" She asked, a puzzling look on her face.

"Was that your work computer?" Agent Fowler had ignored her, again.

"Yeah, why?" She asked.

"Did it have sensitive information on certain projects that are ongoing in the White House?" He asked, his tone was quite inquisitive.

"Not exactly?" She replied.

"Clarify, what does that mean?" Agent Fowler asked again.

"Well asides the usual encrypted software that I used for White House security; I don't think there's anything else…"

"Did you say encrypted? What is the unlock process like?" He had cut her off again, but this time he was looking back at her through rear view mirror.

"Well, there is an algorithm that generates a new pass code every morning, and even then it's a simple copy and paste. I wouldn't know any pass codes even if I tried. Whomever took my computer will have only my streaming subscriptions" She explained.

"So, you're saying that your computer holds no government secrets?" Agent Fowler asked again.

"All encrypted" She replied.

In the ensuing silence, Carol could hear Agent Fowler mutter several times, and from his facial expressions, he was distraught.

For good reason as well, A highly rated agent who had worked at the White House for almost a decade, starting his career in his mid-twenties as a junior agent, fresh off of a short, but impressive stint as a Navy Seal. He had been recommended by a now retired agent and after a few years and stellar accomplishments, including Agent of the Year on two separate occasions, he was tipped to run point on the then President, which he did.

Then came President Wallace, and with him came a brand-new challenge. He had been relegated into the shadows, and despite having to do underground, off-the-books operations for him, he had become a force to be reckoned with at the White House. Agent Cooley could be in all the photos if he wanted to, but the real person running point on President Wallace would always be Agent Fowler.

He was all that, and now he was this; a baby-sitter to a socially awkward software developer who seemed.

"Damn all this!" He cursed. They had come up on the highway.

He was a highly rated agent, and now not only did he get his professional streak ended by this unwanted passenger, but he also has to clean it up while she antagonizes him!

"Imagine going from saving The President from gunfire in Prague, to chasing after a computer thief" he sighed as he spoke to himself.

"Actually…" Carol seemed to want to speak, the look on her face gave her guilt away.

"What it is" He replied impatiently.

"I got a file from the Director of the CIA and as I was going through it, I saw some numbers that looked like coordinates"

"And?" He replied, asking.

"I could not sleep and after the flash drive had exploded- because they said it would- I tried to remember it and I wrote out a couple viable options and tried to figure out what it was. Where it was" she said.

"And these possible combinations, how many were there?"

"Three hundred, and fifty. I think.." She replied, rather guiltily.

"You think? And how many did you search on the Internet?"

"A couple, like two hundred-ish" Her voice had not become louder.

"Tell me you used at least used a private browser" He seemed to be pleading.

"Shit." She muttered.

"Damn it! You had one job! Didn't you!" He yelled, refraining himself from tugging at the steering wheel.

"I'm sorry, okay? There's not much you can do when your mind is a curious as mine!"

"And you thought it wise to mess with important government information? Because you were bored?" Agent Fowler was seething with rage.

"I said I'm sorry!" She yelled back; little did she know she was not making the situation better.

"Alright, call Ethel. Tell her to clear the President's afternoon."

"Ethel?"

"Yes, Ethel! Call her!" Agent Fowler ordered; he was not patient enough to repeat himself that much.

"But I don't have her number" Carol was confused.

"Yes, you do." Agent Fowler insisted.

"I don't, I never got around to getting it from her" Carol defended herself, searching in her bag for her phone. The light jabs into the bag soon turned to aggressive search, then to a frantic, emotional search that Agent Fowler had noticed. Still, she kept searching, tapping her coat pockets and her fanny pack to find it, all to no avail.

"You've lost that one too, haven't you?" He asked, looking back at her through the rear-view mirror. He was disappointed. Couldn't she do anything right?

"I'm sorry" Carol muttered, barely audibly too.

"You're sorry?" Agent Fowler questioned, speeding past a traffic light.

"Hey watch out! And yes, I am sorry." She blurted out, all the while trying to lean forward. Agent Fowler was driving at speeds way past the limit.

"I'm sorry, okay? I'm sorry because I'm good at my job! I'm good at staying behind a desk and tapping at my keys! I'm sorry because I'm scared of airports and flying and all that crap!" Carol had begun to tear up.

"Carol, ma'am, please calm down" She had started screaming in his ear, muffling her words as she struggled to not burst out crying.

"I'm sorry. I'm sorry. I just get nervous, then I get clumsy, then I forget what I'm supposed to do. Not like you have any of those problems" She responded, sniffling.

There was silence, only bothered by the sniffling from the back seat, the other drivers who horned rather furiously at Agent Fowler and his guest, as they sped past traffic light after traffic light. Carol thought about how many tickets he would have gotten off he wasn't White House Staff, in a White House vehicle, nonetheless.

"Do they still get tickets?" She asked herself, realizing that she had regained her composure, and was once quieter confident.

CHAPTER NINETEEN

Now they were a few blocks from the White House when Agent Fowler's radio seemed to buzz. Quickly he reached for it.

"Agent Fowler here"

Carol could not hear what was on the radio, but she could see his face from the rear-view mirror, and he did not look happy.

"Copy that" He finally responded sighing.

"What was it?" She finally got the courage to ask as they sped through the already opened front gates.

"The perp escaped, and with it your devices. A small unit at the FBI is tracking your phone as we speak"

Carol could not respond. Instead, she slumped back into the chair and let her thoughts wander.

She was sure she had to get a new phone soon, but she was in the middle of a rather tight situation with a rather strict man who would not have stopped by a monlie store, even if she had asked politely.

They were now in front of the White House, and as Carol saw Ethel come up from beside the car, and without her signature smile too, she knew that it was not going to nice, or fun.

"The President would like to see you, Ms. Duncan." She requested, turning back towards the stairs as soon as she was done with her statement.

Agent Fowler was now standing beside her; he had opened the door and was waiting for her to leave the vehicle.

As Carol walked last him and up the stairs that led to the front entrance, He could see that she was visibly shaken. In what even he could categorize as "off-character", he offered to walk her to the Oval Office, and even going as far as helping her carry what was left of her bag.

"Thank you" She responded dryly, her eyes seemed to wander, as if they wanted to conspire with her legs to make a run for the front gates, and towards a life without the burdens of the responsibility of her actions.

"You said something about being nervous, didn't You?" He asked as they walked past the front desk.

Carol could only nod, she looked like she was going to cry.

"Well, I remember my first tour abroad. I think it was the days when I was shipped off to Yemen, right? So, I was young soldier, top of my class in the academy, but on the field, that was the first time I had heard enemy fire"

"Un-huh" Carol didn't mean to sound uninterested, but she could feel her legs give way under her, and not in the way she would want them to.

"Huh. Anyways, the moral of the story, is that I had to brace myself for whatever was going to come, and fast. I had had 15 seconds, you have less than that, because we're here" he said, letting go of her hand.

It was then that Carol realised that she had walked up and towards the Oval Office at Agent Fowler's pace. Her legs had begun to shake again, and she felt like she needed a seat.

"You can do that inside the Oval. Come on" Agent Fowler said, urging her to get in.

Despite her unspoken pleas, and stubborn stance, she was in. Right there, with his sleeves rolled up, and his back turned and towards a window as he tried to make a call, stood the President.

As Caril stood, he reckoned that leaning against the door was better that going further in and grabbing a seat. So, she stood there, frozen in time as the President seemed to bargain with someone on the phone, telling them to push dates and hasten the departure of "all of them".

"I don't care. They're previously trained, and besides, they are not going to warfare are they? This is basic espionage here; they just need to steal information as they usually do for a living!" He shouted, startling Carol, who let out a little squeal, but cupped her mouth almost immediately with her own hands.

"I want the one for the embassy shipped by tomorrow afternoon! Get their identities to them by tonight!" He said, before angrily tossing the phone at the table.

"Good day Mr President" Carol greeted rather weakly. He had turned to face her and was peering rather angrily in her direction.

Then, without taking his eyes off of her, he turned to his desk, where he picked up a pair of glasses and out them on, a weak smiling floating across his face as he did. Carol thought he looked at her like he pitied her.

"Carol! Come on and have a seat!"

"Thank you Sir" She thanked him, walking rather weakly to the seats, before falling awkwardly into one.

"Do you want anything to drink? Water perhaps" He asked.

"No, Mr President, Sir. Thank you" Carol responded. She wondered if he could hear how dry her throat was by the sound of her voice.

"Well, you sound like you need it there" he said, walking back to his desk and dropping the glasses he had worn

"Don't mind me" He said, turning to lean on the desk, "I just have a little bit of a problem with my eyes, and it seems to be getting worse as I get younger" He joked, smiling at her.

"Sir, I'm sorry about what happened, I…" Carol blurted out; her eyes had begun to tear up again.

"Easy, easy. I don't blame you. Hell, ask Fowler about Prague and he'll tell you somethings you wish you did not hear." He spoke rather kindly, with his hands moving in circular motions and a smile plastered across his face.

"Look, just like my eyesight, I had made a mistake with my mind's eye. I was going to ship you away to far away Russia with nothing but a small unit of information in a flash drive that you could not even revise those tiny bits of information if you wanted to, and why is that?" He continued.

"Because its destroyed?" Carol offered.

"Exactly! It is destroyed. A small shard of information like that and I was already going to send you off and into no man's land, where the chances of you getting caught, or you blowing your cover are greater than the chances of you surviving the winters there, even with a heating system in place."

"Huh?"

"Oh, this has been proven mathematically. Yeah, some CIA guys did it as a joke. Or was it the FBI? I don't know?" President Wallace rambled. "But here's the thing, alright? You might need to go into the field soon, but not today, you hear? I had Ethel set you up with an office and an intelligence team that answers only to me, you understand?"

"Yes Mr President" Carol replied.

"Also, one more thing, you would be given a new, encrypted computer, and whatever phone you get for yourself will be connected to the closed internet of computers that are aware of this operation, do you understand that?" President Wallace continued.

"I understand Sir" she said, standing up.

 Good, now head on home. Agent Fowler's headed that way, he'll drop you off along the way. Ethel's also outside with a bottle of water for you" he said, ushering her out, and in quite a hurry too. He seemed to be eager to get back to working on something.

As Carol unlocked the door to move out, he called to her.

"Hey Carol, about your old phone listen. It's taken care of, we've disabled it, the PC too."

"Thank you Sir" she said, standing awkwardly, the door was now ajar, and in the corridor of the Oval Office was Agent Fowler's head poking in.

"Oh, don't thank me! I couldn't do it even if I tried. Thank your new co-workers!" He spoke. "Uhm, Fowler, take her home, please." He called to Agent Fowler, who responded with a knowing nod.

Carol turned and in a rather quick shuffle of feet, fled the corridor of the Oval Office. As she came up to the flight of stairs- the same ones she had taken that began this wild rollercoaster ride of natural secrets and potential espionage- she was accosted by Ethel, who, reading the room, only stretched the bottle of water in front of her, which Carol grabbed rather hurriedly.

"She'd have to sign this NDA some other time then" Ethel muttered, shrugging. Agent Fowler had just walked past her as well, and she was sure she heard him mutter a greeting, like a true gentleman in a hurry.

Carol was sure she was going to be sick, but she would rather be out of those premises than find out the state of her bowels.

She was now in the reception lobby, where she could be seen speeding past the watchful eyes of the receptionist, Juanita.

Outside she hurried into Agent Fowler's parked car, slamming the door as hard as she could and poking her head out of the window to beckon on him to walk faster.

Soon, he was out the front door, waving his arms as he questioned her actions. She didn't reply, how could she? All her words at that point would only come mixed with the tears that had welled up several times.

She was not angry, neither was she frustrated, but the fear of the President's wrath if something of the sort had repeated itself stuck to her.

Would he fire me? Would I be arrested for divulging government secrets to the public? Will I be jailed without a fair trial? What if he loses his cool?

As she questioned her very occupation, Agent Fowler had pulled out of the front gate of the white House.

"What happened in there? Are you good?" He asked. For the first time since they had first met that morning, Carol could detect sincerity in his voice.

"Nothing" She chose not to speak, as her stomach had begun to hurt again.

"Alright then"

In what could be described as "awkward", seeing that that had both trades words on various levels of emotions, the ride back to Carol's house could qualify as surely quiet, and uneventful.

It had been a long day, and with trips to and from the airport, and a rush of emotions she had not planned for. Carol was sure she would just get home, curl up in her bed, under warm blankets and cry herself to sleep. Her life had changed so much in the past day, and she was not sure if she was ready for it to change anymore.

Agent Fowler, on the other hand, was sure he felt pity for her.

"I mean, she is young, inexperienced and afraid, who wouldn't" He thought, stopping at a red light.

It was almost six in the evening, and Agent Fowler thought to put on the radio, but he decided against it. They both needed time with their thoughts.

Soon, he was on her street, and before long, her house came in view.

"Were here" He announced, looking at her through the rear-view mirror.

As soon as he stopped the car, He could hear the car door slam shut. She had gone down before he even stopped the vehicle!

As he watched her move towards her house, he thought to go help her with her bags, but he decided against it. She could handle herself, and she didn't need him meddling.

As she turned the key into the door, she could hear him speed off in the incoming darkness. Layton sure wasn't home, and she had forgotten to place orders for food.

"What exactly did I do right today?" She thought, as she pushed her door open.

With thoughts that felt like guilt encroaching on her already clogged mind, a voice at her back startled her immensely.

"Hello, I hope I'm not disturbing?" Came an unfamiliar voice.

Carol stopped in her tracks, turning her neck slowly towards the stranger. Assuming the worst, she clenched her fists and was about to attack first when she saw who had startled her.

"Hi" was all she could say, and for good reason. It was not every day that a handsome stranger talked to her, even if he was at her front door invited and probably had murderous intentions.

"Hi, again." He said, smiling. "I hope I'm not disturbing or anything. I just moved into the house next door, and I thought I'd come check on the neighbors"

"That is very kind of you, I'm Carol" she said, reaching out for a handshake.

"Darrell" He replied, as they locked eyes, and hands. Right up to the awkward withdrawal and the quiet sighs of regret.

"Did you travel? I saw the suitcase and I hope you don't mind me asking" He asked, pointing awkwardly to the suitcase.

"Yeah, I did. Actually, I did not. Yeah. I was supposed to, but it did not work out" She explained, rather unsuccessfully too.

"Yeah sorry about that. Well, I will be around, and I see that you have to rest, so I will not disturb you. Have a good night" he said, backing down her the staircase that led to her house. Soon, he was on his own side of the fence, and waving, all the while smiling.

As he disappeared into his home, Carol caught herself smiling.

"Girl come on!" She urged, grabbing her bag, and heading inside.

"Layton!" She called, but he did not respond. He was probably out, either playing whatever sport he played, or partying at a friend's.

"What sport does Layton play?" She asked herself. With no answers come forth, she proceeded to invade his room, but the trophies he had collected confused her more.

Layton had track and field medals, a football MVP award, a basketball third place medal. All of which she had missed out on.

Sighing, she locked his room as she left. It was when she had crashed into her bed that she realised that she had not eaten anything that entire day. This did not make it any better, and she was equally lazy to get up and make something. Instead, ah turned in her bed, and must have fallen asleep because when she woke up the next morning, she could hear Layton downstairs in the kitchen, where he had made a pan crash on the tiled floor.

Resignedly, she got up and decided to open her windows before heading down to confront him. As she shifted the blinds, she groaned in agony, because there in the street, in a dark blue suit and glasses to match, stood Agent Fowler, ready to take her to work.

CHAPTER TWENTY

"Man, if I have to sit through another geography lecture, I am positive that I will lose it!" Harry had slammed every door she walked through, and for good reason.

"My back hurts. I think I need to lie down for a bit" Gemini groaned. He then proceeded to crash on his bed, letting out a sigh of relief as he sunk into the bed.

"Lucky you, I have to go back there soon" Jabez said, the bed under him seemed to not welcome him, so he turned to pacing the room, doing so ever so frantically.

"What is up with you, man?" Skunk asked. He was bare chested, and nursing what seemed to be a bullet scar on the right side of his abdomen.

"What is it? They're shipping one of us over to Russia tonight!" Jabez announced. "The worst part is that I don't even know who it is, or if Russia is code for something"

"Code? Could it be?" Aria asked. Her blue eyes had widened as she asked, twinkling in the light that shined from above.

"Its code for the freezer the size of five countries" Gemini said, sitting up in his bed.

"Huh? What is that?" Harry asked. She had sat up on her bed.

"You guys are painfully ignorant, it hurts" Gemini said, holding his forehead in his palms. "Russia is code, for Russia!"

"Oh" They all said, almost in unison.

"What kind of dumb person makes the code for a code the same as that code?" Skunk teased.

"Listen, you guys can play dumb all you want, but I have to sleep. I am the one going to Russia. I have a job at the American Embassy, according to the CIA agents that appeared out of nowhere yesterday, I had an interview there- which I aced btw- and I have to resume work in a few days." Gemini explained.

"Wait, how did you attend an interview in Russia she you were here?"

"I don't even know, man. But there's footage of me in a blue suit sitting in various offices and answering questions" Gemini offered. That was all he knew.

"You can speak Russian, right?" Jabez asked.

"Yeah, I can" Gemini replied, he adjusted his stance and was now standing up right, as though the pain in his back had disappeared.

"Me too" Skunk echoed from across the room.

"Me too" Harry said, "Thirteen months in a metal cult that also sold stolen US contraband and you catch a few things"

"I don't speak Russian, what do I do?" All eyes turn in utter disbelief towards Aria. Harry had her mouth open; Skunk had run up after hearing her confession, and Gemini stood, watching her in what could be said to be pity.

"Yep, you die first" he said, crashing back into the bed.

"Gemini!" Harry called, she turned in surprise. "I'd expect that from big dum-dum over here, not you" she continued, pointing at Jabez.

"Wait what? Who's…"

"Its basic math's, I'm sorry Aria, but you have to know the land to be able to farm on it" Gemini defended his stance.

"I don't speak Arabic, and I did well in Dubai" Skunk offered, shrugging his shoulder as he defended his colleague.

"Were you infiltrating a government while in Dubai?" Gemini asked.

"No, just shopping for my mom, it was her seventieth birthday" He shrugged again.

"That is not exactly espionage, now is it?" He said, folding his hands behind his head and proceeding to close his eye.

There was silence, and that was partly due to the fact that Aria was doing her late-night ritual where she solved complex equations to help her fall asleep, and she was silent about it as well. Skunk was asleep, cuddling his blanket, his hair surprisingly intact as he turned rather violently. Gemini and Jabez were both out, but for entirely different reasons; while Gemini was in a debriefing, Jabez was trying to sneak into winery for a drink. A feat he had failed at several times prior.

"Hey, don't listen to him, he's just dumb and he doesn't understand anything about you" Harry called out to Aria, saying.

Aria only gave a knowing smile and nodded in response. "They are right, you know?" She said, all the while facing her equation.

"How so?" Harry asked. He had spent time defending this woman.

"They are right! I can't speak Russia, I never got around to learning" Aria confessed.

"You see?" Harry cheered. "You're not so useless after all" Harry added, starting to hug Aria. who stretched her hand out, with a shy smile on her face.

"I want to believe that I'm more useful than their children" She kept smiling.

As the girls talked about each person's durability, Jabez who had managed to get last the front door security was now trying to be past the chefs and kitchen attendants. Although they could make a mean spaghetti, they always looked mean, and he sure did not want to get caught. Sneaking into the pantry, an old, secluded room with foodstuffs on a wall, and an exit that seemed to lead towards a secret room.

"Got ya!" He whispered, relishing in his victory. As he walked down the stairs, he heard a staircase crack under him. In the darkness, he slowly alighted from the staircase with a desire to make no more noise, but then, in a matter of seconds, there came a dozen flashlights and cocked guns staring rather menacingly at him.

"What are you doing in here soldier?" a voice asked, from behind all the lights

"Uh, I was looking for…" Jabez said, he was however cut off by the voice.

"Well, whatever you are looking for isn't down here, and I know I speak genuinely when I say that you are not Lieutenant Easton's type." The voice shouted, like it was giving orders. It was Lieutenant Mendez said.

"I should have known" Jabez muttered. Someone had turned on the lights, and Jabez was instantly grateful that had not used their firearms on him.

In what he had envisioned to be a tiny room, probably with a secret stash of alcohol for Director Colby and the few other soldier he thought he had smelled alcohol on. Instead, it was a massive, underground sleeping area, and before him, with rather menacing looking eyes, and a smirk that both ridiculed and scorned, every male personnel he had ever seen on the island.

They all slept with firearms, what about them! Jabez made to stand up, but the guns that were trained on him as he does make him change his mind.

He just hoped the faulty AK-47 was not among these guns.

"Look boys, I'm sorry. I was doing a little bit of exploring and I came up your little room here" Jabez tried explaining, waving his already raised hands in a plea for mercy.

"You were looking for booze, weren't you?" Lt Mendez asked.

"As a matter of fact, probably."

"There is no probability here, you're the sloppy drunk that is going to ruin this mission, and sadly, you'll take the others with you" Lt Mendez said, walking forward.

"I said I was sorry, it's just…"

"Just what? There is no justification for breaking and entering! I have half a mind to have you disciplined, right here, right now!"

"Is that legal? Can you do that?" Jabez was calk as he asked, maybe it was because he was genuinely curious, or just out of the sheer joy he had gotten from agitating Lt Mendez for a while now, just to get a reaction.

"You bet your grey goatee that I can!" Lt Mendez sure was agitated, he had begun to sweat.

"The only downside to all of this is how close to my face you'd get. Creepy stuff." Jabez muttered. The Lieutenant had gone to get his radio, he planned on asking permission from the Director to discipline the trespasser.

"Send him my way, I need to talk to him next" Sha had said over the radio, much to his anger.

When Lt Mendez returned, he did what Jabez had described as "The Downside". The thing where he'd get uncomfortably close to a person's face in a bid to look more threatening.

"Listen here, punk. I don't care if you have to go on some secret mission, or if the Director handpicked you herself- who, by the way, is the only person I answer to! - you have to respect other people's boundaries, do you understand?" He barked, his spittle settling uncomfortably on Jabez's face, and lips.

"Crystal" Jabez replied. He seemed to have been blinded by the shower, as his eyes were shut tight.

"Now get up, and scram! The Director wants to see you" He ordered, to which to soldiers grabbed him by the arms and threw him up the stairs, and towards the kitchen.

Once outside, he thought to rain curses on them all, but see it fit to save his strength. He would risk antagonizing them any further.

"Just a few more days and I'll be gone, like Gemini. No need to get an unwanted beating and bruises that hurt when I shower." He thought, to which he decided to kick the door and make a run for the exit of the kitchen.

Once outside, he saw himself under the light of the full moon, with his soft gaze barely grazing the skin. unlike its fierce sibling. Suddenly, he stopped in his tracks, choosing to enjoy the moonlight as he said in hands into his jacket pocket and strolled leisurely towards the Director's quarters.

CHAPTER TWENTY-ONE

"Sir, I will strongly advice that we go with the unbearded look, just like in the picture on your passport"

"And I strongly advice that you choose your next words wisely! Do you know how long it takes to officially enter the beard gang?" Gemini retorted, stroking on his sideburns.

"Okay sir. Just a little trim. You have to look as innocent as possible" the barber replied, He had been almost too patient with his client, especially when you are a soldier in the United States Army.

"What are you saying? That I don't look innocent? That I look like a wild beast?"

"Yes, that is exactly what Lance Corporal Jobowski is saying, Gemini" came Director Colby's voice as she resurfaced from the kitchen, a cup of hot cocoa in her hands. Resignedly, she sat on a chair, and from her position watched Gemini and his barber quarrel.

"Do you even know how to cut black hair?" Gemini asked, a look of triumph on his face.

"Yes Sir, Indeed I do" the Lance Corporal replied.

"Shit." Gemini sighed, falling back into the chair. "If you mess up my stuff, I'm coming for you" He warned, grabbing a mirror so that he could monitor what was going on.

"So, what are we going Sir?" Lance Corporal Jobowski asked for what seemed to be the hundredth time.

"The low fade man, and do whatever you want to do with the beard" he said, resigning to his new status as being beardless.

"Alright Sir" the Lance Corporal replied, taking his clipper to the scalp of his stubborn client.

Before long, Gemini's hair had all been taken off. leaving a smooth buzz cut, a light face on the side, and small goatee that could only the spell the word "nerd".

"What do you think, Sir?" The barber asked, right after he was done.

"I'm not going to lie, this has all the undertones of a split personality, but in a good way"

"What is even that?" Director Colby yelled.

"What?" Gemini asked, turning to face her.

"What did you say?" She asked.

"I meant that I looked like two different people, but in a good way" He explained.

"Can't you just say it simply? Why do you have to make it sound so complicated?"

"Isn't that what my identity is about? Top of his college class, with a major in communications, a minor in psychology?"

"Point taken" she said, sipping on her beverage. "Where even is this Jabez of a man? While I was in the kitchen, I got a radio message that he had broken into the sleeping area for male soldiers" she said, looking at her door, hoping it would hope soon.

"What even is his problem?" Gemini asked.

"Honestly? Nobody knows. "Director Colby shrugged as she replied.

"Did you not have therapists who ran point on his case? Can't you ask them?" Gemini inquired.

"According to them, he was always well mannered in therapy sessions"

"Well, typical psycho behavior, don't you think?

"Or maybe he's not mischievous?"

"I know problematic when I see it, Director Colby" Gemini said, getting up from the chair. With the fresh haircut he just had, his face seemed to betray his muscular physique.

"You do realize that he might be the least messed up of all of you, right? Except Aria, of course, sweet soul."

"Your sweet soul does not speak Russian, what's the big idea there?"

"That is just where she'll fit in. You see, Aria is a rather skilled woman, and one of those skills happens to be breaking and entering. The Russians are organizing a pop-up tour of the Government House in a week or so, with you at the Embassy to validate arrivals and delete records, she will help us get access into the Kremlin."

"So, we should be done in a week's time? Nice" Gemini boasted, tapping his barber on the soldier.

"Not exactly, what is getting into is computer records, employee data. The real price, the real information bank is somewhere in the Government Office. She will validate Harry, Jabez and Skunk as government house employees, giving us a window of a few weeks to a couple months to find this information bank and tap it." She explained.

Almost immediately, Jabez walked in, he had opened the door without knocking, and he sure was met by the displeased eyes of Director Colby.

"Am I interrupting something?" He asked, his tine was rather dry, or bold, depending on who you were in the room.

"Have a seat and listen" Director Colby instructed.

"Do you want a haircut, Sir?" The Lance Corporal asked rather softly.

"I thought you guys would never ask!" He said, jumping excitedly into the chair, clutching a mirror in his hand.

"Now I want something that says, 'I'm bold, beautiful, and I get all the girls', can you do that?" He asked.

"You get Kremlin Security Guard" Came Director Colby's voice.

"Wait, what?" Jabez turned to Director Colby, a confused look in his eyes.

"You will look like a security guard who works at the Russian government house" She reiterated, taking another sip of her beverage.

"Just like me, but I'm Embassy man" Gemini said. Jabez turned his head to the sound of a familiar voice that he was sure he didn't see it original owner.

"Hello Man-child" Came a fresh shaven Gemini.

"What?" Jabez screamed, spring out of his chair.

"What are you doing now?" Gemini groaned, Jabez was now doing backwards walk towards the side of the room where Director Colby sat, nursing her now lukewarm cup of cocoa. When he was within whispering distance he asked Director Colby if she had been running a cloning program like the ones the conspiracy theorists on the internet had talked about.

"For heaven's sake Jabez, the man just had a haircut. He ships out tomorrow and I had to have him look the part" She was genuinely tired of his shenanigans and would much prefer it happened a few thousand miles away, on another continent.

"Ships out? What about the rest of us?" He asked.

"You will all ship out at different times, Gemini here is the first piece of the puzzle."

"I'm the embassy guy, I'll watch to make sure you guys get through and all. Plus, you get the interesting part of the job, just as long as you can figure out how to do it" Gemini said.

"What is that supposed to mean?"

"If you think Agent Gemini here has insulted your intelligence, then that shows how little of it you possess, but I'll explain. We found blueprints of several rooms in the Kremlin, but never have we seen the design of the Main Government Office, and naturally, with blueprints, we cannot pinpoint the exact location the exact location of the information bank" Director Colby explained.

"Information Bank?" Jabez asked.

"Yeah, its inside the Government office, they say it contains missile codes, nuclear warheads from the USSR and their locations, everything. The hope deal, right?"

"I'm pretty sure you guys just defined 'suicide' to me" Jabez scorned.

"Yeah, it is. Fun right? I'll be in my Embassy tapping away at a keyboard when you'd be executed for high treason, Olak"

"Olak? What is that" Jabez asked, then he gasped. "Did you guys call me Olak? Oh, come on! Olak? Tell me I don't look like a Pietro"

Gemini burst into laughter so infectious that the Lance Corporal had to hold himself from snickering, and Director Colby sipped at her beverage, stifling her own laughter.

"That isn't funny. I demand a revision of names! What did Skunk get?" Jabez asked.

"We don't know yet, the Creative team at headquarters has not finished plotting oh back stories for everyone. Your new identity was a preview that Gemini insisted on" She explained, sipping what remained of her beverage.

"What name did they give you, Gemini?"

"Humphrey Jonathan. Real classy" He replied.

"I'm not going to lie, and I hope this does not come off as racist, but that is the whitest thing I have ever heard" It was his Jabez's turn to laugh.

"I knew this would happen, now I need a revision as well" Gemini said, turning to Director Colby.

"Sorry boys. There will be no such thing" She replied, strolling into the kitchen. "Now leave my house, Let the Lance Corporal have enough space to clean!" She ordered from inside the kitchen.

"Don't I get a haircut?" Jabez called, but she did not respond. All they could hear was running water.

"Thanks for nothing, Jobowksi" Gemini said, he and Jabez were out the door.

"You're welcome Agent" The Lance Corporal replied softly, but he was alone, and to his duties he went.

CHAPTER TWENTY-TWO

"Did you crack it? What do you mean by 'incapable'?"

"What sort of incompetence is even that?"

"I'll need to up my game then, we need an insider on this this one as well"

Carol could hear conversations between her new neighbour, Darrell, and someone on the phone. As he saw her approaching, he seemed to end the call in a hurry, sporting a smile that cut through mischievous and shy with an emotionally androgynous knife.

"Hey, Carol. Your driver didn't come today?" He asked, concern in his voice. He had shifted to accommodate her under the shade as they waited for the bus to arrive.

"Yeah, he had to go out of town. He'll be back soon"

Agent Fowler had been recruited to go with the President to Iowa for a meeting with certain political chieftains. Fearing for his personal safety, He had gotten Agent Fowler and Cooley to work as his personal details. Although he was safe, Carol was left without the comfort of a ride to the office. She hadn't taken the bus in a few days, but with all that had happened in the past week, it sure felt like an eternity.

"You work at the White House, huh?"

"What?"

"Oh, I'm sorry if I'm being too forwards, I see the number plate of the SUV that picks you up, I got curious. You don't have to tell me anything, besides, I was just trying to make conversation" He apologized.

"No, It's fine. I do work at the White House, but my work is mostly computer repairs and software installments"

"So, you're the person I would call if I need a 2.0?"

"What?" Carol asked, letting out a little chuckle.

"I'm sorry, it was just a stupid joke"

"Oh, I don't think I got it, or heard it for that matter. Sorry." She apologized.

After what had seemed like an awkward early morning attempt at a conversation, Carol was more than happy when her bus started coming in a distance.

As soon as her bus was right in front of her, she jumped in, throwing a breathless, almost inaudible "goodbye" at her neighbour.

"Aren't you coming, I thought we worked in the same areas!" She yelled, over the sound of the engine.

"No, I work downtown, see you later!" He said, waving as the bus took off. It does off into the distance, disappearing around a bend.

On the bus, Carol discovered that she was not alone. Usually, these early morning buses, especially when they left from her side of town, were usually empty, but somehow, by the time she was coming back from work, they were usually filled.

In the back seat, sat a figure. As they took the journey, Carol could feel this eerie need to look back, so as to protect herself in any eventualities. Even she did not know why she felt this way.

"Was it because of the guy at the airport?" She thought, clutching to her bag ever so tightly.

As she turned back to have a look at whomever it was, she could see him staring back at her, but instead of a cold stare with black apparel and bloody teeth, there was a young man, in a tye-dye shirt, peering at the landscape.

"For 6:43 in the morning, you seem pretty energetic" Carol commented, but he had reached his stop.

As he walked past towards her, Carol held her breath and clenched her fists, preparing to strike before he does, if harming her at his stop was his ruse.

"Hay, Good Mornin'" the stranger said, sporting a smile that was accompanied by a small wave.

Before she could reply, he was out of the bus. The last she saw of him was when He tried to cross the street.

The rest of the drive was uneventful. There were people in the bus, but they were a handful of civil servants who had hurried unto the bus, tired from the previous day of work, but still obligated to resume the next day.

Her stop, a few blocks from the White House usually had more potential passengers than any other. From the factory workers who had to get to work early so that they could fulfil their daily quota of fabrication, to the civil servants whose offices were located at several other districts.

The occasional police officer, who probably had been told by his partner to meet him halfway to work and he would pick him up with the squad car.

The student, or student. Back-pack carrying, energetic kids who were mostly Layton's age or younger.

As she alighted from the bus, these were the characters that waited their turn to get on the bus.

As she walked towards her new office, she noticed that the mobile store where she had bought her phone was open, and they seemed to be having a sale for accessories.

Already late for an early morning with Director Colby, she sped past, resisting the urge to enter and inquire.

"Maybe after work, I will" she said.

As she walked, she heard a honk behind her. It was Kevin, sitting majestically, one hand on the wheel and with his seeing glasses placed on his forehead like badass, he called to her.

"Hey Carol! Is that you?" He shouted.

"Hey Kevin! It's been a week, I think?"

"Yeah, that was one crazy night, I still think about it sometimes" he replied, peering at the road before him.

"Huh? What?" Carol was not sure she had heard right.

"That night, don't you remember? I thought you got fired, to be honest" Kevin replied innocently.

"Ohhh, I didn't. I just got reassigned is all" she replied.

"Well, reassignment looks good on you! I gotta go, I'll catch you on the flip side" he said speeding off and towards the back gate.

Carol walked on, sighing. Who else thought she was fired?

Was she fired?

Was this reassignment a sort of lull to cut her off once it was all done?

She questioned her position, all the way down the secret elevator that opened when she tapped on a rim of a flower vase that stood a few meters to the Oval Office. The elevator would take her down to her new work area, an incognito, Impromptu division of the CIA that provided remote support for the Russian Mission.

Asides herself, the other members of this special team included Alvares Sullivan, also known as the Sultan.

A ruthless hacker who once got into NASA broadband service just a few hours after a reputable firewall company had installed an upgrade at sums that ran into hundreds of millions.

After linking his home internet with that of NASA, he then encrypted his connection, using scraps of the same firewall he had ripped in half.

Rumor has it that he had gone on to using the free internet connection to mine a few cryptocurrencies, hence his nickname, The Sultan.

Within a month, he had amassed a net worth of over three hundred million dollars, prompting audits into his sources of income.

He was however arrested, forfeiting half of his wealth to the US government. Although the other half has never been found, The Sultan was placed under mandatory employment with the CIA and would have to take a mandatory pay cut for his first 5 years of work, with various degrees of pay cuts till he was debt free.

Despite this, the Sultan drives a rather rare sports car, and it is reported that his salary goes to charity, along with other large sums that be com untraceable over time.

Although he was a teen when he began his quest for notoriety, he was now a man, and well into his thirties. A look at him was enough to tell that he lived the privileged life, his choice of turbans and robes whenever work permitted it was more reason why he was called what he was called.

In a group that is out and about, there is always the one that would rather go home and watch a television show. That person would be Brendan.

Asides from her non-gender specific dressing, and her preference for the male variant of her original name, Brenda, she was an overall nice person. With a sharp mind, fueled by an inability to hold social communication for a lengthy period of time, Brendan spent her childhood teaching herself about computers and engineer. By the time she was thirteen, she had made her first project, a flying airplane that bullies in her neighborhood, a small community in Long Beach, had destroyed.

By the time she was eighteen, she had already been two years into a four-year course at a tech school in Tennessee.

A programming genius, with a knack for creating engineering solutions, it was understandable to Carol she only waved and avoided eye contact when she walked into the office.

"I like your shirt Brendan" Carol announced, sporting a welcoming smile, but her effects were met with a slight nod.

"Good morning new boss!" Came another voice, but this time it was from the makeshift kitchen besides the office.

"4-42, good morning"

"Nah, don't say it like that!" He poked his head from inside the kitchen.

"Like how? How did I say it?"

"Like that. Bland as hell" he said, returning to the kitchen. "Anybody want a sandwich?" He yelled, to which Carol obliged.

"One PB and J please, don't remove the crust!" She replied.

"Coming right up!" Came the chef's voice again, like a child that had just gotten a candy cane.

"How do you pronounce it then; I want to learn"

"Not like how you do. It's not 4-42, it's four forty-two. There is no decimal"

"Got it, 4-42"

"Just call me Teo, please. You're dumping on my swagger right now"

"You do realize that I'm your boss?" Carol asked, smiling.

"Are you a cool boss, or the type of boss that wakes up with a couple of drones t-bagging their house?" He said, setting her sandwich on her desk.

"Are you threatening me?"

"How would I. Didn't I just make you sandwich?" He said smiling.

He had taken several bites of his own sandwich and had thrown it on his table alongside two freshly opened cans of soda.

Teo Han was a lot like Layton as far as Carol was concerned. They were both impressionable, but highly self-opinionated, they were both good at what they did, and finally, Layton's annoying behavior almost made them indistinguishable. That, in itself, was a white lie, because Layton stood above 6'0 and was rather thin, as compared to Teo Han, a chubby kid who looked shorter than she did if she wore heels.

Teo Han had been born in Japan, right before his parents moved to the USA when he was given an IQ test and he was shown to have an IQ of about 132.

Now at seventeen, and with an advanced degree in software engineering under his belt, NASA, the FBI, and the CIA scouted him to freelance on various projects, the latest being the Russian espionage.

"Where is Sultan?" Carol asked as she waited for her computer to connect to the encrypted server the CIA had provided.

"I don't know, check his socials" Teo Han suggested.

"Socials?" Carol was puzzled.

"Oh, this is your first time working with Sultan. He takes a work break every week to go to party in Dubai, he probably chose today" Teo Han said, shrugging.

"Doesn't he know how serious this is?" Carol screamed.

"Hey, chill out. He'll be here tomorrow" Teo Han replied, "So what information do we have concerned this Office?"

"Brendan was supposed to work in it" Carol said, immediately feeling sorry do putting her on the spot

"I created a 3d layout from the few videos of the office that we have and that are on social media." Brendan spoke.

"Woah, when did you have time to do that?" Even Teo Han was shocked.

"I taught a bot to 3d design anything" She replied, shrugging.

"Brendan, that's impressive." Carol commented, to which Brendan seemed to nod, before turning back to her computer. Almost immediately, they both got an e-mail notification as she had sent it to both of them.

"Thank you Brendan" Carol said, before going back to inspect the 3d model.

She then forwarded it to Director Colby, who thought it wise to send it to the tablet and phone she was to give Gemini, or Humphrey Jonathan.

CHAPTER TWENTY-THREE

"Here you go" she said, "Its loading right now, but what you should see is a 3d model of the Presidential Office in Russia. Study it, see it you can find anything" She added.

"Will do Ma'am" Gemini said, running up to the helicopter that was supposed to pick him up and to the nearest airport for his flight to Russia.

He had been given a key to a safehouse, which in reality was a room in a large apartment building, but with access to the underground sections from the elevator.

"I see you're ready to go serve your country?" Came the pilot's voice. It was the voice of an elderly man, one who was used to commanding.

"Yes sir. I am."

"That right there is a True American! I'm General Eisenhower, nice to meet yam!"

"Likewise, Sir. I'm a huge fan of your military reforms, Sir!" Gemini's eyes widened; he was being taken to the forefront by his own hero!

"And I'm a fan of your courage, my boy. When you get back, the highest honor ever awaits you, and I'll be there to deliver it."

"Thank You Sir." He smiled heartily.

Back on Unimak Island, Director Colby watched as the first part in an elaborate plan to overthrow a war before it happens, fly away, and towards enemy lines.

As she stood there, right beside the makeshift helipad, she received a call from a number registered to the White House.

"Hello, this is Director Colby"

"This is Agent Cooley and we just got robbed in Iowa" He replied, deciding to go straight to the point.

"Robbed? Is the President okay?" She started walking towards the camp.

"Fortunately, there was no violence" Agent Cooley replied.

"Then what happened?" She was curious.

"A family came up to Mr President for a picture and we obliged, then came another family, but this it was a man carry a child in a baby carrier around his chest."

"Go on" Agent Colby had started recording.

"He takes the picture and leaves, going into the hotel."

"What Hotel was this?"

"Golden Inks'

"Go on"

"As we are about to enter the car, the president makes to call his wife, the First Lady, but the phone is no longer there, his handkerchief too!"

"Have you been able to access CCTV footage?"

"Not yet the Hotel needs clearance from the owner, and he is unavailable."

"Hold on a sec, alright? Golden Inks, was it?"

"Affirmative ma'am"

"My guys are getting that footage as we speak"

There a brief silence, during which Agent Cooley seemed to be giving out commands, shouting at the top of his voice. Half the time he had sounded out of breath.

"Got it. I'll be sending it to you now, including a life feed as well, do well to find this perp"

"Thank You Ma'am"

"And where is the President?"

"He has been escorted back to his hotel room by the other top agent on this assignment, Ma'am"

"Wait, so he had two of you on the field, and he still got robbed?"

"It was a loose moment Ma'am; it will never happen again"

"Now go chase that perp!" She commanded, ending the call.

Immediately, she reached out to the Todd Bell, the Iowa chief of Police.

"Hey, Todd. Your president just got robbed, I want you to be every possible 10-8 on the streets and searching for the people in a video I'm about to send to you"

"Robbed? In my city?"

She could hear him seethe with rage.

"Easy there old chap, think about your sugar, and your heart"

"I'm fine, I'm fine. Listen how about we catch up some other time, we got work to do"

With that, he had ended the call. Knowing Todd Bell, he would have suspects by midnight and a line up by seven the next day. She just wished he would take a break. Life does come at you fast when you were an adrenaline junkie in your younger days.

Not only was her plan in motion, and quite delicate, she now had two cases of stolen mobile devices. Immediately she sat down at her table, in her cabin, she drafted an email to deactivate The President's phone.

"Who knows where the Vice President, and The First Lady are right now? Who knows what could have been stolen?" She pondered.

A status report from Gemini made her phone buzz and she picked it up to see.

"At other helipad. Airport in 1h. Flight in 1h15m. Humphrey out"

She had dropped her phone again, but almost immediately, it rang.

"Unknown Number? Who could it be?" She wondered, answering the call with a hush tone.

"Director Colby, I swear to god! I hope you started deploying our task force!"

"Yes Sir, Mr President"

"It's the damn Russians, Colby. They probably know were coming! I hope you a few tricks up those rolled up sleeves of yours!"

"We have a 3d model of the Government Office in Russia, as we are currently scanning it for the location of the information bank"

"Excellent! Get me a jet! Get me out of this town! No more meetings! Fowler, tell my wife to shut down her book tour for the time being!"

"Mr President, Sir. There is no need for alarm. Our men have it covered" She pleaded.

"Covered? I almost got shot, by someone I wanted to take a picture with! What if he had a gun? What if, Colby?"

"I can assure you, Mr President. Nothing of the sort will happen."

"Well, I don't believe you. Hasten the launch. Send in the next agent, you have 46 hours to do so."

"But Sir, I-" He had ended the call.

Director Colby wanted to scream, but at almost the same time, she heard a knock on her door.

"Who is it?" She called.

"It's Aria, ma'am." Came the voice.

CHAPTER TWENTY-FOUR

"...keep that in mind, do you understand?" Darrell seemed to be in a hurry, and rather angry at whom he was on the phone with. This made Carol rather uncomfortable, as she made to hurry up the stairs, and into her home.

But just as was expected, she called to him.

"Hey neighbour? How was work today?" He asked, waving at her. On his face was a rather friendly smile, his teeth seemed to shine in the light from his front yard, where he was sitting, nursing a glass of what looked like gin.

Carol sighed, she thought to give a hurried "hello" and scurry up to her front door, but he seemed to want to have a conversation. They had been neighbors for a few days, but it still felt new to him. Carol wondered why.

"Maybe he is actually nice" she thought, walking across her lawn, towards him.

"How was work?" He asked again.

"It was good. Really good. I got settled in on a new project and I'm really looking forward to this new chapter of her life" Carol lied. She hated her new assignment. The only upside was that she was given a significant increase in terms of salaries, but it sucked in general; her coworkers were either absent, non-responsive, or just a little too familiar, or loud.

"That's great. Kinda sounds like my old job" Darrell replied. Carol sensed that he was trying to make conversation, and she was not having it. Normally, she would not even consider talking to someone for that long, but it was worse at the moment, as the grocery bag she carried was getting heavier by the second. Under her breath, she cursed whoever reared the chicken she carried.

"Where did you work?" She found herself asking, regretting her decision immediately.

"Oh, Belgium. I worked as a contractor for the government."

"Oh, that great. I work for the government too." She replied, a sense of pride in her voice.

"That's good on you, so what do you do?" He asked, excitedly. Something about his smile had begun to irritate her, it felt almost like he was torturing her on purpose by letting her stand there, clutching a heavy grocery bag, her fingers growing number by the second.

"I work in Internet Security at The White House" She replied almost immediately, sporting an accomplished smile. She had learnt how to lie. A few weeks ago, this question would have had her stammering for minutes on end, but she saw herself as well-composed, and without her eyes twitching. Agent Fowler may be stuck up, but he sure was a good influence on her!

The only downside was losing feeling in her fingers.

"Listen, could we continue this sometime? I really, really need to put down this bag" She begged, almost as soon as she saw him try to mouth another question.

Before He could say goodnight, she was already up her stairs, stopping only to smile as she opened her door.

"He likes you; you know?" came a voice behind her, causing Carol to jump, crashing her knee into a kitchen stool as she did.

"What the heck, Layton?" She yelled, nursing her knee.

"I'm sorry, but don't you see what the universe has done for you here?" Layton had his hands raised, almost like he was declaring the will of a thousand gods. Carol could only smile. She couldn't be mad at him for long, and he knew that. Again, he had used it to his advantage.

"Come off that type of talk, you know you're always saying stuff like that" She hissed, turning to her chicken. She took it to the freezer, with her mind running through recipes she could think of. It was a Friday, and although she had to be at work the next day, she was sure to be free on Sunday.

"I'm not, give me one time where I was wrong about a guy that liked you?" Layton asked. He was seeking vindication, and they both knew he always got it.

"Not this time, baby boy" Carol whispered, a mischievous smile on her face. He had distracted her from her thoughts, and she was about to unleash hers on him.

Slowly, she turned. On her face, she brandished a smile that reeked of devious revenge, but Layton was having none of it.

Again, he asked, "I'm still waiting, prove me wrong, Carol" he taunted.

"Ivan, the guy that worked at the mobile store where you bought my new video game controllers last summer?" Layton had already started listing out witnesses, like an attorney who was closing up a case he was sure he had won.

"He asked if we were okay with the controllers! That doesn't count!" Carol defended herself, she was certain that this was her fight to win.

"Why are you forgetting that he incessantly asked for your number? Carol, he gave us bad controllers so that we could come back to the store! He even offered to pay for gas!" Layton yelled, his hands were raised, and he laughed as he recalled his sister's suitors, and their shenanigans.

Carol, on the other hand, was business like. She had not won an argument with her brother, and she felt obligated to win this one.

"Did you want me to date someone that was manipulative?" Carol asked, her eyebrow was raised. Her gaze was so intense that Layton stammered as he tried to answer.

"No, no! You know I wouldn't... Come on Carol!"

"Aha! I thought so!" She said triumphantly, moving her feet along to a tune she had begun to hum.

Layton slumped on the couch in defeat, and Carol resumed washing the vegetables she had brought back from the grocery store.

"Finn Crawley, Remember him? Finn? Ring any bells?" Layton whispered, reveling in his comeback.

"Damn you, child!" Carol cursed, turning slowly to face her brother. "Layton, you win." She surrendered, standing awkwardly.

"How many times did you have to cancel your dates?" Layton asked mockingly. "Three? Two? Four?" He continued to ask, his eyes glistening in the living room lighting, and a smug smile plastered on his face.

"It was six dates, Layton" Carol muttered.

"Huh? I can't seem to hear you over the sound of my victory, please speak louder"

"It was six dates, okay?" She yelled, immediately covering her mouth. She had yelled so loudly that she was sure the neighbors had heard her.

"Damn. You really broke his heart. The last time J checked his Socialgram, he was following the AlphaBros, and possibly every gym within a 30-mile radius. Body builders too'

"The AlphaBros? What is that? Eish" Carol asked. "Whatever it is, it sounds misogynistic" She added, shuddering as she turned back to continue preparing dinner.

They were out of leftovers, and she had not cooked in almost a week, and all they had was organic vegetables, a big chicken, some fruit, and ramen she bought from the high-end store she always avoided she grocery shopping.

"It is" Layton replied, shaking his head slowly. "I couldn't watch a video to the end, your boyfriend had like 4 fire emoji comments on it too" He added.

"God, I broke him, didn't I?" Carol said, sighing in regret.

"Yep, you did. Break those noodles too. Not everyone like theirs like tied up shoelaces" He ordered.

"You'll eat them how I eat them, how we're all supposed to eat them, you hear?" She said, hissing.

"Well, I'm going up to my room, I have a tom of homework to not mess up, see you in 20."

"Yeah, thanks for helping" She called out to him, but he was already up the stairs. But he had heard her.

"You're welcome!" He called back, shutting his door.

"I know that boy's playing video games right now" She sighed, continuing her work.

"Work! damn" She immediately gasped. She had just remembered that she had files to run through.

As she cut through the lettuce and washed them under running water, she was grateful that the files she had to either read, sign, or validate were all in a small flash drive, and not in paper form.

"Who's gonna carry that? Not me!" She said to herself, giving a small shrug.

She was uncertain what detailed information the files held, but she did seem to have a fair knowledge.

Cutting slices of tomatoes and placing them into a blender was not enough to stray Carol's mind away from looking for patterns.

"Maybe, the guy that stole my phone wanted to get information about the White House? About the President?"

The President!

All Carol could figure was that he had abruptly returned from his trip, and that he was angry with everyone.

He had requested for Teo Han, after which the boy returned, his face looking rather sunken. Rumor had it that his phone was not encrypted, and his security system was not up to date, and that Teo Han was responsible.

"President Wallace's phone got stolen too, didn't it? Damn, he was right to be paranoid"

According to the files she had gotten from the Director of the CIA, and several memorandums she had Teo Han pick up from the Director of the FBI, she was to familiarize herself with the agent in the field, as well as several other that she would be likely to activate in case of "critically, unavoidable emergencies? Whatever the note said." Carol caught herself muttering, but she was grateful that she did not have to be in the field.

"Russia is cold, isn't it?" She asked herself, shrugging as she could bring herself to answer. "I'll look it up, definitely".

CHAPTER TWENTY-FIVE

"Gemini, come in"

The walkie on his side table buzzed, but it was not enough to wake him from his sleep

Tired, and not used to the cold, his first day undercover as a clerk had been literal hell, but unforgivingly cold.

This was not his first time in the field, and neither was it his first time in Russia. But this supposed familiarity did not seem to keep him immune to the sting that came with the cold. It seemed to cut through the fabric on his many layers of clothing, grabbing him by the sides and making it impossible to breathe.

"It's that goddamn global warming, I tell ya" His boss, Bernie Post had said, after he caught him turning up the heater.

For a man who had spent almost half his life in foreign lands, Bernie post sure did know how to retain an accent.

"Kholodnaya Pogoda, huh?" He had asked after he had caught his new employee toying with the thermostat.

"Yeah, real chill" Gemini had replied. He still had his coat on, and that combined with the scarf he wore to match his blue suit didn't seem to keep the cold at bay.

"Listen, Humph, you'll get used to it." He had said, tapping him on the shoulder. "Now, get to the front desk, you have papers to sign." He added, the cheer in his voice was gone, and with it the smile he had worn as he walked past initially.

Whatever was buzzing didn't seem to make him want to get up, although he heard it loud and clear. Gemini thought of sacrificing the warmth of his many blankets for a routine check-in with the Director and decided to stay in bed.

"It'll go away" He groaned, raising a blanket over his face, and turning towards the wall.

As soon as the buzzing died, he sighed and went back to sleep. He was now an employee of Unites States government and he had to keep up appearances, he couldn't risk being late and losing his cover.

*

"Gemini! Come in!"

Director Colby was at her wit's end. The President was furious with her and demanded extra security details following his arrival in the capital, and even more for his wife, the First Lady.

"Gemini, come in!" She called again, hoping her point man was not in danger.

"But how could he be? He just got there, right?" She asked herself, thinking to radio the others and ask for information on his whereabouts.

Unlike his usual disposition, it was unlikely for Gemini to not answer a radio call for status reports.

She thought to ask Skunk about his whereabouts, but that would be a breach of protocol. The only other option was to activate an agent that lived nearby, but the mission was too delicate to let any other person in on it.

"He's probably sleeping. I know that." She thought, shrugging. "He better be awake soon and with travel details of all visa applicants too" she muttered, running her fingers around the rim of a glass that used to hold a shot of rum.

"Well, unto the next one" she told herself, sighing in anticipation for the wreckage she was about to bear witness to; Jabez, or Maksim Egorov.

"Jabez, come in" she called.

After a rather short buzz from the static, and to her surprise, he responded.

"Maksim here, how can I be of service?"

"Good morning soldier, how is Russia treating you?"

"Quite cold, like if death had a freezer" He replied, his voice was light, as he tried to sound as casual as possible.

"And how are the living conditions?" She asked.

"Cold, the rooms are always cold. Basically, everything here is cold" He replied.

"Tell me about the job, what do you see happening at the Kremlin?"

"Well, Director. Whomever had this identity had a pretty shitty job. I've had to stay as a guard in the most unholy of places, and that is just me being generous with words."

"Stick to the plan, Agent." She said, sighing. "Any contact with other agents?"

"I think I saw Gemini when I went over to the Embassy to validate my stay or something like that. Then I saw Skunk give me the middle finger. His job is worse, imagine being a mailman with that sort of uniform, and those colors, ugh"

He seemed to spit, before apologizing in Russian to someone who walked past him.

"Stay on the mission, Agent. Don't forget that. I will be speaking to Aria and Harry soon, have a good night's rest"

"I work night duty! What sort of shitty agent did You guys make me?" He yelled into the radio, but Director Colby had cut him off.

"Chaotic" she said, hissing. "Talking to that man is like trying to pet a wild animal. Never ends good"

As she reached to get herself a refill, she heard a loud thud outside. Hurriedly, she looked outside the window, hoping to get to safety in case of any danger, but all she could see was a soldier that had thrown a crate to the ground.

The figure standing over a smashed crate that seemed to contain ingredients was none other than Lance Corporal Jobowksi.

"I didn't even need to know that" She sighed, shutting her window in anger. Slowly, she walked over to the counter where she kept her drinks, a makeshift bar, if you will.

As she stood there, pouring herself a glass of white wine, Director Colby realised that she had not decorated her cabin to feel like her.

"Damn, I got to get to that. I'll be here for a while" she said, cursing her forgetfulness.

It was not as if the room was in a state of disarray, but She had always been particular about these types of things.

"That rug should not be there" She commented, scoffing at the design choices of the former inhabitants of the cabin. "And what type of person has triangle shaped mirror?" She continued, entering the bathroom.

Lost in soliloquy, she did not hear her phone ring. It sat on her desk, buzzing, and wailing out her ringtone; a calming melody played over the sound of crashing waves.

When she finally heard it, the call had ended. Hurriedly, she rushed to the phone. There were only two people that knew the phone number Director Colby used to receive or give information during her stay at Unimak Island. These two people were none other than her husband, and the President. Not even Carol, the new recruit who had been instrumental in discovering the hidden attacks in the first place.

As Carol picked up the phone, she sighed yet again. Her guess was right, and it was the President. Her Husband had been understanding of her intense work schedule and activities. Although she was forbidden by law to give him full details, he seemed to want to know less, only promising her a weekend away as soon as she got back.

"It's Him" she said, keeping a straight face. She knew he was going to call again, and that he was going to be very raw with his words, and that he was going to demand a better output, but she did not mind.

Soon, he called again, and she was there to answer, bracing herself for the onslaught that was President Wallace.

"Good evening, Mr President" she said softly, taking a deep breath, with her eyes shut. Let it rain, she thought.

"Well, a good evening to you too, Director Colby" Came his voice.

Her eyes widened. Numerous thoughts ran through her mind at once.

Why was he so calm? Did the White House medical staff give him something to sedate him? Was this a drunk dial? He didn't sound like he was slurring, and he did sound genuinely happy, so she listened as he continued to speak.

"Well, I just wanted to congratulate you on your deployments and the success you have had so far. This is a win for all of us. Nay, this is a win for America" He proclaimed.

"Thank you Sir, we would not have been able to do this without your visionary leadership" She responded, flinching at the dryness in her tone. "But why would I not? I had expected a war, and he came with flowers!" She told herself, listening as The President went on about how the security situation worried him, and that he felt like the cyber-attacks were the first wave of massive attacks again the United States.

"I can assure you, Mr President, that our agents will be to the root of all this, faster than the speed of light, even" She bragged, wincing as soon as she remembered Jabez.

"Your agents? Even the funny one? I don't even mean the good type of funny; you know?"

"Sir, I can assure you that Jabez, or Maksim, as he is now known, will be on his best behavior"

"Even after the airport?" The President asked. Licking his lips loudly in triumph as he heard Director Colby gasp. "You thought I wouldn't find you, did you?"

"I'm sorry Sir. He is a bit of a wildcard, Sir. But I can vouch for him and say that he is a good agent." She was on her feet and pacing the floor of her cabin.. "Here comes the war, damn you Jabez" she cursed under her breath.

"That kid is 19 years old, Director Colby. Your guy lands in Russia and he already fought with someone? A kid?" President Wallace questioned.

"Sir, I had my guys access the security footage of that store and…" He had cut her short. All she could was sigh and trace the eye bags under her eyes with tired hands.

"Yeah, I saw that too. Our guy packs a mean punch, I'll tell you that."

"Yes sir. But he got jumped, Mr President. He had no choice but to defend himself."

"Why didn't he stop? The kid was done, his friends had run away. Why not get out of there?" President Wallace would not give in that easily, and now he was questioning her at top of his voice.

"I think we can both agree on that Sir." She said, "I spoke to him this evening, and he apologized to me about his misgivings. He also said to apologize to you as well" She lied.

"He better be sorry and mean it too! This was supposed to be an under the radar type of mission. We don't want our assets behaving like miscreants and getting caught on tape too!" He yelled; Director Colby was sure she heard a hand descend heavily on a desk.

"I can assure you that my team at the CIA headquarters has destroyed both tape and it's digital footprint from off the internet." She said, reassuring him.

"Good. What about the other agents?" He asked.

"Well, I spoke to a few hours ago, and they are settling in nicely. Right now, I'm waiting for sunrise so that I can communicate with them." Director Colby replied.

"Good. Where are we on getting me a secure mobile device?" He finally asked. "I'm using a backup and even I can tell that a preschooler can hack it" He continued.

"Well, Mr President. I have instructed my finest cyber security expert to present an upgraded Mobil device to you in a few days. I'm afraid that you are stuck with the backup for a couple days"

"Uh, if you say so. Listen I have to get to dinner with my wife. Keep me updated!" He yelled, ending the call.

As soon as the call was done, Director Colby slumped onto her bed. She had been pacing all this while and was suddenly out of breath.

As she lay on her bed, trying to catch her breath, she thought to call Director Taylor of the FBI, firstly to thank him for his information gathering and with helping place the agents in strategic points.

Fighting every urge to lie down, she grabbed her phone once again, forcing herself to sit up as she did.

As soon as she sat erect, she let down a yawn, and with eyes that watered, she dialed the Director's number. To her surprise He responded immediately.

"Good evening Director Colby" He greeted, his tone as meek as ever.

"Good evening Director Taylor, uh I just wanted to thank you and your team for gathering the necessary intelligence report necessary for my team to embark on this phase of the mission."

"I was only doing my duty, Ma'am. Thank you anyways." He responded dryly.

"Thank you again, Director."

"Have the agents been settled in? Are there any complaints about the living conditions that safe house have provided?"

"Absolutely none so far, all thanks to you.

"And the ones in charge of gathering intelligence about the Presidential Office, and the reservoir of information?"

"All in place, we await an opening at this juncture."

"That is absolutely splendid." He replied, and Director Colby was sure she detected a tone of excitedness in his voice. "Then you should consider taking advantage of a pop-up excursion by Government House staff. It's sort of like an open day, but for students, and tourists"

"Is that so?" Director Colby asked, her eyes widening with joy. She was pacing the room again.

"Yeah, it came up on a government website a few hours ago..."

"When does this happen?" She asked.

"In a few days. Look, I'll send you the link. Have a look then. If you need my help with intelligence gathering, you know what to do. Look, we are not done cataloguing information for all your agents, so advise them to not get caught for at least a day, or two. Please"

"Yeah, about that" She had stopped pacing.

"I know about Agent Maksim and his back-alley brawl. I personally alerted the CIA after my guys brought it to my attention. Please tell him to refrain from such activities, please." Director Taylor explained.

"I already did, you have nothing to worry about" She lied again, but Director Taylor was having none of it.

"Well, I hope for your sake that he heard you. Have a good evening Director Colby. I'll forward the links and details to you right away; we both have work to do." With that said, Director Taylor ended the call.

Almost immediately, she saw that she had been emailed a list of links that redirected her to several sites.

Just like her room, she stared scornfully at the design choices of the website designers.

"Why in hell would someone go with a pink and green design? If you're designing websites, how then are you a retarded moron?" She cursed, perusing the information. As she scanned, she came upon an invitation for students and for the general public to come for an open excursion.

"...That only admits 500?" She asked. "I just need to get two people in there. This would not be an issue" She muttered.

As she read further, she discovered that digital passes were to be made available to all that were willing to show up, and that they were to be available the night before the event.

Scrolling down, she came upon a list that showed the list of people that had indicated interest to be reminded to vie for a pass, her eyes widening once again.

"What? Fifty thousand? How is that even possible?" She said, gasping. "Damn Russians!"

Although she had grown rather tired, she knew she had to message through to the White House team. They needed to be sure they got the passes to both Aria, and Harry.

Skunk and Jabez, on the other hand would not need them. They both had identification cards that showed them as long-serving members of the staff that worked at the Government House.

With heavy eyes, she wrote a message to send with the links to Carol, with a notice that said to send them to all other member of her team. As a heading, she used the words; "Treat as Urgent" marked in red and larger in font than the rest of her message. But her eyelids had become too heavy, and she could not find the strength to send it.

A few minutes later, and rather tipsy from using alcohol to cope with her stress, Director Colby lay on her bed, fast asleep, but not before letting out a sigh.

CHAPTER TWENTY-SIX

"You do realize that we have no backstory, right? I mean, like where are we from?" It was Harry that was talking. She had been staring at her new identity for a while and finally spoke out, startling her fellow agent, and roommate, Aria.

"What?" Was all Aria could ask.

"I mean it! Look at your Id. It only gives you the basic stuff, nothing too deep. We did not even have any sort of debriefing, unlike the boys."

"Does it matter?" Aria asked, she was exhausted. The little information they were given stated that they had to pretend to be tourists, and that involved long hikes to tourist sites, uncomfortable buses, and a lot of food, some of which seemed to make her sick. Unlike Harry, she was not very chatty, and she was disappointed by how her quiet time in the shower had been disrupted by the ever-chatty Harry.

"I mean, if someone asked, what are we?" Harry asked her at the top of her voice.

"I don't know, what do you think?" She replied, regretting instantly her attempt to engage.

"Students? Tourists? Lovers?" Harry suggested.

"What? What did you say?" Aria asked.

"Nothing? What do you say?" Harry retorted, almost immediately.

The shower was ended abruptly, and Aria stormed in the bedroom they shared. Despite having separate beds, Harry had resorted to almost living on her's and although it upset her, she did not say anything about. Inwardly, she hoped Harry would understand what her facial expressions meant.

"Do you mind?" Aria asked, beckoning to Harry to get up from her bed. She had been laying down on her clothes and did not seem to be in the mood for apologies as she only shifted and allowed Aria access to them. Then, unrepentantly, she lay back down on bed, jumping and ruffling the sheets in the process.

They had to be out in the city night life, so as to take picture for fake social media accounts that had been created and managed by several FBI agents.

Harry was already ready. In her dark, baggy jean trousers, and with a bright red graphic T-shirt to match, she was all set, except for the black leather jacket that hung by the door. Without flinching, and despite Aria's pleas, she watched as her roommate slid into her dress for the evening. Aria had on a white woolen gown, a brown beret to compliment her stilettos and a fur jacket to match.

"You look way too good" Harry announced, her eyes staring at Aria. Aria was sure she was uncomfortable, but that was the price she had to pay.

As the left the apartment, Aria complained about the weather, cursing as she walked in the biting cold.

"Come on, you got on a fur jacket, you'll be fine" Harry encouraged, looking out for their driver.

"I'm not. That meat dish we had earlier didn't quite like my insides, how sure are you that I would not have a breakdown while we are out?" She complained.

"You won't! Trust me, don't you?" Harry encouraged her. "Look we got the fun part of the entire job, let's just go out, and I promise you won't taste anything that makes you sick, okay?" She promised. Their taxi had arrived, and after conforming the plate numbers, they were off and into the night.

The journey was made in silence, as they both knew that their conversations would be hinged on the mission they had, a mission that they did not want to be compromised. Instead, they resorted to taking in the sights.

"Moscow at night, huh? Who would have thought?" Harry finally spoke.

Almost like a signal, the cab driver, a balding man who looked like he was well into his fifties, spoke out, striking the type of never-ending conversation that Aria had hoped too about.

"Is beautiful, no?" He asked, his English was weak, but he made sure to get his point across.

"Yes it is, Sir. Yes it is" Harry replied wholeheartedly, beaming with a full smile.

"No please, call me Dima. Everyone calls me Dima" the cab driver insisted.

"Alright Dima, how is your night going?" Harry asked. All Aria could do was hold her breath, hoping the conversation would not involve her.

"Ayy, is slow. Very slow. You lady want to have fun in Moscow, no?" He asked.

"We sure do, Dima. Tell him Aria" Harry beckoned, tapping her counterpart's shoulder.

"I'd rather not speak, Kiki" She whispered.

"You'd rather not gather Intel? Is that it?" Harry whispered back, cupping her hands over her mouth as she spoke.

"I want to, but not like this. Keep me out of your conversation, thank you!" Aria requested. When Harry saw that she was firm on being left alone, she shrugged, and with another smile, she turned to Dima, the cab driver.

"So, Dima, was it?" She asked.

"Ah yes. You American?" The cab driver replied, asking.

"Yeah, we are American"

"Ah, the people that talk funny." He said, sporting a mischievous grin.

"We don't talk funny, Dima" Harry replied, laughing.

"I believe you then. What bring you guys to Mother Russia?" He asked, turning the wheel to the left, and overtaking a rather fancy looking car in the process. They were almost at their destination.

"Well, we got a break from work and my friend here is just done with her masters, so we decided to see some sites as a form of celebration"

"Ah, congratulations. No wonder she quiet. Smart people always quiet"

"Dima! I'm smart too!" Harry protested

"But she the one with Masters, no?"

"Fair point, but you get only one star now" Harry said jokingly.

"Please no, American woman. No one-star. Last internet attack wiped my information from driver registry."

"Internet attack? What happened?"

"You don't know this? Big attack shut down half of Moscow! One electric car drive in circles for 19 hours. Another ATM send out only one person money, and this man is in Ukraine for work summit! Is crazy!" He said, tapping at the steering wheel.

"I don't know about this, Dima. Sorry about that. Five stars for you" Harry replied, eyeing Aria.

"Ah, thank you. I have just one more question, eh..."

"Kiki, its Kiki" Harry replied.

"Eh, Miss Kiki. I want to know, Are you people in the rainbow?"

"In the what?" Harry was amused.

"The rainbow, eh? I see them in the street. They kiss themselves; they hug like women. I also see women in them, with the color on the paper, and on the t-shirt, are you them?"

"We're just friends." Aria finally spoke.

"Ah, is good if you are rainbow or if you are not. Dima don't hate on anyone."

"Thank you Dima, but my friend here, Mia, is an old pal of mine. She's basically my sister at this point."

"Is good. Is good" They had gotten to their destination, and Aria had left the car, stepping onto the pavement, and breathing in the cold, Russian air.

The restaurant they had chosen for the evening was quite inexpensive, but in her opinion, the fact that it overlooked the Red Square in all its nightly glory made it an even better pick.

Soon, Harry was out of the vehicle, and their driver, Dima drove off. As they walked towards the restaurant, Aria was sure she was him wave at them with his free hand till he was past a bend, and out of sight.

Inside the restaurant, Aria was particularly impressed with the decor, and for some reason, it looked better than it did on the many review apps she had to go through to find it. Wooden seat accompanied the tables in fours, which were themselves covered in tablecloths. The lighting was low enough to ensure privacy, but just about right in case the customer needed to create memories.

As they sat, a smiling woman came up to their table. her thin, jeweled hands holding menus and her apron, a jotter.

"Welcome, good evening" she said, speaking Russian.

The pen she had tucked behind her ear helped keep her thick, black hair in place, even then, it shone in the dim restaurant light. She looked like she was in her early fifties, and according to the pictures on the wall that led to the kitchen, the wife of the owner of the restaurant.

After she had offered the menus to her customers, she walked briskly away from them. She went back to other customers but kept a keen eye on her new ones.

"So, what do you wanna get?" Harry asked, closing her menu. It was obvious that she had made her choice.

Aria only shrugged. Her Russian was not that good, and she had a difficult time understanding what was written.

"What's this?" She asked, pointing to the Pierogi, a Russian dish of dumplings served with potato and onion filling.

"Oh. That? It's a type of dumpling, Pierogi" Harry said.

"Is it vegetarian?" She asked.

"Yeah, I think so. If it was the Pelmeni it would have had meat, and the Pierogi is usually vegan, so yeah"

"Vegetarian." Aria corrected calmly.

As soon as she closed her menu and dropped it on the table, the woman was back.

"Have you beautiful ladies decided what you would like to order?" She asked. Standing with her hands by her side, ready to grab her notepad, and her pen.

"I'll have the Stroganoff. Beef" Harry replied in Russian. Returning the smile, she handed the menu back to her.

Aria, however, struggled to communicate her order.

"Can I get the Pierogi, please?" She asked politely, but the woman only smiled and looked at her. A sort of embarrassed smile, partly at Aria's helplessness as she tried to communicate her order, and partly at herself, because she could not pick out a word her customer was saying.

"She would love the vegan Pierogi, please?" Harry finally intervened.

"Vegetarian" Aria corrected again.

"Vegetarian Pierogi" Harry said, almost immediately.

Again, the woman beamed with a hearty smile, and after a small courtesy, she disappeared into kitchen, leaving them to wait.

"What if we get caught?" Harry suddenly asked.

"What?" Aria did not hear her.

"I said, what if we get caught?" She asked again, but this time slowly.

"Why would you even think that?" Harry asked.

"I don't know, have you seen this mission?" Aria asked in return.

"Yeah, I live it. But what makes you feel that way?" Harry asked again.

"Think about it, okay? The US government puts together a team that is clearly dysfunctional and makes them embark on a mission halfway across the world to steal secrets from another government they think is harming them. Does that make sense?"

"Well, You…"

"I'm not done" Aria announced. She was whispering, but her tone was still angry. "They kidnapped us because I'm quite sure I didn't come here on my own! Now I'm in a country I've never been in before? And to what? Trying to steal something that we don't even know if it actually exists?" She opined, raising her head as the woman resurfaced close to them. In the tray she carried were two dishes, the Stroganoff, and the Pierogi.

Harry thanked her, commenting that the food smelled heavenly, but all Aria could do was give a thumbs up.

As soon as she had set them down, their heads were bowed again, and they continued arguing.

"This type of shit happens all the time! Don't you see movies?" Harry whispered.

"But this is real life, isn't it?"

"It is, our lives are movies, Aria! How many times have you been in deadass horrible situations?" Harry asked.

"Countless times, but that is beside the point!"

"What then is the point?"

"That I have a bad feeling about this!" Aria confessed. There was quiet, all they could hear was the dinnertime chatter of the other customers that sat beside them.

"Oh, I didn't know that. I'm sorry you feel that way, but nothing is going to happen to us" Harry offered, grasping Aria's hand in hers.

"I feel like it will, and I'm always right" Aria was adamant in her pessimism

"Not this time, it won't" Harry said, grabbing a spoonful of her Stroganoff.

"I'm never wrong, Harry. Plus, you forgot to take pictures, we have an appearance to keep up with, remember?" She admonished.

"Shit, shit!" Harry gasped, setting her plate in place for Aria to take photographs.

"There, I'll forward it to that weird email they said to forward it to." She said after she had taken pictures.

"Do you even know the names of our social media accounts?" Harry asked in between mouthfuls.

"I think it's in our files. Or not? I don't know, honestly. I've never been one for online presence" Aria replied, shrugging. She had finally bitten into a Pierogi dumpling, and as she ate in silence, she begged for two things; that Harry stop interrupting her, and that her stomach does not react negatively to the Pierogi dumplings.

CHAPTER TWENTY-SEVEN

Carol was still looking for her glasses when her phone started buzzing uncontrollably. In a panic, she fell out of her bed, hitting her back hard on the hard, tiled floor of her house. The coldness seemed to seep way to fast into her spine, that she jumped up, wincing in pain. Her phone kept buzzing.

"Who the hell is even that?" She wondered.

She quickly grabbed her glasses and checked her phone.

"Hidden ID? Must be the Director" She thought.

"Hello, Carol. I have important information to divulge to you. Please check your emails and make sure to write back to me" She read a part of one of the texts she had gotten.

"Too formal, way too formal" She thought, straining her eyes to find the clock that she had hung in her wall.

"4:37" she said sighing. There were two thoughts in Carol's mind at that moment; go back to sleep and get to her emails by morning or get to them now and lose hours of much needed sleep.

Without thinking twice, she took the latter option, jumping unto her bed. Right as she closed her eyes to get some more sleep, her phone buzzed again, making her let out a loud groan of complain.

With reluctance, Carol grabbed her phone, hoping to find another message, but this time it was a call, and she answered it.

"Hello" She greeted.

"Good morning, Carol. This Director Taylor of the FBI" came the voice from the other end of the call.

Almost immediately, Carol sat up in her bed. She had to expect a call from him, and his tone seemed like he had important information to give.

"Good morning Sir" Carol greeted, even she was shocked by the alertness in her voice.

"I had passed sensitive information to your superior, the Director of the CIA. Has she made you aware of the developments in our little project?" He asked.

Hurriedly, Carol opened her laptop. There were no new messages from Director Colby.

"Apparently not Sir, I don't see anything in my inbox."

"That is unfortunate. Regardless, I'll be sending you some files that contain links to a possible entry point to getting the information we need. Please go through it, and give me your feedback as soon as possible"

"Okay Sir, I..." Carol said, but he had ended the call.

"The nerve on that preppy, stuck up..." Carol cursed, before holding her lips shut. If he could get her number, what exactly was stopping him from turning her phone into a listening device.

In a final show of defiance, and tiredness, she retired to her bed, but not before setting the alarm clock for seven in the morning. Agent Fowler had said he was going to pick her up by nine, and she did not need the whole day to get ready.

Slowly, she slid into a deep sleep, so deep that it took Layton to wake her.

"What?" She asked. Her eyes were still heavy with sleep, but she managed to sit up.

"He's here" Layton announced.

"The Agent? The one that picks you up?" Layton explained. He was leaning against her door, and with his free hand he tugged at his full, dark, curly hair.

"What?" Carol asked again.

"The agent that picks you up is at the front door, Carol" Layton offered, shutting the door as he left the room.

It was only then that Carol came to the realization that she had missed her alarm.

Hurriedly, she peeked out of her window, and staring back at her was Agent Fowler, in his signature suit, but this time it was deep blue, and for the sake of the sun, he had with him a pair of glasses, and an umbrella.

"Crap!" Carol cursed, rushing to the bathroom. There went her plans to marinate the chicken for later, and she still had the files sent to her by Director Taylor to review!

Hurriedly, she brushed her teeth, and slid into the shower, braving the cold water and taking her bath as quickly as she could.

As soon as she was ready, she sped out to the front door, throwing dollar bills at her brother, and leaving for Agent

Fowler's car.

"You're early" he said.

"I'm sorry, okay?" Carol was instantly on the defensive. Moving about that quickly had given her a headache, and her stomach hurt because she was hungry. She was definitely not in the mood for another back-and-forth argument with Agent Fowler. All she could think about was getting some snacks from the White House kitchen.

"If you say so." He commented. As soon as she was in the car, he slammed the door short and strolled the driver's seat. Slowly, he undid the umbrella he had been carrying and lifted his sunglasses, placing them just above his brows.

As he strapped himself in, he sighed. He had been punctual and respectful enough to wait for her, and all he got was a flimsy apology! A sudden welling of rage made his chest hot, but as she reversed away from her house, he made sure to take deep breaths, hoping Carol would not trigger his anger with so much as her breathing loudly.

Carol, on the other hand, used the seemingly uneasy silence to go through the files that the Director of the FBI had sent.

To her surprise, it was about thirty pages of possible identities, in case the agent's present ones got compromised

"I'm not going to go through that right now, hell no" she thought, swiping past them. She, however, could not help but respect Director Taylor for the amount of work he had out into the mission.

According to previous reports, he had sourced for old social media accounts bearing the same names as the agents and edited the pictures in them, replacing them with expertly edited photos of the agent, making it look like old accounts. All these, with bots that interact with the new profile He and his team had also sourced.

"Impressive stuff" She muttered, raising her eyes to look at Agent Fowler. He seemed angry, but he had never smiled at her, so it was hard to tell when he was happy, and when he wasn't.

There was also a brief bio of all the agents in the field, but these pieces of information were still lacking photographs. Carol thought it strange that she was running point on this operation and doing what the President had initially set out to do, but she still did not know who the agents were. She thought to ask, but quickly decided against it. If anonymity was going to be the key to a successful operation, she was all for it.

As the pulled up to the end of her street, she noticed the stranger she had seen a few days prior. He was on the phone, looking rather suspicious as his eyes darted in all corners. Carol looked back as they drove past him, and he seemed to be looking at her. Although the glasses were tinted, and probably bulletproof as well, Carol could not but feel unsafe.

"Hey, Agent Fowler?" She called; her voice was almost in whispers.

"Yes, Carol." He sounded solemn, and he kept his eyes on the road.

"Could you perhaps give me lessons in self-defense sometime?" She asked.

"Why would you want that?" He did not expect the question. All he wanted was a proper apology, and at this juncture he knew it was not forthcoming.

"I don't know. I just have this feeling that I'll need it. Will you help me" She pleaded, instantly regretting the rather foolish decision to make her voice sound like she was begging.

"Okay then. What are you doing tomorrow evening? I hit the gym by five in the evening, maybe we could go together?"

Carol bit her lip. She had wanted to spend Saturday cooking and cleaning, as well as brushing up on important documents, but all those things will have to wait. Except the cooking, and the cleaning. She already knew Layton was going to be of no help, and he was sure to come up with an excuse, like sports practice, or a hangout with friends.

"Sure. Will you come pick me up?" She asked. "Please?" She added almost immediately. She needed a favour from the man and being as humble as she possibly could seemed like the best way to go.

There it was. His chance to punish her for her earlier misconduct, but would he take it? Was he going to use this to his advantage, or was he going to give in, and forgive? Carol was not usually a bad person, she just...

"Agent Fowler, I asked if you would come pick me up, please." She tapped his shoulder, waking him from his thoughts.

"Fine. But remember that this is you invading in my personal space, and that I have no obligation to take you with me" he said matter-of-factly.

"What?"

"I have no obligation to..."

"I understand that, but you don't have to be angry about it" She protested. She had slid back into her seat.

The rest of the journey had such an uncomfortable silence in the air, one would swear it was mixed with the air conditioner.

"Thank you, and I'm sorry about earlier" Carol said. She had been sulking the entire time, but the urge to make peace was stronger than ever.

"I forgive You" Agent Fowler replied, sporting a knowing smile. Jackpot!, he thought.

As they pulled into the gate, a yellow sports car with red detailing on the side sped past them, almost crashing into the fields that led to the parking spaces.

"Who the hell is that?" Agent Fowler asked angrily, and to no one in particular.

'I don't know, but I think I have an idea" Carol replied, exiting the vehicle.

And she was right. It was The Sultan.

"Ah, you must be my new boss! Greetings, I'm The Sultan" he said as he saw he walk towards him. His arms were out and extended, and not for a hug, but for a regal pose that exuded influence, power, and affluence.

"Good morning Mr Sullivan, it's a pleasure to finally meet you" Carol greeted, stretching her hand out for a handshake.

"Who is this Mr Sullivan?" He asked, his eyes darting about, drowning in an embarrassment that only he felt.

"How about I show you to our office" she said, leading the way. "Shall we?" She continued when she saw that he had not been following her.

Of all the stories Carol had heard about The Sultan, she now saw reason to believe them. Although he was a literal wizard at cyber security and all types of hacking, his eccentric personality, seemed like his greatest possession. He seemed to walk with his head held high, so much so that Carol wanted to ask if it hurt his head. He was neither Muslim, or religious for the matter, but he was on the verge of changing his legal name to "The Sultan".

"First name, 'The', last name 'Sultan' Cool, right?" He bragged as they got into the elevator.

After a short silence, he spoke again. "Ugh, I see why I didn't come to work now" he said, scoffing at the worn out look of the elevator. "This is real nasty, look at that rust" he commented. And he was right, but Carol could not quite put her finger on what she found more nauseating; the worn-out elevator, or his attitude."

"So, what's the deal here, what are we doing?" He asked, crashing into his chair. The chair creaked in why could be termed agony, and Carol was sure that any more pressure would send him flying out.

"Well, today I assigned data to all the employees to catalogue unto digital libraries that would serve as information residues for this case. Next we…"

"Woah, woah. Let me stop you there. Director Colby only told me to supervise here. She said, and I quote 'Sultan, you are so cool, go over to that secret task force and oversee it. Give them a cool nickname too" he said. pretending to read a message from his phone.

"Mr Sullivan…" Carol made to continue, but he hushed her.

"Please, It's Sultan" he said, stretching his arms in the regal manner she had come to hate.

"Mr Sullivan" Carol was adamant. "I am sure Director Colby gave you no such directives, and that my authority and jurisdiction in this matter directly from the President."

"What do you think about 'Underground Espionage'?" The Sultan asked.

"I like it" came Teo Han's voice from the kitchen. Both Carol and The Sultan gasped in fear. Teo Han seemed to have put in an all-nighter. It was evident because he was wearing the same clothes as the previous day.

"How long have you been standing there man?" The Sultan asked, clutching his chest. Rather easily too, his silk robe-like outfit left most of his chest in public view.

"All morning. My hands hurt, and this is my sixth cup of coffee, so my hands shouldn't hurt, is that alright?" Teo Han asked. His glasses were tucked rather awkwardly in his hair, and his sky-blue shirt was spotted with brown stains.

"Oh, that is not normal, but it doesn't compare to my shroom high at Flaming Individual" Almost like a flash, he turned to Carol and asked, "Did I ever tell you about Flaming Individual? Aw man. It was 2018 and I was..."

"Where is Brendan?" Carol asked, completely ignoring The Sultan and his story.

"Oh, Brendan's on their way home. Probably there already by now, to be honest" He answered, staring at his watch. He then proceeded to stare at it awkwardly till Carol snapper him out of it. Teo Han gasped, and with almost the same breath, smiled a sheepish, almost mischievous type of smile, and disappeared into the kitchen, probably to make another cup of coffee.

"Wait, is he?" Carol asked.

"Going to make another cup of coffee? Yep" The Sultan answered. He was admiring the gold rings that adorned his fingers. "You know, it's kinda like my shroom high at Flaming Individual, did I ever tell you about that?" He asked, but as he turned to face Carol and possibly entertain her with stories of his conquests, he discovered that she had vanished into the kitchen.

"Well, suit yourself. You'll have to pay to read it in my book then" he said. He had now turned his chair and was facing the table that was assigned to him.

Teo Han could not possibly drive himself home, so Carol made him sober up at his desk, as she lulled him to sleep by using a piece of paper to fan his face. Then, she set out to work, running fail-safe options for their upcoming projects and the best possible way to retrieve the information they needed.

The Sultan on the other hand, spent his time checking himself out, so much so that Carol likened him to apes and how they groomed each other. Except that this one was evidently lonely and had no one to groom him.

When he finally got around to doing some work, he discovered that he had left his laptop in his car.

"Well, don't worry about it everyone. I'll go get it!" He said, darting for the exit.

Carol looked around to see whom he was referring to, but she found no one. Teo Han was still asleep in the corner, and Brendan was probably at home building some breathtaking contraption with her massive 3d printer.

Resigning to her fate as the unofficial baby-sitter to a bunch of criminally genius tech heads, and Brendan, she sighed, and got back to work, hoping to finalize her stimulatory exercises and get home to her chicken.

"The Chicken!" She gasped, grabbing her head between her hands. "Pizza it is". She said, returning to work.

The atmosphere at Carol's underground office had been quite heated for a few hours. Partly because it was no longer news that in a few hours, the agents would have to embark on what Teo Han had deemed "a literal shit show, like that one series about vampire soccer players"

The heat was unbearable, and so was Brendan's tapping away at the keyboards. Carol thought Brendan was resourceful, and a great worker, but being around Brendan could also be uncomfortable. Stealing a glance at her employee, she wondered if Brendan thought the same about her.

"Do they even work for me?" She muttered, noticing that The Sultan had yet again disobeyed her orders.

In the few days he had been around, he had successfully destroyed the coffee maker in the room that served as a kitchen, which he promised to fix, and buy a better one. Worst of all, he had disobeyed direct orders to not work on the project in any other place than the room assigned to him.

"Where is Mr Sullivan?" She asked, looking around the small, hot room they all worked in.

"Sultan. He's having it changed legally" Teo Han answered. He did not raise his head from his computer.

"I don't think I care about that. What I care about is where he is currently" Carol retorted, rather angrily too. They were given a direct order by the President, and he couldn't even carry it out.

"I don't know, ask Brendan" Teo Han said, shrugging. His eyes were fixated on his laptop screen. Deadline was approaching, and he had to prove himself.

"Cafeteria" Brendan said, with their back turned to Carol.

"Thank you Brendan" Carol replied, gratefully too. She felt like she had just been accepted a rather reclusive person who was way better at her job than she was. She felt like high school again, and she had just been accepted by the cool kids. With this feeling of accomplishment, she scurried towards the elevator, hoping to bring the heat she felt to Sullivan.

"I'm not calling him that stupid nickname" She muttered as she entered the elevator.

As she walked out of the elevator, and towards the cafeteria, Carol suddenly came to the realization that she had not eaten anything in a while. The adrenaline that fueled her work had waned drastically as she left her left her computer.

"New plan, okay?" She muttered to herself, "Get something to eat, and then give the pretentious punk a piece of my mind". Carol was sure she could feel her stomach biting and her legs were becoming weaker. By the time she was down the flight of stairs led to the corridor that opened up in the corridor across from the cafeteria, she had begun to feel dizzy.

"Two doughnuts, one large soda" she told herself, braving the pain. Finally, and after what seemed like quite a toil, she was at the cafeteria, but The Sultan was nowhere to be found.

"Damn, prick!" She cursed. She had looked at every table, but the purple turban and yellow silk robe he wore were nowhere to be seen.

After a fruitless search, Carol walked towards the counter, turning to inspect the cafeteria for one last time, before greeting the attendant with a painful smile. She was positive her stomach was going to cave in.

"What are we having today?" The attendant asked, greeting her with a smile so professional, Carol almost believed she was happy to see her.

"Chocolate doughnut, with sprinkles too, and a large soda" Carol replied, turning her back to the counter in the hopes that it would make time move faster. As she stood there, she came to understand why Teo Han always had a stash of sweets and snacks, and why Brendan always…

"Well, Brendan probably runs on a nano nuclear reactor" She joked, realizing that she had never seen Brendan leave for either a lunch break, or to use the bathroom.

Just as she was about turning to answer the call of the attendant who seemed to be come with her order, she noticed someone enter the hall. It was unmistakable, and equally unbearable to look at, but it was The Sultan, in all his glory.

"…Ma'am?" The attendant called again.

"Oh, right. Thank you." She said, smiling at the attendant. She was not supposed to pay, seeing that she was a staff, but she, like every other staff had a ration, and the moral obligation to leave a food tip. Carol took her tray from the attendant and slid a twenty-dollar bill over to her. Now she had to face the egotistic persona of The Sultan, and she was sure to be brutal with her words.

As she walked over to him, she rummaged through her mind for the meanest words she could say to him that would get her point across, and still not get her in trouble with Director Colby.

"Carol?" Someone seemed to want to get her attention, and as soon as Carol heard the voice, she knew who it was.

"Kevin?" She said, turning to him.

"Yeah! Long time no see. I mean, I do see you, but you're always with these new guys that nobody had seen before" he said, whispering as he turned to see if The Sultan was listening. He wasn't. Instead, he was on his phone, making a video.

"Yeah, I got a new gig. President's orders." She spoke. "We're coding a new interface for the president's personal security system. Top stuff" She lied.

"Sounds fancy. Word was getting around that you guys were fighting a cyber war with Russia. Word being turban guy" Kevin replied, pointing stealthily to The Sultan.

"What?" Carol fought to hide her shock. Her nervous laugh did not seem to cover up the anger she felt. Again, and surprisingly, she felt energized. All she wanted was to get on the phone with Director Colby and get The Sultan out of her team.

"Yeah, he told Lara, the web design chic. Yeah, he tried to make a move on her yesterday" Kevin said.

"He's just saying that. You know how guys like him like to brag about stuff that didn't happen, right?" Carol hoped to the heavens that she sounded convincing.

"Yeah, yeah. If you say so. Just keep him in line, okay? Lara said she had half a mind to report him to HR if he persisted. Shelton from the night shift said she threatened a sexual assault lawsuit, and we both know how that goes around these parts." Kevin then proceeded to take a slurp of his beverage. As he did, Carol could feel her stomach untying itself as the rage she felt vanished. She needed to have seat, and fast.

"Thank you Kevin, I gotta go" she said, walking off.

"See you around!" He called to her, taking a bite of his sandwich.

Carol then made her way to where The Sultan sat. He seemed to be on a live stream, and Carol had half a mind to swipe his phone and smash it on the floor, but she didn't.

"Damn it, who am I kidding? I don't earn as much as he does!" She cursed, instead taking a seat beside him.

"Look who just joined us, you guys!" The Sultan seemed engrossed in his live stream that he did not see Carol take the seat opposite him. Despite her annoyance, Carol sat rather quietly and ate her doughnuts, and it was only when she took a sip of her soda that he seemed to notice her. As he did, his face beamed in excitement, and he announced to his viewers that he had just been joined by his boss.

"Mr Sullivan, I would like to talk to you" Carol said. Even she was shocked by her calmness.

"Okay, give me a sec. I got a request to join feed" he said, waving off her request.

Carol had had enough. In a blind fit of frustration, she banged on the table, causing Kevin and the few other customers in an otherwise customer to look at their table. The attendant did not seem to pay attention, as she could be heard blowing gum bubbles in the background, providing a bit of comic relief in what could be described as an increasingly hostile space.

"Can you chill?" The Sultan asked, returning to his live stream.

"Chill? Don't I look chill to you, Mr Sullivan?" She asked.

Groaning, he set down the phone. "You don't, and it's not exactly good for my spiritual space, so could you try to be happy? Smile too, thank you" he said.

"How dare you? You do realize that we have a deadline to meet, and all you think of doing is playing turban and getting some random teenager some screen time with your online presence?" Carol whispered. She knew Kevin and the others were looking at them.

"Easy there boss, we don't want to mess up The Sultan's live stream, now do we?" He said, smiling nervously at the camera.

"Oh, I plan on doing just that. Mr Sullivan, get to work immediately, or I would have to call the Director on you" Carol announced.

"Sorry kid. If anybody asks why you're sad today, tell them Carol Duncan stopped you from winning a thousand bucks" The Sultan said to the kid that had joined him on the live stream. "Alright then, I'll catch you all on the flip side! Till then, stay ruling your worlds!" He said, turning angrily to Carol as he turned off the live stream and tossed his phone to the table. "Are you happy now?" He asked.

"Yes, I am. If you don't mind, we have simulations to run, and agents to keep alive."

"We just have to direct them to whenever the information bank is, right? Easy peasy" The Sultan replied, shrugging.

"We do not yet know what type of lock is operational on the information bank, and even if we did, we'd have to go through about half a quadrillion possible combination for each simulation. So no, it's not 'easy peasy', Mr Sullivan, and we would all appreciate it if you got to work.

The bot to run the programs is in place, but we did not have enough time to give it the full Sentient X dosage that Brendan synthesized, and that is where the human, you, comes in. So, if you would be kind enough to return to work, your country would really appreciate it." Carol felt like pleading with him.

"I heard about that on the tech streets, I thought it was just a myth? Wait, Brendan did that?" The Sultan asked, completely ignoring her pleas to get back to work.

"Yes, she did. The crazy part is that she made a programmable, quasi-sentient bot to help her create the Sentient X bot, and that she programmed then original bot to sabotage itself and end its own life once it was done." Carol thought to indulge, that it was somehow possible that it would make him want to go back to work, but it wasn't. The Sultan made to speak again, but she interjected.

"But that is beside the point! We need you to get back to work!" Carol was done with her doughnuts, and she was feeling full, but she knew it would not last.

The sugar rush that chocolate sweetened junk and large portions of soda gave could not be compared to a proper meal.

"Alright, alright. I'll help" The Sultan finally said, after being lost in thought for a while.

"Thank you!" She replied, standing up to leave.

"Right behind you!" He called out to her, but she was already at the far end and out of the door. Bit he had no plans of going back to work, instead, he snuck out of the cafeteria, and sped off in his car. As Carol walked up the stairs and towards the elevator, she heard the roar of his engine, and in the distance, she saw his white convertible speed past the open front gates.

"Son of a bitch!" She cursed, hoping the director would call her and she would table Alvares Sullivan's matter before her.

"Pretentious wannabe" She cursed again, tapping vigorously on the elevator door. Carol decided that she was not going to call him "The Sultan", at least not to his hearing.

"Hey Carol?" An oddly familiar voice greeted her. Carol froze in shock. Nobody was supposed to see her use the elevator. Carol turned with fear in her eyes, and who it was shocked her even more.

It was Darrell, her neighbour! What was he doing here? Was there a tour? Did he follow her?

"Hey, I just came over to say hi. If I'm intruding, I could back off, if that's fine by you?" He apologized and turned to walk away, by Carol called him back.

"I'm sorry, I was not expecting to see you here! What are you doing here, even?" She asked.

"Well, I'm working security and surveillance for the President. Yeah, I told you I was a contractor, right?" He explained, beaming with a smile. He wore a black suit, the basic fit, just right for an agent, but classy, nonetheless. To Carol, it seemed like a big shift from the grey sweatshirts and cargo pants he usually wore.

"Yeah, you did mention that. I just thought you were in engineering or something" she said, laughing at her mistake. He joined her, and a short while, they laughed heartily, so much so that Carol almost forgot her "The Sultan" problem.

"No, I don't do engineering, But I do know security. My last client in Belgium recommended me. He's this big guy in the government that had gotten threats from an anonymous source, who later turned out to be a separatist cell that had not yet gathered any traction or public sympathy- Am I boring you?' He explained, but stopped he saw that Carol had zoned out.

"No, no! Not at all, I just have an employee that is a pain in the ass is all" Carol explained hurriedly. He seemed like a nice guy, and she did not want to seem rude, or unwelcoming.

"Tell me about it. An employee of ours almost lost his life because he went out drinking in Algeria once. The drunkard blurted out our mission to the entire bar and was captured by opponents of the guy we were supposed to protect. We had to go get him, and we lost the terrorist leader. He fled to Cuba" Darrell said.

"You do have a lot of stories, huh?" Carol joked.

"Yeah, that's what happens when your life is an adventure" Darrell replied, shrugging.

"How about you tell me about them, over a plate. Your place?" Carol suggested. "Damn you Layton!" She said under her breath.

"My place is a mess, so I can't accept that, sorry. How about a night out in the town?" He asked.

"Sounds good. But it can't be soon, I have a lot on my plate right now"

"Well, not too far away either. I'll leave you to it, you seem like you have to get back to work"

"Yeah, I do. It was good running into you here"

"You too, take care." He replied, walking towards the Oval Office.

Once she stepped out of the elevator, and was in her office again, she noticed the change in the temperature, and that she had begun sweating again. For a second, Carol felt herself sympathize with The Sultan, but she soon shoved her feelings to the side. He, like everyone else in that room, had a job to do. Leaving your job because of a discomfort, no matter how little, or big, was tantamount to being lazy, and disrespectful.

"Guys, where are we with those simulations?" She asked as she settled in her work chair.

"Almost at 40%" Teo Han said.

"40?" Carol could not believe her ears. They had broken out their best processors for this task, but it seemed impossible to even execute. The heat from the processors made the room even hotter and harder to work in, yet they worked. There was silence for almost an hour, and all that could be heard was the whirring of cooling fans, and the tapping away of keyboard, accompanied by the occasional sigh, or the crackle of a good wrap.

"Sullivan was supposed to work on escape protocols!" Carol yelled after a while, sighing.

"I got it covered" Brendan whispered, but Carol was sure she was hearing things.

"What? You got it- how?" Carol asked. She had yet again been dumbfounded by Brendan's efficiency.

"Yeah, we kinda did have it covered already. We both know that The Sultan is kind of lazy, so we did his job. We, Brendan. Don't hoard all the credit" Teo Han interjected. All Brendan did was shrug and go back to work.

"How?" Carol could not believe her ears.

"It's kinda simple, really. In the eventuality of a breach in obtainment protocols, the safest way to escape is in plain sight." He said, shrugging.

"And how did you prove this?" She was still skeptical, so she had to ask.

"Oh, we didn't. Sentient X did. She's a real smart lady." Teo Han said. "Woah, I guess Brendan do solve it. Well, I helped, I added the necessary variables."

"Oh, thank heavens." Carol was relieved, and she turned to go back to work. Suddenly, she realised something and turned back to face Teo Han.

"If you knew that Sullivan's quota had been solved, why allow me to go fetch him?"

"I didn't know you were going to hassle him about that. You know what? How about some praise, alright? Brendan and I have done the work of at least a hundred CIA programmers, and in record time too, so how about some credit, and I don't know? A pat on the freaking back?" Teo Han burst out. Carol had never seen him upset before and she immediately apologized.

"I'm sorry, Teo- I mean, 4-42" she said remorsefully. He was right. She was being hard on them, but it was all because of the type of pressure she was under. Several times in the last few days, she had woken up to several texts from Directors Colby and Taylor, instructing her to cut down on her sleeping and get to work. She knew that they were under pressure from none other than the President himself, and although the cyber-attacks had stopped. There seemed to be pockets of random attacks at several points in the US, and these random points were untraceable, as they followed no known pattern.

Before leaving for work that morning, Carol had read about a family that lost everything because hackers had turned their entire savings into cryptocurrency, tripled it in an hour, and then purposefully lost the amount on online gambling sites.

"Sad stuff" She had said, but she felt responsible for it regardless. She however felt proud, because she was going to be in the team of people that foiled the plans of these supposed Russian cyber terrorist attacks, by holding the entire government ransom with a large file of information on the Russian government that their field agents were to steal as well as unlock the Russian internet system in few hours.

With renews conviction, she looked at the time.

"3:37" She muttered. They were going to be for the night, again. That way by 1 in the morning, or 8 AM, Russian time, the agents would leave for their mission before then, and she would have to catch them on the road.

"Uhm, Carol. Could you pull some strings and get another AC unit in here?" Teo Han asked.

"Yeah, let's see how it goes today. If we're lucky, we can get two." She responded, beaming a smile.

Carol felt lucky to have the team that she did. She had always thought it felt good to have people better than you on your team, that way they're capable of pulling their own weight, and without unnecessary supervision too.

The night was still quite far away, but Carol felt like it would come sooner. She was also nervous, and she wanted to feel like she wasn't the only one.

"Maybe the agents are having a meltdown. Hopefully not" She muttered, getting back to work.

*

It was around six in the morning that Aria heard the telephone in their room ring. She had not slept throughout the night and was lost in a sea of her own thoughts.

In a part of her mind, she found it funny that she had urged Harry to get some sleep, but she was the one awake, and surprisingly, scared. Somehow, the language barrier seemed like less of a blessing than a curse.

If she could not understand what a person was saying, how would she know if she was in danger? How would she read signs? How would she communicate for help if need be? The best she could do was a terrible Russian accent, but that was as insufficient as her confidence going into the mission.

What was worse was the fact that she was supposed to be on the mission with four others, but she had only been in contact with Harry, as her cover and Harry's were merged together. If one blew open, the other would too. No one would believe that she was not aware of Harry's intentions, especially if she was found out to be American, the same people the taxi driver had accused to carrying out cyber-attacks on Moscow.

The facts that their covers were intertwined made Aria more anxious. She was not used to depending on anybody, more or less a wild card, like Harry.

"She is basically the Female Jabez- whatever his last name is" She muttered. Standing up from her bed seemed to make her eyes hurt as she struggled to get to the bathroom. As she washed her face in the sink, she realised that she had not gotten enough sleep.

Sighing, she walked back to her bed, hoping it was still 1 AM, and that she had a few more hours to catch some sleep. It wasn't. The telephone rang almost immediately she pulled the covers over her eyes.

Letting out a loud groan, she tapped at her roommate's shoulder till she was awake as well, and together, they answered the call. Harry was not entirely awake, so she sat in her bed, rubbing her eyes, and trying to get a grasp of her surroundings.

"Aria here" she said, picking up the telephone.

"Good morning Agent Mia Walker" Came Director Colby's voice.

"Right. That's my name now" She replied unenthusiastically.

"Please hold while I connect the other agents to the phone call, and please get Agent Kiki Chambers to join in on the call. Sensitive information is about to be divulged to all Agents." Director Colby instructed. As soon as she was done speaking, Aria heard a beep, and then static. She had been put on hold. That was her cue to wake Harry up.

"Harry! Psst, Harry!" She beckoned, shoving the shoulder of her fellow agent. Harry had sat up in her bed, but she was yet again sleeping.

"Harry! Wake up" Aria shouted, startling her roommate.

"I'm up! I'm up!" Came Harry tired, sleepy voice.

"Good. The Director just called, she has information for us, and she needs us to listen. Right now, she us trying to get the other agents in on the call we're having" Aria explained.

"Agents?" Came Director Colby's voice soon after.

In the background, they both could hear the other agents' voices.

"Here. Tired, but here" Came Skunk's voice.

"At ay cap'n" echoed Jabez.

"Present" Gemini said.

"Alright then, now that I have everyone's attention, I would like to use this opportunity to thank you for wanting to serve your country. I know this has all been on short notice, and you have had to put aside a whole lot for this mission to be an actuality, your country thanks you for your service, and your president as well."

"You guys better pay us good!" Jabez's voice came over the phone. Aria was sure she heard a chuckle from either Skunk or Gemini.

"Agent Egorov, I assure you that you will be adequately compensated by your country. If you don't mind, I will now play a prerecorded message from the president that carries all his good wishes towards you and your mission today" Agent Colby announced, right before she tapped the play button on her computer.

"Dear Agents, it's I, your President. I have no intentions of sounding formal right now and I want to relate with you

guys on a personal level. All I want to say, really, is thank you. Thank you so much. Thank you for agreeing to do this..."

"It does not feel like we had a choice" Aria muttered.

"...despite the flaws and clogs. Thank you once again, and please, remember what I just said. God bless America" The President's message had ended, but it felt Aria wondering about what she missed because she was not paying attention for what seemed like five seconds.

"Alright Agents, you have 30 minutes to prepare yourself for the day ahead. After that, you will move to Room 86B on the third floor for supplies that you would need. Please note that despite the severity of how being caught will be, you are advice to not carry lethal weaponry into the Kremlin. See you in twenty-nine minutes" Agent Colby said, ending the call as soon as she was done.

Almost immediately, the phone in Jabez's room rang. Sighing, he picked it up and answered. "Ma'am?" He spoke.

"Listen, Agent. I want you to be on your best behavior today, alright? You are the one with the most experience on this team, thus, you are the official leader. You have not really stepped up to his position in times past, but I hope you would try to live up today, because we are all counting on you" Director Colby knew that she could not overemphasize his importance to the team.

"I know that ma'am. I also know that I have to be at work before all the other get there, and I have to be there right away. I'll stop at the apartment room on my way there. Besides, I've been dressed and prepared to move for almost 2 hours" Jabez said. In reality, all he had to do was tighten his tie, and find his cufflinks, but he knew that he was ready.

"Thank you Jabez, and good luck out there today." Director Colby said.

"Thank you ma'am" He replied, ending the call by himself. Jabez then proceeded to have a seat. Ever since he had that incident at the camp, this was the first time he had any weakness in his legs, but this one was not as a result of alcohol, or a cold.

It was the shivering reality that although he had done a lot of stealing and looting for the US government, he could get caught this time, and that even worse, he could get denied by the US Government and left to rot in Russian jail, or worse; killed.

"Damn it!" He cursed, reaching for his suit, and jacket. He still hadn't found his cufflinks, but when he reached into his jacket pockets to find his head warmer and gloves, he found them.

"Well, first bit of luck today, let's hope it continues, shall we?" He said, leaving his room. As he got into the elevator to go down to the third floor, he made to tighten his tie, but he found that he did not need it. He needed to breathe.

On getting to the third floor, he soon realised that it was sort of deserted, the rooms were filled with furniture, but they looked deserted, like they had no owners.

"This is a safe house, isn't it? These cheeky bastards have it hidden right there, in plain sight" he muttered to himself, all the while loosening his tie a little bit more.

Room 86B was on the far corner of the left side of the building, and although it was missing the "6" from the door, it looked more secure than the other rooms. On the door was a lock that did not seem to need any keys.

"How the hell, do I get into this..." He muttered aloud, looking towards the other end of the hallway.

"Access denied" came an automated voice.

"What the!" Jabez jumped in fright. He had not expected to hear anything, let alone a loud voice that startled the courage out of him.

As he looked closely at the door, he noticed a faith red light that seemed to beep over the lock on the door. Above it was a small scribble that read "What IS your name?"

"Easy, right?" Jabez said to himself. "Jabez Glee" he stated proudly.

"Access denied" came the automated voice.

"What? Uh, Matthias Blair?" He said, "Maybe it's a trick question?"

"Access denied." The voice said yet again.

"@sugardaddygotbread?" He spoke. He was dealing with the CIA, and possibly the FBI, so he was sure they knew about his internet history and troll accounts.

"Access denied" The voice was unrelenting.

"Is? Like the present?" He thought, realizing that the word "IS" was capitalized in the scribblings. He took a deep breath, and in a tone shrouded in regret, he said "Maksim Egorov".

"Access Granted." Came the voice, followed by the faint green light turning to a bright green. As he stood at the door, Jabez thought he heard movement inside the room. He would soon discover that Room 86B was lined in the inside with about half an inch of steel.

"Welcome, Agent." Came the automated voice again.

"Yeah, thanks." He said, looking around. It did not look like much from the outside, but inside was to be considered a small apartment, like his upstairs, was a rather large room, filled and carefully stocked with all kinds of weaponry, and ammunition.

Jabez began to have a look around and was about to pocket a Glock 42 when a phone rang rather loudly. Again, Jabez was startled, and before long, he had found the phone. When he had answered it, he discovered that on the other end was Director Colby.

"Ma'am. I found your secret stash" he said, his eyes darting across the room.

"Not mine, Agent. It belongs to the United States, and at decided intervals, agents in need of weaponry, cash, or protection. They are usually at liberty to take whatever they want, at their own discretion."

"Yes! This SAW MAP 22 has been calling my name!" He exclaimed in delight.

"Unfortunately, this does not apply to you, Agent Maksim. You are to only take the bag assigned to you" She instructed.

"Damn it! Not even one pistol? The small ones?" He protested.

"Absolutely not Agent. This is a stealth mission, and as I am sure you are aware, the security is tight at the entrance to the Kremlin, and for security staff. Therefore, we cannot afford our Agents going in and firing guns, not even if it had a silencer." She explained.

"So, what do we get? Huh?" He said, walking over to the bags. As he stood, he opened the one marked with his newly assigned alter ego. "A taser? And tape?" Is that a pair of gloves? An earpiece?"

"The taser is in case you have to neutralize an enemy that is beyond your reach. The gloves are to protect you from the tape. Please do not hold the tape without first using the gloves, Agent. That tape is a very strong sedative, it's still experimental. Just apply it to exposed skin of whomever you want to sedate, and they will pass out in no time. Note that the tape should not touch you. Our labs recorded a report that the test subjects had symptoms of drowsiness and general body weakness for weeks after administration. Treat this information as urgent. That earpiece is for communication, please keep it in your ears till the mission is over" She declared.

"Yeah, yeah. Got it. I might not even need it though." Jabez said, picking up the gun he had already dropped.

"Agent, we can all see you. Please drop the weapon" she said.

"Shit." Jabez cursed. He could not even have a gun to protect himself? "What did you give the other agents? Did Aria get makeup brushes that turn to daggers?" He protested.

"That is none of your concern, Agent. I believe you have a job to get to?" Agent Colby said.

"Alright, alright. You guys suck, you know that?" He cursed, walking towards the door.

"I just hope that sulking does not get in the way of your mission, agent."

Jabez did not answer, instead, he stormed out, brushing past Gemini and Skunk who had come down together.

"Hey, easy there man! Is that how you greet your buddies?" Skunk asked.

But Jabez was in the mood for neither pleasantry, nor banter. All he could say was, " I hope they gave you both a water gun" and he left, tapping at the elevator button rather furiously.

"What is his problem?" Skunk asked to no one in particular, because it was beyond clear that Gemini did not have the answers.

"I don't know, man. I think that's him on a good day" Gemini replied. Laughing at Jabez's antics, they both walked towards the end of the hall.

"Have you been here before?" Skunk asked.

"I think I came up to this floor once when I was lost and didn't know how to find my way to my apartment. Plus, my room is directly above this one, and where I'm from, you know all your neighbors." Gemini replied. As he came up to the door, he peered at the lock. "This is new" he said.

"What is?" Skunk asked him.

"The lock, it used to be a safety lock, wjrb numbers. Now it looks like the voice activated type. This model doesn't just read your voice, but the vibrations and frequencies. That way you can't open it with a recording." Gemini explained. "What IS your name?" He read.

"Easy. Venedikt Yuriy" Skunk interjected. "Is? It's a trick question, but at the same time, it isn't. My name is no longer Jeffries, at least not for the time being" Skunk explained.

"Shit, I was going to lay out my entire name on his goddamn computer" Gemini said, laughing as he entered the room.

Upon getting inside, he seemed to freeze, prompting Skunk to rush in. He too froze, and both men stood in awe of what they saw; weapons from every conceivably weapons manufacturer of repute, spy gear that they had only seen on agency brochures and acquisition sheets, and the bags on the table.

"Agents! Welcome" Director Colby announced over the phone.

Gemini and Skunk jumped in fright.

"Director Colby, is that you?" Skunk asked. He was looking suspiciously at every corner of the room.

"Of course, it's her, dumbass" Gemini said. He had regained his composure sooner than his counterpart.

"On the bags that are placed on the table are name tags, please do well to take your assigned bag and leave." She instructed.

They both took their bags and turned to go, but Director Colby called them back.

"Gemini, please choose a pistol from the rack. I would personally recommend the Glock 19" She instructed.

"How come I don't get one?" Skunk protested.

"Easy. It's because you're not as cool as me" Gemini bragged.

"Agent Venedikt, it is because Agent Humphrey will be stationed outside Kremlin premises. You, on the other hand, would have to go through security checks and bag searches."

"Is that why I get a case of earpieces and a change of shirt?"

"The plan that would be communicated to you through your earpiece involves a contingency situation where you would be asked to exit the building as a civilian if need be." Agent Colby explained. "Now, I would advise that you two be on your way, you both have jobs to do today".

With that, they had left. Harry and Aria, however, were nowhere to be found.

Agent Colby could only sigh. With she remote access key, she secured the safe room, and then proceeded to call the room that the remain in agents occupied.

After a couple rings, Harry answered.

"Ma'am?"

"Agent Chambers, I would really advice that you come down to the safe room and get the packages assigned to you. The drive to the Kremlin is an hour and a half away, and you are already late as is"

"We're sorry ma'am, but Aria had a slight issue with her health." Harry explained. Director Colby thought she sounded out of breath.

"We'll see about it. What is the problem?"

"She seems to be having a panic attack. She says that the fact that she cannot understand Russian makes it seem as if she's going in blind." Harry explained.

"She has you, doesn't she? Tell her that! Come on, we don't have all day" Director Colby barked. She wanted to feel sympathetic, but she had an entire team at the White House that needed to be asleep in a few hours. There were also rumors of attacks in several quarters along the east coast and it was all trending on social media. The United States had to retaliate, and quickly too.

"She's up, Director. We are on our way to the third floor" Harry suddenly announced.

"Good, I'll be waiting." Director Colby said, ending the call.

Slowly, but with calculated step, they made their way towards the third floor, and towards the safe room. To save time, Director Colby opened the door by herself.

Inside, she instructed them in the same manner that she and done the others, and they were soon out on their mission, armed with listening devices and two flash drives that carried a virus the CIA had synthesized to steal the information they needed.

"Harry, you get a pair of glasses that would help us direct you on how to configure the system" Director Colby said finally, as both women left the safe room.

*

"Check, check. Show time is upon us" Director Colby announced. Her team was in place and ready for action. Jabez had taken his place as a security detail for the tourists to all places except the President's office. He did not have clearance to be in there.

Skunk was assigned to be on cleanup duty in case any of the tourists made a mess. Both Harry and Aria were to be part of the lucky few that got to experience the tour.

"The tourists are in" Director Colby announced. She had left Unimak Island was back in Washington at a CIA facility, which she had cleared out by ordering everyone to take a day off, then she brought Carol and her team in. Surprisingly, the Sultan was in, and ready to work.

Brendan and Teo Han had both gotten remote access to a couple of feeds, ranging from digital cameras that the tourists carried, the security footage from select cameras within the Kremlin, and the glasses that Harry wore.

"Jabez, Skunk, be at attention. We have outside support in the person of Gemini. Gemini come in" She called.

"Here" he responded.

"Remember, Agents. Do not touch your ears, no matter the circumstances. You could sabotage the mission, and honestly, don't let the movies lie to you, you do look stupid when you do it." She instructed. "Harry, Aria, you are to stay in the back of the tour group, alright? Do not get noticed."

"Noted" Harry said.

"Try to actual casual, Aria. Please loosen up your shoulders" Came Director Colby's voice again.

"Yes Ma'am" Aria responded. She felt quite nervous, so she stuck to Harry's side.

As the tour progressed, Aria seemed to grow more tense, so much so that she had to leave to use the bathroom.

Could you not hold it in, we're this close to reaching our goals. Satellite scans show that The Russian President's office is empty. The only agent positioned there is ours, and according to camera One feed on that floor, we have a security guard, but he would not notice anything for a while.

"Sorry ma'am, I had to wash my face." Aria apologized, hurriedly exiting the bathroom.

"Shall we then proceed?" Director Colby asked.

"Affirmative." came everyone's voice, except Aria's.

"Aria? Are we clear to proceed?" She asked again.

"Yes Ma'am" she responded faintly.

"They're coming up on the Presidential floor now, guys once you are there, Agent Venedikt will pass an EMP to you, all you have to do is trigger it and throw It into the office, it would give us control of the cameras for about 10 minutes. This should give you enough time to plant the virus" Teo Han called out to them.

"Where do we do that?" Aria asked.

"Yeah, how do we do that?" Director Colby asked.

"Oh, right. If our 3d model simulation is correct, there should be a lever beneath the right edge of the President's desk. Just push it in and the floor under the desk will open to show a small opening that you will then stick the flash drive into."

"Just that? Sound like a piece of cake!" Harry said.

"Not exactly. You would have to get it out. The systems are quite dated, and we cannot hack into it remotely. We thought we could, but we were proven wrong. We will have to transfer the information to a computer, possibly in the safehouse.

"What in hell?" Harry wasn't happy. "If I have ten minutes to be in the office, how long will the data theft take?"

"About 25 minutes?" Teo Han responded.

"What? Ma'am, who is this guy? Isn't there someone better I could talk to?"

"Of course, blame the tech guy. All you agents are the same" Teo Han said, falling back into his chair.

"Hey shut! Both of you, I don't want to hear anything else!"

"Harry, you have 9 minutes to be in that office, after that all the forces in that building will be gunning for you."

"Ma'am do you think that is enough time?" Carol asked.

"We're barely scraping the honey pot here, but we can work something out, right?" Director Colby replied. "Gemini, at my mark, set your clock for 5 minutes, once the timer ends, I want you in the parking lot to pick up Harry, Aria and the Flash drive.

"Noted, ma'am" Gemini responded.

"We're coming up to the office right now. I and Aria are en route" Harry said. As their tour passed by Skunk, he handed over a small white casing to her.

"This is it?" Harry was surprised.

"It only has one charge, Agent. After that it's a worthless piece of fried plastic and wires. Use it wisely" Director Colby instructed.

"Will do Ma'am".

As the delegation walked past the office, the tour guide made mention of renovation plans and how they weren't supposed to go in there. With the delegation already down the corner, Harry and Aria sneaked away and back into the office. The doors were wide open, and they could have walked in, but Teo Han warned them about the pressure plates that would send off silent alarms.

"Listen, slide the EMP in, it has no weight and shouldn't trigger any plates." He instructed.

"Done" Harry said. Turning to Aria, she instructed, saying "stay here, if anybody asks, you're a lost tourist and you cannot speak Russian"

"I can't speak Russian, really" Aria said matter-of-factly.

"See? You're really convincing" she said, tapping her fellow agent on the shoulder. "Is the EMP armed?'" She asked her voices in her ear.

"It is, NOW!" Teo Han said, to which Harry rushed in.

As she stepped in, she giggled. "I just stepped on one of those pressure plates. Let's just hope your bite sized EMP works" she said, scurrying over to the President's desk. "Lever you said?"

"Yeah, a lever."

Harry ran her hand under the table till she suddenly stopped. "Found it" she said, flicking the lever and stepping back.

Underneath the table, a couple of tiles seemed to slide on their sides, giving way for what seemed to be a part of a seemingly never-ending connection of wires, underneath which lay what they were waiting for.

"Found it" Harry said. She then proceeded to lift up the wires and after reaching into her bag and getting the flash drive, she inserted it into the port.

There was a sound of applause, but Director Colby quieted them down. They were not out of the waters yet, she said.

"I have a better plan, alright? In place of me standing around totally doing nothing, how about leave it here to collect as much information as possible, then Skunk comes to get it later." She suggested. "You guys put the most nervous agent you have as a lookout, doesn't seem right, or fair to me. To any one in fact."

"Agent Venedikt, what do you say? Can you handle the extraction?"

"At night? Then yes, but I'll need an EMP. Those pressure plates are active till the President is within half a yard from his office." He responded.

"Good, I'm out of here." Harry responded. She had closed the secret hatch and was darting out of the office.

Once outside, she grabbed Aria's hand and dragged her all the way back to the tour.

"Out in less than 3 minutes. You don't have to worry anymore, Aria" she said.

"Director Colby, Ma'am. We're going to need that car ASAP" Harry requested.

"Gemini is enroute. Also, Gemini, your return journey should involve him getting an EMP"

"Noted, Ma'am" Gemini said, pulling out of the alleyway he had parked in.

"Harry, Aria, excuse yourself from the tour in a way that would not cause suspicion. Your ride should in the parking lot any moment from now." Director Colby instructed them.

"Already done… Excuse me, sorry, I didn't see you there"

"What was that?" Director Colby asked, she could not see what had happened clearly.

"We bumped into some Asian dude; no big deal" Harry replied.

"Aria, Harry, I'm almost here. You coming?" Gemini asked.

"On our way." Aria answered as they both rushed to the entrance.

"Over here!" Gemini yelled out as soon as he spotted them.

Aria and Harry ran over and hopped into the red saloon car.

"What's the rush even? The tour isn't even started yet"

"Exactly, we could go back to deliver the second EMP to Skunk" Harry said.

"But what do we tell the guards?" Gemini asked.

"Aria, how about "Rock, Paper, Scissors"? The loser gets a fake bloody period?"

"No need. I'm doing it regardless. I've never been good at games." Aria gave in.

"Okay, it's settled. We're coming back, but with a bloody period and lack of menstrual pads as an excuse, okay then. Let's go." Harry urged, but Gemini had already sped off into the distance.

*

"It's been hours since we gave him the EMP, do we wait any longer, or do we reach out?" Aria sat on her bed was painting her nails, when Harry came out from the bathroom looking really worried.

"He's probably given it to the Director already, chill out" Aria replied nonchalantly.

"Chill out? You don't know how wrong these things can go?" Harry retorted.

"Well, I do, and imma tell you to chill." Aria said. "Remember how I was today? Look at me now, I'm chill. You should be too" Aria tried to encourage her roommate, and for all the selfish reasons she could think of too. She was finally at peace, and she did not want anything, or anyone, to trigger her and make her anxious.

As Harry paced the room, the telephone rang, and she rushed to answer.

"Ma'am?" She said, her tone was in hushes. Like she risked being heard, and exposed.

"Hello, Harry. Have you heard from Skunk?" She asked.

"No Ma'am. We thought you'd have an idea where he was." Harry was shocked to learn that even the Director had no ideas about his whereabouts.

"I don't. That's why I called. I hoped he had contacted you all, but I'm yet to receive word that he did. Did you deliver the EMP to him as agreed?" Director Colby asked. She needed to confirm it for herself.

"Through Agent Jabez, yes." Harry answered.

"Agent Jabez surely gave it to him, He made sure to tell me and even Skunk confirmed that he had gotten it" Director Colby seemed to concur with what Harry had said.

"We are worried as well, Ma'am." Harry knew she was past worried. She had a bad feeling, and in her experience, they weren't always wrong.

"I just hope to the high heavens that he is out in the city for celebratory drinks or something of the sort". Director Colby said.

"Us too, Ma'am." Harry replied, turning to Aria who was polishing still polishing her nails.

"Did you notice anything strange about his behavior today? Was he off? Did he look like he had to do something?" Director Colby asked her questions in quick succession, but Harry kept her answer at a bare minimum for all.

"No Ma'am. He seemed like Skunk; you know?" Hard replied.

"Alright then, have a great night's rest." Director Colby said, ending the call as she did.

Harry knew that protocol was to report him as AWOL and declare him missing. But she was sure the Director had issued the AWOL signal. It would take a few more hours to declare him missing.

"You need to chill, Harry. Skunk probably followed son fine chic home. He'll be fine." Aria said. "We had a win today, of course he would be out to celebrate" She added.

"With our prize? That is so reckless, even Jabez would consider it wrong!" Harry surmised. All she could do was sleep. Maybe she would hear something about him in the morning announcements, or maybe not. Ah had grown to love their small, dysfunctional family, and although she did not show it, she had developed a rather soft spot in her mind for them.

Soon she had fallen in a deep sleep, and the thought that had troubled her seemed to fade away, yet they made their way into her dreams.

Before when the Director was to call, Harry was already awake.

When the phone rang, she rushed over to it and answered.

"Did you get any sleep at all?" The Director asked. Even she was shocked by how tired Harry sounded.

"I did, Ma'am. I just woke to use the bathroom" Harry lied.

"Well, I'll have to break it to you. Skunk was found yesterday by a stranger. He had been beaten in an alleyway and robbed. Whomever did it, took the flash drive." Director Colby announced bitterly.

"What?" Harry could only gasp in shock. A loud gasp that some Harry from sleep.

"As painful as it might be, we have an agent in the hospital, a lead and weeks of tireless work, all lost. Whomever took the flash drive better have NASA Level decryption strewn on their carpet floor." Director Colby bragged.

"Do you think it was planned, ma'am?" Harry asked.

"I don't think so. I mean, I have no strong opinions at the moment, except those that would involve having to divulge this news to the President."

"I hope he understands." Harry prayed, but Director Colby only laughed, and then she ended the call.

*

There comes a time in the life of everyone that they sit, think, and reevaluate several decisions and how it had affected their lives. That time had come in the lifespan of the special team that the President had sanctioned and supported. Now, he had begun to lose faith in the rag tag team of clearly unproductive miscreants that were secretly recruited.

Over a period of five months, funding for the agents had been cut drastically, especially in the face of low productivity. With little or no input, or feedback, things had begun go fall apart, and as with the mission, so had the rest of the world.

News of little pockets of what critics and analysts deemed to be calculated attacks spread throughout the world. Once, and in what seemed to be an isolated fire incident, the Chinese Embassy in Russia suddenly caught on fire, killing a total of three people, alongside an Embassy employee who had just begun duty.

In the midst of all of these, the agents tried severally to steal the information again, but it was lost, and this time. there were no openings for any form of infiltration. The Russian President had returned from his time abroad, and there was a call for an employee audit. The agents were left with no choice, and they had to find new lives.

It had been several months since the mission to steal Russian secrets failed and the agents were now living seemingly normal lives, devoid of close supervision. The last time Director Colby heard about Jabez, he was a sale rep at a car dealership and had him a beautiful German girl that he lived with.

"It is best to find new covers, seeing that the old ones were almost blown. Relocate if you must but know that you are safer where you presently are." She had announced, right before telling them that they were to be unsupervised for a couple of days, pending review of certain details.

Days soon turned into weeks, and soon the weeks formed months. With no word from Director Colby, the CIA, or the FBI, the agents presumed that the mission had been called off, and soon began to blend into Russian society.

After recovering from his injuries, Skunk was now religious and worked as a bartender in uptown Moscow. The ladies would flock to the bar, and he soon became an attraction in his own right. Gemini thought it best to still be employed by the embassy and stayed put.

Harry began making band music and was a local celebrity, while Aria had gotten into a school that taught Russian, she also worked part time as a waitress. Before long, she was well versed in the language and was able to communicate with little difficulty.

Director Colby had decided to take the drought of ideas to rekindle the spark between her and her husband. In a careless series of decisions, which were unlike her, she abandoned her duties and decided to unwind.

She felt like she needed it, and in spite of the fact that the timing was wrong, she did not mind.

"I'm becoming more of Director Colby, then Rachel Colby" She muttered as she boarded the plane to go meet her husband.

She was in for a two-day mini holiday Hawaii when the President called, requesting her presence. Although she had put Carol in charge, the President did not take it lightly that she abandoned an already failing mission.

Aware of her mistakes, as she got into the Oval Office, she immediately began to explain, but President Wallace would have none of it.

"It's been months, Director! Months! At this point, I think I would have to call a vote of confidence on your little project." The President was in a fit.

"Sir, I-" She tried to speak, but President Wallace quickly interjected.

"I have waited for several months on end for a formal report on how you conquered Russia, but I have got none. Why is that so, Director?" He asked calmly.

"Sir, our project in Russia could be deemed as stalled, but my team-" He cut her off again.

"What team?" He asked. His temper had begun to rise.

"Sir?" She asked.

"Your team had long been reassigned, Director."

"By whom, Sir?"

" By me. Besides, you seem tired and unable to carry on. Therefore, a resignation letter would be marvelous from you." He stated.

"But Mr President, Sir. I feel fine, and healthy"

"That was an order, Director!"

"Alright then, Sir."

"Thank you"

"But Mr President, I would really love to still be in charge of my team. With myself inchargex we are sutenti attract more success"

"No thank you, Director. How about you have a look around, Director. Does it look like you are doing anything? A while ago, you had a beat-up agent with a couple broken bones and another agent who developed a complex case of hypothermia, all because you hired an agent you had a drinking problem! A drinking problem, right from camp! As it stands now, the vote of confidence will not go in your favour, and that is probably for the best too" President Wallace said.

"Sir, if you could give us one more chance, we will prove ourselves to be-" She tried to explain again, but yet again he had cut her off.

"No more chances, Director Colby. Have a nice day."

Sad, and rejected, Director Colby walked out of the Oval Office. She was sad that she had lost control of everything, but a part of her wanted to quit a while back. Now she could focus on love, life, and everything in between.

As she walked down the stairs and towards her new life, she wanted to call her closest employees and tell them, but she decided against it.

"They will find out eventually" she said. She was free, yet she felt burdened with the fact that she had sent lives across the Atlantic in a blind effort to curtail faceless attacks that were still going on. She had managed in securing the White House, and its environs, but the man on the street could still get his identity stolen and end up in debt, and it would not be because he showed his card at a bar, or because he got mugged or kidnapped.

The cyber-attacks were becoming more by the day, and Director Colby had half a mind to believe that the reports of similar attacks in Russia, and China were not fake news, neither were they mistakes.

As She stood by her car, she heard a familiar voice call to her from behind her.

"Director Carol, is that you?" said the voice.

"Yep, it is. Who's asking? Oh, it's you." Rachel Colby said, her eyes had begun to water, but she braved it, and soon even General Larry Eisenhower thought she was just under the sun.

"How are you, Ma'am?" He asked.

"Good. Good. Are you going to see the President?" She asked. She knew he was going to see him, she just needed to confirm.

As they spoke, Director Joaquin Taylor of the FBI seemed to have alighted from a car that had just parked by the main entrance. In his usual fashion, he walked over and gave his share of pleasantries; the emotionless, yet heartfelt kind.

"I'm sorry you've lost your job, Ma'am. It was a pleasure working with you" he said, before nodding awkwardly and walking away. As he did, General Eisenhower turned to Carol in shock.

"Were you not going to inform me? What even happened?" He asked, he wanted to sympathize with her, but he was in enough shock already.

"Professional errors, failed plans, you know the drill, right? Well, somebody had to pay for it. I guess I got the axe first. Maybe Carol Duncan gets it next, I don't know. I'm not even supposed to know anything anymore"

"I'm so sorry Ma'am. Do I speak to him on your behalf? I mean, it isn't official yet, it is?" He asked.

"No need, General. I needed a break regardless. I just hope those agents get a new, vibrant leadership and a plan that was not doomed to fail from the beginning." She said, stepping into her already opened car.

As she drove off towards the front gate, General Eisenhower could only sigh and continue his march to the Oval Office. He had stopped getting updates on the mission and consultations to tactical maneuvers after a couple of weeks and he did not bother to ask. If he was asked, he would have thought they had worked it all out by themselves.

As he climbed the stairs, he surmised that the meeting would center on Project Russia, and he was ready to urge for Director Colby's reinstatement.

Tense, ominous silence like that had not flooded the inner walls of the oval office in a long while. General Eisenhower was sure that he could feel it resting heavy on his shoulder, and all these was just a minute after he had entered.

Inside the Oval Office was the Director of the FBI, Joaquin Taylor, who had already been seated. He sat awkwardly, tapping his fingers on his knees as he did. He nodded to him as he entered the room, doing the same thing to Admiral Grant less than a minute later. The President was nowhere to be found.

"Hey, I called to you right up from downstairs, you didn't hear?" Admiral Grant asked his lifelong friend as he sat on the couch beside him. General Eisenhower did not see him when he entered, and now wore a look of surprise as he was startled by his friend.

"There's a whole lot on my mind, Buster. But we'll talk later" General Eisenhower replied in whispers. He was looking nervously at the side door. He knew he had a moral obligation to plead Director Colby's case, and he intended to fight to the last.

Without warning, The President stormed into the Oval Office, and all eyes turned towards the loud bang of the door, and the stifled groans of a manly voice from the outside.

Angrily, he took his seat at his desk, and said nothing. His brows were furrowed and slowly, his anger turned into bleak frustration and before long, he had his hands in his palms.

The other people in the room watched as he slowly peeled his face away from the buttress of his hands and made to speak. But he stopped almost immediately. This time he made to loosen his tie, and in a fit of silent rage, he threw it against the wall beside him. A figurine of an old president came crashing down, and almost immediately, the door creaked open. It was Agent Cooley.

Evidently nursing a limp in his foot, he walked rather painfully over to the President and whispered into his ear, causing his eyes to widen. The Agent walked out of the Oval Office soon afterwards, but the uneasy silence had not yet left. Not until the President had cleared his throat rather noisily and was sitting more comfortably in his chair.

"Gentlemen. I regret to announce that Rachel Colby, formerly the Director of the CIA will not be joining us for this sensitive meeting. Although information discussed here would be communicated to her on due course, she is to have no say, and will have to only relay this information to her successor" he announced solemnly.

There was silence. General Eisenhower had a lot to say, he was itching with protests and counter arguments, but the President's word was final, especially in cases like this where he was running the show. So, he kept quiet, hoping the next opening would be perfect for him to speak.

"So, a few months ago, we all sat in this room, and we all agreed to undertake a project that I'm sure is regrettable, especially in hindsight, was rushed, and apparently foolish" he continued. He then paused to study the faces in the room. Seeing neither raised hands nor pursed lips, he continued yet again.

"I would like us to recall said agents, and if need be, compensate them accordingly" he paused again, but this time he had grabbed the office phone and was making a call. Then he continued, saying " In a few minutes, the interim overseer of this mission will be joining us. He'll handle the recall process and possible further redeployment"

"Mr President, I would..." General Eisenhower had finally decided to speak, but he was quickly hushed by the President who had a finger up as he spoke on the phone.

"Yes? Send Mr Boyd up, thank you" the president murmured into the phone.

"Boyd? What the hell?" Buster had turned to Eisenhower. "Did you know about this?" He asked, whispering so that he would not be heard.

"I don't know, I am just as shocked as you are!" Eisenhower whispered back.

"This better be good, or I'm walking out" he whispered back, covering his mouth as the conversation intensified. "You know he's a nut job right? You remember that first meeting? How the hell did he get Secretary of Defense?" Buster blurted out.

"I'm sorry, what's the disturbance about?" The President had raised his head from his call and was wearing a puzzled look.

In response, they both waved to him, prompting him to return to his call.

"He's probably going to us to blow up Russia." Buster was at it again.

"Shush, you're a grown man." Eisenhower said, to which they both laughed. They suddenly stopped, as Director Joaquin Taylor of the FBI was staring intently at them.

"Good! Let's have it then!" The President seemed to be in a better mood than he was when he walked in. The broken figurine was still on the floor, but all he could do was look apologetically at it.

"Gentlemen, as a precursor to the rest of our meeting, I would love it if we don't agitate each other during this meeting, please" he urged, getting up from his desk as he spoke.

"Alright Sir, I would love it if you looked at some numbers that I ran as we sat here, that is if we were to pay the agents for their time. There is a…" Director Taylor made to speak, but The President had yet again interrupted someone in the room.

"Director? Director. I'm sore but you'll have to take this up with the new head of our taskforce here. In all honesty, I want to have nothing to do with this case. If the Vice President didn't fill in for me on the trip to Bolivia, I'd be La Paz right now" he said.

"Okay Sir, but I hope this meeting will treat the welfare of the agents as a priority, just as Director Colby would have wanted" came General Eisenhower's voice. All eyes turned to him.

"What Rachel Colby would want is not our priority at the moment, General. Yet again, thank you for your concern" came the President's reply. "Ah, Secretary Charles, glad you could join us" he said, excitedly, ushering the ever-cocky Charles Boyd to a seat.

In an almost vindicative tone, and with an air of authority, he took a seat apart from the three men that sat with him. He was wearing a rather expensive suit, and his perfume wafted rather strongly into the noses of all that sat with him.

"Gentlemen" he finally spoke, stealing scornful glances at Director Taylor, and then the General. Admiral Buster was sure he would flip him off if he looked at him, but for some reason, he didn't.

"Now, Gentlemen. Shall we begin? Mr Secretary, do you want to do us the favour?" The President asked, clasping his hands together. Smiling in unison, both men shared a knowing glance before the President took his seat, leaning against his desk.

"Mr President, Gentlemen. We have been chasing out own tails for months on end with nothing as tangible as a single lead, or shred of information. I want us to recall the agents. I mean, the cyber-attacks are not as frequent as they used to be, social media is focused on other issues now too." He said, shrugging.

"Mr President, I am of the opinion that we…" Director Taylor tried speaking, but He was interrupted, but this time it was by Secretary Boyd.

"Easy there, Director. We haven't even laid out certain terms yet. As I was saying, this fruitless mission has cost us money, time, manpower and our pride as a nation. So, I suggested to the President that we withdraw our forces, or whatever we choose to call this rag tag team of miscreants put forward by Rachel Colby and get us some real soldiers. Hell, we could even get our sleeper agents to step in and make us proud." Charles Boyd stopped. He had run out of breath and was less than gracefully looking for his handkerchief.

"A withdrawal with full reimbursements for their efforts, I presume?" Director Taylor asked.

"Yes. Yes. Of course. We could do that, or we could secure our future" Secretary Boyd said, a sly grin was plastered across his face and be looked mischievous.

"What do you mean? What does that mean?" Buster asked. He had leaned forward in his chair, and he had an inquisitive look on his face.

"Easy, Buster. I just made a suggestion, alright? Jesus!" Secretary Boyd replied exasperatedly.

"I also want to know what securing our future would entail, Secretary Boyd." Director Taylor asked in his calm manner. He was too busy with the numbers and details that he forgot to read emotions, especially that of the President, who was back in his chair and was biting a fingernail.

"Gentlemen, the President called to me and educated me on what was going on, right under my own nose, I might add. I mean, the office the team used was so close to mine, I think we shared tap water. Anyways, we're all Americans here, we know our history, right?" He paused, hoping for nods and grins, but all he got was blank stares and an occasional frown.

Sighing heavily, he continued, saying. "Look, how often has loose ends come back to bite us where the sun doesn't shine, huh? How many times have had to experience a national crisis because some nut jobs couldn't keep a secret, huh? How many times do we have to go through the same things before we learn, gentleman?"

He paused again, but the reaction was the same.

"All I'm saying is that we secure our legacies. If the Russian government discover that we attacked them with what was beyond the lines of harmless, good old espionage, it could start a war!" He finished. Again, he was breathless.

"Three times." Came Buster's voice from the bad end of the room.

"What? What happened three times?" The President asked.

"He said 'huh' three times, Mr President" he replied with a straight, emotionless face, causing everyone to go into a laughing fit.

"You think this is funny? Huh?" Secretary Boyd was in a fit of his own, and he burned a bright red from rage.

"Four times" came Buster's voice again, causing the room to erupt with laughter.

"Alright, settle down. You're all grown men with four hundred plus people waiting for your decision." The President announced, snickering as he did.

"It is funny, really" Secretary Boyd started. "What will be funnier will be the look on your faces when you're seventy and have to face war crime charges at the Hague!" He barked, and for the first time, the room actually took his serious.

"It will be funny when you're bundled up because of war crimes you committed to defend your country. It will also be funny when the media uses that opportunity to dig up things from your past; a parking ticket, a drunken brawl in an alley, and the most brutal of all, that one time you said the n-word along with the African American rapper on the radio" he spoke solemnly, eyeing his audience and watching them cower as he spoke, even Buster. The Admiral had a legacy to uphold, and jail time would ruin that.

Secretary Boyd was now walking around the room slowly, as an invigilator in an examination hall would do. He was scanning his audience, or as he saw them, his prey. From Director Taylor's nervous lap tapping, to General Eisenhower's shaking of feet. Even the President was biting deeper into his fingernails.

Finally, he had gotten to the other end of the room: a raised platform that President Wallace had specifically ordered to practice speeches on. With an ability he was long due to overgrow, he leaped unto the platform, startling both the President, and Director Taylor.

The two soldiers in the room seemed to have followed him with their eyes and did not flinch when he leaped.

"So, what you're saying is that we would have to put down our agents?" General Eisenhower asked.

"Good to see you finally caught on. Welcome" Secretary Boyd replied, sporting a derisive smile.

" I want to let it be known that the General's question is valid. What do we do with our agents when they get back?" Director Taylor asked.

"In all fairness, we should compensate both them and their families, but it would be ideal that they die painless deaths. All of them." Secretary Boyd replied.

"So, your soldiers get taken out by friendly fire? And all because of a hunch?" If General Eisenhower was furious, he was sure to always hide it, but this time he did not, as his face burnt a bright red.

"Technically, they're not our soldiers. They're disposable agents with tons of deniability" The President answered. He was now seated on his desk again. All eyes were now turned to him and so were their questions.

"We trained them, Mr President. They may have failed a singular mission, but they are still valuable to the cause" General Eisenhower protested.

"Valuable? We have a thousand agents that would have done what they were supposed to do, flawlessly too!" President Wallace replied.

"Mr President, we do not have to put down our own men." Buster finally spoke again. "Can't we make them sign an NDA?" He asked.

"Will that be of any help?" The President spoke, but he was referring to Secretary Boyd.

"Director Taylor, care to answer?" Charles Boyd requested. His tone was laden with pride as he stood on the platform.

"Of course, we can, there isn't a rather long process to getting one drafted. I could call my team and we could get a full functional NDA by tomorrow evening" he said, meaning to brag.

"That wouldn't be necessary. As was originally the intention of the president; we would have to wait for a qualified team to be put together," Secretary Boyd lied, much to the bewilderment of every occupant of the room.

"What? Hold on!' Buster was on his feet. "Mr President, I'm sorry for the outburst, but I don't think we have right leader here to handle the transition process. Could have Director Taylor run the show instead?" He asked.

"I'm sorry Buster, but we need a decisive thinker. Secretary Boyd remains. Also, you are here in an advisory position, and I think I'm behind the idea of securing my legacy, please go ahead to comment either a counterclaim, or a demerit of our direction, thank you." The President replied calmly.

General Eisenhower could only sigh. He had already made his decisions a while ago and just needed a small group to do just as he pleased and support his schemes. He had found Secretary Boyd (or was it Boyd that found him?) And they had bonded, probably over good whiskey.

"Gentlemen, all in favour of this decision, please raise your hands?" Secretary Boyd asked. Only his and the President's hands were raised.

"Those against it? Please raise your hands" he announced, to which both military officers lifted theirs. Director Taylor was hesitant for a second, as if he was pondering certain things, but he finally lifted his.

As Secretary Boyd watched as the three men claim to "do the right thing", he was sure he felt a bit of amusement. I mean, the main advocates for sparing lives were soldiers with several kills and quite a reputation.

"It's almost ironic" he thought, smiling to himself, "but yet again, they were soldiers, and their kind doesn't leave anyone behind. Ever"

"Secretary? Do we have anything else to discuss? I'm sure these gentlemen would love to be on their way" came President Wallace's voice.

"Nothing else, Mr President. They're free to go." He said, returning to his seat. Slowly, they made to file out of the room, leaving Secretary Boyd and The President.

"Gentlemen, please inform Rachel Colby that she is to transfer all sensitive CIA data to Secretary Colby's desk, pending the installment of an interim" he had called out to them, and he spoke rather solemnly.

In silence, all three men filed out of the Oval Office, lost in thought. As expected, Buster first spoke out, and with his usual outburst.

"I don't believe it! You mean to tell me that President Wallace put the most volatile man we know of in charge of the most volatile mission ever? Come on!" He exclaimed immediately they were outside of earshot.

"Easy, Buster" Larry Eisenhower urged. In reality, he was talking to himself. He needed to calm down and think, and Buster would not make it easy for him to do so, especially when he was in one of his infamous fits.

Director walked beside both men quietly, pondering and searching his vast mind for solutions to their current problems. Although he was almost the same height as both men, his slim build was dwarfed by their large, post-muscular build. Both men had been fit in their prime, and they dominated their chosen military fields, while he dominated the areas of research and self-development.

As they walked down the stairs and towards the main entrance, the uneasy silence had once again enveloped them, and it was not until they had to go to their various cars that Director Taylor spoke.

"Gentlemen, who will tell Director Colby about the happenings here today?" He asked.

"I will. Buster, will you come with me?" General Eisenhower said, before turning to his longtime friend.

"Sure, sure. But we're going for drinks afterwards." He said excitedly, snapping his fingers as he mentioned drinks.

"Alright then, we'll do that too" General Eisenhower yielded, sighing. Sometimes he wondered how he was the single one, and how Buster had convinced him to let him marry his sister.

"Director Taylor, you could join us if you want" Buster offered, but he was soon turned down.

"Oh, no. I don't drink alcohol, but thank you. I hope your inebriation brings you ecstasy" he said, right before hoping in the back of his SUV and signaling his driver to take off.

"What a weird little guy" Buster remarked as they both watched him drive off.

"Oh, please. If anything, he's taller than you. You're just built like a pint of beer, is all" Eisenhower joked, running off. He was being chased by his longtime friend.

*

"The two men in charge of our nation's armed forces, and they're playing like children in the parking lot of the White House. Disgraceful." Secretary Boyd said scornfully. "Are these the people you put in charge of planning one of the biggest information heists in American history?" He had turned to the President who was nursing a glass of scotch.

"You know, I used to think that we would pull it off and never get credit for it. Now I'm grateful that we were so incognito with it all" he finally spoke.

"I may not be an expert, Mr President, but yet again it doesn't take an expert to see that your elite team of planners have failed you. So yet again, I thank you for calling to me" Secretary Boyd had now taken a seat on one of the chairs inside the office, where he placed his glass of scotch on the desk beside him.

"Sorry about all that not including you at the onset, Charles. I thought I had it under control, to be honest" President Wallace said, downing another gulp of the scotch. He then proceeded to pour himself another bottle, but this time he did not attempt to nurse it, instead, he chose to pour the contents of his glass down his throat.

"So, our plan to tie up loose ends is still on, right?" Secretary Boyd asked.

"Of course. And make it look like accidents too." President Wallace added.

"That settles the 'How', now we gotta ask 'who', Sir. The military is out of the question as we've already seen, the CIA's loyalty will not with us, and even if the FBI handled killings and such, they wouldn't still move against their director, now would they?" Again, Charles Boyd was breathing heavily.

"Private contractors? Ms. Colby hired a few guys for me a while back, where do you think their loyalty would lie? To her? Or to me?" He asked, but Secretary Boyd had no answers for him. Instead, he had stood up and now walking towards the tray that held the bottle of scotch.

"I'll look into it. In the meantime, instruct whoever is in charge of this team to organize their return. We'll move from there. Plus, it gives us more time to know what to do with them" Secretary Boyd said, moving towards the door. "If that will be all, Mr President, I would like to take my leave, I have certain dealings to attend to" he continued.

"Have a good one, Boyd" President Wallace said, turning in his chair to face the windows. By the time he swiveled back, Secretary Boyd had disappeared into the hallway. All President Wallace could do was sigh and pour himself another drink.

As he walked in the hallway, Secretary Boyd got a call. When he had gotten a look at whom it was, all he did was sigh, and look back to see if he was being followed. All he saw were the curious eyes of Agent Cooley who he had passed on the way out of the Oval Office. Hurriedly, he walked towards the flight of stairs and answered the call.

"Yeah, hello?"

"Is our plan going as it should?" A voice asked over the phone.

"Yeah, yeah. I just spoke to the man. The sheep will be in the slaughterhouse soon." Secretary Boyd answered. He was walking fast and towards his car.

"And the Rook? Is she out of the way?" The voice asked.

"Yeah yeah, resignation's coming in soon" He answered. His eyes were darting in all corners. He had never gotten a call when he was not in a secure location, and especially not when he was in the White House!

"Excellent, keep us posted. No mistakes, no excuses." The voice said again, ending the call as soon as it finished speaking.

"Shit" he muttered. "Airport, I have to get to somewhere!" He barked to his driver.

*

Despite an early morning call and an itinerary of things to do before she was to come in at the office, Carol felt a little bit more energetic that she usually was. It was the last lap, the final, few seconds in a race that had exhausted her in no small measure.

In the last few months, her schedule had involved more of brainstorming, so much so that The Sultan joined in. Even in the midst of admirable effort, they all came up short, including Brendan.

After the first month, there was a lull that rested over the little underground office. Even Brendan dropped in creative solutions to the problem they had.

As the days progressed into the second, Yep Han would stay a week without coming into the office, and Brendan would spend hours on end reading blockchain engineering eBooks. Carol realised that she worried less about productivity and soon began to feel guilty for her drop in output.

By the second month, Carol would come to the office thrice a week, mostly to get away from Layton and his antics, and also to get a look at Darrell, her neighbour. He would offer her a ride to the office at times, but she would refuse. Agent Fowler was not as regular as he was before, and they only met at the gym he had invited her to.

By the third month, she decided to work from home, in other words, doing absolutely nothing. The only thing she feared at that time was her salary going back to normal as she had elevated her taste and was even saving for a car.

"Curse you Sullivan" she cursed. It was around the fourth month that Carol realised that she was actively stalking his social media, and that she was already saving to buy a car she had seen him flaunting. She was into her second payment and would get it by the fifth. Going back to her previous salary would put her back by a few months, years, if she was to take her ideas of getting a better programming degree seriously.

By the fifth month, the office had been deserted, and Director Colby was unresponsive. Teo Han had spread a rumor in the office group chat that she was on a trip in some exotic land. Although it was against current protocol, Carol was sure that she needed it. Rachel Colby sounded tired in most of the phone calls, and she was in charge of monitoring the agent's day-in and day-out routines, as well as delivering messages at midnight.

There was a frustration that had built up in the hearts of all involved, and now they were being called in to help kill their already dead mission?

"Well, good riddance" Carol muttered.

"What! I can't hear you over the sound of my totally awesome mixtape!" Came Kelvin's voice at the other side of the car. He had offered to take her in to the office, and she had no choice but to answer. She also wanted to ask him for a ride to the showroom to get a refund after a twenty percent deduction of the fees she had already paid, but she couldn't pressure him. He was a sweet soul, and it felt like she was taking advantage of him.

"I love it!" She yelled over the loud music. Kevin had sent her links to his music. He had concluded that his next step in life was to be a rapper, and like his car doors that were always stuck, Kevin knew nothing about keys. His self-engineered project sounded worse than her little cousin Kalia's Sunday rendition, but she had to listen regardless. Carol had a half a mind to turn it off, but she was not one to hurt his feelings.

"...the world would do that, soon." she thought.

*

"Carol! You've got Aria and Harry, right? I've asked you a thousand times already!" Teo Han was furious. He had gotten a dye job on his hair in a fruitless attempt to look like an idol, but it had failed woefully.

"Maybe that was it?" Carol thought. She was sure that even Brendan resisted the urge to laugh every time she looked at him.

The Sultan, as usual, was nowhere to be found, and they had to do all the work by themselves. Not that it was even to be considered work. They were tasked with getting the agents past Russian customs and checkpoints by bypassing airport firewalls and validating evidently expired identity profiles. Easy stuff.

With ease, Brendan had gotten Skunk past airport security and towards his first-class flight back to East Philadelphia.

Teo Han was in the process of getting Jabez, upon his request, to Las Vegas. As he put it, he had "cash to lash, babes to smash!"

His second assignment, Gemini was enroute the airport. His suitcase had malfunctioned, and he was done fixing it.

Harry and Aria were to return to Washington. They were the first to undergo the debriefing exercises.

As Skunk was about to board his flight, the telephone in the office suddenly rang.

Carol, in her role as the leader of the son defunct team, picked it up to answer. On the other side of the call was Agent Fowler, and he was as business-like as always.

"Carol Duncan, the president is ordering a reroute. All agents are to return to Washington directly." He said, ending the call almost immediately. He did not sound as if he was in the mood to entertain complaints.

Slowly, Carol turned to her team. "We're to bring them all back to Washington." She said solemnly.

"Son of a bitch!" Teo Han cursed. Slamming on his keyboard.

He had just risen from his computer in a bid to get himself a victory coffee as a celebration for a job well done. He had gotten Jabez on a flight enroute Vegas, and Gemini's passport had sailed past customs and immigration.

After his fit of rage, he ran to his keyboard to get through to his assignments, but they both confirmed that they were already enroute their destinations.

"Damn it" Carol cursed. They would have to stay at work till they all landed and were then transported to Washington.

"What if they don't come? What do we do then? You think if I were these guys, I'd ever step foot in Washington anymore?" Teo Han was throwing a tantrum. Unlike other times, this time it seemed justified. They are sure to labeled incompetent, and forgetful.

Carol got on her phone and texted Layton that she had sent him a few bucks for both lunch and dinner, that she was going to be late.

"You're doing this again? What happened to working from home?" Layton asked over the phone.

"Trust me, after today, none of this will happen" Carol said, but she felt a quick sting of sadness. Ah was going to be out of a routine, and if she was unlucky, out of a job.

"You better! See you soon sis. Oh, can I go out tonight? I got a date. Possibly. I don't even know yet" he asked.

"Layton, if you managed to get a girl to want to go out with you, then you can go. I gotta go, there's so much to handle here" she said, ending the call.

"Alright fellas, shall we begin?" She yelled as an attempt to urge them on. She immediately regretted it, so much so that she did not bother to turn when she heard Teo Han curse.

*

If they had expected fanfare, they were awfully wrong. In what seemed like a funeral profession, the agents were ushered into the Oval Office by a rather stern looking agent fella.

"Looks like *blond muscle* here woke up the wrong side of the freaking bed. Hey easy" Jabez said as Agent Fowler had to nearly drag him into the Oval Office.

They had been on flights after flights and had less gotten sleep that was required. Although none present could complain about room service at the hotel where they were kept, they still wished they had more time with their beds.

Aria yawned as she took a seat. That was her first night away from all of Harry's snoring and she still did not get to enjoy it. Skunk wore only the shirt he was given, deciding to go against the suit he had gotten. So did Harry, as she showed up in favorite pair of blue jeans, the ones that had just enough room for an ankle knife.

Jabez and Gemini were dressed like the gentlemen they weren't, fully draped in a two-piece navy-blue suit, complete with custom White House cufflinks and ties with eagle embroidery.

They had all been seated for a few minutes when Carol and her team walked in.

"Who are these suits?" Jabez asked. They all turned to face the tired looking group as they stumbled towards the remaining seats. Carol heard something about a bet, and something about "the other voice", but she was too tired to pay attention.

"I take it that you must be the other voice?" Gemini thought to start a conversation, and also solve a debate that had raged in the last three months of the mission. He was talking to Brendan, who more than always was not in the mood for a conversation.

"Oh, no that's not her" Teo Han interjected. Carol thought his voice sounded different, and he stroke his hair as he spoke. He was the most energetic of the bunch, as he was on his sixth coffee.

"Right, he's sitting next to that cute girl" she surmised, nursing the small headache that had started because she smiled at his antics.

"Who is it then? It's not you is it?" Jabez asked. "Because that would be weird, and you might just be in the wrong profession too" he continued, smirking at his own joke. When the others finally got it, it was both too late to laugh, and there was too much tiredness that lay massive, unbreakable chokeholds on the others.

"That's me" Carol said, ending the awkward silence.

The agents stared at her in disbelief.

"Shut up!" Jabez yelled. Spring from his sit and pacing to the end of the room. He was laughing wildly. Gemini sat in disbelief, so did Skunk, who shifted himself to the edge of his seat and stared at her, both in disbelief, and shock. All Harry and Aria could do was stare at them, confused and completely in the dark, as did Carol. Teo Han had focused his attention on Aria. Brendan was busy solving a virtual puzzle, oblivious to what was going on.

"I don't understand, what's going on here?" Carol asked, but to no one in particular. She had not sewn their pictures and had not heard much of their voices, but from their files, she would tell that the tall one with the rather loud personality, hair that seemed to have started greying and far older than the rest, was Jabez. Jabez Glee, in full.

"Oh, it's nothing. We just had a bet about what the other voice looked like" Gemini offered an explanation. He was the only one that fit the description as being of African descent. That put the rather casually dressed one as Skunk. Slowly, she had begun to understand that they meant, and the reactions they put up. Although she did not show it, Carol had not envisioned them to look the way they did, well, at least, she thought they looked some other way.

It was then that the President stormed into the office, alongside several agents who held several of his effects. He had been at the unveiling and public launching of an e-library, which was basically a tall, statue-like monument that was placed at several parts of the state. They featured a QR-Code that let people get free, easy to download books. He had been called to unveil the one at the state university and owing to the fact that he had numbers to skyrocket, and a Vice that was somewhere in Bolivia, he had to go to this function, even if it meant eating into the time he was supposed to have with the agents.

"Darrell, could you hold onto this for me?" He asked, handing him the souvenir he had gotten at the event. President Wallace had been accompanied by Agents Cooley, Darrell, and another agent that looked like he could have a full hair of head, but sported a buzz cut.

"Thank you" he said, taking his seat. He had taken off his suit jacket and was no sitting at his desk, all business-like. In actuality, he was studying a set of speech cards that Secretary Boyd had sent to him. Although he thought the tone was too harsh, and way too revealing of his future intentions, he preferred to improvise, and so he did.

"Ladies, Gentlemen. Thank you for showing up today" he started, intent on keeping it as casual as possible. "We've had a hell of a quarter, right?" He asked.

The room was then filled with a mixture of enthusiastic nods, approving smiles, tired, nonchalant smirks of approval, and the emotionlessness of a seemingly absent-minded employee. Then He continued.

"I'm sure we've all had fun, we've all been frustrated, and we've possibly been made angry, that is why I want to use this juncture to thank each and every one of you, for your service that is. Your country thanks you and although the American on the street cannot know about what has happened, they will be going to sleep safely tonight because you thought to step up and do the right thing" he continued.

Then, in his usual manner, he got up from his chair, and came to rest on his desk, but this time he sat fully on the desk, letting his leave swing under him

"Uh, Mr President?" Carol called to him. There had been silence in the room for a little while as the president was rummaging through a couple of cards and scribbling on them.

"Yes, Carol?" He answered without looking up from his cards.

"If the team is to be disbanded permanently, do we still need to monitor the cyberspace for threats?" Carol asked. She knew better than to be out of a job, not at the moment, at least.

"Yeah, that sounds important, doesn't it? In the light of this disbandment, there will still be frameworks put in place to maintain the integrity of not just the cyberspace of the White House, but all of America as well" President Wallace replied.

"Oh, okay. Thank you Sir" she answered, sinking back into her chair, sighing with relief.

"Secretary Boyd was supposed to show up, but he informed me that he had to go monitor some investments somewhere" President Wallace continued. "Carol, could he so kind as to meet Ethel and have her compensate our agents? Also, have her get them enlisted on a mini-pension thank you." He said, looking around the room as they all sported smiles.

"I'm on it, Sir" she replied.

"Matter of fact, everyone gets raises!" He announced. Even Brendan looked up from her tablet and beamed a smile.

"On behalf of all of us, I just want to say that we are grateful, Mr President" Gemini said. He had risen to his feet and was about to speak, but President Wallace looked like he was in a bit of a hurry to get back to seemingly pressing paperwork.

"It's all in a day's work, agent, and thank you for your service. If you don't mind, I would love to get back to some paperwork, Carol and her team will lead you to collect a little token of your country's appreciation. Have a good day" he said, jumping off his desk and walking briskly towards his chair.

Slowly, they filed out, each giving a little salute as they left. The last person to leave was Jabez, who protested Rachel Colby's absence.

"Agent, we all have to move forward here. She has no more jurisdiction in this case, and neither do you. I suggest we all move forward and wish for the best in our future endeavors." President Wallace said, waving a hand towards the door. He wanted to be left to his duties, and he needed Jabez to not distract him further.

Once outside, Jabez quickly joined up with the test of his now disbanded team, and they seemed to be engaged in a conversation about their various futures.

"...way back in Boca. Yeah, I'd like to go to Argentina, probably Cuba as well" he heard Harry say.

"In all honesty, going back home would really be it for me right now" Gemini said.

"What home? Africa?" Aria asked.

"Yeah, I think my cousin is getting married soon. My old social media account is still in the family group chat, and I check it from time to time" he announced.

"On second thought, I don't think I like Vegas that much. I mean, it sure as hell is electric, fun and all. But I really want to go back Russia, or bring Russia to me, you know?" Jabez interjected. He sounded emotional as he spoke.

"That Anya chick? She's cute" Skunk commented.

"Yeah, she is. I've not been gone for that long, right? I could tell her I went to see some family members, right?" He asked.

"Family members? She doesn't know your true identity, does she?" Aria asked Jabez.

"Yeah, not exactly. Does it matter?" Jabez retorted.

"You don't love her, move on" Harry blurted. She was staring at the windows, and the city in the distance.

"What?" Jabez had turned to her.

"If you love her, she would not have been kept in the dark by you" Harry said bluntly, looking Jabez in the eyes.

"I don't love her? What are you saying even?" Jabez felt guilty at his foolish attempts to hide who he was. Anya was a sweet woman, and he loved the smell of her hair, but she not knowing who he really was seemed truly unfair. He hoped that she forgave him, wherever she was at the time, and also that Harry was wrong.

"Follow me, please" an unfamiliar voice spoke. It was Darrell, and he was ushering them towards a waiting area. Ethel was in the city running a fee errand and was not available at the moment.

As he walked in front of them, Gemini could not help but wonder where he had seen him before. He was one to forget a face, but the one looked way too familiar. As they all walked, he continued to ponder.

"Was it the army?" He asked himself. But it wasn't. He was unfamiliar with his tall, tanned physique, which would have been the reverse if he had been in the army with him. Gemini Aldo found it hard to place the voice, and the accent as well.

"Was it European? Why did it sound so forced?" He asked himself further.

As a master of disguise himself, it was easy to tell when a person was faking an accent, and although it was unnoticeable, Gemini realised that their guide was not speaking as he normally would.

"In here, please" Darrell had ushered them to a waiting room. An air-conditioned large space complete with lounge seats, highchairs, and even a bean bag in the corner. The grey on the wall perfectly completed the black undertones in both the furniture, and the upholstery that held the television.

Once inside, they all chose seats and mostly kept to themselves. Despite their earlier chattiness, the President's remarks had layered the hearts of both the agents and Carol's team with a bit of solemnity.

Jabez, unlike his usual self, sat in a corner and tried to remember Rachel Colby's cell number, cursing all the alcohol that he had ever taken as the reason behind his forgetfulness.

Harry and Aria engaged in a shell of a conversation, and they soon decided to keep to themselves. Skunk tried his best to avoid Teo Han and all his questions about Aria. They had worked together for almost half a year, and he still did not know anything about her, and he was not to ever get the opportunity. As all these happened, Gemini was lost in thought, and so was Carol.

"That agent that escorted us here, you see him around often?" Gemini asked Carol. He had been staring intently at her for a while. Mostly out of bewilderment, because of the way she sounded when she made announcements in the then Director Colby's place.

"Yeah, Darrell? He's my neighbour" Carol offered.

"Really? How long has he been working here?" Gemini asked. He felt like he was up to something, and although he couldn't place his finger on what it was, it still bothered him.

"I didn't start seeing him at the office till a few months ago, why are you asking?" Carol retorted.

There it was. In Gemini's mind, it was clear. Darrell the agent was a spy. It was now left to figure out where he was from.

"If you're thinking he's not what he says he is, then you're wrong. He's a security contractor, and he was recommended after a stint in Belgium" Carol was quick to defend her neighbour. Whenever Agent Fowler could not make it, he had stepped up and given her a ride to work.

Gemini then made up his mind to find out where he had seen the face. He might be off-key voice, but what if he got assassinated by someone they could have foiled? Or what if the next President stops the now incoming salary.

Before long, Jabez was out of his funk. It was then that he looked around where he had chosen to sit and mope and realised that he had gotten a bucket of ice, and even better, champagne.

Slowly, he handed over several cups to all but Brendan, who was decided against all manner of social interaction or contact. Then, without thinking of the toast he wanted to propose, he proceeded to pour out what he deemed the life blood of the mission, exciting on the tongue, but not so easy on the eyes, or on composure.

When they had all drank what was contained in the bottle, Jabez thought it wise to start another conversation.

"So, hair guy!" He called out, referring to Teo Han and his rather bold fashion choice. "What do you do here?"

"Uhm, the same thing as everyone anyways." Teo Han confessed. "I code solutions to tactical problems and emergency issues within the US military" he added, adjusting proudly in his seat.

"Right, right. I'll text you when I need to rob a bank" Jabez replied with a straight face. Teo Han thought to laugh, but as he saw that he was not joking, he then shut off his laughter and tried to ask questions. It was then that Jabez started laughing, so much so that Darrell had to peek through the door to ascertain what was going on.

As he did, his eyes and Gemini's locked for a few seconds, and afterwards, all Gemini did was smile. A smile of decidedness and decisiveness. He knew where to look and he was going to search till he found it.

Ethel called her office, and it was communicated that she was going to be away for another hour. There was nothing their grumblings could do to change it, but they grumbled regardless. Some, like Jabez and his crew, had nowhere else to be, unlike Carol, who had pulled an all-nighter and was about to go a full day without sleep.

"I have to call Layton" she mumbled to herself and excused herself from the room. Outside, she saw that Darrell was not at his post, but at the other end of the hallway, making a call.

Carol then went the opposite way, and when she came up on a side bench, she fell on it, and then she called Layton. She was not feeling as tired as she thought she was, but she still felt like she needed rest. She had eaten, had a few too many breath mints, coffee as well, but she had not had a single minute of sleep.

Guiding the agents towards new destinations took more time that she had expected, and then she was supposed to have them in the White House before evening. At exactly 3:17 in the afternoon, she sent out authorized White House vehicle to go pick them up, and by 3:56, they were all seated, awaiting the President who was running late from a public function. After a short meeting that turned out to be 45 minutes long, she now had to wait another hour.

"At this rate, it'll be 9 when I get home, aw what the hell?" She cursed, vowing to not show up the next day.

She had tried Layton's number twice already, but it just rang till it didn't, leaving her with an automated message, and frustration. Resigning to her fate, she decided to let go of having a thawed-out steak dinner when she finally got home. Instead, she would settle for pizza, and yes on the extra toppings as well. She needed to go to sleep feeling fuller than she was supposed to.

"'Bloated' is the word" she thought, walking back to the waiting area.

It was almost five, and Carol was sure she felt like disobeying direct orders if it meant she got a nap.

*

The next few weeks were just as Carol as expected; boring. She now had less work to do, and more time to spend on herself, but even this feeling was not unique. Everyone seemed to want to find something that made them feel less jobless.

Sing there was no longer a team. Gemini resorted to finding Darrell's true identity, and he sent so many emails with scrappy prices of evidence that Carol had to chalk his address up as a spam account, although she did not stop reading them. Her curiosity had gotten the better of her, but she had an even more worrisome question,

"How did he get my email?" She had pondered severally, but with no visible response.

Aria had moved out of state and was planning a trip to go see her parents. She had not seen since all the trouble they had, and she hoped that absence had made the heart grow fonder. Harry made to go with her, but Aria was strongly against it. She needed to do it alone, and although they had gotten really close in the past few months. she was not ready to share that part of herself just yet.

Jabez had been trying to reach Anya since a day after the meeting with the President. He was going to tell her everything, but he had discovered to his mortification that she had blocked his number. Jabes had become heartbroken, and for almost a whole week, he set aside his sobriety and indulged in as much vodka as he could find. By the third day, he felt like he was going to die, but he braved it all, vowing to continue when he was feeling better.

He was seated in the house he had bought with his pay when he got a call from a hidden number. Nonchalantly, he picked up the phone and answered it. It was Rachel Colby, but she came bearing bad news.

"Well, I know it's probably none of your business, but I honestly just wanted you to know" she said.

"What isn't my business? What wrong?" Jabez was nursing a headache, but he managed to sit up from his bed.

"Skunk was driving on the interstate when he crashed into an incoming truck. The driver fled and left him to die. That was last night, well we can all agree that he was a tough man. He died just a few minutes ago. We'll be having a small state burial in a few days" she said, her voice breaking as she spoke.

There was no response, only a loud crack, and awkward static.

"Hello? Jabez? You there?" She tried to reach him again, but the number was suddenly not available. Sighing, she proceeded to call on others to relay the terrible news to them.

Unknown to her, Jabez had smashed his phone into the wall in anger and was now sitting on the floor of his apartment. Sniffling was all he could do, as the tears refused to flow. He had not cried in a while, and he desperately needed the tears to flow. Yet, he got nothing.

The others did not take the news well, so much so that Rachel Colby thought to withhold it from Aria. She got wind of her trip to possibly reunite with her parents and she did not want to ruin her mood.

Gemini was still investigating his own case when she called. He had just finished going through the case files of all foreign soldiers that had fought against the insurgents in Northern Nigeria in the past. He had recognized several of them, most of whom he fought besides, but there was nothing on Darrell.

Yet again, he got the strong feeling that made him think that he had not seen the man anywhere, and that maybe it was just a picture. He then remotely accessed the files from his stint as a worker at the American embassy in Moscow and was scouring the database for files he had worked on. It was then that he got her call. It read as "Hidden Caller ID", but Gemini knew whom it was.

"Director?" He said as soon as he answered.

"Agent. I have some bad news" she said, giving him time to brace himself.

"Let me have it" he replied, sounding unconcerned.

"It's about your fellow agent, Skunk" she said, once again giving him time to process it.

"What about him?" Gemini asked.

"He got into an accident last night. Ran into a truck. He died about thirty minutes ago" she said solemnly.

"Shit!" He cursed. "When's the funeral?" Gemini asked, sighing.

"A few days, we need to put together a small group his known family members that can get here" she replied.

"Stuff like this isn't supposed to happen" he said, taking his palm to his face. "Thank you for call Madam Director, I'll be there in a few days to pay my respects" he said, right before she ended the call.

Sighing again, he looked at the time on the wall clock above his work desk. It was 6:12 in the evening, and he suddenly thought it wise to go for a drink.

"A couple swigs, just what I need" he muttered to himself as he donned a jacket. It was cold outside, and he needed to cover up. After finally dressing, he put on his favorite accessory; a Swiss knife he had custom made a while back, it was tailor made to his grip and was sharp on both sides. Before long, his taxi had arrived, and he was driven into the night.

Death had always taken a toll on Gemini, and although he had learnt how to mask it, he felt like breaking down and crying his eyes out. In the last few months of their mission, he had really bonded with all his fellow agents and a loss, especially one that was as uncerimonious as Skunk's hit hard.

His taxi had pulled up on *La Villa*, his favorite restaurant in all of Washington, located a little into the eastern part of the city, it offered a variety of African dishes, and drinks. That way you can get as drunk as you would want to, but not on an empty stomach. It was his home away from home, a place where he could get the feel of being in a typical Western Nigerian party setting, the ówambè, without the sickening feeling that had kept him away from home for almost two decades.

As Gemini walked into the restaurant, he started to tingle with nostalgia. It was all the same, just as he had left it. The seat, fashioned from some of the most durable wood he had ever seen, had the same carvings as they had a few years prior. The lights were the same; a bright orange that illuminated the space through which the magic happening in the kitchen travelled through.

Even the neon lights on the wall that spelled restaurant's name was the same. A few bulbs had died already, but it was almost like an unwritten tradition to not get rid of them or change them.

As he sat on the wooden chairs, he began to feel a surge of nostalgia. Basking in the ambience, Gemini found himself nodding to the sounds of the drums playing over the speakers. It was the talking drum, and although it was a song with other instruments, the talking drum was doing a solo.

"Worth all the noise complaints I've gotten" he muttered to himself, allowing the music to minister to him. For a second, Gemini was lost in a world like the one he once knew, a world that he longed for. Then came the waiter.

"What will we be having, Sir?" he said, causing Gemini to open his eyes. Instead of the proud, robust man that wore an *agbada,* who usually boasted of being to speak any Nigerian language that the customer wanted to converse in, there stood a thin, tall kid, about twenty years of age. His hair was cut low, and his beard was shaved neatly. For a second, Gemini did not speak, as he needed time to adjust himself.

"Goat meat pepper soup, please" Gemini replied, clearing his throat.

"Coming right up" the boy said, returning to the kitchen. Gemini watched him go, following him till he disappeared beyond the curtain made out of beads and strings. As he looked at the rest of the restaurant, he came up on an old, balding man, who sat in a chair beside the kitchen door. Gemini had not seen him before, but he had on a green *agbada,* and he held a cane in one hand.

"Could it be?" He gasped. His favorite restaurant owner had grown old, and he couldn't dance as he used to. It was then that Gemini realised that he had not been in those walls in almost eleven years, since his first time in America.

"Death comes to us all, damn it" he said, sighing. His pain had followed him, even to his happy place. Gemini knew he was growing older, and just a few weeks ago in Russia, he had seen a white speck in his hair which he thought to be the snow, but it wasn't. He was greying, and he only chalked it up as growing old.

"How old was Skunk? 29? Was it?" He asked, but no one replied. The restaurant was empty, save for a couple who sat with their two young children.

The boy had emerged from the kitchen again, and in his hands, a large tray that held a bowl of pepper soup. As he walked towards him, Gemini began to see the resemblance between the loud, funny kid that ran through the restaurant as his father served delicious food, and the grown man that held his meal with steady hands.

"There you go, Sir. Enjoy" he said, dropping the pipping-hot plate on the table. As expected, the aromas from the artfully prepared goat meat pepper soup wafted into his nostrils, once again filling him with delight. Hungrily, he devoured the various meats that filled the plate, alongside the complementary palm wine that was supplied.

It was then that it dawned on him. He had come to a realization that he once overlooked. He was sure he had gone over the files a few times, but he did not see it.

"With contact lenses and a fake beard, anybody can look like someone else!" Quickly, he emailed a few documents to Carol and paid the fee for his meal. He needed to make calls and clear his head, a night in the city air was sure to help him. Before leaving, he made to greet the old man, but he was asleep.

"I'll tell *Baba* that you came by" said a voice behind him. It was the attendant, and he was beaming a smile.

"Thank you" Gemini said, beaming a smile. He left immediately, as tears had begun to gather in his eyes.

Outside the restaurant, busy Washington night appeared to dull in comparison when compared to the insides of the *La Villa* and he suddenly felt empty.

Then came the paranoia. As he walked towards the intersection to find a taxi to his next stop; a liquor store to grab himself some tequila, he suddenly beta to feel like he was being watched and followed. He had not felt it before, but he thought to walk inside an alleyway next to the street he had just crossed. There he would wait for the assailant, knife in hand.

Gemini was right, but he was also wrong. He was being followed, but not by one assailant, probably a petty thief, but by suits who appeared to hold machine guns.

"Light it up" Gemini heard one of them say, and immediately, a barrage of bullets began to pour into the alleyway.

"I guess Director Colby would have to make another call then" he said, laughing. Tears had once again gathered in his eyes.

Gemini had been dead for almost month. The news had shocked everyone at first, but the shock was now lower than it formerly was. Skunk's burial was carried out in a worse mood than was expected, as everyone was still in shock over Gemini's murder.

Skunk had been in an accident, but Gemini had been executed. The eyewitnesses said that the killers all dressed in black and carried weapons that were way above what the gangbangers on the street corners could get their hands on. They were said to have moved in squads and seemed to have military training.

Although the President and Secretary Boyd had assured him that they were not involved in the killings, Jabez was not satisfied by their speeches and reassuring words. He had stormed into the President's office, wrestling Agent Fowler to the floor, and making his way in.

They had sat him down and calmly told him to go home and that they had stationed soldiers round the clock to protect him and what was left of the team that went to Russia.

Still, Jabez was not impressed, and neither was Carol. Right after his outburst in the Oval Office, he had met her waiting for him outside her house. Apparently Gemini had been conducting an investigation based on several oddly familiar faces he had seen at The White House.

"Your neighbour?" Jabez had asked.

"Exactly! He's Russian! His real name is Pietro Vitalis, born in 1987." Carol had replied.

The files contained several information about Pietro and his team that was stationed at various places within the Capital city.

"Do you think he's part of the team that is taking us out?" Carol had asked.

Jabez not sure, for all he knew, Pietro, or Darell, and his team could have been sent with the same mission as he was, and that he was going to be hunted by his government as soon as he failed.

Still donning the suit, he wore to the burial, Jabez requested to see Pietro.

"He's gonna be at home, it's his day off today" Carol replied.

"Exactly, we need him unawares" He replied, storming towards the front yard, where he hijacked an SUV and with Carol in tow, drove to her house.

Once he was on her street, he parked a few blocks from her house and studied her house and Pietro's.

"We need to question him, alright?" Jabez said turning to Carol who was seated beside him. She was clutching her laptop and staring at him. Jabez had to snap his fingers to bring her back from her thoughts.

"Sorry, I've just never seen you so business-like" she said.

"Yeah, I don't want to die yet. I'm sure I have a kid with a Brazilian that I need to confirm. I can't do that when I'm a corpse, now can I?" He replied, smirking.

Carol stared straight ahead, and she did not say anything.

"It was a joke!" Jabez said again, tapping her on the shoulder.

"I know, I'm just studying the house. If it's anything like mine, the back exits should leave to the intersection"

"Good job. Oh, about the kid in Brazil thing, I wasn't kidding. I get calls from Rosinda every time I use my old number" he said, starting the car again. This time, he let it roll till they were just a stone throw from Carol's.

Jabez was now rummaging through the crevices in the car, "Alright, if this SUV is anything like the others, there should be a gun here somewhere" he said.

Soon, he found a small pistol in the glove box.

"Sweet!" He said, smiling as he brandished his new friend, right before tucking it behind his suit. "Act natural, okay?" He said to Carol. She was sweaty, and her glasses were sliding off of her face as she tried to pull them back up.

"Hey, smile a bit". When Carol turned to him, Jabez was baring his teeth, but she was not amused.

"No? Okay then, ruin the mission, see if I care" he retorted, slamming the door as he stepped out. He was not walking towards Pietro's, his eyes fixed in the windows in case the Russian gentleman was intent on surprising him with another visit to a funeral home.

Carol followed closely behind him, eyeing her own front door. It was a Saturday and Layton was at home. He had taken permission to have a few friends over, but she knew he meant to have a party, especially as she had gotten up abruptly to go to work.

"Keep an eye out for our friend okay?" Jabez said as he reached back to tap Carol on the shoulders. She had repeatedly bumped into him, but he had decided to be patient with her.

"In case he escapes?" She asked.

"In case he fires at us" Jabez replied as he climbed up the stairs that led to the doorway. In all honesty, the latter was more plausible. They were, in fact, home invaders.

That was not to be the case as Pietro was already at the door, holding a bottle of scotch and two glasses.

"Come on in guys, I've been expecting you!" He said, leaving the door open as he walked back in.

"What the fuck?" Jabez muttered as he turned to Carol. His face held a dozen questions as he turned back to the door, and then back to Carol.

"What just happened?" She asked, tapping on the shoulder of his grey suit.

"I have absolutely no idea, but I'm about to find out" Jabez replied. He was undoing his tie and wrapping it around his right knuckle.

"Here" he said again as they walked on in the doorway. He was handing her a small knife; the same one he had used to open the car. "You might need it" he said, pushing the door all the way in. There they stood, waiting for an attack, but none came.

Jabez peered inside, but there were no assailants or bad guys waiting for them. Instead, all he could see was a nice house with tastefully selected furniture. The decor leaned towards an earthy green with brown couches that complimented the walls perfectly.

"Clear" Jabez said as he beckoned on Carol to come on in.

Together they walked into the parlor, where they saw another gentleman sitting on one of the couches. Immediately, Jabez reached for his gun, but the man, an Asian gentleman called out to him with a truce.

"It's okay, Mr Glee, I'm a friend. So is Pietro. At least we should be, since we all have a common enemy, don't you think?" The man said, taking his cup of herbal tea from the table.

"Right, and who are you?" Jabez asked, his gun still trained on the man.

"Jin Xu, but you can call me Jerry" he said.

"I'll call you what I want to call you, alright?" Jabez retorted. "Is that Ginseng tea though?" He asked. The aroma was all over the room.

"Yes it is" came another voice, causing Jabez to turn to the staircase. It was Pietro, and he was clutching a laptop under his arm.

"I got it on the trip in, good stuff. I never for around to using it for myself, but I'm glad somebody else appreciates good tea. You can have some if you want?" He said, taking a seat on one of the couches.

"No thanks, could be poisoned" Jabez said, putting Carol behind him. She had come out of her cover when she saw Pietro.

"Carol, please have a seat" Pietro beckoned, but Jabez kept her in place.

"No siree, she's staying right here" Jabez said, holding her in place.

"Mr Glee, you much need to sit down for this. We have news that affects us all" Jin Xu beckoned.

"Nope, thanks. The only sitting I'll be doing is on your asses when the CIA comes over and cuffs you both" Jabez replied.

"It's about Skunk, and Gemini. We know how they were killed" Pietro said.

"No shit. So does everyone who worked on the case we worked on together. Now, tell us something we don't already know, will you?" Jabez retorted.

"He meant that we know how they were killed. Along with who killed them" Jin Xu replied.

"What?" Jabez asked.

"We had lost agents in similar manner, and ad we did a little digging, we found taped recordings of the deaths of the agents; mine, yours, and Jin's" Pietro replied, turning the laptop to face Jabez and Carol.

In the clip that was playing was a man breathing heavily as he waited at a junction. As he sat in what seemed to be a huge truck, a radio beeped beside him.

"Target inbound. Over."

"Roger"

After this brief conversation, the truck gets revved up and the driver begins speeding towards what looked like a highway.

Soon, the driver comes up on the main junction where the truck smashes into an incoming vehicle. The truck catches on fire, and the driver scampers to safety.

Soon, the driver is at a safe distance where they report back to what seemed to be a control room, and then the video goes off.

Immediately, another video began playing. In this second clip, a body cam shows about half a dozen masked men seated in suits, all armed with military grade weapons. A walkie buzzes to life and after a short, inaudible conversation, someone signals the rest of the crew to move out. In the distance, Jabez and Carol could see Gemini sprint into an alleyway, right before the cam gains on his position. A commander gives a signal and then the bullets to flying in. After all the rounds were exhausted, the assailant with the body cam goes in on Gemini, revealing his bullet-riddled body.

"Jesus" Carol gasped, looking away.

"How did you get that? Did you do this, huh?" Jabez said, raising his gun again. He had begun to tear up, and he used his free hand to clean his face. When he took the hand back to Carol, he could feel her shaking.

"No, no!" Pietro replied, raising his hands. Jin Xi followed suit. Jabez was agitated, and he could fire if they made any sudden movements.

"We know who did, at least we think we do. That's why Gemini was talking to us!" Jin Xi revealed.

"Talking to you?" Jabez asked. He could not believe what he was hearing.

"Yeah, yes! He found me out, and then I helped him find Jin!" Pietro replied.

"Found you out?" Jabez was still asking questions.

"He told Carol everything! Tell him, Carol" Pietro beckoned.

"He- He didn't…" Carol managed to speak.

"The emails! Did you read them?" Pietro asked. Jabez could fire at any moment, and in the spirit of gaining trust, he had left his gun upstairs when he went to get his laptop.

"Yeah, no. I mean no! I thought he was just looking to share what he had seen in Russian, and I thought it was a need-to-know thingy and I didn't need to know- I'm sorry" Carol was rambling. It was evident that she was still shaken from what she had just saw.

"Those emails have details of everything we had accomplished. The rest is here" Jin said. "For a while before his demise, Gemini had undertaken a private investigation. His target was Pietro, and his cover as Darrell. But then, he caught Darrell and after hearing about how he had lost his men in incidents and how the Russian government and some secret organization was after him, he sought to join forces. Gemini was still skeptical, and that was when he and Pietro here caught up to me" He continued.

"What's your deal? You Russian?" Jabez asked Jin.

"Chinese Intelligence. I had lost a few of my men in a sting operation in Russia. We were able to retrieve sensitive information from the President's office at the Kremlin, but it led to a dead end. You see, China had been under cyber-attacks for a while, and the hacker's signals traced back to Moscow and Washington" Jin explained.

"Wait, sensitive information in the Kremlin? That was our steal!" Jabez protested.

"I'm sorry, but I saved you a whole deal of trouble and months of deciphering that would end in nothing. Besides, we stole it off the work of overzealous foreign students in a tour" Jin replied.

"Those women were our agents, you idiot!" Jabez charged forward, his gun pointed at Jin. Suddenly, he stopped.

"Look, why would Gemini work with scum like you guys?" Jabez asked.

"Because our governments are not the enemy, and that it's something else. Something more dangerous?" Pietro explained.

"Huh!" Jabez scoffed. "What could be more dangerous than the might of the US Army? And why didn't Gemini talk to me about it, huh?"

"First off, we don't know how strong this shadow power is, but they are strong. Secondly, he said uh were out partying in Vegas or something" Pietro replied.

"Oh" Jabez said, lowering his gun. "But he should have called!" Jabez said as he fell on one of the brown couches.

"He did, he sent a screenshot of his call log too" Pietro replied. He tapped away at his laptop and then he revealed a screenshot.

"16 missed calls? Sorry I was busy, but I missed them all" Jabez said.

"Of course," Jin Xi replied. They were all seated, except Carol.

"Have a seat, Carol" Jin Xi requested.

"Now why is this shadow power after you? After us?" Jabez asked as soon as Carol was seated.

"We used what we call a drill protocol to get the information we have. The good thing with this is that the information never stops pouring in, and the bad thing is that the…" Pietro explained.

"The information never stops pouring in. Yeah, I have information on my old laptop to disgrace every president of Peru, ever. Did your tunnel get discovered?" Jabez said.

"Unfortunately, yes" Pietro continued. "Turns out they're just as smart as we are. They not only know who we are, but they're watching us as well" He sighed.

"There are other videos showing how our agents were killed, but we won't show them, for her sake" Jin Xi said as he pointed to Carol.

"Thank you" was all she could mutter.

"And for ours as well, we're not cold machines with no feelings" Pietro spoke again, this time he was looking Carol in the eyes.

Carol could not hold his gaze, so she looked away, and so did he.

"Here" Pietro said again after that brief silence. His hand WS stretched out and in it were two identical flash drives. "For you guys" he said.

Jabez made to grab them, but he stopped. "How do I know they're no spyware?" He asked, raising his right eyebrow.

"They're not. They'll keep us alive for as long as possible" Jin Xi said.

"They better" Jabez said, scoffing. "Alright, that's it. Come on Carol, we're heading out. As for you guys, pray we see something that makes us not want to call the CIA in here" Jabez said as made for the door.

"Mr Glee, wait."

Jabez stopped and took a look behind him. It was Jin Xi.

"Mr Glee, I would advise that we don't take this matter to our governments, that's why we are still in Washington. Pietro had all his agents killed as soon as they stepped foot in Moscow, and so did I. If you could give us enough time to find out who is behind these killings, it'll be much obliged. Also, tell Carol to forward those emails to you, we'll be in touch, okay?" said Jin Xi, after which he gave Jabez a tap on the shoulder and left.

Jabez scoffed as he exited Pietro's house. How foolish did they make him out to be?

They wanted him to commit treason?

Maybe working with them was what got Gemini killed! Still, if they were right, that meant that both Harry and Aria were in danger.

As Jabez made his way to the SUV, he called Harry's burner, but there was no response. The same thing happened when he called Aria's.

"Can you trace a burner?" He asked as he stormed into the SUV.

"What?" Carol was startled, but she managed to speak.

"Can you trace a burner?" He asked again.

"Yeah, yeah. I mean no. I mean, you're not supposed to, but I can. We'll need my computer at work" Carol replied.

"Coming right up!" Jabez said as he started the car. Soon they were speeding on the highway, heading for the White House, and her underground office.

*

"You think they'll help us?" Pietro asked Jin after they had left.

"Nah, not chance in hell. I'm sure they're headed to the CIA right now with those drives" Jin replied, returning to his cup of tea.

They both laughed.

"They're not that dumb, are they?" Pietro asked after the laughter had died down. There was a look of seriousness and worry on his face.

"I know she is, Mr Glee is a wild card" Jin replied.

"Yeah, he is. You should've seen him when they returned from the Motherland"

"I mean, he's a wild card. A wild, rabid card with impulses like that of a dog that just had a taste of blood" Jin replied. The smile was gone from his face.

"Jesus Christ! He's going to rat us out, isn't he?" Pietro was now worried.

"Either that, or Ms. Carol will fold under the undue pressure we've mounted on her and blurt out our existence to the President himself" Jin continued.

"Jesus man, are you always this pessimistic?" Pietro asked.

"Nope. Realistic, that is why my passport is on me at all times, and why I have a bag packed upstairs in case I have to disappear" Jin replied. He was on his way upstairs.

"We're good, you hear?" Pietro yelled out to his counterpart. but he was out of earshot.

*

"Should we tell Director Colby?" Carol asked as they dashed into the elevator. Surprisingly, no one was around to raise an eyebrow over the stolen SUV or the fact that it had been returned and parked illegally White House lawn.

"You mean the one person that could've believed us if she still had the power she had?" Jabez retorted.

Carol did not reply. She knew what Director Carol had gone through in the months after her dismissal. She was not as powerful as she used to be, and that was not even politically. Her body had become weak due to an excessive intake of alcohol, and the stress of the mission. The last they had heard from her was a month and a half ago, when Skunk died.

"Thought so" Jabez said again, sighing.

The last ding of the elevator was followed by a thud; they were not underground. The office was dark, and no one was around. It was not unusual to see Teo Han spending his free time there, but he was not around today.

"Quick, where did Harry and Aria say they were headed?" Carol said, beckoning for a response

"Minnesota, I think?" Jabez replied. He was unsure as he had not been paying attention.

"Minnesota? Forget it" Carol sighed as she tapped away at her keyboard. "I'll just have to hack their emails then; do you know Harry's?"

"RagingPhoenix@Bloodstinger.com" Jabez blurted out.

Carol gave him a quick stare, then she resumed typing.

"What? I'm a big fan of her former band. I might have sent a few mails telling her how much she rocked from a burner email, but don't tell her!" Jabez confessed.

"Harry's in a band?" Carol asked. Her eyes did not shift from the screen as she spoke.

"Yeah, 'was' is the right word. The whole thing dissolved after the drummer got called by his dad to come work on

Wall Street. Raging Phoenix and SummerCold did not like that" he said, snickering.

"SummerCold?' Carol asked again.

"Yeah, lead singer. You should have seen his Twitter feed that whole month, he got banned for hate speech, I think"

"So, what part did Harry play"

"Guitar, backup singer. The girl can rock out"

"Got it! She got a debit alert in Minneapolis, apparently she bought something called a Howler at an adult store"

"Oh, spicy. Look it up" Jabez requested.

"On it already" Carol said, smiling mischievously. "Oh god" came her voice again, followed by a look of terror.

"What is it?" Jabez asked as he hurried to her side. When he saw what was on the screen, he gasped.

"Oh god" he echoed.

"Right?" Carol said, scrolling down the search results.

"Wait, do you think they're-?" Jabez asked.

"They're what?"

"Harry and Aria, do you think they're- you know what I mean right?" Jabez asked again.

"Dating? I don't know, I mean I didn't know them that well. I mean, I don't even know you that well"

"Right. Fair point"

"Right"

"But they did spend months holed up together in Moscow, do you think?"

"What do you mean by holed up?"

"Holed up?"

"Don't say 'hole' okay?"

"Right?"

"Good"

"It just makes so much sense now" Jabez sighed as he slid across the room.

"I mean, they kept to themselves, and they didn't come to the guys for anything"

"Anything?"

"You know what I mean"

"I wish I didn't, honestly" Carol sighed as she made to shut down the computer. But Jabez stopped her.

"How about we take a look at this?" He said, revealing a drive he had gotten.

Carol sighed. She had made up her mind to shelf this for later, but Jabez was sure to be insistent, and she didn't have a will that was as strong as his.

"Fine" she said, taking the drive from him. Quickly, she inserted it into the computer, and it began to load up. Then came the pop-up screen, followed by a file titled "Everything".

"Everything? Original" Jabez commented, but Carol didn't reply. Her curiosity had gotten the better of her as she clicked on the file. Inside was a large collection of random files, short video clips, images of paper photographs with blood splattered on them.

Among the files were Russian agents that had been killed, as well as Chinese agents that had ala been killed. Beside these photographs were death certificates, and 480p clips that showed the murders. One particular one stood out. A fire at the Chinese Embassy in Russia.

"Shit I was there that day!" Jabez exclaimed.

"What?"

"Yeah, yeah. I had to deliver food to Gemini. See, I had lost a sports bet to him the day before and I had to bring him food for a week" Jabez continued.

"Did you see anything?" Carol asked.

"I don't think so, I just saw a fire down the stress from there I would take a bus to where the American Embassy was" Jabez explained.

"They've been on you guys this entire time" Carol sighed.

"We seem to be the last of the kill mission. I have this feeling that Harry and Aria are next" he sighed as he ran his hand through his head.

"Holy shit! Holy shit! " Carol suddenly exclaimed. It was a kill order slated to happen in downtown Minneapolis. The description of the car to be used was also underneath the order, signed by something called "Xavier".

"That's where the girls are!" Jabez exclaimed. "We have to call them, check the emails, is there any mention of a number.

"Uh, yeah yeah. Harry purchased a disposable number a few days ago"

"Try calling it!"

"It won't work! They use these types of numbers to register for illegal sites or to give someone a wrong number."

"Try texting it then!"

"On it." Carol replied as she frantically typed out an SOS message.

"What did they say?"

"Nothing, nothing! Oh, its seen! Harry's seen it!"

"What is she saying?"

"In traffic, can't talk right now"

"Ask her to check if she has a tail. A black Mercedes with random alphabets for plates"

"She says she sees a black Mercedes, but it HSS no plate number"

"Tell her to get out of there!"

"She's sending a voice note!"

"Play it!"

"What is up dick faces! Did you guys miss us. We're in traffic right now, and Aria's driving- oh, hold on, someone is trying to tell us something! ONE SEC SIR!- Go back to your car, fucking dumbass. Let's chat never, shall we?"

Jabez was not going to hear it. He reached forward and leaned into the mic.

"You listen to me you midget piece of shit, that guy is probably armed and wants to execute your lesbian ass! Get the fuck out and run! Come on!" He screamed into the mic, before storming off into the kitchen.

Carol could hear him scream into the think walls of concrete that surrounded them. He had not ended the recording, so she tapped on the send button for him and gave him his space.

It was then that she remembered that she had packed her breakfast into a small foil wrap when she left the house that morning. Resignedly, she unwrapped the toast that was now cold and dug in, sighing as the pain in her stomach reduced. All that was left was worry, and panic. Who knew if they would come after her and her team next? Possibly even Director Colby too!

"Come on, let's get moving. Get the drive, I'll be waiting in the car" Jabez said as he stormed out.

"Where are we going to?"

"Your place, technically" he said as he tapped impatiently on the elevator door.

"Why?"

"Isn't it obvious? They need to tell us everything they know, and more! Soon there'll be someone with a kill order out for me, and I need to know the man that's pulling the trigger or at least the person or people who sent him." Jabez said as he stepped into the elevator.

"Hold!" Carol requested, she immediately unplugged the computer and turned off all the lights. Soon they were on the presidential floor again. Without waste, they made their way to the SUV, but there were agents checking it out.

"Come on" Jabez beckoned as he walked towards the main parking lot.

Inside he sighed as he took in the cars that were available.

"Make a choice" he said, tapping Carol on the shoulder. "Pick something classy, maybe a nice dark shade of blue, and without trackers, you know, a whole package"

"How about this one?" Carol said as she checked out a Sedan.

"Oh, the rumors are true. You have no taste" Jabez mocked.

"It's safe, and nobody will go looking for a Sedan from 1996"

"It's a 1999 baby, but still, a 1965 Mustang looks better than it does"

"Remember, no trackers!"

"Fine" Jabez grunted. "Knife please?" He said, beckoning for his penknife.

"Oh, I have it here somewhere" Carol said as she checked her dress. She didn't not have it on her, so she checked her bag, much to Jabez's irritation. He groaned as she rummaged through her bag, first bringing up her half-eaten sandwich, then the knife reared his head, and she tossed it over to him.

"Merci" he said as he worked his magic on the key. Before long, the door swung open, and he reached under the steering wheel to hotwire the car. "Get in!" He said as soon as it roared to life.

"Where did you learn that?" Carol asked.

"Ghana. A local teen did it to my car. When I caught him I made him teach me as punishment, then I gave him a couple hundred dollars. Last I heard he had a shop where he sold spare parts, and a warehouse" Jabez explained as he drove out of the parking lot.

"You're actually a good person, and not a total asshole?" Carol asked sarcastically.

"Haha, very funny. Sandwich, now" he demanded. "Don't even hide it, I saw it from the kitchen" He added, reaching into her bag.

"Hey!" Carol yelled as she struggled her sandwich with Jabez.

The Sedan grumbled a few times, barking as it requested to be returned to its state of inactivity. But still it, surged forward, towards the gates, and then away from the entire building, enroute to Carol's house, where she had just promised to make Jabez another sandwich in place of her cold one.

*

The news reports had soon started coming in. Harry had been killed in what police were deeming a drive-by gone wrong. Aria was hospitalized, as a bullet had gotten into her skull. She was under intensive care, and as such, was not accessible to anyone other than her doctors.

Director Colby had tried reaching out, but she did not have enough time, or resources to help as she always did. She had stated that she was late for a therapy session with her new doctor and as such could not talk much. All she had for Jabez was "stay hidden, I'll blow over. Hopefully".

Jabez knew he had to do just that, and no better place to do it than at Pietro's. The trio were working round the clock to ensure that none of them ends up dead on the news. Jin was a prolific hacker, and so was Pietro. Jabez, although his excesses were glaring, was an excellent detective and he knew a whole lot of things about basically everything. Together, they worked for about a week to find out who was ordering the hit on them. Carol helped as much as she could, but with her day job getting in the way of her committing hours to her new cause, she was almost always a consultant.

It was then that Jabez learnt about how Jin and Pietro had met each other.

After the death of his field agent at the Chinese embassy in Russia, Jin and the other members of his team had been extradited back to China where they were debriefed on their mission. Their outreach out in the USA, of which Jin championed, had successfully stolen the president's personal mobile device, as well as his fingerprints. Still, they found nothing. The US was not responsible for the cyber-attacks that had rocked Beijing a few weeks prior.

After their supposed successes in both Washington and Moscow had come to be dead ends, the team was sent home and released after they had been thoroughly debriefed and made to sign NDA. All was normal until they started dying in what seemed too random to be accidents, but these accidents seemed to happen to only Jin's team.

His second in command, a cyber expert codenamed "Panda" was soon killed in his own home.

"Electrocuted by a washing machine he had bought on his return from Moscow" Jin said, sighing.

The others either were in car accidents, or they were mugged and beaten to death. All deaths happened within a space of one month.

It was then that Jin began to notice shadows all over places he visited. It was as if he was being backed into a corner by what seemed to be foreign nationals.

"I knew I was a prized asset, and Chinese Intelligence could not come after me, so it must have been the Russians, but when I confronted one of these men that had followed me home on a rainy evening, I found that he was something else. In his pocket was a badge that just had his name and a watermark that looked like a fall asteroid" Jin explained.

It was then that Jin knew he had to disappear. He had soon sent his daughter to live with her grandmother and under a fake name of "Jerry Chu" he moved to the US with only one clue; coordinates he had found in the man's ID card.

"Those coordinates led me to Pietro. At first I thought he was some kind of leader for these killers, and I was ready to get my revenge for my team"

"Boy, did we fight. We even shot at each other" Pietro yelled from the kitchen. He was fixing himself breakfast.

"Yeah, remember when I asked if you were part of the Asteroid Gang" Jin asked, laughing. Pietro joined in the laughter.

"What was it that I said when you asked me?" Pietro asked as he held his stomach in pain from a laughter.

"What type of ice-cold bullshit is an Asteroid Gang?" They both echoed, and then they began rolling in laughter. Jabez just sat there, waiting for them to finish guffawing and get back to the story.

"It was then that I found out that I was also a target, and that I was also last on the hit list. Apparently, my team from Russia had died as well." Pietro started his own part of the story.

"Why do you say it like that? You didn't know them?"

"Nope. I was assigned to the White House under a fake name; Darrell, and they were sent to other parts. We were to report directly to our commander back in the Motherland. I don't know who they are, till this day. But I heard that an agent died in China, from food poisoning, I think. The only person I knew personally was a young agent that was sent to shadow Carol. Every morning, he would get on the same bus as she did, and report back. A simple job, until he got shot when he wandered into the wrong neighborhoods"

"Or he was kidnapped" Jabez said, sighing.

"Oh, he was kidnapped. Tortured, starved. I could look at the pictures, even If I wanted to. Soon after this, I was supposed to return to Russia, commander's orders. But I stayed back, and why? Because I was afraid. I've heard stories of unsuccessful agents and how they get treated. I was not going to take that risk" Pietro continued.

"Jesus" Jabez gasped.

"The extraction letters came again and again, but I ignored them. Then, our sleeper agent in China got killed"

"You got two in China?" Jabez asked.

"Yeah, he wasn't activated, and nobody knew about him. But I figured out the if he could get killed so gruesomely, that it had to the Russian Intelligence. I mean, they were the only people that knew of his existence. I went ghost, and I started going into the database through the backdoors they had thought us in training. I used the dark web and for days on end, I would read through lots of information concerning Russian Intelligence. It was then that I found a breach"

"A breach?" Jabez asked.

"Yeah, some other hacker. I thought that was how they had captured and executed the sleeper agent, so I dug deeper, till I decrypted the information that the hacker had let slip. I was now getting half of the information they were sending out and receiving. Then some coordinates came in, and they matched Jin's location. I thought he was their leader, or something. So, I booked a flight to China to find him, only to wake up for my flight and find him kicking my front door in"

Jin laughed in the background.

"Man, it was something. I mean that lamp used to have a floral design on a vase on top of it, now it's just a stand." Pietro said, pointing to a stand in the corner.

"Tell him about the frying pan" Jin laughed again.

"Oh, yeah yeah. A few days after our fight, we were going to make omelets, so we got pan off the wall, but it had a bullet home right in the middle of it" Pietro said as he pointed to the pan.

"We still made our omelets" Jin said, laughing as he took his seat again.

"I must say, Mr Glee, without your friend, we wouldn't have as many leads as we do right now"

"Gemini?"

"Yeah, he really helped us" Jin said as he walked back into the living room.

"How?"

"Your friend was a tech wizard. He designed the remainder of the tunnel I had programmed. He gave us more than the 40% my initial program was giving, and on top of that, the videos were no longer pixelated. In all honesty, he didn't want to involve you. He wanted to get it done and take the risks for himself. He only consulted with Carol for a while, but for some reason she stopped answering her emails. Then, we got news that he was dead, murdered by the same people he swore to stop"

"Real sad, we had plans for drinks after this was all over" Jin said.

"He said he knew a good place for Nigerian food, and he was going to take us as soon as we had stopped whoever was coming after us" Pietro concurred.

"What, he never offered that to me!" Jabez was shocked.

They both shrugged.

"We spent months freezing our asses off in Russia, we were brothers!" Jabez protested.

"Big whoop, I spent 20 years in Russia freezing my ass off, where's my medal?" Pietro said as she stood up from his seat.

"Rub it in, will ya?" Jabez yelled as Pietro walked into the kitchen. They were having canned soup for breakfast, and he was on his third serving.

It was then that a beep came in.

Jabez and Lin rushed to the computer that sat be for them. Pietro had heard it too, so he ran from the kitchen with his bowl in hand.

"What does it say?" He asked as he ran towards them.

"Request for debriefing... Secretary Boyd, make time to be Durban in a few days. The details will be communicated shortly"

"Secretary Boyd?" Jabez gasped as he spoke. The dodgy bastard must be up to no good!

"We need to go to Durban!" Pietro announced.

"Did you guys see that the details will be communicated shortly?" Jin asked.

"Yeah, yeah, we'll wait. Pack your bags people!" Jabez said as he hurried upstairs.

I'll text Carol about fake IDs. I heard you can make them in the White House." Pietro said.

*

Soon, the details came in and they were ready to leave. The prompt also included a hotel reservation and a pickup location.

By early morning the next day, Carol was knocking in the door, with fake IDs in hand. Jabez was the one to receive them, accompanied by a key to a US safehouse that held several weapons they might need if the occasion arises.

"Thank you Carol!" He said as he walked back in.

Everyone was in a busy mood. Pietro was darting up the staircase to help Jin carry a bag that had gotten stuck in the doorway. Jabez had packed his bags and was ready to go. They were to take the old Sedan he had found in the parking lot of the White House.

"No one has come of it yet?" Carol asked him.

"Surprisingly, yes. Imagine if we had followed your lead and carried that Aston Martin that was sitting pretty in the corner" Jabez said. sighing.

"You wanted a fancy car, not me!" Carol protested.

"Not from what I remember" Jabez teased.

"You know what? Forget it" Carol said as she tossed his new identity at him.

"Stiles McCoy? Really?" Jabez sighed.

"Yep, you said you wanted that name, remember?"

"I didn't- nice one, Carol" He replied. She had given him a taste of his own medicine.

Carol laughed, but she stopped to greet Jin who was now coming down the stairs.

"Hey Jerry!" She greeted.

"Hi, Carol. Good morning".

"You're still going with Jerry Chu, aren't you?"

"Yep, old trusty Jerry Chu" he said, tossing his passport into his back pocket.

"All set?" It was Pietro and was standing atop the stairs.

"Yep" they all echoed.

Soon they had all filed out of the house and were stuffing the trunk of the Sedan with their bags. Then, they said their final goodbyes and left for the airport.

"You know, I've seen you with more men in the past couple of months that your entire life, and I must say, I'm proud of you"

It was Layton, and he had come out to watch them leave. He was clutching a beverage, and he spilled almost all of it as he turned to run into the house, seeing that Carol was chasing him.

*

"...Yep, we're here. In a cab actually"

They agents had landed safely in Durban and were now enroute the safehouse in a taxi. Jabez had thought it wise to call Carol on the burner phone they had gotten upon arrival.

"Yeah? Let me say hi to the others" Carol was at, so ah couldn't talk.

"Carol wants to say hi" Jabez said as he passed the phone over to the others.

"Hi guys" Carol whispered. She was not in the upper levels again, and her new coworkers seemed white nosy.

"Hey Carol" they echoed.

"See? They're safe" Jabez said.

"Alright, I have to go. We'll catch up later!" She said, ending the call.

The car was now pulling up on the safehouse. It was a small building, bordered on the right by a medicine store, and on the left by a restaurant. It was still the early afternoon when they landed, and although they were tired, they all decided to try out the restaurant as they waited for another notification from the laptop they used to track Secretary Boyd.

His itinerary showed that he was in town, but he was at the other side of town, probably enjoying a nice warm bath after flying first class into Durban.

After they had settled in, they decided to have a nap. With one person taking a shift to watch the laptop for any more information. However, this was not to be the case, as all three men promptly fell asleep a while after that.

The next time anyone in the room stirred was the next morning. It was Jin that woke up. He quickly woke the others up, and they all checked the laptop, blaming each other for their deep sleep.

"It was a pleasure having such a high-ranking member of the Cabinet of the United States here, we are glad that... Therefore-. At your convenience, we would love to have you- hidden factory in Wuhan. Here are-. Also, we are of the strong belief that you were followed into Durban, this is being taken care..."

"Taken care of?" Jabez asked as he turned to the others.

"Get down!" Jin yelled. Then came the shots, loud and determined. "Wuhan is deep in China, what do they want there?" He asked amidst the gunfire.

"I don't know! We should be asking you!" Pietro yelled back.

"50 Cal, real classy" Jabez commented as they made their way towards their own weapon stash.

"Here!" Pietro yelled, handing Jabez two Saw Map 22s".

"We all know that they're coming up the stairs right?" Jin said as he reached for an M4 Carbine, right after pocketing a Glock 19 he found on the shelf.

"We're ready for them, correct!" Pietro hollered. He was holding an M16 AA.

Soon, the door was breached and in came about half a dozen men with assault rifles.

"Clear!" Came a voice, followed by static on the radio.

In the dust that followed their breach, they did not seem to have notice the three agents leave, but not before Pietro had thrown a grenade to the floor of the safehouse.

All three men hurried downstairs, clutching their rifles.

A shot rang past the agents, hitting the fuel tank of a nearby car and causing it to explode.

"On the roof!" Jabez called out as they till cover behind a car. The car windows soon come crashing to the floor as the sniper was relentless.

"Quick, grab that mirror!" Pietro instructed, beckoning to Jin.

"1 shot left" Pietro said, turning to Jabez. The trio share a mischievous smile, followed by a countdown

Jin checked the mirror he was holding, and from the angle, he could see the sniper struggle to reload.

"Now!" He yelled.

At his signal, Pietro and Jabez turn to the sniper and open fire on the top of the building, injuring the sniper who retreats.

Sensing that he would get away, they rush to the building, but they are soon sent back into hiding, but this time they were inside the medicine store. The owner had left it open and fled.

"Reinforcements!" Jabez yelled.

In front of them and charging were about a dozen armed men, all surrounding them and opening fire.

"Shit! Shit!" Someone yelled as they ran across and towards safety, but they get caught in the crossfire.

"Now we've got civilians dead?" Jin asked.

"Where?" Jabez asked. He could not raise his head as they all had their weapons on them.

"Hey, get to shooting. He's dead already!" Pietro urged. The assailants were still shooting nonstop, and they had to fight back.

"Wait, what if we don't?" Jin suddenly asked.

"What?" They both asked.

"Cover me!" He requested as he crawled to the back of the store. Jin had seen what looked like an exit behind the white curtain and he wanted to check it out. It turns out that he was right. There was an exit in the back, and it led to the end of the street where they could not be found out by the assailant.

Bringing good news, he crawled back to his counterparts and told them of his plan.

"Who is gonna cover for us to escape?" Jabez asked.

"How about these bad boys?" Pietro asked, brandishing two more grenades.

"Right! Let's go then!"

"Cover fire!" Pietro requested. Jabez and Jin emptied their barrels, while Pietro threw the grenades to the street. As they crawled to safety, they could hear the assailant tell each other to fall back.

The escape route was a narrow road that could only fit one at a time. It led to a small ledge that they had to climb to get to the other side of the street. As they made their way, they saw the sniper seated on the floor, nursing an injury to his hand. Their shots had hit him and taken out a finger and from their vantage position, they could see that he was in a lot of pain.

Jabez drew out a pistol from his back to end him, but Pietro stopped him.

"What if the others hear you?" He said as he pressed his hand firmly atop the barrel of Jabez's gun.

"Does it matter? We could just do it quick. He can't even hear us!"

"But they can, alright!" Pietro insisted. We need to go, they're probably in the pharmacy by now! Get moving boys!"

"Fine!"

"We've all got our passports right?" Jin asked.

"We're leaving?" Jabez asked.

"Do you want to stay, you're absolutely free if you want!" Pietro replied.

"I've got my passport; how do we dispose of these guns?" Jin asked.

The trio was now descending the heights they had climbed. The street was underneath them, but they were now atop an uncompleted storey building.

"There are stairs here somewhere, come on" Pietro urged as he searched the floor for staircases.

"Here!" Jabez yelled. He had found a way down. I was just planks and scaffolding, but it was worth something.

The streets were devoid of cars and people, all thanks to the attacks they had just survived. Everyone had their doors shut, so it was almost impossible to ask for directions. The trio stayed to the side of the road. They knew that the assailants would be looking for them to "take care of them" and they had to be careful. Therefore, every incoming car was a target until they were proven otherwise.

Soon, a yellow cab came passing by. The driver was already reversing when they stopped it and begged him to take them to the airport.

"A thousand rand" the driver announced.

The men looked at themselves, asking if they had any cash. Sighing, Jabez pulled out fifty dollars and handed it to the man.

"It is worth more than a thousand rand, trust me" he assured the man. With a questioning look written across his face, the driver sped off in the direction of the airport.

*

As they alighted from the cab, Jabez's burner rang. It was Carol. She sounded calm, so that means that she had not heard anything about what had happened.

"Hey guys, what's up? Are you going to the site already?"

"No, not exactly" was Jabez's reply.

"I don't understand, you were supposed to be there an hour ago"

"Yeah, they knew we were coming, we got ambushed."

"What?"

"Yeah, long story. We're at the Durban airport right now, we'll be in Johannesburg in a few hours, then it's Washington from there." It was Jin that spoke.

"What the hell happened?" Carol had begun to worry.

"Well, the person we were tailing had people that were tailing us. We obviously cannot go back to Pietro's, or Washington, if we're being honest. We got jumped by guys with military grade weapons". Jabez spoke again.

"Oh, okay. Just text me the details"

"I think we'll need more than details. We'll need your skills, the drive, and a new computer, probably something that can withstand a grenade? Do you have any of those?" Pietro spoke.

"No. I have seen any of those I'm afraid. Look, I'm rummage through office supplies and see what I can find" Carol said.

"Good. And you'll need some stuff from my house. I'll mail a list to you, but you'll have to go through the backdoor, okay?" Pietro instructed.

"Alright, be safe guys. See you in a bit" Carol said.

"Yeah yeah, we survived. We don't need pity, we're invincible" Jabez blurted, but she had needed the call.

"Ditch the guns, now" Pietro instructed.

In a single file, they all went into the men's bathroom where they dismantled the gun. In separate stalls, they threw the dismantled guns into the toilet bowls and flushed it down the drain.

"Sorry Janitor" Jabez muttered as they left the toilet. His toilet had begun to overflow with water.

The attendant at the desk was kind, but there no flights available to Johannesburg till the next morning.

"I'm sorry Sirs, but the first flights out of Durban is slated for 7 Am tomorrow" She had said with a smile. "If you want to buy a ticket now, I could fit you in the economy class" she added.

The trio had booked seats, with Jabez paying for them out of his pockets.

"The city's not safe, you know?" Pietro commented as they tried to leave the airport.

"That is true, we already flushed our protection down the toilet" Jin added.

"Gee, I wonder who would tell us to do that" Jabez said, staring Pietro blankly in the face.

Will all this in mind Jin, Pietro and Jabez had to sleep in the airport that night. They found a spot in the waiting area, but the three men could not find it easy to sleep. Instead, they stayed awake, trading spy stories and bonding.

Jin was the first to start. He had worked to Chinese intelligence since he turned eighteen, and he had been working there for about 14 years.

"How many bullets have you taken?" Jabez asked.

"Oh, you're on!" Jin replied as he stood up. With his shirt up, he showed Pietro and Jabez a series of scars on his chest.

"Small rifle, close range. This was '07, I think" he said as he touched a scar on his stomach.

"That's nothing, check this out" Pietro was on his feet as well, but he was baring his back. "3 to the lower back, barely grazed my kidneys. I had infiltrated an Anti-Putin cell and my immediate superior was mad at me because I was going to take over and run his cell, so he shot me in the back." Pietro said, laughing.

"I'll do you one better" Jabez finally spoke up, he too was on his feet. "Brazil, right in the chest." He said, baring his chest. "I had just had a drug kingpin arrested, so I decided to go on a little joyride with his wife. Apparently the police were too corrupt to even let him think about his crimes for a bit before releasing him. Okay, so here's the story. I'm doing something called a banana split with his wife- mind you I'm coked out of my own mind right? - and he shoots me, right in the chest, last thing I remember was his smug face when he shot me. He sure wasn't making that face when I saw that he had been extradited to the US and jailed for 30 years, I think" Jabez said.

"How are you not dead?" Pietro asked.

"Cocaine, bro. It's Ironic because it saved my life. Also, I might have came as he shot me, because Rosinda has a white baby that looks just like me" He added, laughing.

They all laughed. In the distance, there seemed to be movement, so they quieted down and waited to hear what it was about. Pietro had already removed his shoes in preparation for sneak attacks.

But it was all for nothing. The noise had come from the janitor. He was grumbling over the overflown toilet and cursing whatever travelled had done it. Jabez tried to laugh, but he held himself.

"How come your toilet got clogged?" The other asked.

"I don't know, maybe a bullet went in the wrong way? I'm unlucky like that" Jabez said, shrugging.

"About bullets going in the wrong way, who wants to see a ricochet scar I have on my left leg" Pietro announced.

"What's the story there?" Jin asked.

"Well, I was in a shootout with bank robbers, you know the usual thing where we wait till they run out of bullets then we close in? Yeah, some asshole shot randomly, and it deflected and somehow found its way to the back of my left leg, right where I was crouching" Pietro explained as he unbuckled his lap to reveal another bullet scar.

"Damn, and I thought I was unlucky" Jabez yawned as he spoke. He looked up at the clock.

"9:56" Jin said. He was yawning as well.

"Who is taking first watch?" Pietro asked.

"I won't" Jabez said, he was already lying down on one of the benches with his arms folded and his face to the backrest.

"I'll do it then" Pietro said, sighing.

"I don't feel sleepy, I'll stay awake as well. I honestly wonder how you can sleep with all that has happened today.

"Simple; I've seen worse, and I can" Jabez mumbled from his resting place.

"What did he say?" Pietro asked, he was facing Jin.

"He says he has seen worse, and that he can" Jin responded.

"Typical American" Pietro answered, shaking his head.

"Heavens no. If the typical American was anything like Mr Glee, we would be fighting a world war right now" Jin replied. They both laughed.

Jabez was now fast asleep, but Jin and Pietro stayed awake and gossiped.

"His name cannot possibly be Jabez Glee, it's way too made up to be his actual name. What do you think his real name is?" Jin asked Pietro. It was almost midnight and everywhere was dark, and quiet.

"I'm thinking Todd. Todd Lebowski" Pietro replied. They both snickered.

"He doesn't look like a Todd, honestly" Jin replied. "Isn't Lebowski a Jewish name? Is he Jewish?"

"I don't know, the only other person I ever saw with a name like Jabez was my friend from back home. Jabez Mitrovic, good kid. I wonder where he ended up"

"Checks out, honestly" Jin replied, shrugging. "What about Glee?"

"Glee? Is that not the old TV show? The one with the blondes and the parties?"

"Yeah yeah! You think he got it from there?"

"I don't know, but it makes sense. Even more sense than Jabez Glee. Whoever okayed that as a spy name needs to be sacked".

"Maybe he was going for cool name, like James Bond?"

"Please, nothing can be as cool as James Bond"

"It's my first and last name, thank you very much" Jabez finally spoke. He had been awake the entire time. "It's not Jewish, my parents were just really religious. I changed it as soon as I could, but as you can see, it stuck. Now that that's out of the way, can we discuss Wuhan?"

"What do you know, Jin?" Pietro asked.

"Not much honestly, I was supposed to visit there with my mother a while ago, but she wasn't up for it. Funny, isn't it? She spends her entire life daydreaming about seeing the sights in China, but once she can afford it, she changes date after date till she says she's not going till her granddaughter turns ten."

"Great, our one Chinese guy knows nothing about China" Jabez said, rolling his eyes.

"Hey, that's racist!" Jin protested.

"How exactly is it racist?" Jabez retorted.

"Because I'm Chinese doesn't mean I have to know everything about China! You don't see me asking you about Atlanta"

"Great strip clubs, bit cocky strippers" Jabez replied almost immediately.

"Wyoming?"

"Nice place, I didn't like the weather that much."

"Maine?"

"Jesus Christ, don't have sex in this town. If you don't, don't do it with a Sheila, gave me three STDs at once"

"Ohio?"

"Ah, home of Martha with the matter!"

"Martha with the matter?"

"Yeah, Martha's her name and her boobs were like matter; they occupied so much space, I almost felt like being Christian so that I can thank god for them!"

"Wait, so you've done it in every city?"

"God no! What am I, a sexy crazy monkey"

"Oh, I-"

"Twice in every state, once in Argentina, once in Brazil." Jabez replied. "How about you guys?"

"12 times, tops" Pietro confessed.

"I've only had sex with one woman, and she was my wife. Well, till she left me for her boss" Jin said

"Ah, so sorry man. We'll get you some when we get back to America."

"If we get back to America" Jin replied.

"Now that pessimism better not see daybreak tomorrow, you hear?" Jabez said, shoving Jin.

"We need a laptop, don't we?" Pietro asked.

"Yeah, and we need to build your tunnel again, don't we?" Jin asked.

"Yeah, but it'll be easier this time. The schematics are in the drives I have you and Carol. Honestly, she just need a steady Internet connection and it'll run by itself" Pietro said, shrugging.

"Now that's what I'm talking about!" Jabez hollered. "See, that's the type of spirit we need here, not yours! This is the attitude that gets you some!" He was talking to Jin.

"Yeah, yeah, blow me!" Jin was sulking.

"I won't, but I know a few ladies on Long Island that'll do it for free!" Jabez was laughing.

"I'm going to bed; you both have to keep watch now" Jin said as he closed his eyes and lay on the bench.

"Me too, Mr Glee you're on guard duty till dawn" Pietro said, laying on the bench he was sitting on.

"Aw, come on guys!" Jabez complained, but they were all quiet.

He grumbled to a while, till Pietro let out a laugh. "Typical American" he said.

"Blow me!" Jabez responded.

"Oh, I won't, but I know some ladies in Moscow that will do it for free" Pietro replied, causing Jin to laugh till he fell off his bench.

30 minutes had gone since they last checked the clocks. Jabez was still sleepy, but he knew that within his tough, carefree exterior, he was just as scared for his life as the others. This fear kept him awake, till it didn't.

It was morning before he felt a tap on his shoulder.

"Come on Mr Glee, the flight is leaving soon.".

It was Jin, and he was holding up his passport.

CHAPTER TWENTY-EIGHT

In the glamorous life of every superstar, no matter what field you excel in, be it making catchy pop songs, or hired killing, there is always a downside. For some, it's the drugs or the alcohol, but for Skunk, it was being called 'Venedickt Yuriy' and having to carry it in a badge when he worked as a cleaner on the ground floor of The Kremlin.

"Aren't you a little too cute to be mopping floors?" His new boss, Petrova, a woman who although she was past her forties, her addiction to cigarettes, and in her words, "the juicy types", did not seem to be satiated.

"We got the cards we get, Ms Petrova" would be his reply, just as Director Colby had instructed.

Although he had been working there less than a week, Skunk was sure he had been assaulted by his boss more times than he could count. She could pretend to slide on the wet floor just to make him help her up, all the while smiling at him, her browned, decaying teeth in full view. Skunk was sure she looked better with a frown.

"She's the whole package. Like bad luck in a bag! And there is nobody I can report to because she's the final authority!"

"Calm down, Agent" Director Colby had said.

"How can I calm down? Even if I had someone to, would they take my word over hers?" He ranted.

Normally, he enjoyed the attention from the ladies, but not this one! Her makeup seemed to get worse by the day, and her clothes always smelt of cigarettes and wetness, like they had not been properly dried.

"...And yet she's always in my face!" Skunk complained.

"It will all pass, trust me she will be out of your hair before you can even know it" Director Colby said. She knew that the best she could do was to try to encourage her agents.

"She smacked me, Director! I was mopping a small hallway in the east wing, and she smacked me across the butt cheeks, then she muttered something in Russian, I've never heard it before, then she gave me the finger and walked down the hall"

"Look, Skunk. I apologize that you have to go through all these, but remember your training, remember that you are there for a purpose, and that she is but a fleeting memory that will pass. All we need is a few days to work over some details that would be sent to each of you" Director Colby said. For the first time in a while, work was starting to feel like work, and she was not having any fun as she usually did.

"Old age. You're a grown woman, Rachel" She muttered.

"What was that Director Colby?"

"Nothing, Nothing. I just recalled the codes to specific protocols." She had lied, but she feared that Skunk was already aware of her lie.

"Oh, good, good. I wish I had heard it as well." He joked.

"I take it that you see your fellow Agent on your way into work?"

"Jabez? I don't think so. I take a back entrance when I get into my workstation, but I think I saw him last night when I was mopping a section of the front yard. He was really going at it with someone on the phone. You should check that man, Director." Skunk said. His voice sounded concerned, but at the same time there seemed to be a tincture of derision towards Jabez"

"I am pleased to inform you that your fellow agent is sane. He was on the phone with me, and that rant was about how shitty his job was. I think we both know someone who feels the same way. How about I check both of them, then?" Director Colby asked. Jackpot. She had gotten him.

"It was a joke ma'am, but really, being security isn't that bad to start with" Skunk explained himself. She had him cornered and the best way to wring himself from her clutches was to apologize.

"He wanted a job indoors, and he said it gets really cold outside. Do you want to switch? I could make that happen right away." She asked.

"Nah, I'm good, Thank you very much. Yesterday a bus sped past me, and my shoes froze. Literally."

"It is good to know that you are hale and hearty, agent."

"And you too ma'am"

"Yes, have a good day." She said in reply. "Resist any urges to retaliate, please" She admonished. He had a history of violence, one that would ruin their mission

"Ma'am, after these days, I don't think I'll be able to have any urges" Skunk replied.

"Also, later today you all will get a couple of files that contain information on several upcoming events"

"Like the open day excursion? I'm in charge of clean up on the same floor as the President's office." Skunk said, rather nonchalant too.

"Excellent!" Director Colby felt herself spring up from her desk as she heard the news. "We'll use that to our advantage. Stay put soldier, I have calls to make"

"Wait, Director! I..." Skunk tried to speak, but she had ended the call.

"I don't believe you, Jabez. I'm sorry, but I don't, Secretary Boyd may be a whole lot of things including stupid, but he's not a traitor. The guy has a Ferrari painted with the flag colors for god's sake!."

"Director Colby, you have to trust me on this- yes I was sober- hold on! Hold on! Shit! She hung up!" Jabez yelled at the mild-mannered cab driver.

The trio had landed in Baltimore, Maryland despite the plans to end their journey in Washington. Caroline had disagreed with them, and honestly they had no choice. Secretary Boyd had the President in the palm of his hands.

"Or in a diabolical handshake" Jin shrugged. Pietro was yawning. 17 hours of flying does take a toll. He took a look at his watch.

"Its past 12, that means we've wasted an entire day doing absolutely nothing" he complained.

"Any word from Carol about the laptops?" Jin asked.

"Nah, not yet. Goddamn it!" Jabez cursed.

"Hey, don't curse so loudly, some of us don't need the noise" Pietro protested.

"We're gonna stay in a hotel right?" Jabez asked.

"For how long though?" Jin was not sure how much money they had left between them.

"A couple nights, tops. Carol will show up, she always does"

"If we want to stay for a couple of nights, we'll need a motel. The more run down, the better"

"May I make a suggestion?" It was the cab driver that spoke.

"Okay, you got any good recommendations" Jabez replied.

"How about a safehouse?" He asked.

"A what-now?"

"A safehouse. How about I take you guys to a safehouse?" The cab driver was shrugging as he spoke.

"What do you know about safehouses?" Pietro groaned from his half-sleep.

"Well, I haven't used one yet, but Rachel Colby says you guys need one"

"Okay, now that is bullshit! Alright? Rachel Colby is somewhere in some fancy spa getting her mind cleansed or some shit like that" Jabez replied. His mind had begun to race. What if the driver was stalling as a way to get him and the others into more trouble? Did Secretary Boyd know of their return?

"That is in fact correct, but you see, you might be using a burner and your location might be still intact, but hers isn't. Madam Colby is sure that her calls have been tapped. That is where I come in, as foot solider, if you will" The cab driver was smiling.

"A what now?" Jin asked as he leaned forwards to look into his face.

"We're a small faction in the CIA that is still loyal to the former director. She may look like she doesn't have the power she used to have, but that is all part of the plan. Carol knew about this, but she couldn't tell you guys. The safehouse is just behind his building, round the block. It's a typical family house, but the windows are bullet-proof, you know? Just in case" The cab had begun to slow down, and soon they were parked.

"Why should we trust you?" Jin asked.

"Because you have no other choice. Here's a key and thank you for not trying to strangle me with your jacket there" The cab driver said as he tossed a key at Jabez. "If there are any safes or locks, the combination is written somewhere directly opposite where the lock is".

"Opposite the safe? What does that mean?"

"I don't know either" Pietro said. He was already outside the cab. His back was turned to the rest as he spoke.

"Neither do I alright? I'm just a messenger" the cab driver said.

"But how exactly do we trust you?" Jin was not convinced.

"Here" The cab driver sighed as he bent over to open the glove box. Jin immediately tightened his fists.

"Hey, come on man. You think I'd want to fight someone at 1 in the morning?" The cab driver chuckled as he got back to his chair. He had seen Jin's clenched fists and was clearly amused. "Here you go" he said again, handing them a paper bag.

Jabez reached forwards to grab it, but the weight both shocked and surprised him. "Nice!" He yelled as he opened it.

"What is that?" Pietro was peeking back into the cab now.

"Christmas" Jabez replied, pulling out a firearm from the bag. He smiled, and so did Pietro. Jin, however, looked at both men and shook his head, right before making his way out of the cab.

The outside air was chilling, and he had begun to grit his teeth.

"How the hell did Pietro stand out here with only a T-shirt on?" Jin asked as he strolled down the street. If his instincts were right, someone would try to attack him from behind one of the bushes.

"Well, that'll be as much fun as anything else right now" he smirked as he made his way to the end of the small street. A signpost at a small intersection read "Holloway Avenue" in big red prints accompanied by other signs, including one for the local boy scouts.

"Hey Jin! Where are you going to? The house is just past here!" Jabez was yelling at him.

"Coming!" Jin replied, cursing under his breath. Before he could catch up, the taxi driver had sped past him, waving as he went. He was also smiling, but Jin did not see it fit to return the favour. However, as he caught up to the others, he had begun to feel guilty.

"...Nice guy, that guy" Jabez was chatting loudly.

"Hey Jin, are you good?" It was Pietro and his hand was on his shoulder.

"Yeah, yeah."

"Say whatever you want dude, we're like family here" Jabez replied excitedly. For someone who HD just come off one of the worst flights of his life, he seemed oddly excited.

He had been given a seat that was not only far away from both Jin and Pietro's position by the windows, but he was also made to seat next to a woman whose baby made it a point of duty to haunt him.

"...I mean, the little fucker vomited on me! Why do you think I had found a store as soon as we landed?" Jabez announced.

"I don't know, maybe you smelled like bad breath?" Pietro joked. Jin only smiled a little, his mind was clouded by other thoughts

"Ha-ha, very clever there Vodka man" Jabez retorted, waving his hand in indignation.

"Hey! That's racist!" Pietro cried. They were now close to the house.

"Oh, come on! I can't be racist, not to you. For all I know we could have had the same ancestors" Jabez said.

"You're Jewish, aren't you?"

"Yeah, so. I wanna make this clear, that I'm Jewish by tribe, not by religion."

"What difference does it make?"

"A lot, kinda like your ignorance"

"The racist man gives a clap back, clever"

"I'm not racist! Ask Jin.! Hey Jin, have I ever said anything racist to you before?"

"Jin's not here with us right now"

"I am" Jin finally spoke.

"Oh-" Jabez, for the first time in a while, had nothing to say.

"You guys may or may not be racist, but you're too loud. We have neighbors, you know?"

"So?"

"So, we need to keep a low profile. There are lives at stake here, can't you guys see that?"

"We can, that's why we're going into this house not knowing what's on the other side, so chill Jin" Jabez replied.

They trio was not in front of the house now. Like every building on the street, it was a one-storey apartment with white paint that covered the entire exterior. In the darkness that was only illuminated by streetlights, it was still possible to see the green highlights on the columns that supported each end of the building, as well as the railing that led up the small flight of stairs to get to the door, which, like every other one on the street looked like it was hand-carved. This one, however was different, as it had a metal door with a 4-pin lock standing between them and it.

"What's the password? Did he tell you what it was?" Jabez asked.

"He didn't have to. He said it would be opposite the locks" Jin replied. He was still at the foot of the stairs.

"That'll mean the pin is somewhere out there? Fuck!" Jabez cursed. It was still dark, and although the streetlights had illuminated the streets, there still was so much they couldn't see.

"Maybe we don't have to see anything" Jin suggested.

"What?" The others asked.

"What's the house number on this house?" Jin asked.

"2248 Greens?" Jabez replied. He had seen the number that was plastered on the side of house on his way up the stairs.

"So that'll mean that the house opposite would be?" Jin asked, but there was no reply.

The silence persisted as both men thought long and hard on his question.

"Ah, fuck it. I'll be right back" he said as he wandered into the street, cursing as he went. He had crossed the road and was peering intently at the house on the opposite side of the street.

Soon he was back.

"3384 Greens" he said as he walked up the stairs. "That's the address of the house at the other side" he said as he tapped away on the lock. Then, he stepped back.

There was a light buzz, then the otherwise dark lock gleamed a dim green around the number pad.

"Viola, assholes" Jin said as he turned the lock. The door opened and Jin walked in first. Halfway in, the others heard him gasp.

"What was that?" Jabez asked. He was checking out the backyard with Pietro.

"Jin yelled. Jin doesn't yell" Pietro asked.

"He doesn't" Jabez replied. They both rushed to the door, and after checking the environs, ran into the house where they met an awed Jin.

"Damn" Jabez finally spoke. The trio had been standing in the small hallway for a while.

"Damn indeed" Jin replied, his eyes still fixated on what they had seen. Pietro, however, was on the other side of the hallway.

"Guys, we have a full fridge!" He announced. The hurried footsteps followed almost immediately. There was bread, cake, all sorts of meats and tiny snacks filled their hungry mouths and made them moan in delight.

"This is so much better than airport peanuts" Jabez moaned, his mouth filled with chocolate cake.

"We have steak, people!" Pietro announced again.

Jin was no longer in the kitchen. He had already grabbed himself a handful of the small cakes and was in the living room. The door was still open, so he locked it, but not before memorizing the address of the house opposite there. It seemed to be a two-way and getting locked in their small paradise was not in his plans.

"Now for the main attraction" he said as he eased into the couch right in front of the many covered computer screens. The plastic covering over the couch made him uneasy and although he slid on and off his sitting position, he was intent on keeping it on.

After all the covers were off, Jin stood back to admire the computers that were in front of him. They were all state-of-the-art models of popular brands and after a little scrutiny, they seemed to be connected to the laptop that sat on the table in front of him.

"We shall" he said as he booted the laptop. As the whirring started, Jin held his breath. It had to work, all of it. It was the only way they could get on the Internet and tunnel back into the servers of his unknown evil that was still actively haunting them.

Jin sighed as his mind raced back to the message they had gotten, about Wuhan. If it was going to be under attack, was there any proof that the attacks would stop there? Will they extend to the rest of the world? Would they try to attack his family? His daughter?

"Hey, what's up?" came a voice. It was Pietro. Jin looks up at him, and he saw that he was alone.

"The American is making himself some bacon, how typical" Pietro said as he settled down. He had a cupcake in his hand, but it was already half eaten.

"Yeah, typical" Jin replied. He quickly returned his gaze to the screens in front of him. More screens were now displaying several messages, and the whir was louder.

"Speaking of typical, you're always moody, my friend, but this one, it bothers me" Pietro said.

"I'm peachy, Pietro" Jin replied as he forced a smile onto his face.

"A peachy person would not say peachy" Pietro was adamant, and although Jin could not stand his nosiness, he was right. Jin was worried for his family.

"Look, I just miss my daughter is all, nothing more." Jin finally spoke.

"I thought so. But don't let it weigh you down, my friend, alright?" Pietro admonished. He was already on his feet. "Time to explore, not so?" He said as he walked towards the stairs.

Jin was more focused on the computers in front of him than everything else, and to him, saving his family mattered the most to him.

"Hey, Jin! How about we do all of that in the morning?" Pietro asked. He had not yet gone up the stairs. In all honesty, he knew how Jin felt, and how he would feel if anything happened to his family. But a restless mind is not ideal, and he needed to rest, increasingly so because of the tumultuous flight they had just endured.

"You know what? We'll get to this in the morning, won't we?" Jin said. He knew he had to rest, especially with the way his back ached when he tried to move on the couch.

Soon, they were both upstairs and choosing rooms. Jin went with the smaller bedroom, a small room that was fit for a growing teenager. Pietro went for the room opposite that Jin's. The two rooms were almost identical in terms of design, size, and bedding. Unlike the main bedroom, where Jabez was going to stay.

"Let him have it, we do not want the American to sulk do we?" Pietro joked as he surveyed the big bedroom. There was still another room left, but they kept it locked, seeing that they had not use for it.

As Pietro and Jin made ready to go to sleep, they could hear Jabez curse as a frying pan fell to the floor, but they paid no attention to it. They had not slept in almost a day and their beds felt cozier than any bed could feel.

*

It was late in the afternoon that Jabez finally woke up. As he staggered down the stairs, he could hear nothing but indistinct whispers and the whirring of several fans.

As he made his way down the last of the stairs, he was faced with a curious Jin, and Pietro who sat on a stool beside him. They seemed fulfilled with their work and conversations. Pietro was tossing a half empty can from palm to palm, stopping only as he saw Jabez.

"Good afternoon American, you finally join us" he said.

"Too loud, need coffee" Jabez said as he wandered towards the kitchen.

"The drives came in today" Jin announced. The silence was awkward, and it had depleted his concentration.

Jabez rushed into the living room. "Carol was here?" He asked.

"No, a message came over the telephone around seven in the morning. It said that we should go for a run and meet the neighbors" Pietro said.

"Meet the neighbors, what does that mean?" Jabez asked. He was now clutching a cup to coffee.

"Some lady gave us a cake soon after we came back exhausted, she said she lived down the street" Jin replied.

"But she doesn't" Pietro added.

"Wait, what?" Jabez was still dazed. He was still yawning.

"Yeah, she's an agent, like taxi driver guy. Apparently Carol is being watched, so the plan was to stick the flash on her co-worker, a Kevin dude, till she was out of plain sight, then some agents put the drive in a cake and had this lady deliver it." Jin explained.

"Seems way too elaborate, honestly" Jabez replied.

"I said the same thing!" Pietro replied, waving his hands in vindication.

"Done!" Jin replied. The computer before him was beeping. He and Pietro then peered attentively at the screen.

Jabez could not be more unbothered. His head was now feeling the pangs of hours of flight travel and homicidal henchmen sent to end them. His head was ringing with every step he took and keep his face to the ground to stead himself felt like torture. Yet still, he took another sip of his coffee, praying it would go away, at least till he found himself some painkillers.

"Or noise cancelling headphones!" he yelled at his counterparts in the living room. They were chatting excitedly about something, and Jabez thought it would be right to go check out what it was.

"We found it!" Pietro announced as he walked into the room.

"Found what?" Jabez asked as he walked over to peer at the screen. The other screens were all flashing, and he could not handle lights at the moment, so his focus was trained to the laptop Jin and Pietro proudly brandished.

"We found the location of what seems to be a factory of some sort, we don't know yet" Jin replied excitedly.

"Factory?" Jabez asked.

A bot was decoding a series of anagrams that spelled out coordinates for a location.

"30.59..." He muttered. "Alright, we have out location, any news about this Boyd Character?" He asked after another sip of his coffee. His head was no longer as heavy as it was.

"Nothing much, just an invitation to *witness the cleansing*, whatever that means" Jin said.

"Cleansing?" Jabez asked. More numbers were not coming up on the screen.

"30.5928° N, 114.3052° E" read the coordinates.

"Wait, isn't that the coordinates for the entire city?" Pietro asked.

"It is. Guys, cleansing? Doesn't that ring a bell?" Jabez asked.

"No" both men said.

"Those aren't the coordinates for a meeting point, they're the coordinates for where the cleansing will take place!" Jabez hollered.

"So where will the meeting take place?" Pietro asked.

"Jin, are there any old factories in the Wuhan area? Preferably one that has an underground system? One that was renovated in the past year, or so?"

"I don't know Wuhan that well, didn't I tell you guys?"

"Do you have anyone you can call? We do have a secure system here, don't we?" Pietro asked.

"An old cop friend of mine, he lives in the city. He's deputy chief of police for the city, I think. I'll call him." Jin said as he turned to the computer to set up the call.

"Pietro? Any Asian connects? Any connects in the black market?"

"One. My cousin, Olav. Black Sheep of the entire extended family" Pietro said, spitting out of the corner of his mouth.

"You're going to have to slurp that up, because we need him now!" Jabez yelled.

"I'll try to read my friends in that area as well, especially some dude named Yedder. Chill guy" Jabez commented as he fled up the stairs to find a phone.

"Yedder? That's Olav's cousin!" Pietro yelled after him. "Small world, huh?" Pietro said as he turned to Jin, who was not paying attention.

He had successfully reached his friend, Inspector Barry's office and he was on hold.

"Inspector Chu, I'm listening" came his friend's voice.

"Barry, it's me!" Jin whispered.

"Jin? Is that you?"

"Yes it's me! Old friend, see I don't have much time, but I have a few questions to ask you"

"I don't know, Jin. Some men came in the other day with questions about you, they looked like secret service, but not like you. They didn't have that smell, you know?"

"Secret service? No, they're not secret service. They're traitors to the People's Republic! Listen, I have a question, okay?"

"Ask anything old friend"

"Did any papers for any sort of massive renovations on the old factories come through your office, perhaps?"

"Renovations? None, I'm afraid, only a rather strange case came through my desks a few months ago"

"What case?"

"Some worker got killed by a rare disease and his employees covered it up. His family made the report as they demanded son form of aid. They got paid, but in what looked like a robbery, they lost everything, including their lives. The armed robbers were never caught, and my boss told me to close the care a few days ago, just hours after the secret service men came by"

"What factory was it? Jin asked.

"The old coal mines that closed down because they polluted the water a couple decades ago. The one with the smiley white man"

"Sir Kelly's?"

"Exactly!"

"Thank you old friend. I'll never forget what you've done for me today!"

"Jin! Before you go. Whatever those guys are, they're ruthless, and they're looking for you. I suggest you stay out of Wuhan for as long as you can"

"Thank you, bye." Jin said as he ended the call. Little did Barry Chu know that his old friend was on his way into, and that he was in a dance with murderous shadows that played dirty.

There was silence for a while as Jin pondered on his decisions for the safety of his family. He knew that their being in China was dangerous, but where would they be safe, especially if unknown gun men had traced him to a house in downtown Durban a few hours ago.

"Well, Yedder can't talk right now, because he's at a dumb funeral" Jabez said as he re-entered the room.

Pietro walked into the room and sat down rather solemnly. He did not speak to anyone, and he kept muttering prayers.

"Pietro! Status?" Jin had grown impatient.

"Today is Olav's funeral" Pietro announced.

"Oh" the other men said as they stole glances of each other. Jabez was feeling guilty, so he made to comfort his friend, but Pietro had excused himself to go get a drink, half of which he poured into the kitchen sink in memory of his late cousin, **a simple auto mechanic in downtown Beijing that was the victim of a stray bullet shooting when rival triad gangs took their fights to the streets,** or so the local papers would report it.

"Local papers, that's it!" Pietro announced as he stormed into the room again.

"What?" The others asked as he made his way towards the computers.

"Any names of newspapers you know. Jin?"

"I don't know man" Jin confessed.

"Really?" Pietro said. He was disappointed.

"―

We did find something already though!" Jin announced. "Some old factories on the outskirts of the city was getting renovated till some guy got into an accident"

"And?" They both chorused.

"My sources say that they had to shut down the factory, and the case. Even the dude's family died in some gruesome way. What's even worse is that the powers that be got so interested in a simple work accident case" Jin continued.

"You think the base is at this factory?"

"I think it is the factory, maybe underneath it as well" Jin replied.

"We're gonna need to investigate this factory thingy, right?" Jabez said.

"Yeah, but we don't have any resources, or guns."

"I can get us guns in China, I mean, I know a guy that can get us guns" Jin offered.

"Alright, good! How do we get to China?" Jabez asked.

"The telephone! The lady said to call when we needed something!" Pietro said. He was already on his way upstairs.

"We are missing something; I can feel it" Jabez suddenly said.

"Like what?" Jin asked.

"I don't know, but we know where we're going to, possibly how we're gonna get there too, but do we know what we're gonna be doing?"

"Or stopping" Jin added.

"The worker, did they say anything about how he died?" Jabez asked.

"Let's see, shall we?" Jin replied. He had started opening case files and newspaper articles that had been deemed unpublishable.

"What do you think we'll find?" Jabez asked.

"The truth? The scary truth" Jin replied as he sighed.

The whirring soon slowed down as the computer had finished processing the information.

"Here!" Jabez said.

"Man hospitalized due to respiratory problems. Deemed contagious." Jin read.

"Wuhan man patient zero in new epidemic?" Jabez read.

"Factory Worker exposed to disease vials, Points fingers at Pharmaceutical Company" Jin read.

The list was seemingly endless, with the bodies of the articles either scraped or deleted.

"Look at all the status of the articles though" Jabez pointed.

"Unpublishable. Fake News"

"All except this one"

"Local Factory Worker's mysterious death; A peek into the silenced minds of journalists, By Agatha Zhao"

"Google her!"

"Disgraced *reporter ends own life in bizarre building jump*"

"Jesus" Jabez muttered.

Pietro had just come down from the stairs. He could read the room and without ask in questions, he walked over the screen and asked, "Another lead, huh?"

"Yep" Jin managed to say.

"We've got a flight that leaves for China around the same time that Secretary Boyd does, but we'll need a serious change of identity"

"What does that mean?" Jabez asked.

"It means that you cannot be American or have a stubble anymore" Pietro replied.

"What stubble? My beard is a chic-magnet!" Jab3z protected.

"Exactly why it needs to go, you're Belgian now. Antony Gerber" Pietro announced.

"Let's have it!" Jin muttered as he turned in his chair.

"You're Canadian-Vietnamese now, Jin. Jonah Nguyen"

"What are you?" Jabez asked Pietro.

"Norwegian. Erling Daamsgard" He replied.

"Where are the passports?" Jin asked.

"On the way, along with out luggage and keys to a safehouse" Pietro answered.

"Another safehouse? Come on" Jabez complained.

"Save your complain for later, American. We might not make it to China with the way things are" Pietro said.

"The way things are? What does that mean?" Jin asked.

"They know we're coming, and they'll be waiting for us" Pietro said casually.

"What the fuck?" Jabez said.

"They know we're..."

"I heard it; I just don't want to believe it"

"Do I need to do anything to my appearance?" Jin asked.

"No-no. You're good. There's just one more thing, eh?"

"What's that?"

"The seats. One is first class. The other two aren't" Pietro said.

"Sweet! You guys are taking the other seats. right?" Jabez said.

"Not exactly." Pietro said. "Jin gets it, we don't".

"You guys, you didn't have to give it to me" Jin protested.

"I was about to say the same thing. He doesn't want it" Jabez said.

"If you're going to be a Canadian-Vietnamese professor of Asian History, go for it" Pietro said. "They also said to find the bulletproof vests in the house, for protection"

"How do we do that?" Jin asked.

Pietro did not answer, instead he walked over to couches and lifted the plastic covering on them.

He then nudged the chair, and a lock became visible.

"Opposite" he muttered, using his hands to run through the various furniture in front of him. He still didn't see anything.

Then he looked over at the ceiling and a combination of numbers were staring at him. Pietro then imputed the numbers into the lock that had opened on the arm of the couch.

Immediately he did, the farthest screen in the set up before Jin eased to the side. Inside the wall were about six bulletproof vests.

"Here, don't take these off till we're in the Chinese safehouse" Pietro admonished.

He also tossed the other vests over to the couch on the couch at the entrance to the living room.

"Jabez would come and find it lying there" Pietro said solemnly, as he climbed the staircase to go and have himself some rest.

The flight was to leave the next morning, and they were given an entire night of rest, and pack a few things.

*

Charles Boyd had just retired to his suite when the telephone rang. Immediately, his heart sank.

"We already spoke today, so what's the problem now?" He muttered as he picked up the phone.

He did not say anything as he waited for whomever was on the other end to speak, but to his relief, it was not who he had expected. It was the hotel receptionist back down at the lobby.

"Mr Charles, Sir? Someone would like to talk to you" came the voice.

"Who's that?"

"She says she's an old friend, that you guys go way back"

His mind had begun to race again. Who could it be? Was it an old fling that had come back to haunt him with a pregnancy report?

"Well, eh.."

"Sir, she's coming up. Ma'am, please you cannot be back there! I'm sorry Sir, she just took your room key and went into the elevator.

"How does she know my room? I'll need to have a chat with your manager in the morning!" Secretary Boyd had become agitated, and anxious.

Who was this mystery person? What did they want with him? Had he offended his leaders? They had given him more time than this to shake of the tails he had gotten, right?

Soon, he heard a knock on his door. He did not open it, instead he went over to the safe at the foot of his bed and armed himself with a gun.

The knock came again, but all he did was secure himself behind his fridge.

"Come out from behind the fridge, Boyd. You look pathetic!" came a voice that he recognized easily.

"What a pleasant surprise, Rachel Colby! I always knew you were too much of a cockroach to stay dead!" He spoke. He knew that she had tapped into the live feed in his room, and that she was watching him at that very moment.

"And you're too much of a bitch to have one master! Is that right, Boyd?" She retorted.

"I really missed our playful banter, you know. Also, I'm not putting my gun down, that way I can pull the trigger and get a slap on the wrist. You, however, will be dead, and guilty of trespassing!"

"How about we play that game, open up traitor!" She said, pounding on the door.

The lock came undone, and she walked inside th3 house. Inside the suite, Charles Boyd was seated on a bear rug covered chair, brandishing his weapon for her to see.

"Some big guy you are, hiding behind a Glock 19 like it's a tank" Rachel Colby commented as she took her seat at the other side of the room.

"I'm the biggest guy in his room. Right now, I call the shots, and my first okay is simple; What are you doing here?" He said emphatically.

"I just came by for a visit, you see?"

"And you've been received. Now, you can either get out or talk your big game"

"Big game? Hell no, Boyd. I'm not like that, you should know me already"

"Are you stalling for something? Are you recording this conversation?"

"Of course, I am, what do you take me for? A newbie?" Rachel Colby laughed for a bit; bit Charles Boyd did not find it funny.

"You know what?..." He was on his feet and waving his gun around in anger.

"No, I'll tell you what? Charley Boy, I'll only say this once, alright? I've worked at the CIA my whole life and I've seen your type every single day I go to work."

"Yeah, what's my type? Handsome?"

"Oh, far from it. Your type is the wise guy. The one who thinks they can go farther than everyone by being two-timing, back-stabbing traitors. You see, those guys always have the life they wanted. A good car from some foreign manufacturer, a spot in some new world order that'll fall immediately they try to build it up" She was walking towards him, and she could see that he was cowering

"Uh-huh? Is that so? How about we have this talk in the White House sometime? That'll be really something wouldn't it?"

"Oh, please. You probably have him where you want him, but not how you would've wanted it. President Wallace might be dumb but his heart's in the right place" she said as she made her way for the door.

"Yeah, walk away. Like you've never done that before!" He hollered.

"Also, I need to tell you something. If some henchmen come after me, Or I see anything like Durban happen around me, I'm having your head on my wall in Alaska" she said with a smile and walked out.

Charles Boyd fell to the floor beside his bed. His head had suddenly become a playground for different thoughts and fears. Exactly how powerful was Rachel Colby?

Was he safe?

Had he been making the right choices?

Was he really not as powerful as she was?

Was she bluffing?

"Thanks for the talk, Charley. You too, Agent." He heard her say over the service line.

"Agent?" He pondered.

Was the receptionist an agent as well?

Had he been set up to stay at a CIA safehouse?

What about the people he had let into his room to clean it up for the past few days?

Suddenly, he got to his feet and ran out to the reception. Instead of a female, he saw a man who was nursing the back of his head. He looked confused as he stared at the already paranoid Secretary Boyd.

Rachel Colby had kidnapped him for a few hours and while they set up their plan, they had him knocked out on the floor of the storage room. Now, he was back and with no idea of where he had been for the past three hours.

Charles Boyd knew he was not safe there anymore. He had to leave as soon as he could. As he got back to his room, he packed his things and called his driver to pick him up.

As he waited for the driver, he began to question everyone's loyalty, and as soon as the driver came around t4 building with the car, he made sure to take the car for himself. Not before leaving the driver a couple hundred dollars to get home.

There was no other place to go, so he drove to the parking lot of the White House and slept there. He had to get ready for his flight in the morning, and this was essentially the safest place he could think of, right in plain sight.

As he tried to get some sleep, he was constantly plagued by Rachel Colby's words, especially when it came to the matters he had connected himself with. He knew she still had a few agents roaming the streets sniffing for his blood, but he did not know who they were. He had successfully terminated a couple of her agents, but one was still free, and after the incidents in Durban, he was sure they had multiplied.

"Rachel Colby, you fucking bitch!" He cursed several times. He wished he was better than her at this game, but with the way things were, he felt like she was always a step ahead of him, even when it didn't feel that way.

Soon, he had fallen asleep, only to be awoken by an orderly who had come down to make sure that all the cars in the parking lot had been warmed before the agents take them out.

"Yeah, thank you" he said as he tipped the grateful orderly.

Charles Boyd looked at his watch. "7:45?" He gasped.

He was going to be late if he spent another second in that parking lot! He was also going to be late, seeing that the airstrip where the private plane assigned to him was parked was about 2 hours from the White House. If he needed to get there, he had to be fast, and reckless. The Accordance did not take lightly to lateness.

*

"The Accordance, huh? What a dumbass name!" Jabez commented.

"I mean, who the fuck wants to join an organization called The Accordance?" Pietro asked.

"Hello Sir, can I tell you about a homicidal cult that wants to destroy the world, we call ourselves The Accordance" Jabez joked.

They were on their way to the airport and the taxi driver had just given them a little bit more information about the evil they were to face.

Everyone was laughing, except Jin. Jabez had already tried to get him to be in on the jokes, but he had declined.

"Easy man, come on!" Pietro said.

Rachel Colby's visit to Secretary Boyd had proved to gather them more information than they had bargained for. After he had fled the scene, she had gone back to the hotel room and downloaded all the information into a flash drive she had been given. Teo Han and Carol had designed it in such a way that even deleted information could still be salvaged.

That was how they got the extra information they had, and the plan of this inter-connected web of powerful men and women in all the sovereign states in the world, called "The Accordance".

"So, it's a cult? Kinda like the illuminati?" Jabez asked the driver.

"Almost like the Illuminati, Sir. Those guys are top guns, and they're so few that we could track th3m for a million years." The driver said.

"So, we're stuck chasing wannabes?" Jabez scoffed.

"Sir, these wannabes have a biological weapon that can reduce the population of the world by 20%" The driver said.

"Well, damn." Jabez would not say anymore.

They were almost at the airport now, so the driver gave them their new identities, and small radios that ensured communication between the three men at all times.

"I'll have to drop you brave men here and take Dr Nguyen to the first-class gate." He spoke.

"Lucky ass" Jabez murmured as he left the car. He had been handed his new identity and from the photoshopped image, he could see that the faster he was no longer Antony Gerber, the easier his life would be.

"Look at that face. Goddamn it, I look like a virgin!' He cursed as he walked towards the airport.

"Have fun!" Pietro said. He was not walking beside him so as not to arouse suspicion.

They soon got checked and they got on the Plane. Pietro had his seat in the front part of the plane, while Jabez sat at the back.

Jabez was almost asleep when he heard a buzz in his ear. It was Pietro.

"Bad guys at my 6 and 5." He spoke.

"Yeah, I see a couple beside me. Who are they fooling, honestly? Anybody can see that they've never had sex before!"

"You can tell that?" Pietro asked.

"Yeah, and they're not looking like they want to join the Mile High Club, or that they're in it!"

"Mile High Club?"

"It's when couples have sex on a plane, forget about it"

"Can you guys just keep it down?" It was Jin.

"Hey, Jin! You know what the mile high club is, right?" Jabez asked.

"It's clearly one of your sexual things and I would not be associated with it!" Jin replied. He also went online, as the static from his own side of the call was deafening.

"Fuck!" Jabez cursed. The couple beside him locked eyes with him for a second and gave him a smile.

"I just locked eyes with the dude, and I think I was wrong. He's a virgin, she's not!" Jabez said again.

"And you think they're gonna do it?" Pietro asked.

"They've already stood up."

"It's about to go down!" Pietro said excitedly.

"I'm proud of this, I really am" Jabez said.

"How many hours till this flight is over?" Pietro asked.

"I don't know. A day?"

"A day? Come on!"

An air hostess had offered him a snack and he was not munching on a medium sized bag of peanuts.

"Man, these are delicious!" Pietro gasped.

"Compared to the meals that Jin is having, they're trash, trust me" Jabez said.

"Wanting more is such an American thing, you know?".

"Criticism is such a you thing. See, I didn't just give the middle to an entire continent, ya'know?"

"I'm sorry, alright?"

"You better be!"

"American, what do you think will happen in China?"

I don't know. We get shot at; we survive. We run away; they chase after us. They corner us, but they don't know that we've cornered them. We come out with guns and fire at all those bastards, ending every last one of them"

"Well, that's an American thing"

"Sure is! After all of that, we go save Jin's family, save them and take them back to America with us"

"Honestly, that's the most important part of this mission" Pietro concurred.

Then came the static again. It was Jin.

"Thank you guys. I just got offered Salmon, and it is delicious" he said.

"Motherfucker!" Jabez cursed.

"What?" The other two asked.

"They gave us sushi the last time I flew first class. Now they're taunting me? These assholes know how much I like Salmon" Jabez said.

"You're a really crazy guy, you know that, right?" Pietro asked.

"Yep, it's an American thing" Jabez replied.

"American thing? What's that?" Jin asked.

"Oh, for Pietro it's literally anything I do. Jin, I would like to tell you that oh friend is racist"

"I already know that" Jin replied.

"What?" Pietro replied. "I swear on my ancestors when this flight is over, I'm kicking your asses!" He spoke.

"Imagine holding a grudge that long. Jesus" Jin replied.

"Seems like a Russian thing, honestly." Jabez joked, to which they all laughed.

*

"So, you're going in through the back, is that so?" Jabez said.

"Jin and I would come at them from the back, right here" Pietro said as he pointed to the map.

It was a few hours since their had landed and they were planning their course of action. The taxi driver had provided them with a map of the factory and how it had changed. All the exits were guarded by armed men who had a shoot on sight order.

"And that's why we're going in through the back?" Jin said again. He and Jabez were laughing, but it was obvious that Pietro did not get the joke, not yet. Soon, he was laughing with them.

"Come on, American. We have to focus here" he urged.

The trio had escaped surveillance at the airport and were now in the safehouse they were provided with. Unlike the others they and taken asylum in, this safehouse was different. In the garage was parked a car, the same one that they would use to execute this current mission.

"We don't get to rest, do we?" Jabez said. he was yawning, and so was Pietro.

"If we want to get this right, we can't" Jin said.

"Look who has home advantage" Jabez said.

"I'll ignore that, okay?" Jin said. He was turning his hands through the walls looking for a lever. Soon, he had pulled something, and the walls came spinning around. At the other side were all kinds of Assault rifles and pistols

"Dear God!" Jabez said as he ran towards the wall.

"Fuck yes, American!" Pietro said.

"Hell yeah!" Jabez said. He had already armed himself with an ACR. "Hey, come and pick a present!" He urged.

Pietro was the first to step forward. He then took an M4A1 and checked it out.

"Bullets?" He asked.

Jin did not say anything, instead he twisted the head of an ornament that was beside him, revealing another part of the wall that had just bullets.

"Merry Christmas, Pietro" Jabez said.

"Same to you, American!" Pietro responded as they both surged forward to grab bullets.

"Wheel's up in ten. There are combat uniforms upstairs, if you want" Jin said. He had grabbed himself a SCAR-11 and as heading to check out the car.

Like children that had been spoiled, both Jabez and Pietro ran upstairs to go check out the combat uniforms.

"Mother of god" Jabez said as he saw the fit they had been provided with. They had been provided with masks that had air filtration devices, and a more current bullet proof that was better than the one they had found at the American safehouse. They also had flares, and padded uniforms that prevented damage.

"Let's try them on" Jabez urged.

"Already on it!" Pietro said. He had tossed his weapon to a corner and was trying on his own suit.

By the time Jin was back from the garage, they had already won their uniforms and were ready to go. They only had to wait for Jin who had not yet suited up.

"We'll be in the garage!" The duo said as they headed down.

"Good" was all Jin could way. He was sure that they both considered this entire thing an adventure, but Jin felt like he had a mission to his country to get it right. The Accordance had to be stopped. Charles Boyd, the American secretary of defense had to be stopped as well, even exposed. But he was a powerful man, and he could play around any allegations that could be brought up against him.

"Death it is" Jin said as he picked up his weapon to go meet the others. As expected, they were excited over the car and Jabez was seated in the driver's seat.

"In the back, American!" Jin ordered as he walked into the garage.

"Oh, come on!" Jabez complained as he settled in the back seat.

It was now time to go.

"Everyone ready?" Jin asked.

"Yes!" Pietro replied emphatically.

"I'm gonna die with no facial hair" Jabez muttered.

"I will be Ignoring that" Jin said as he started the car.

Soon they were on the road, heading for outskirts of the city. As expected, there were no active police officers on the roads as they had all been paid to not be vigilant. They however came across some police officers on a road that were stationed a few miles from their destination, but they did not make any moves.

"Corrupt bunch" Jin cursed as he drove past them.

Soon, they were on a road that led straight to the frontage of the factory, so they had to stop and review their plans.

"I see a couple guards up front, we have to take them out" Jin said as he fitted the silencer over his pistol.

"How about we all attack from the front?" Jabez said.

"Stick to the plan, American" Pietro said.

"Okay, cool" Jabez said as he fitted his silencer over the mouth of his pistol. He was grumbling, but he was not as audible as they would have wanted him to be.

"Let us get this right, okay?" Jin said as he fitted his mask over his face.

The trio was now sneaking towards the entrance. The guard was quite easy to take down as Jin put two bullets in the back of his head.

"Out back, on me" he whispered to Pietro.

Jabez followed the entrance and took out a few more guards.

"Pietro, on me! We've got a few coming this way!"

"Safe."

"On my six, thank you"

"Safe."

Jabez had taken out all the guards and was now waiting for the duo to come up on his position.

"You guys had all the fun, didn't you?" Jabez asker as they came up to his position.

"Yep!" Pietro replied.

"Screw you guys" Jabez replied. They now had to deal with the second wave of guards who were now approaching their position.

"How did they know we were here?" Jin asked.

"I don't know! But I think it's time we introduced ourselves!" Pietro said as he put away his pistol and grabbed unto his rifle.

"Fuck yes!" Jabez hollered in response. In the distance, they could hear several voices that were gaining on the position by the second. The trio took cover behind a metal wall and waited for them to come.

As soon as the voice were close by, they opened fire, killing off almost half a dozen assailants.

"Clear!" Jin yelled. They had to move forward and secure more positions.

The gunshots had alerted more of the assailants. Soon, they had guns trained on their position, but even these ones were also eliminated.

"Plan B!" Jin yelled.

On command, the others secured the exits and face him enough time to steal information from a computer they had come across. As Jin sought to override the defenses of the computer, Pietro and Jabez fought off another wave of assailants.

"Clear!" Jin soon said, at which they moved again.

"We have to down to the other levels!" Pietro said as he cracked open an elevator.

"They'll be expecting us!" Jin said.

"Exactly!" Pietro replied

As they got on, he opened the repair hole in the ceiling and made them crouch there. Then, he set the elevator to take them to the next floor, right before climbing out and into the repair hole.

As the elevator opened, there came a barrage of gunfire. The assailants were waiting for them on the other side of the door and had opened fire!

As Pietro stayed crouched, he counted the rounds of the guns.

"Now!" He said as soon as he heard the last gun fire.

He was now inside the elevator opening fire. Soon, he was joined by Jin, and then Jabez who opened fire on the assailants.

"There! Another computer!" Jabez pointed out to Jin. "We'll cover you!" He said as Jin ran in the direction of the computer.

As expected, more assailants were coming but Jabez and Pietro promptly took care of them.

"Hey! I saw a map!" Jin said as he rejoined them. "There should be a flight of stairs right behind one of these doors!" He announced.

"Alright, Gentlemen! Reload!" Pietro admonished.

As they made their way down the stairs to what could be the third and final floor, they came in contact with a few of the armed men on the stairs.

"These guys were planning an ambush!" Jabez said as he fired down the stairs.

"Good thinking Jin!" Pietro said as they made up on the foot of the stairs.

"Here it is, alright?" Jin said as he made to open the door.

"Here it is!" Pietro and Jabez hollered.

With a swift kick of the foot, Jin cracked the door open.

"What the fuck?" Jabez cursed. The room was dark and devoid of life. They could only hear stifled moaning and labored breathing.

Suddenly, the lights go on and the trio found themselves in a sort of laboratory.

"Hey, look!" Jabez called out to his counterparts.

"Jesus" Pietro muttered.

On the other side of the room was an experimentation facility. The two rooms were demarcated by glass, but the trio could still hear the chained men and woman begging for their lives.

"Amazing, isn't it?" Came a voice. Soon, a hooded figure walked out from behind the chained body, his hands in the air as if brandishing his achievements.

"Now, who the fuck are you?" Jin hollered. The trio now had their guns trained on this figure.

"Me? I am but a servant of the greater purpose- don't even try to shoot, it'll just bounce back and put holes in your head" the figure said.

"Yeah? How about we come over there and put a few of those bullets in your head!" Pietro yelled.

"Yes, you will be coming over here, but not like that" The figure said, then he tapped away at the watch that sat on his wrist.

A knock-out gas had soon begun to filter into the room, causing the trio to make for the door.

"It's locked! Fuck!" Jabez said, his eyes had begun to sway as he spoke.

Soon, Jin was passed out on the floor, and so were Pietro and Jabez.

"Please, bring our guests over to this side of the room" the man said as he turned to his experiments.

As they remained immobilized, some of the henchmen came over to the room and dragged the unconscious bodies of the trio over to the other side of the room.

There, they tied them up and left them to regain consciousness.

*

"So much for gas filtration headgear" was what Jabez could hear as he regained consciousness.

"Hey, what?" Jabez tried to speak, but his mouth was heavy for some reason. His legs and hands were also immobilized. His neck was stiff, but it turned when he tried to. To his sides were both Jin and Pietro, tied as he was.

He had been caught! They had been caught!

"Shit!" He cursed, but his words did not make it out his mouth. His lips were also heavy, and his eyes hurt when he held them open for long.

Soon, he had begun to hear groaning beside him. The others had woken up, but they were just as immobilized as he was.

The man that had spoken to them was also in the room, but his attention was diverted. A henchman was giving him information and his attention was solely on this person. Soon, the henchman was out of sight and his attention turned to the trio he had just caught.

"Gentlemen, welcome back" he said in a mellow tone.

They did not respond, so he continued.

"I'm sorry we had to be introduced like this, but I am the one they call Uno, of The Accordance" he said.

There were still no replies.

"I see that the poisons have not seated off yet, so we shall do this again in 10 minutes, okay?" He said as he turned his back to them.

"Oh, they have. We're just thinking of ways to kick your ass!" Jabez was the first to speak.

"I'm sorry, what?" Uno asked.

"Yeah, so far we've found 5!" Pietro hollered.

"I admire the industry, but there is no way you are escaping today. Your chances are almost none-existent, I'm afraid.

If you guys are willing to share, I would love to hear what you have" Uno said as he pulled off his cowl to reveal his face.

"That's 6 ways, dear god!" Jabez yelled.

"You look like you got that cowl as a birth present!" Pietro yelled.

"You look like a bad dumpling!" Jin yelled.

"You look like every horror movie, ever!" Jabez added.

"I can assure you that I have heard those and a thousand more every day of my life. I must introduce myself again. I am Uno of The Accordance, and this is my work. I do not think I appreciate guests dropping in uninvited, but here we are." Uno said.

"You know, I always had a vision for a better world. A world where the assholes that put me down did not exist. A world where people like my goodly neighbor lived in abundance. Now, that was until my goodly neighbor tried to molest me. I had taken refuge in his house on a rainy day to escape from my bullies and he made certain, disgusting moves on me. I had to run out, towards my own bullies. They rescued me. You see, they later took my lunch money, but at least I still had my dignity. Then I started thinking; is there anyone that is truly good in this world?" Uno explained. He had people cover the mouths of Jin, Pietro and Jabez as he spoke.

"Now. since no one can be good, why not be good enough to make the world a better place, devoid of sentimental attachments and people you deem are good, or bad!" Uno continued. "What better way to bring about this balance than with the men that the people have deemed good enough to wield power? The same people who had been elected and appointed into public office to be GOOD! I found those people, and here are they" he said, ushering some people out into the open.

In a single file, several high profile faces in several world governments made their way out into the open.

"There goes the bitch!" Jabez cursed as soon as he saw Secretary Boyd.

The secretary walked gingerly over to where Jabez was being held and slapped him across the face.

"Ohhh! Is that how you say hello, Mr Secretary?" Jabez asked.

"You fucking piece of shit! You've made me agitated for the last time, you heard?" Secretary Boyd yelled.

From the shadows came a figure that only Jin could be familiar with. It was Inspector Chu.

"Hello, old friend" the inspector greeted, but Jin did not respond. Instead, he struggled to get free, tears running down his eyes.

"Easy, Jin. Please" Inspector Chu admonished, but Jin would not listen.

"How could you?" Jin finally spoke. He was sobbing at this point as he played his old friend's betrayal over and over again in his mind.

"Jin, please" Inspector Chu had no other words.

"How could you!" Jin yelled at the top of his voice.

"Easy there, Agent Jin" Uno finally spoke again. "Yours is the happiest, honestly" he said as he ushered another person from the shadows.

"Hello, Pietro" came an all too familiar voice. It was Borya Fedorov, the head of the Foreign Intelligence Service. The same person that had sent Pietro and his fellow agents on the missions to America, and China

"Director Borya?" Pietro gasped.

"It is good to see you, Pietro" Borya Fedorov said.

"I cannot say the same for you" Pietro said as he spat on the floor.

"You can despise me Pietro, but I am your superior and I still have jurisdiction over you" Borya Fedorov gloated.

"Power is everything, folks! Look at my circus, there's too much of it! Powerful men who sold their allegiances in exchange for more power! Splendid!"

"Is that what you did, huh Old Friend?" Jin asked Inspector Chu.

"Shut up, Jin!" Inspector Chu commanded, but Jin was not yet done.

"Is this how bad you wanted power? Huh? Your place as a deputy super-intendent was not enough? So, you sold your whole station, and for what? So that you can be superintendent?"

"We both know that position was mine! I've served this country for almost three decades, and what do I get? A desk job monitoring infants who are only in it for the salary!" Inspector Chu was riled up.

"Oh, come on! The entire precinct had a vote, and you weren't chosen! Ming Xu suffered the same fate in Beijing, and I don't see him here whining like a kid!" Jin retorted.

"Ming can settle for peanuts, but I cannot! You hear me!" Chu was still shouting.

"I swear on the gods, I'll break out of here and make sure you pay"

"No, you won't!" Inspector Chu was now speaking soberly.

"And why is that? Huh?" Jin asked.

"Because I can't let you, I'm sorry, old friend' Inspector Chu was holding a gun.

"Chu, wait!" Jabez and Pietro pleaded, but it was too late. Inspector Chu had shot Jin twice in the head

"You son of a bitch!" Pietro yelled, ripping his restrains off. In desperation, he surged forward and overpowered Inspector Chu.

"You bastard! I'll kill you myself!" He yelled into the old man's ears.

"Let them go! Don't fire!" Uno yelled at his henchmen. Jabez was now free. Alongside Pietro and an overpowered Inspector Chu.

Hurriedly, they make their way out of the factory with Inspector Chu in tow.

"You're gonna die today you old fuck!" Jabez yelled as they escaped.

"What now?" Pietro soon asked. They were at the car and Inspector Chu was on his knees with his hands behind his head.

"What now?" Jabez turned. Be had been pacing for a while.

"Yeah?" Pietro asked. His gun was still pointed to Inspector Chu's neck. The old, treacherous inspector was already saying his prayers. His eyes were tight shut as he muttered and whimpered.

"What now is that we get this old fuck back to the safehouse and torture him till he tells is everything he knows, that's what's gonna happen now!" Jabez yelled. Pietro nodded in agreement, but this only made Inspector Chu whimper more.

"Get up! Get up you old fuck!" Jabez urged as he dragged Inspector Chu to his feet. Suddenly, he stopped. He was now looking Pietro in the eyes. Pietro had noticed him pause, but he had not had enough time to make it out as anything.

"Duck!" Jabez then yelled, falling to the floor beside the car. Pietro did the same, but the good old Inspector, who had the same agility that a man his age would, did not. Instead, he became a source of the blood splatter that Pietro and Jabez were now being showered with.

"Red dot, huh?" Pietro yelled at Jabez. Whomever was shooting was still trained on their position.

"Yeah!" Jabez concurred.

"Do you see him, American?"

"No, but he's out there. The only thing keeping him from us is this here sports car" Jabez replied.

"Here!" Pietro yelled as he tossed the contents of Inspector Chu's pockets to Jabez.

"Breath mints? Really?" Jabez asked the almost headless body of the Inspector, right before he tossed it to the other side of the small road they had parked beside. In a small flash, he saw the red dot from the sniper land on the body, and then disappear.

"Heat signatures" Pietro said. Jabez only nodded. The Russian had said his mind.

In the distance, they soon started to hear chatter, and the quick movement of feet. Soldiers were coming up on their position, and they needed to move.

"Hey, can you hot wire a car? Jin had the keys!" Pietro asked.

"Stupidest question I ever heard, honestly" Jabez chuckled as he crawled his way into the driver's seat.

Pietro was to be the look out and judging from the lights on the assault rifles that were circling their position, their outlook was not looking good. Jabez would have to hurry.

"I heard you!" Jabez said, cursing under his breath. Soon, the car roared to life, and Pietro struggled into the back seat. "Drive!" He commanded, but Jabez was already down the small road before he could finish.

"Hey! Why does it feel like that sniper wasn't for us?" Jabez asked as they sped past the small group of law enforcement they had passed on their way in.

"Now that you say it, I think they didn't consider us sniper-worthy"

"Yeah, because they could have taken us out, like that!" Jabez snapped his fingers. They really were sitting ducks, especially if that sniper had the heat signature vision they taught he had.

"The sniper wasn't a bad shot either. I mean, he took out the Inspector's head!" Pietro added.

"Whoever that UNO guy is- the ugly motherfucker wanted us alive. That's why he sent those foot soldiers. The ones that were circling us. I mean, they didn't even shoot when we sped off!"

"Yeah, yeah! He was ugly. Were those burns? Or genetics?"

"Yeah, it looked like a side of his face had tried to switch with the other side, eww"

"Crazy bastard, he probably did one of his experiments on himself"

"Yeah, probably"

"Hey, shit!"

"What?"

"The drives!"

"What drives?"

"The ones Jin was stealing!"

"Shit!"

"Yeah! We need to go back!"

"Oh, fuck no!"

"Maybe we could find his body?"

"We need to go back!"

"Don't you turn this car around, American!" Pietro begged. "We don't have that type of ammo!"

"Shit!" Jabez cursed again. All their efforts so far were useless, and they had lost a colleague to an ugly-looking psychopath and his handful of brain washed political appointees.

The rest of the journey happened in silence, as Jabez tried to find out who had seen with Secretary Boyd.

After a while he had come up with absolutely no one. Under his breath, he cursed himself for not being observant. Pietro was mumbling words as he stirred in his back seat. It was then that Jabez realized that they had left their guns in their hurried escape.

"How exactly did you expect us to get back there?" He berated Pietro.

"We could go and get it!" Pietro explained.

"Oh, you think those guys- the ones that came out of the building with guns to our heads! - you think they'd just leave assault rifles lying on the floor? You think they'll not mount surveillance? Come on!" Jabez cursed as he swerved past what seemed to be drunk drivers.

"Hey, watch it!" Pietro yelled from the back seat.

"That wasn't my fault!" Jabez retorted. The car, a bright red convertible seemed to have been driven into a wall, or whatever that loud crash was. The duo drove on, as Jabez knocked over a couple of trash cans on his way back into the garage.

"The neighbors will not be happy, you know?" Pietro observed.

"Fuck the neighbors!" Jabez retorted. He was too on edge to care about trash bags, or neighbors. All he wanted at that moment was to be behind the steel doors at their current safehouse, probably with a half-full shot glass to his face.

Soon, they were locked in the safehouse. As soon as Pietro activated the safe lock on the house, he fell to the floor. Like Jabez, he had come to the realisation that he was missing a soldier. Quietly, he sobbed but like Jabez, it soon turned to crying. Before long, they were both drunk, sprawled on the kitchen floor, and taking turns to empty a large bottle of vodka.

"I can't trust my government, American" Pietro cried. "I thought I could, but even my superior is a bag guy. Who knows how deep the lies run, huh?"

"You're lucky, honestly. At least they don't think you're a fugitive, like me. Apart from Carol, and Director Colby, everyone else thinks I'm a bad guy. I can't even be on American soil freely, and I want a pizza" Jabez cried, he was shaking as he hugged Pietro tightly.

"Come on, we can get pizza in Italy, right? There's a pizza place here somewhere"

"Not like New York Pizza, there isn't" Jabez complained.

"We sure lost Jin, didn't we American?" Pietro asked. His tone was less agitated, it was almost like he had come to the realization a second time.

"We lost him" Jabez said. He was on his feet, with the now empty bottle of vodka in his hand. In a blind fit of rage, he smashed the bottle on the far living room wall, sending small shards of glass flying everywhere. "Someone has got to pay, honestly" he said emphatically as he turned to Pietro.

"Fuck yes, American!" Pietro urged.

"Someone has got to pay for our brother's death!" Jabez yelled.

"In the morning, could you call that American woman. The one that helped us?"

"Carol?"

"No, the older woman"

"Ms. Colby? Sure. We need her"

"What do we do about the evidence, the one Jin collected?"

"If I know Jin, he probably made a backup in the cloud storage for this place" Pietro explained as he walked towards the computers. As expected, there was a pop-up window with files that were actively downloading.

"The beautiful Chinese bastard! He was the smartest of all of us!" Jabez exclaimed as he rushed to embrace Pietro, causing the latter to drop the bottle of Vodka in a loud, crashing thud. But they did not seem to care, as the two drunk men danced around in a circle.

"I think I might have to vomit" Pietro announced shortly. With his hand clasped over his mouth, he rushed towards the upstairs bathroom.

Jabez fell to the couch behind him, watching the pop-up window load.

"17 percent" he muttered as his eyes began to become heavy. He made to check on the doors again, just to see that they were secure enough, but his legs failed him. Instead, he fell to the couch again, and thus began his sleep. The only thing that seemed enough to jolt him back to consciousness was Pietro shoving at him, a cup of coffee in hand. When Jabez looked at the wall clock, it was well into the afternoon, and Carol was on a secure video call guiding them through the encryption process for what she described as "way too much information".

*

"Way too much? Why would you say that?" Pietro asked as he handed over a scalding hot cup of coffee to Jabez. He wasn't looking and some of the contents spilled onto Jabez's hand, the heat awakening him faster than anything else could have.

"You fucking piece of shit! You almost burned my arm off!" Jabez cursed as he dropped the cup on the table. It was then that Pietro turned to him.

"Could you keep it down? I can barely hear her, and we have a world to save, don't we?" Pietro admonished him. He didn't seem to care about whatever pain Jabez was in, and honestly, neither did Carol.

"Agent Jabez, we strongly suggest that you take your pouting to the other room, thank you very much" It was Director Colby that spoke from the background, causing Jabez to stop in his tracks.

"I'm sorry ma'am" he said as he took a deep breath in a last attempt to pull himself together.

The flashbacks of the previous night had started to haunt him, and it although he hoped it was a dream, Jin was nowhere to be seen in the room. He wasn't in the kitchen making a snack, and neither was he behind the computer screen as was characteristic of him.

"He's really gone, Agent Glee. The best thing we can do is to get ourselves in an orderly bunch and try to avenge him." Director Colby spoke again.

Jabez tried to be as coordinated as he possibly could, so he cleared his throat and shrugged as he spoke. "Yeah, yeah. We need to do that"

"Good. We can do a ceremony for him after we've had his killers behind bars, or better yet, with a bullet in their skulls" came her voice again. "If you will excuse me, I have a meeting with the President, and the good old Secretary Charles Boyd. You people better figure this shit out, I'm about to go digest some. Besides, we still don't know if the President is pure evil, or just stupid. This meeting should clear somethings up for me"

Pietro muttered a farewell greeting, and Jabez raised his now half-empty cup of coffee in a salute, right before disappearing into the kitchen.

"What do you have currently?" He could hear Pietro ask Carol right before he left, but he wasn't paying attention to that.

Jabez Glee had lost soldiers before, but this one seemed to hit him the hardest. Jin had never shut up about his daughter and how he was going to take her on a world tour when all this craziness was over.

"Damn, I never even got him a slice of that American cookie" Jabez snickered as he stumbled into the bathroom. The bathroom was dark, so he felt for the switch and turned it on.

"Mother-!" He cursed, regretting his actions as soon as he did. The bathroom lights stung his eyes and made his headache worse. Blind with pain, he reached into the cabinet and when he had found painkiller, he chewed on a couple of them, right before dunking his face in the tap water.

As he tried to raise his head, the pain seemed to sting a nerve on the back of his skull, causing him to groan and curse even louder.

As the pain quieted down a bit, he sighed and then proceeded to wash his face. His sunken eyes caused him to sigh again.

"Damn Russian. He out drank me, and still got up earlier than I did to work on the computers" Jabez muttered under his breath.

Then, he sighed. The eye bags showed that he had put himself under too much stress in the last few weeks. He considered himself lucky that the jetlag alone had not yet grounded him.

"After this, I might have to go back to drugs, and then check myself into rehab once I've had enough" Jabez joked, but he knew that the sorry case that stared back at him from tired eyes was even more laughable.

"Hey American! You need to see the news!" came Pietro's voice from down the stairs.

"Coming!" Jabez yelled back, immediately regretting his outburst. The painkillers did not work as fast as he thought they had, neither did the coffee.

"Hurry up!" came his voice again.

Jabez was infuriated. "I hope it's worth the screaming, honestly!" he said as he descended the stairs.

"...Reports from the autopsy claim that Inspector Chu was murdered in what seemed to be an execution. The Wuhan police district has released a statement; they claim that the late Inspector as killed after he allegedly refused to cooperate with local thugs, gangs and even the elusive triad bosses that still control underground Wuhan..."

"Bloody Chinese reporters don't know he was the cancer that had infected their city!" Pietro yelled at the television.

"Maybe they do, maybe they're saving face"

"What the fuck are you on about, American?"

"Think about it, okay? What if Barbecue Face runs the media too?"

"Go on"

"I mean, think about it for a sec, okay? The police statement sounds like something they would say if they knew he was bad shit, and they were bad shit as well!"

"Okay, you need to take more painkillers" Pietro snickered as he walked past him, and into the kitchen.

"It's the classic cover-up alright? I've seen this stuff too many times to not see it coming a mile away!" Jabez was unrelenting.

"You talk like someone with a blindfold on" Pietro said as he opened the freezer to grab himself a bottle of water.

"I might have a blindfold on, but my other senses are heightened!"

"Honestly, I'm praying for you to be wrong"

"Why?"

"Nothing. I have it handled."

"Now I'm worried, what did you do, Pietro?"

"I may have gone to the media with an anonymous tip a few minutes ago, call it an hour. I told them that their beloved Inspector was a piece of dog shit"

"What!"

"Anonymous tip! I said anonymous, didn't I?"

"You fucking piece of crap!" Jabez could barely believe his ears.

How did Pietro not know to not trust the media? Why would he go to the media without proof? Was he working for them too?

Weighed down by numerous thoughts and a nagging headache that seemed to get worse by the minute, Jabez stormed the living room, his eyes searching.

"Hey calm down! I already told you, they don't know who I am. I encrypted the source for the message." Pietro explained as Jabez walked away. Cursing Jabez's paranoia, he tossed the now empty bottle to the recycle bin.

"Are you working for them? Huh!" Jabez yelled as he walked back into the room. He had found a gun, and although it had no bullets, he was still going to use it to achieve aims.

"Hey, calm down American, eh?" Pietro replied casually. His back was turned to Jabez as he tried to read the upper most part of the kitchen cabinets.

"Answer me!" Jabez barked. The headache raged on, angering him the more.

"Woah, easy!" Pietro had now turned around. The smirk on his face was no more, as it had been released by a panic. "Easy, American!"

"Are you working for them, Pietro!" Jabez barked his questions, wincing as he felt the headache even more.

"No! No! Why would you think that?" Pietro asked. His hands were suspended in the air.

"Why did you contact the media then, huh?"

"Because-"

"Talk faster you piece of shit!"

"Because I wanted them see the Inspector for who he was, okay? Not the all-loving crap they're actively peddling! I sent a video and everything! Apparently Jin had a body cam in his gear, and he was feeding the footage directly to the computers here!" Pietro explained.

"Fuck!" Jabez cursed. The headache had made it harder for him to even think, and he was starting to get dizzy.

"They haven't released the footage, not yet! I thought it was because my email had gotten sent to their spam folder, but now I think it's because they're hiding the truth! I was skeptical because I didn't want to believe you, okay? I wanted to believe that this UNO guy didn't control the entire city, but he does, and I was wrong! For that I'm truly sorry, American, but I would never betray you!" Pietro explained.

"You better be telling the truth you vodka-sipping piece of shit!" Jabez said as he backed away, and into the living room.

"The footage is in a folder labeled 'PLEASE DO NOT WATCH' okay?" Pietro called after him from the kitchen.

"Shut the fuck up!" Jabez cursed. He wasn't convinced yet. With a shaky hand, and heavy eyes, he opened the video. As Pietro had said, it was a body cam and he could hear Jin's last words, right before the Inspector murdered him.

Swallowing what felt like a boulder in his throat, he went over to the emails, and sure enough, Pietro had used a burner account and had been very explicit about his distaste for the departed Inspector. In the email, he urged the media houses to share his sentiment and report the truth.

"You know that gun has no bullets, right?" Came Pietro's voice from behind him. When Jabez turned around, he had a smirk on his face, and he looked almost amused.

"Shut the fuck up" Jabez cursed.

All Pietro did was laugh, and hard too. Soon, he was rolling on the floor, clutching on his stomach. This only angered Jabez the more, but he needed to lie down more than anything.

"Grow up!" Jabez said as he walked over Pietro on the living room.

"You need to lie down, American. If I was evil I would have taken you out before you could even point that thing at me, you know? Get a nap, there'll be soup for you when you wake up!" Pietro said as he sat up, but Jabez was already up the stairs.

"It better be chicken noodle soup, you piece of shit!" Jabez cursed as he slumped unto his bed. Soon, he was asleep again, this time the soft pillows cushioned the sharp pain in his neck, and his back had stopped hurting as much as it did before.

*

"Reports are coming in, and we are being attacked by what seems to be a contagious virus. Residents are advised to stay indoors during these times as we try to contain the spread"

"More than 100 have been confirmed casualties so far..."

"Health workers have been charged to be brave in the face of a contagious virus"

"The use of nose masks has been deemed mandatory and although movement had been restricted, anyone who deems it fit to go out of their residence should wear one at all times"

"The Wuhan Government has made provisions to enforce a total lockdown..."

It was a week after Jin had been murdered. Pietro and Carol had worked tirelessly to find out the plans of the group they had come to know as the Accordance. According to several reports by now deceased journalists, they were "a virus that had infiltrated several government houses, political parties, and even religious organizations..."

"...their one aim? An unholy unity under the rulership of a man known only as UNO, the first of The Accordance; a scientist who is said to have 70% of the world's weapons, both biological and otherwise, in his hands, or in the hands of the people he controls" Carol read.

It was a meeting day, and although she had been on a video call with them for about five hours already, it seemed like they had not done any work.

"*As gathered by Charlie Hudgens*. Can we reach this guy?" Jabez asked.

"With a medium, we can. Says here that he committed suicide a few days after he published this article on his blog. The poor guy fell to his death from a skyscraper in Seattle.

"Shit" Jabez cursed. "So we have no leads, huh?"

"Not exactly. We do have information via Jin's tunnel that the final phase of the plan, as well as an antidote is at a private location that is known only to the members of the Accordance"

"I assume that you have this location?"

"All we know is that it's deep in the inlands of China, and that its probably an island, and that it has a cloaking device of sorts" Carol explained.

"In other words?" Pietro asked.

"Untraceable, except by invitation, of course" Carol replied.

"Invitation, how?" Jabez asked.

"Right now, Teo Han is running a small virus through to the Secretary. All we need to get access is for him to pick up the phone and answer the call. Then, we'll use his voice to finish the AI system that'll help us decrypt the invitation that he received an hour ago"

"How long till he gets this call?" Pietro asked.

"forty-six seconds, hopefully" Carol explained. "He's currently in a meeting with the President, and he'll need to pick up the phone, especially when it comes directly to him, and not through his secretary" Carol further explained.

"Cool, keep us posted." Jabez said.

"Call's in. We've got exactly twenty seconds till he's pissed off and ends the call, but that should give us enough time to get a sample of his voice. I'll let you guys in" Carol said. Almost immediately, the entire room was filled audio from the call to Secretary Charles Boyd.

"...Exactly, Mr President. That's why we need to sell some of our nukes. I know congress will be a stumbling block, but we need to tale a stance for peace, and profit- Yes, who is this?"

In the background, the President seemed to be skeptical about the Secretary's proposal, but Charles Boyd was paying more attention to the call he had received, and the silence at the other end was starting to make his short temper even shorter.

"Listen here you piece of shit. I could decide the fate of all Americans if I wanted to, so if you think prank-calling and not saying anything would affect me, then you're sorely mistaken! Have a nice fucking day!" He swore as he ended the call.

"Sheesh, what a nut job" Jabez said.

"I don't blame the guy, I mean, we prank-called him while he was trying to get nukes for a guy that looks like barbecue chicken. If I was him, I'd be pissed as well" Pietro laughed.

"We've got it. Decrypting now" Carol said.

"Good, we're waiting" Pietro acknowledged.

"That's odd" came Carol's voice again.

"What is it?" Both men chorused.

"There are no coordinates, no venues, no addresses, nothing" Carol said.

"What? How's the meet supposed to take place then?" Jabez asked. Pietro was giving him a questioning look. It seemed like they were all confused.

"I don't know. Here, has a look; I'm forwarding it to you now" Carol replied.

The invitation soon appeared on their screen, and sure enough, there was no mention of any locations, pick up spots, or coordinates. All they could see was a message that read thus.

"Brother, you are invited to a party that'll be held to celebrate our latest wins. Our virus has spread to the ends of China faster than we expected, and in a week, we will be looking at worldwide spreads, as well as a meeting with certain officials of the UN in a bit to retail our antidote.

You know where the party's going to happen. Cheers!"

"...You know where the party's going to happen?" Jabez asked.

"It seems like they've been there before" Pietro added.

"Yeah, a summerhouse for murderous public servants" Carol added.

"But we do have the antidote, right?" Jabez asked.

"Yeah, just the formula. We haven't managed to synthesize it. The labs haven't come up with a clear-cut result yet. Honestly, we need to get it in the hands of the professionals" Carol explained.

"Hey, we'll need you to grab us a copy of the Secretary's itinerary for the next two weeks. We need to know where he's going to go, who he's going to see, and who he's going with. He cannot be the only one that has been compromised" Jabez instructed.

"Already on it" Carol replied. "It's been fun chatting with you gentlemen, but we need to call it a day, or night. It's almost 5 in the morning here" She added, right before signing off.

"Thank you Carol!" Pietro said. It was almost evening, and although they were still fugitives of the Accordance, and the Wuhan Police, they still had to get groceries. Their seemingly endless supply of food and drink had begun to run out, but thankfully the drawer of cash they had found hadn't.

He was arming himself with a pistol when a notification came in. The loud *ding* sound caused Pietro stopped in his tracks, and so did Jabez.

"What was that?" Jabez asked.

"I recognize that sound, it's a notification, from the burner email I used a while ago" Pietro answered. He had already let his coat fall to the floor and was on his way towards the computers.

"I thought a burner email meant that it would disappear after sending the message?"

"Yeah, so did I" Pietro replied. "Someone found a way to reply, obviously".

"What does the message say then?" Jabez asked.

"Uhh, you might want to see this" Pietro said. He sounded worried, so Jabez rushed to the computers.

"Fucking hell" Jabez gasped.

They had received three messages from what looked like another burner email, except that this one was untraceable and had no return address. In the messages were short letters, followed by video clips, one of which was playing at the moment.

In the first video, there was an old Asian woman lying down dead on the far end of the room. She was in a pool of her own blood, and presently, a child was being dragged into the frame. The child, no older than ten, was made to kneel, and then despite her screams and pleading, was shot in the head. Her lifeless body fell to the floor, leaving Pietro and Jabez speechless.

"Fuck" Jabez finally spoke. He was pacing the room slowly. Then, he stopped, and with eyes widened, he gasped and lunged towards Pietro.

"That's Jin's kid!" He announced. Pietro gasped as well. "Play the other videos!" Jabez commanded.

Soon, the second video clip was up for display. The message that it was in Portuguese. Jabez already knew what it was about, so he braced himself.

"Rosinda!" he gasped.

Her bloody, lifeless face was in the grasp of one of the men in the video. Like the other men in the video with Jin's family, they were dressed in black, and masked.

Bent over on a window was a child, no older than six years. It was obvious that his mother had tried to help him escape, but their hideout had been breached before she could help him out of the window.

"I'm so sorry man" Pietro tried to comfort him as he held on to his shoulder, but Jabez wrung himself free, aggressively too. As soon as the video ended, Jabez was out of the room and Pietro thought he heard a bottle smash on the kitchen wall, followed by cursing and kicking.

Pietro was left alone and wondering whom they could have gotten to in the third video. His links to family and friends were scrubbed from the database as part of his confidentiality agreement when he joined the Secret Service, so they could not get to him. Still, he delayed watching the third video as h braced himself for whatever it had in store for him.

With a shaky thumb, he clicked on the third video.

"Sophia!" He gasped. Tears had begun running down his cheeks ad he watched her being shot at as she tried to enter her car.

Sophia Velasquez was a desk agent at the secret service. She had resigned about two years prior, and although they had worked together on several missions, they had never officially met. He only knew what she looked like, and although she had seen him during the numerous debriefs she had to undertake, they had never been properly introduced. That was until he went Christmas shopping in Moscow.

It was a cold day, and seeing that it was Christmas eve, the bigger malls were filled with all sorts of people. Pietro, like Sofia, had decided to shop at the same convenience store on their way home from a fruitless day of trying to get groceries. She had noticed him in the stalls and while she tried to place his face, he disappeared into the whole foods aisle, only to resurface behind her. He had grabbed her by the hand and placed a Swiss knife on her side, and with the most authority he could muster in his voice, asked her who she was.

A scared Sophia had introduced herself, but not before she dropped her crate of eggs. She was visibly shaken, and he had offered to take her home, as well as pay for her stuff as an apology.

Still shaken, she had accepted his offer but only when he insisted over and over again. The walk to the car was not devoid of the questioning stares of the shopkeeper who had clearly seen him grab her by the hand in the security feeds. Sophia said that he looked familiar, and she thought she had seen him before.

"Yeah, I work in Finance" Pietro had lied, but when she explained that she had been a desk agent at her previous job and that she had handled debriefings where she saw someone that looked like him, he knew she had been a desk agent at the Secret Service.

"...several times, too" she explained.

The duo had decided to meet up for drinks later in the week and soon started seeing each other. Although they had been on and off for a while, as their relationship had been plagued by cheating rumors and arguments, Pietro still felt like he had put her in danger.

"How did they know about her?" He asked himself. His legs were shaky as he let his hands run through his hair. He was lost in thought, and the urge to go out and get groceries was no longer there.

Hell, he would not even eat even if a feast was set in front of him.

Sophia was dead, she had been shot upwards of seven times. The assailants, all dressed in black had opened fire on her as she bent over to put her shopping bags in the back seat of her car.

Pietro could taste the salty tears on his cheeks, and he did not bother to clean them off. There and then, he vowed to end the life of his Superior whenever he meets him.

*

"We ran background checks on several pharmaceutical companies, yes. It was a long search, and Brendan is taking the day off, but we found one, Phoenix Pharmaceuticals. There haven't been any reports of illegal or unethical activities in the company, and the Managing Director happens to be a close associate of Director Colby." Carol announced.

It was three days after the invitation was delivered to Secretary Boyd, and it was also three days since Teo Han had hacked into the personal server used by his personal assistant. Unfortunately, there was no mention of any flights to China, or an Asian country for that matter. Not yet.

"Thank you, Carol, I-" Jabez tried to speak, but she interrupted him.

"Wait, something just came in! We got a meeting place. Its somewhere in the inlands of China, I mean, I can barely pronounce it. I'm sending you the coordinates now"

"*Diaoyu Island, 25.8061° N, 123.5952° E*" her message read.

"Wait, isn't this place the cause of feud between China, Japan, and Taiwan?" Pietro asked. He was monitoring the news reports and had barely been paying attention, till now.

"Is that so? Apparently not, obviously. UNO has it" Jabez replied.

"The records show that the islands belong to China, maybe he bought it from them?"

"If we're looking up the same article, Ms. Carol, it also says that the island is uninhabited" Pietro asked.

"Apparently not" Jabez said, shrugging.

"Look, we can argue about all this, or we can devise a way to get there soon. Secretary Boyd has a way. He's a diplomat with the highest level of clearance. His itinerary says that he is to be in Beijing for a consolidation meeting with several leaders of industry. And please, just Carol is fine, thank you" Carol interjected.

"Lucky bastard, but not for long. I mean, we can't even activate agents that live here in Wuhan, or anywhere for that matter. The travel restrictions are so convenient for them, but not for us" Jabez complained.

"I'm sorry, but you guys are alone on this one. Director Colby and General Eisenhower will support in the best way possible, but there will no outside assistance after that" Carol explained.

"I understand. Just get us enough guns and a way in, that's all" Pietro said.

The room was tense, and Carol felt like she had to address it. There wasn't anything she could do, especially when she was halfway across the world, and at a hideout because Director Colby thought she was at risk, especially because of her part in the missions, but she had to say something, Jabez and Pietro looked like they needed some emotional support, and quick.

"Gentlemen, look." She started, but her words seemed to fail her. Even she could feel the pressure that they felt.

She heaved a heavy sigh, and then continued.

"Gentlemen, I know all this is overwhelming, and you're losing your shit at a fast rate, but trust me when I say that you're not alone. I know it may look that way, but you've got some of the best minds backing you on this one, and I assure you that you'll make it out. Alive. You'll make it out alive" She blurted. Her hands were suddenly cold, and she could barely breath, but Carol had spoken her truth, and that was all that matters.

The event to decide to all was hours away, and the agents were as nervous as they could get, even if they didn't show it. Carol, Brendan and Teo Han had been literally stashed in an undisclosed location for a while till it all cleared out, and they were working around the clock. They were nervous too.

Director Colby however, had a rock-solid disposition. She was calm and collected, and in all honesty, she needed to be, especially when she was to procure a pilotless jet from a Belgian billionaire she had put away during her days as a field agent.

*

Lars De Smet was a small-time arms dealer that had made it big retailing weapons of mass destruction to countries at war, especially in the later parts of the 20th century. Civil wars, African dictators, and interracial conflicts were his biggest markets and he made quite a fortune.

Most of the times, he had also sold to rebel forces in exchange for large parcels of the lands they so fought to protect, at the same time selling to the government of the day in exchange for rather exorbitant amounts, as well as stakes and seats in power. By the time the Kosovo war was over, De Smet was sitting on an illegal empire that made him filthy rich.

That was until he was brought up on war crimes, fraudulent activities, illegal sales of firearms and weapons of mass destruction, employment of child soldiers etc. Leading the charge was a young Rachel Colby, or Leah Creed, as she was known in his inner circles. She had attached herself to him, and he had taken a liking to her. Like a father and his daughter, he showed her his dealings and taught her almost everything he knew.

Before long, he was brought up at the Hague and she was the key witness, alongside several child soldiers, and a few paid actors. Nobody knew the difference, and most of them were still afraid of him to come forward.

Lars De Smet was put away with several life sentences, but 30 years later, he was released silently due to several health complications at the age of 87. He was pronounced bankrupt, but the numerous bank accounts under various aliases proved otherwise. The old man was retired, but his investments had gotten him one of the biggest private islands in Chile, where Rachel Colby was arriving in a helicopter presently.

It had rained all day, but the evening was uncharacteristically warmer than usual. The guards, however, were cold as ice and although she looked a frail old woman, they didn't take chances as they made sure she wasn't carrying anything.

Lars De Smet had agreed to a meeting, especially to see her face. The old man had grown fond of her, and although she had ruined him and taken a large chunk of everything he owned, he still had a soft place om his heart for her.

"Leah! Come, have a seat" he called to her as she came down the stairs that led to the fireplace he was resting beside. The moon was out, and in the dim light of both the moon, and the fireplace, she could see that he was well, unlike the doctored images the courts had gotten. His makeup artiste also did a good job, honestly.

"I don't go by that anymore, and you don't look a day over 60!" She spoke.

"Ah well, you put me behind bars didn't you, if you didn't I'd look better than those Asian boys that make music"

"You know K-pop?"

"Yeah, yeah. Those guys. Why wouldn't I? My granddaughter is obsessed with those guys, my god it makes me sick."

"Let's cut to the chase here-"

"What chase? I'm an old man for god's sake! What am I chasing for, eh?" Lars joked.

Carol could see that he was trying to lighten the mood, or fight through the awkwardness of their meeting.

"Look, kid. I know you want something, and honestly I should have Ernesto over there put two in the back of your head, right after Riccardo his twin brother cuts off all your fingers and toes" he said as he pointed to the mean looking guards who stood menacingly outside the cabana.

"I-" Rachel Colby tried to speak, but Lars wasn't done.

"Look, I'm an old man, and I honestly don't have that much time, so how about I put the hatchet to the side. I'm not burying it though, by Madonna I'm not" he said.

"I need a favour, Lars" Rachel Colby finally spoke.

"I know, I know" Lars said. "Look, as long as it doesn't make that much of a hole in my retirement fund, you've got it" he announced.

"I need your drone plane" Rachel Colby said matter of factly.

"Dear Christ! You should have asked for my left testicle first!" He said as he laughed at her demands.

"It's for the greater good, and in all honesty, it'll benefit you too" she offered.

"Really?" Lars asked. "How so?" He looked like he wanted to be amused, but Rachel Colby was just getting started with him.

"We both know that buying what could only be considered as the biggest private island in Chile is more than a retirement plan, Lars." She started, smiling as she noticed him shift in his chair.

The fire crackled relentlessly. Lars was silent, but he smiled softly. The Leah he knew was still there, and she was doing what she did to the Kosovo generals to him.

"We both know that you're a businessman, and that you're always in the mood for profit. We also know that your back may have given out, but you're still pushing. I mean, you're pushing everything! Am I right?" Rachel Colby laughed heartily. She could see that she was working him.

"I mean, a senior citizen like myself has to pau for the dementia medication, don't you think?" He joked.

"Cut the shit." Rachel Colby wasn't having it. "We both know that this island is the capital of your new business ring, and that you have more than one drone aircraft, matter of fact, you just procured a dozen more, haven't you. I mean, your retailers in Lagos need to get their stuff faster, right? And the porous airspace could not pick up a drone in stealth mode, so that cuts out bribing border officials, like that" she snapped her fingers.

"What do you want, Rachel" Lars asked. His tone was less hearty than usual, and he wore a smug look on his face now.

"A drone jet. Don't worry, we'll return it once we're done. We just need to save the world, that's all." She replied.

"You know what? Fuck it. I could do without one of those things anyway" Lars said. He was laughing nervously, even so because he knew that Rachel could see my cower. It wasn't always a good look to concede in front of your employees, especially when it comes to a compromise, and you're on the losing end of it all.

"Good. It would be best if I leave with it too" Rachel added as she stood up to leave.

"Right now? Do you know how much those things cost me?"

"I know their market value, and I know you got it for less than that from the German company that makes the models you use. How much less did you even get it for? Forty percent? fifty? sixty percent?" Rachel asked. She had begun to feel impatient.

"I got it eighty percent less than the original price, okay? If there's one thing you learnt from me is pay small, sell big, am I right?"

"Well, what you are is wasting my time" Rachel asked.

"Ernesto!" Lars called to his bodyguards, all the while staring intently at Rachel Colby. She was staring back, as well. Right in the eyes.

"Yes Boss?" The hunky Latin man came forward and stood with his hands behind his back, awaiting instructions.

"Take Ms. Colby to the hangar and let her have a pick, okay? Also, shame on you, Ernesto! You too Riccardo. You do realize that this woman had a Smith and Wesson pointed at me the entire time, right? Work on your frisking skills, goddamn it!" He cursed.

"Thank you Lars" Rachel finally smiled. She waved at him as she left, brandishing her weapon before putting it back into the pouch she had concealed it in.

Ernest then led Rachel towards a waterfall on the far side on the cabana, right beside it was a steep cliff. Rachel Colby clutched to her weapon as she walked on behind Ernesto. Then, just as they were close enough to the waterfall, he opened a small opening in the wall, and revealed a retina scan, which he promptly worked, causing the waterfall to come to a stop.

A door opened on the wall that formed the background for the now ceased waterfall and Ernesto entered first, followed by an ever cautious Rachel Colby.

"An elevator?" She asked patiently as she observed the keys on the side of the wall.

Ernesto only grunted in a reply. He did not look exactly thrilled to be accompanying her to where she would basically be stealing from his boss, while blackmailing him with the very livelihood he was actively involved in.

The elevator doors shut, and the descent began. On the dial, Rachel counted 3 floors before the small thud and easing sound as the elevator door slid open.

As she entered the large hall, she wondered what Lars had stashed on the other levels. The old man was cunning. He could have the real Mona Lisa painting there for all she knew.

Lost in thought, she did not hear Ernesto cold remark to her.

"Make a pick, hangar doors open when you press start the jet" he said as he made his way back to the door.

"Wait, why does that one have *Mr Blue Sky* written on it?" Rachel asked. In the far corner of the hangar was a jet with the Electric Light Orchestra song title scribbled on its side in the band's custom font.

"That's his favorite one. I guess it's yours too. Take it, but make sure you bring it back" Ernesto explained as he closed the elevator door.

Rachel Colby was left with several options, but *Mr Blue Sky* looked like the favorite pick, so she went with it. She already HD experience flying jets, so figuring out how to get the million-dollar hunk of metal to obey her wasn't a problem. Before long, she was out of the hangar, and on her way to the hideout.

"She took it, didn't she?" Lars asked Ernesto as he resurfaced from behind the waterfall.

"Of course, she did."

"And the tracker, it's on it, right?"

"Yes sir."

"Good boy, Ernesto. Now go google frisking" Lars said as he took a spoonful of caviar to his lips.

*

The day had come, and the duo, dressed in rather expensive tuxedoes, had been picked up by the jet at the local airstrip. The journey was about 3 hours and during that period, the men were debriefed by Rachel Colby herself.

"Gentlemen" she begun. "You're being transported to the Diaoyu island by a rather expensive jet. Please do well to not let it he caught up in your mission. By caught up, I mean do not destroy it. It is your way in, and your way out. You are to infiltrate this ceremony of the assholes we have come to know as The Accordance, and stop them before they can launch phase 2 of their plans"

"Which is? You never told us that part" Jabez asked.

"Phase 2 is the global spread of this virus we have all come to know as Corona. We have the antidote, but we do not need casualties. Suicide agents of this Accordance have been placed at strategic places around the world with one aim in mind, to be weaponized as the leaders of these Nations watch and cheer. Presently, we've discovered about three hundred of these agents, but there are a lot more out there. Stop UNO before he can weaponize the virus in the bloodstream of these agents and get out. If anyone gets in your way, attack with extreme prejudice. Remember, everyone there is an enemy, even your Superior. That is for you, Pietro" She admonished.

"I understand ma'am" Pietro replied. He was intent on killing his superior, even if it was the last thing he did that day.

"The jet will drop you guys off just beyond the shores, find a way into the ceremony, and infiltrate. Introduce yourself as the guy that sold the most NFTs last year, or something. You've got the suits to prove it, so be it. Once you see UNO, end him. He is the key to all of this, and the good thing about building a hive mind such as he has done is that they cannot function without him, so that is what we'll exploit. Is that clear?"

"Yes ma'am!" Both men echoed.

"Jet's ready for the drop off" Carol said from the background.

"You hear that gentlemen? Have fun, kill bad guys" Rachel Colby said.

The jet soon came to rest a few hundred meters from the main building, and the duo alighted to join the soiree.

"What the fuck is this beauty?" Jabez commented.

The Accordance was having its gala at what could only be described as an architectural wonder. The building was designed in such a way that it could not be seen from above. With reflective panels that mirrored it surroundings, you had to have infra-red vision to see the people in or around the building. From the sides, it looked like a diamond, with glossy exterior that portrayed a welcoming aura, betraying the murderous intents that went on within its walls.

"This UNO guy has a big ego, doesn't he?" Pietro commented, to which Jabez concurred.

The guards at the front gates were welcoming, and although they were skeptical about admitting any more persons, they decided to me them in, under close surveillance, of course.

"Well, come in Mr Tomasz. We've been expecting you. I hope you don't mind me asking, but who is your partner here?" A rather skinny looking attendant asked them as they made their way in.

"Bodyguard" Jabez replied with an air of authority and importance.

"Well, it's just that we can barely find you on the list, and we do not have room for even a plus one as it stands, so-"

"Listen, what's the name?" Jabez blurted.

"It's- its"

"It's nothing, okay? Now look here, nothing? I got courted by this really scary guy to join whatever this is okay? I'm just here to give it all a look, I'll be out as soon as I have an appraisal, and by the looks of this place, your quota will be alright, real quick, you understand me?"

"I think I do-"

"I didn't sell three billion in NFTs to have you think, Nothing. Good day" Jabez said finally as walked away. Pietro followed closely behind.

"Guards at the door, we dealt with them" Jabez radioed.

"Good, nice improv Mr Glee" Rachel Colby radioed back.

"Please, call me Tomasz Jon. Bitcoin expert" he said as he tugged at his collar. "Time to mingle"

"Pietro, glasses please" Carol asked.

"Noted" Pietro radioed back as he put on the glasses he had been given.

"Connecting, now!" Carol announced.

In the party before them was almost all the second in commands in the world governments. Several heads of service, ministers and even Presidents of small countries were among the attendants as well.

"My god, that's the President of Lotvia" Rachel Colby gasped.

"You know the guy?" Teo Han asked. He was also in the room as had taken a break as the code he had embedded in the glasses transmitted wavelengths that gained them access to the live footage from the cameras at the party.

"Yeah, we met at a party where I helped broker peace between his country and Indonesia. I thought he was a cool guy. I mean, we played golf together" Rachel Colby explained.

"Well, they can't all be winners" Teo Han shrugged as he returned to his computer. The hack was complete, and they had access to the live footage from the event.

"UNO's in a suite downstairs. He's heavily guarded with soldiers that have military grade weapons. I'd advice that you stand down. The plastic guns you smuggled in can do you much good, but they're not good enough. Disarm some guards before you attack, or better yet, stand down. I'll alert you when he's free" Rachel Colby announced.

"Oh shit" gasped Teo Han.

"What is it?" Carol asked.

"It's Nothing" He replied.

"Then why did you gasp?" She asked.

"I mean it's Nothing. The guy, he's showing something to the guards, and they're look to our guys" Teo Han explained.

"What?"

"Nothing googled Tomasz" Teo Han explained.

"Shit" Rachel Colby cursed. Her plan was falling apart, and all because some acne-infested attendant was too zealous and googled a fake name. "Change of plans. Boys, disarm some guards now, and make your way towards UNO. Now!" She barked.

"Go time" Jabez said as he turned to Pietro.

The guards were making their way towards them, so the duo blended in with the crowd. Soon, they were past the search party and after a quick trip down a hallway as instructed by Carol, they met up with a few armed guards. It was obvious that the guards had not been intimated of the breach, and they greeted them cordially.

"Hey, gentlemen, could you show us to the bathroom, please?" Jabez asked.

As soon as they guards turned their backs to them, Jabez and Pietro knocked them out and took their weapons.

"M-16s? Too classy" Pietro commented as he reached into the unconscious man's pouch to grab extra bullets.

"Alright guys, enter the elevator on your left" Carol instructed. "Fifth floor." She added.

"Done" Jabez replied. They had promptly entered the elevator.

"Just in time, too. You've got hostiles coming to your position, and it seems like they've radioed UNO's location. Expect heavy fire" Carol added.

"Sure thing" Pietro added. "You ready, American?" He asked Jabez.

"Born Ready" Jabez answered as he cocked his gun.

"Alright, you're going to have to crawl into the vent above you for a bit. The hostile on floor five have set up a perimeter of sorts. You're going to come up on some heavy fire soon" Carol added.

"Just like the factory" Pietro added. His eyes glistening. Jin's death was still being felt, even at that moment.

"Yeah, just like the factory" Jabez concurred as he climbed into the vent.

As expected, the elevator was lit up with bullets as soon as the door swung open. Then suddenly, they stopped.

"Hey, do grenades bounce?" Jabez asked.

"What? I don't know!"

"Let's find out then!" Jabez said as he threw a grenade hard against the wall of the elevator. Sure enough, it ricocheted out of the elevator, and as soon as it exploded, a couple of grunts were heard, followed by complete silence.

"The gunshots have caused a panic on the upper levels. Also, your presence helped us get more footage from the lower levels too. Gentlemen, it's almost poetic because we have UNO, Boyd, and Pietro's superior, all in one room"

"Fuck yes!" Jabez hollered.

"Hallway is clear, please proceed" Carol instructed.

The duo then jumped out of the vent and made their way to the only door, which was at the end of the hall.

"25 armed soldiers on the other side, what's the play, gentlemen?" Rachel Colby asked.

"Decoy fire, hit them when they reload?" Jabez asked Pietro.

"Good call American" Pietro said as he fired a warning shot.

Sure enough, there came a barrage of bullets, causing the duo to find cover.

"Are you counting too?" Pietro asked.

"7 more!" Jabez replied.

Soon, the shots came to an end, and then they made their entrance. Jabez and Pietro then singlehandedly eliminated all the hostiles they could find, leaving only the three men who were at the far and of the hall protected by the steel wall that covered a part of the bar they sat at.

As they made their way towards the men, Charles Boyd began to pout as was characteristic.

"Listen here you sons of bitches! I-" he hollered, but he was soon interrupted, as Jabez had put a bullet in his skull.

The once talkative Secretary of State fell to the floor, lifeless and limp.

"Get out from behind there! I'm not going to say it twice!" Pietro hollered. He was going to get his own pound of flesh, and nothing was going to get in his way.

"Pietro, I command you to stand down!" His superior yelled, but he was shocked to see that Pietro did not flinch.

"You piece of shit! What did she ever do to you!" Pietro hollered. Sofia's death had stung him more than he could ever imagine.

"Pietro-" His Superior tried to speak, but he was shot in the leg. The old man cursed and groaned in Russian; bur Pietro was unfeeling.

All the while UNO had gone behind the bar and was fixing himself a drink. Not even Jabez's commands to not move could stop him.

"Oh please, spare me that crap. I mean, I just saved forty percent of the problems of the planet a half hour ago and you think I wouldn't make myself a drink?" He asked.

"A half hour ago? What do you mean by that?" Jabez was puzzled, like everyone else. They all needed answers.

"You didn't think I knew you'd come snooping around on my servers, huh? I could fix the leaks in my information dispensation system as easy as the alphabet, but I led you on, I told you what you needed to know. Yes, I activated my weaponized agents a half hour ago, but that was just a small chunk, for show, honestly. The real fun happened when I woke up this morning. I think it was the first thing I did" UNO replied, chuckling as he took his Martini to his lips.

"I'll fucking kill you, you bastard!" Jabez roared.

"No, thank you. In fact, your Russian friend needs to die, don't you think? He's killed his nemesis, right?" UNO asked. With a swift movement of the hand, he took a pistol from behind the counter and shot at Pietro twice.

The Russian agent fell in a heap, right beside his dead Superior.

"No!" Jabez roared as he rushed to his side.

Pietro had been shot in the chest, and he was bleeding faster than Jabez could apply pressure on the wound.

"American" a fading Pietro asked.

"Yes, brother?" Jabez asked, his eyes welling with tears.

"Kill that cockroach, and then have a toast, okay?" Pietro groaned. "I'll- I'll be fine, go!" He muttered as he struggled for breath.

Jabez turned to the bar with a vengeance, but UNO was gone. He had escaped through a trap door somewhere in the large backdrop of the bar.

"Jabez, I know now's not a good time, but to your right is a mainframe. It has schematics, graphs, the entire thing. We need you to help us get it, and then destroy it, okay?"

"Sure, whatever" Jabez replied, gritting his teeth as he held back tears.

"Alright, Mr Glee. Your plastic gun also doubles as a holder for a flash drive, so if you could get it out from behind the barrel, that would be nice". Carol instructed.

Jabez then plugged the flash drive into the mainframe, but them after what seemed like a change of heart, he took a grenade and after taking out the pin, tossed it at the computer.

"What the fuck was that?" Rachel Colby barked.

"Download isn't complete" Teo Han announced.

There was radio silence from Jabez. In the cameras, he could be seen making his way towards the elevator, but before arming himself first.

The angered American agent opened fire on everyone that crossed his path, despite warnings to stand down from Director Colby.

"Damn it, Glee! This is why I don't take you on missions!"

There was still no response.

"He just killed the Lotvia guy" Teo Han announced.

"Damn it Glee!" Director Carol barked, but she was ignored.

Soon, footage picked up Jabez, but this time he was tossing grenades at several parts of the building in an attempt to burn it all down. A large number of those present at the meeting were soon dead, but he didn't stop.

As soon as Jabez was satisfied, he then overturned Teo Han's control of the jet and after putting on stealth mode, took off.

Director Colby was furious. She attacked the screens with her chair and destroyed anything that moved in her path, forcing Carol and Teo Han to exit the room.

Jabez was gone. The world was under attack from a virus, and her friends at Phoenis Pharmaceuticals were not close to synthesizing a cure.

*

"...It is said that Secretary Boyd was reported dead in his hotel room as a result of food poisoning and allergies that the hotel administration had not taken into consideration..."

"The Secretary of State would be given a state burial and buried in the Presidential burial grounds..."

"It had been said that a lone terrorist was responsible for those attacks on a summit held in respect of several heads of states at the inlands of China. The Peace summit, which was strategically held in a disputed area of land was a supposed to be a panacea for world peace, until a terrorist struck. Details shortly..."

"The terrorist had been presumed dead or missing. He is said to be Jabez Glee, and of American descent. The American government deny any affiliation with this man, and claim he was working for either Al-Qaeda or of a personal hatred for peace and harmony amongst nations..."

"He is said to be heavily armed, dangerous, and if seen, to be reported to the police. Good night and be safe. Remember, the corona virus is still a rampage. Wash your hands and isolate if you have symptoms. Also remember that social distancing is important, and as such, stay six feet away from others, at all times..."

Printed in Great Britain
by Amazon